The Blackfeet Boys

Warriors By Day – Lovers By Night

Part I

By
TJ Johnson

Copyright © 2010 by TJ Johnson

Library of Congress Control Number:
2009909965

ISBN 978-0-9819932-1-8

Published By
Hard Title Publishing

www.ItsFiction.com

As young men, Windtalker and Kiyo developed excellent hunting skills during the warmer months, and in winter, they learned how to fight an enemy and kill on the field of battle. However, their desire to be together forces a plan long in the making. Making their way through the snow, they hurriedly make their way west from the plains of Montana, and begin crossing the treacherous, difficult ridges and rivers in the Glacier Mountains. The mountains harbor dangerous animals and tenacious warriors, but they refuse to turn back. They seek a valley far from their homeland where perhaps they can live in secret together, but their journey is wrought with adventure and numerous near death experiences. They use their well honed skills, and the powerful love they share, to survive every obstacle, but can they survive in the wilderness alone?

Comments:

"The thing that I love about your writing is how wonderfully you develop your characters. You make me really care about what happens to them. Then, on top of it all, you are able to develop a plot line that makes the book impossible to put down. I have lost a lot of sleep because I read into the wee hours of the morning, (that's why I hate you!!!). But, I love you because of the amazing stories that you write. I have just started 'The War Apart-Part 1' and am already hooked." Bruce Foulkes Santa Ana, CA

"5 out of 5 stars! What a wonderful story, it is so rare - especially in gay fiction to have a story fold around you like a comfortable blanket. The characters are so rich and their environments and emotions are presented in such vivid detail that the reader feels like they are in the story themselves. Simply wonderful." By Todd Seibel (Austin, TX)

Books by TJ Johnson

The War Apart - Part I
(A Josh & Zeke Story)

The War Ahead - Part II Revised 2010
(A Josh & Zeke Story)

The Will
(A Brett & Chase Story)

Stranded
(An Austin & Ryan Story)

The Raceboys
(A Jack & Thad Story)

A Writer's Fantasy
(About His Favorite College Basketball Star)
(A Shane & TJ Story)

Gay Grifters
(An Eric & Tyler Story)

Coming soon:

Crosshairs
(An Eric & Tyler Story)

The War Beyond - Part III
(A Josh & Zeke Story)

The Blackfeet Boys Part II
(A Kiyo & Windtalker Story)

Rock Solid Part III
(An Eric & Tyler Story)

Web Site and Release Information:
WWW.ItsFiction.com

Dedication

To my pal Mickey, one of the best dogs I have ever loved. He is missed every day. We got him from the pound, and often joked that we paid about a dollar a pound! He ended up being worth a whole lot more.

See the rocks in your path not as obstacles,

but as opportunities to climb higher!

The Blackfeet Boys – Part I
'Warriors By Day – Lovers By Night'

ONE

The scholars and historians of both early American and Indian history often proclaimed the Blackfeet Indians as the most feared of all the North American tribes by Indians and whites alike. The tribes thought nothing of committing the cold-blooded massacre of the warriors protecting an enemy village, but also the slaughtering of old and young alike, including women, children, and dogs hiding in the various tipis. They fought with overwhelming brutality, indiscriminately, and felt no remorse for the lives and families they destroyed. Every Blackfeet warrior spilled the blood of their enemies everywhere, including onto their own bodies as a symbol of success. Their battle-axes, clubs, tomahawks, and spears were all permanently stained with dried blood from previous battles. They fought to steal, to overwhelm, and to survive.

If their tribe or village were attacked, the Blackfeet women and children took part in the annihilation of the captured wounded, as well as the corpses of their enemies. They didn't follow the Sioux example of cutting the heads off their enemies and displaying the scalpless noggins on sticks, but with great vengeance, they utterly destroyed the anatomy of the fallen warriors. If their enemy remained alive, they cut off body parts, including ears, nose, fingers, genitals, peeled their skin, cut open their gut, cut tongues, drilled eyes with sharp sticks, and slashed heads from ear to ear. The children pounded the skulls with the largest rocks they could pick up. Bigger boys and women stomped the chest of the wounded until the ribs cracked and the chest cavity fell in. The entire village took out their revenge for the attack with great exuberance and tenacity. For the Blackfeet widows, it became a bloody catharsis, and literally an eye for an eye. In the nineteenth century, the words for forgiveness or sorry did not exist in their language. They felt no remorse or tenderness for their enemies. To the tribe, it was simply kill them before they killed you.

Permanently scarred from seeing so much bloodshed at their tender ages, the boys and girls alike toughened quickly. The boys turned into hunters by their mid teens, and with more experience and training, by age eighteen or nineteen they became warriors that hunted humans.

For centuries, tribes became enemies after one group of warriors stole pelts or food from the other, but when horses arrived, thieving became an art form, a topic of every meeting, the price for marrying an old man's daughter, a gift for their sons, and stealing became the goal of every brave. It was a badge of high honor to pilfer the exceptionally valued horses from an enemy tribe or even another band of Blackfeet. The Blackfeet tribes absconded with more horses than all the surrounding Indian nations together.

They kept the best horses, while trading the weaker stock for food and weapons. Their favorite swindle was to welcome a group of white explorers into their camp, feed them, smoke the peace pipe, trade their horses to the men for goods and supplies, and then wave a friendly goodbye when they left the following morning. Later, a small pack of warriors would trail the explorers for a few days until they were far enough away that the white men would not want to give chase or return for revenge on the village. Late in the night, they would steal the traded horses back and gallop away laughing. As more white men came west, they traded the same horses repeatedly, after stealing the animals once again.

Like most of the tribes, a successful raid of horses bestowed the victor a high honor among his fellow tribesmen. They also loved counting coup, the art of riding right up to the enemy and tapping him with the butt of their spear and galloping away while yelling nasty epithets. Once out of arrow range, they insulted their enemies by showing their naked butt, slapping their behind, and calling them every foul name they could think of. Not every man in the tribe was the best hunter, or the best fisherman, but from early childhood, the fathers trained all young men to be the best warriors. If the tribe recognized an exceptional warrior in their camp, they would encourage their son to spend time with the man, hoping to improve their skills. They knew for their band of tribes to survive, everyone must defend the village and their families from all enemies. The Blackfeet chiefs wisely never waited for a possible pending attack, but with careful and cautious analysis of the scouting reports after spotting an enemy tribe, they immediately went on the offense by riding all night and attacking at dawn.

Some tribes to the west were friendly to the early small squads of whites that came west, but as their numbers grew, many leaders began to fear an invasion of more and more whites. Santanga, a highly skilled and experienced war chief, delighted in driving the white men from the Blackfeet's vast lands in the northeast. He sent warriors out to attack every beaver and buffalo hunter they could find, bringing scalps and severed ears back as a testament of their overwhelming success. However, every time he thought they had killed all the white explorers, more would come.

When the wagon trains began their trek through their lands, he watched the large trails of dust announcing their arrivals. He spit and cursed them, and along with his older warriors, he planned to annihilate them all. He gave new orders to his men. They were to attack the trains in large numbers, demonstrating how powerful they were. He told them not to kill everyone, but make some watch as they tortured the living. After they won the battle, they rounded up the women and children and made them watch and listen to the screams, as one by one they cut the remaining wounded men to shreds. Their knives would slice off toes and fingers like sausages. They stripped bare the helpless, captured white men so they would not bloody the clothes. They

2

mutilated their genitals by stomping them and then quickly cutting them off. Noses and ears came next, followed by tongues. Blood squirted and sprayed on everyone, but they didn't stop. Using sharp skinning knives, they would peel the skin of the men like peeling an orange. They would rub sand in the open wounds to increase the pain. Just before the men would pass out, they would gut them with a sharp cut across their belly button, spilling their intestines on the field before their eyes. Their scalps came off in whole slabs, and then finally, they would slit their throats. Tossing the cadaver aside, they would start on the next man with great energy. The gruesome scene never once caused a Blackfeet warrior to throw up.

Once completed, they would kill the older women, choosing only the pretty, younger, childbearing ones for slaves. An Indian woman lived a difficult life and often died young. They secured the white women as replacements, thus increasing the number of childbirths. They killed all of the young children, except during winter when food was scarce. At those times, they would put a leather leash around a child's throat and march them to camp like captured cattle. Once the killing was completed, Chief Santanga allowed two of the oldest boys to live. With a thin knife, they striped their faces and arms with long cuts as a visual testament that the Indians attacked them. They would put them on horses, and order them to ride east to warn whites if they came west, they would horribly kill them all. He intended to demoralize the whites and make them afraid of the Blackfeet warriors. He thought this treatment would stop the march of the whites to the west.

What the Blackfeet warriors did to the white settlers was not much different from what they did to any enemy tribes that attacked them. If ten of their men died in a skirmish or an attempted raid of horses, once the battle was over, his men and women would hold no mercy for the survivors. They tied the limbs of victims between strong horses and ripped them apart. They cut off the limbs while the fallen warriors were still alive. They gouged eyes. They hammered knives in one ear until the tip showed on the other side. They made enemy children chew the flesh of their families. Knees and feet were broken with rocks, and sand forced down their throats. In a few hours, hardly a blade of grass on the entire battlefield remained free of the spilled blood. They left not a single captured enemy alive, though some escapees watched the gruesome scene from the safety of the forest. The warriors looted the village and then burned it to the ground. The vultures circled overhead as they rode out of the enemy's camp victoriously, shouting and pumping their bloody fists into the air.

Not all the members of the tribe believed they should slaughter innocent white women and children, but fearing reprisals, they said nothing. Their leaders believed if they didn't attack the whites with the goal of total obliteration, then the whites would wipe away the entire tribe. News of the white man's disease called smallpox reached the camps, bringing great fear to everyone. The blood of the Indians lacked the antibodies to protect them and they acquired no medicine to stop the fatal pandemic.

Their shamans revealed dreams of white men marching across their hunting lands in one long line, as if ants queuing for a fallen buffalo. Over and over, the mystical men warned the chiefs of the vast numbers of whites heading their way. There were no scientific tools to prove these men were right, but in fact, they were. Almost every day, another ship docked in New York's harbor filled with immigrants. During the warmer months, every week a new wagon train set out from Saint Louis to the west. For every hundred settlers killed, three hundred would head out once again.

The Tiltanga family consisted of a father, mother, grandmother, two girls, and their only son they called Kiyo. The grandmother told stories of their ancestors going back centuries. She carried a large, soft-tanned, deer hide, with hot knife markings like a crude family tree. She often told stories of her childhood and the stories her grandmother told when she was a child, and during the long cold nights of winter, she spoke nearly every night. She was their entertainment as well as a teacher.

Kiyo Tiltanga reached his eighteenth birthday last winter. His best friend lived in the next tipi, as the families were close. Windtalker Nitana's family consisted of his parents, two grandparents, and a pestering sister. Kiyo and Windtalker's family trees were similar, and they grew up playing together as soon as they could walk. Their fathers taught the boys how to make weapons in winter and expanded their hunting skills in the warmer months. Now almost grown, everything they wore they made themselves from the skins of animals they hunted and skinned. It was a source of pride to make your own clothing and weapons. They wore the traditional black moccasins that also identified the young men as members of the Blackfeet tribe. They were not born with black feet, but the soil of the northwest was very fertile, and running across it barefooted as a child soon gave the boys their traditional dirty black feet.

They taught the boys how to fight, especially in the last four years, as they protected the families while their fathers went to war. They spent the early morning hours fetching water for their mothers, but the rest of the day they remained in the forest hunting. They rarely ate lunch in the village, preferring to eat on the run and going farther away from the village hunting for game. Sometimes, they had to replace a lookout on a high mountain overlooking the village, but mostly they stalked everything considered edible. On a bad day, they brought home prairie dogs or large rats, but on a good day, they killed a deer, elk, or moose, providing plenty of food for their families. They did not attempt to hunt or kill a buffalo, grizzly, mountain lion, or panther, because these kills required the skills of numerous older hunters working together. Buffalos were essential to their diet, as they were not farmers but rather voracious meat eaters. They left the other big animals alone unless attacked.

Together, they became the best hunters in the village, bringing back plenty of game for their families, and extra game for the village. Everyone liked them, calling them tishiwas or twins, as you rarely saw one without the other. The boys looked very much alike, with their dark tanned skin, long black hair, deep brown eyes, and slim muscular frames. Kiyo had a scar on his left arm from a badger bite and remained the taller of the two at almost six feet. In the warm season, when their fathers were not away attacking other tribes or wagon trains, and thus could stay home and protect the village, the boys would go alone on longer overnight trips while hunting bigger game. It was on such a trip they learned they had more in common than any villager thought.

At the end of a long day of trailing a nimble fleet-footed moose, and before they could make camp, a thunderstorm raced over the mountain, drenching the boys with cold rain and bombarding them with hailstones. Shivering as they sloshed through the wet melting snow, they searched for cover until finally, they found a dry area underneath a big overhanging rock. They pulled their hides and gear from the packhorse and flung it under the rock, they hobbled their horses but let them feed on nearby grass. They spread out a hide to sit on, but starting a fire with the wet wood was not possible. They ate some dried jerky from a rabbit fur lined pouch and decided to sleep. They took off their rawhide loincloths and laid them on a rock to dry out. Naked, they pulled another hide over them and lied down to sleep. Kiyo could hear Windtalker's teeth chattering, as did his own. They moved closer together for warmth, hands began roaming, arousals happened, and soon they were kissing. It was a wild passionate first time for the boys to spend an entire night together. After keeping their feelings completely secret all of their lives, it felt like a dam of emotion finally broke free, leaving them spent from adrenaline, but deliriously in love.

The next morning they did not discuss their actions. In fact, they did their best not to talk at all as they continued searching for the moose. The following night, it did not rain, but they slept together anyhow and once again kissed and cuddled. Their secret lovemaking began over two years ago, and they knew they were in love with the other. However, they also knew that no one must ever know.

Like most tribes, the Blackfeet Indians handled the oddness of two males behaving like a couple in similar ways. If a boy was effeminate, but smart, he attached himself to a shaman and learned how to be one. They often respected a slightly feminine acting shaman, thinking he must truly be possessed with rare gifts, and he never worried about having to fight in battle like the other boys. Shaman rarely lived long lives, as a few incorrect dreams or an unsuccessful potion might result in a revengeful death. However, if the village caught two boys experiencing sex together, any number of bad things could happen. Generally, they killed, mutilated, or scarred the offending boys, while they treated some like slaves. Banishment from all tribes usually ended in death, as the abandoned boys usually starved while trying to live on their own. Most tribal leaders preferred banishment, knowing starvation provided more pain, as well as the constant fear of being eaten alive by a mountain lion or other predators.

Kiyo and Windtalker were pretty sure their tribal chief would have them killed, because it happened to two older friends several years ago. They also feared separation from each other by selling the boys as slaves in trade for horses from opposing tribes. A slave in an enemy camp would experience a short miserable life.

Not long after Windtalker's eighteenth birthday, they began making plans to leave the tribe forever. They felt it was the only choice they had to both survive and be together. All winter long, they stored supplies, weapons, hides, cooking and skinning utensils, as well as seeds and sacks of wild corn, and hid their possessions in a secret cave. The winter was the only time of the year the nomadic tribe stayed put, instead of following the trail of the buffalo across the plains in the warmer season.

Their fathers gave each boy a horse when they turned fourteen and they trained the animals well. With just the slightest touch of their thighs, they could silently maneuver their horse through any obstacle. They could fire their bows with great accuracy on a full gallop and they were deadly with spears. This was the way the great hunters of the tribe took down the buffalo. To make their escape, however, they needed a packhorse. To steal one from their family or another member of the tribe would be a great insult, and the entire tribe would seek revenge and hunt them down. They needed to find a wild horse on their own.

All winter they made their plans, but on warmer days, they hunted the gullies in the mountains for wild horses known to hide from the winter storms in the deep gorges. They found none. They saved up worn pairs of moccasins and repaired them, as active hunters often went through a pair of moccasins in just six weeks or so. They saved buffalo bladders to carry water, and made many bags of jerky and cornmeal. They planned to leave on the night of the first big spring rain, as they knew the rain would mix with the melting snow, hiding their tracks and their trail to make it nearly impossible to find them. They would also ride for days, stopping only to rest their horses. They prayed they would find a packhorse soon and before the village returned to the plains. The forest would hide their trek while the plains would make it easier for a good scout to see them.

The spring sun woke them early in their tipis. They fetched water as usual, ate some leftover hot stew near the fire, and set out on their horses to hunt game. The men were away after a scout spotted a white hunting party killing buffalo on the plains near the edge of the mountains. They were on the trail of a deer and tracked it to the entrance of a ravine they knew to be a dead end. They went about a quarter mile into the gulch, tied off their horses, and set about on foot tracking the animal with great stealth. Their moccasins made no sounds as they carefully crept gently along the trail.

Kiyo decided to climb the ridge so he could see down into the ravine while leaving Windtalker on the main trail in case the deer tried to bolt down the trail. Kiyo hoped to get behind the animal and force him towards Windtalker and certain death from one of his pal's arrows. He had just reached the top of the cliff when movement down the trail behind Windtalker caught his eye. Quickly, he fell to his belly and crawled behind a rock. Prudently, he peered out through the crack of two stones. His heart sank as he spotted the unmistakable colors of a Shoshone warrior. The man appeared to be alone with a bow over his shoulder, a big hunting knife at his side, and a spear hung loose in his right hand. Kiyo assumed he was a hunter because he, too, was tracking the deer, but now he also tracked the larger hoof prints from Kiyo's and Windtalker's horses. The warrior smartly valued two horses more than one deer.

Kiyo searched the trail ahead for Windtalker, but could not locate him in the cover of the forest. Carefully, he moved along the ridge being mindful to avoid scattering rocks, but urgently searching for a glimpse of his friend. The minutes slipped by and the hunter began speeding up his search. Kiyo knew about where he had left Windtalker, so he assumed he must have moved deeper into the ravine.

Suddenly, he caught sight of Windtalker briefly, but he could not fathom how to signal him. He cautiously waved his arms, but Windtalker never looked up, while assuming Kiyo had reached the top, ran along the ridge to the end, and descended as planned. Finally, Kiyo caught just a glimpse of Windtalker before disappearing in the foliage again. Kiyo looked back to his left, while discovering the Shoshone warrior was but fifty yards south. Kiyo's eyes rapidly searched the trail until finally he saw Windtalker once more.

Quickly, Kiyo threaded an arrow, aimed it in front of his friend, and fired. Windtalker nearly jumped off the trail as the arrow slammed into the dirt just three feet ahead of him. He recognized the arrow immediately, as the boys had made their arrows together for years. He looked up and saw Kiyo signaling quietly by taking his hand like a knife and pretending to slit his throat. He then pointed behind Windtalker. Then Kiyo pushed his hands downward with open palms; a signal the tribe used when enemy warriors approached and the families should silently hide.

Windtalker looked behind him, snatched up Kiyo's arrow, scattered snow, and left the trail. Kiyo began making his way off the ridge as quietly as he could in case the warrior discovered Windtalker. Forty yards from reaching Windtalker, the Shoshone warrior stopped when he found their horses. He pondered whether to pursue the game, kill the riders, or just steal the horses.

TJ Johnson

Wrongly assuming the hunters were grown male warriors, he took the safer route and began untying the horses, because without horses, the hunters would probably die in the snowy gorge.

It had begun to rain with a snowy mix, but the Indian tied the horses one after the other and was in the process of maneuvering them to leave the gully. Kiyo saw him and nearly panicked when he saw him leading them away. He climbed on a rock overlooking the trail. He turned towards the deep end of the gorge and let out the sound of the hawk. It was a sound he had practiced all of his life and one that Windtalker knew well.

Windtalker crept out from his hiding place and listened once more, then took off running back down the path. Kiyo threaded his bow. The warrior tried to hurry along, but didn't want to make too much noise. The wet snow began pouring down harder. When the warrior was but twenty yards away, he spotted Kiyo just as the boy let go his arrow. The warrior almost managed out of the way, but the arrow caught him high in the left shoulder. He pulled his bow up and tried to fire back, but his wounded left arm didn't work well. He dismounted and lifted his spear. Kiyo fired again catching the man in the thigh of his left leg. Filled with rage, the man attempted to run towards him. Kiyo fired again but missed.

Windtalker heard the Indian yelp at the impact of Kiyo's first arrow. He threaded his bow as he ran. Kiyo searched for cover but found none. The big warrior was within range of a certain kill. Kiyo placed an arrow across his bow and fired again, but the warrior dodged the hurried attempt. Suddenly, the man stopped, and brought back the spear with his right hand. Kiyo feared for his life and rapidly tried to place another arrow on his bow, but he was too frightened.

Before the Indian could fire, Kiyo heard the zip of Windtalker's arrow. It caught the Shoshone warrior in the back of the neck, came through and out his Adam's apple. The sudden immense pain forced the man to drop the spear. Windtalker didn't hesitate but fired again, putting a second arrow deep in the man's back. Kiyo finally fired and hit the man in the heart, and the warrior went down like a stone, his life quickly drifting away.

Windtalker ran up and cautiously checked to see if the man was alive, but he was rapidly bleeding out. "It's all right. He's dead. Come on down."

Kiyo hurried to him. "Thanks, he was about to kill me with the spear. He was stealing our horses. I had to stop him."

Windtalker laughed. "Well, you might as well have used rocks, as you didn't even nick him good. Come on and let's strip him of his weapons."

"We'd better hide his body in case he has friends nearby."

They quickly took his knife, bow, arrows, spear, and a tomahawk, plus his kit of supplies, including a valued flint rock used for starting a fire. They dragged his body into the brush.

Suddenly Windtalker grinned. "We finally have our third horse. We

8

can go now."

Oblivious of the cold wet snow sliding down his back, Kiyo's eyes lit up with excitement. "Do you mean now, or go back to the village and leave in the night?"

Windtalker wet his chapped lips with his tongue while thinking. "Well, there are some things I would like to have at the village, but how would we keep the new horse a secret?"

"I guess we can't say goodbye to our families and friends, but we've always known that."

Windtalker added, "Most of the men are away tracking the wagon train. They can't afford to send many warriors to track us, and with the wet snow, it is probably best we leave right now. The snow will hide our trail."

The boys remained deep in thought for a long minute as their bodies became soaked with the cold rain snow mix. Kiyo finally agreed. "If we leave now, the icy rain will wash away our tracks, hide the blood spilled by the Shoshone warrior, and we'd have a horse. We'll just have to hope we can find game soon, as we don't have much food."

"How far do you think it is to the secret cave?"

Kiyo replied, "About two hours ride. Do you think we should go to the cave first?"

Windtalker nodded. "Yes. It is a risk as someone might spot us, but I doubt anyone else would be out in this weather. If we get our cache of supplies, we'll have a greater chance of success, but we must hurry there, load, and ride as far west as we can before nightfall."

Kiyo agreed. "Help me scrub away the markings on the horse in case we run into more Shoshone."

Using mud and leaves mixed with snow and rain, they scrubbed away the colors on the horse's rear flank, and then used the warrior's tether to make a loop around the horse's neck. Together, they left the gorge and turned east in the direction of the cave.

They were quiet and careful, but moved as fast as they dared, hoping to avoid any other Shoshone hunters. Reaching the cave safely, they attached the supply frame they made months ago to the new packhorse, tied on their supplies and bundles of extra arrows and two extra bows, the captured weapons from the Shoshone hunter, and kissed in the dark of the cave. They were about to commit tribal treason, but they knew they wanted to live unencumbered for the rest of their lives. They felt they had no choice. They were now homeless without family or friends, but together they were free.

Taking a different route west, they bypassed the area where they were hunting in case someone discovered the body of the Shoshone they killed. As soon as possible, they made their way up the western ridge towards the higher mountain and out of the area, and hopefully, out of range of anyone looking for the warrior. By late afternoon, they were in the bottom of two gorges to the west, and making their way a bit south to make travel easier. The rain let up but they were cold. By late afternoon, they came upon a cave. They checked for bears or mountain lion tracks near the mouth of the cave, found none, and cautiously entered the cave.

They hid their horses behind a blind of brush, hobbled them, and set about breaking off dried limbs off the trees. It took a half hour before they felt the warmth of a fire. The snow was melting so they knew the temperature was above freezing, but they were still cold. Once the fire grew, they ate some jerky, and made some cornmeal cakes cooked on a hot flat rock next to the fire. They drank water from a bladder, laid out a few hides, stripped naked and hung their clothes on sticks to dry, and then huddled together for warmth. They knew perhaps one of them should have stood watch, but on this first day of their journey to freedom, they felt exhausted from the short battle, the decline of the adrenalin rush afterwards, and the long ride to get away. They fell asleep dog-tired but deliriously happy in each other's arms.

TWO

It had been a few days since their escape from their tribe and the killing of the Shoshone hunter. Kiyo climbed a tall tree and watched for a half hour, but could not spot any attempting to follow them. They had been in this territory of the mountains before when they were younger and the tribe needed to go deeper into the mountains for a particularly harsh winter, and to get away from swarming bands of Sioux warriors determined to catch them after a particular bloody raid and the theft of many horses right before the first major snowfall.

A week later, they began feeling confident no one was tracking them, but daily they did things to hide their trail to prevent other hunters from attempting to catch up with them and steal their horses. They walked through streams for long periods, departed the water on long stretches of rocks, and stayed away from larger well-worn trails by moving parallel in the forest. They finally managed to kill a deer, and ate well for several nights, carried some cooked beef with them, but abandoned the rest to the scavengers, as they didn't want to take the time to cure the meat. The weather improved with the Indians noting longer days of sunshine and blue skies. The snow continued to melt but the nights remained cold.

Mile after rugged mile they climbed steep mountains and descended the rough terrain on the other side. They were often in the sun during the middle part of the day, but the rest of the time they were in the cold dark shadows of the tall mountains. A few days later, more rain fell washing away most of the snow. The timing of their escape might have been a little early, as a possible late blizzard could certainly kill hunters so high in the mountains, but they were young, tough, highly trained, and in love, and determined to survive.

It had been a long first month on their journey, eating on the run, chewing game when they could get it, and finding a few berries to still the grumbling in their empty bellies. They relentlessly continued moving west and as far away from their own Blackfeet people as possible, but by doing so they feared capture by another band, and either forced into slavery, or worst for them, a forced march back to their tribe. For the better part of two years, they planned and talked about this trip, but now that they were doing it, and yet, they were not sure of where to go. As boys, they heard stories of the mystery lands to the west, and tried to recall every detail, but every day they went up yet another mountain ridge, and down to the next riverbed.

Sitting near the fire to stay warm, Windtalker said, "I think we must find a secret valley full of game and good water, but difficult for anyone else to enter."

Kiyo grinned. "If it is difficult, how are we to find it?"

11

Windtalker laughed. "Oh we will find it, because we have to."

"How are we to live? We don't have enough hides for a tipi."

"Once we find our valley, we'll make camp and hunt deer until we have enough hides to make a small tipi."

"It might be easier to build a lodge like the white men."

"How so?"

"Do you remember when we found that abandoned lodge built with the white man's tools? They built it in a square using the tree logs and mud."

Windtalker laughed. "I thought it was weird looking, but it did look warm."

Kiyo added, "And dry. I can't wait to dry out in the summer sun."

"Me, too."

The next day, they crossed a stream and saw a large trail just a bit south. They walked their horses through the water cautiously while listening for any sound. Suddenly, Kiyo lifted his hand for Windtalker to stop and remain still. Kiyo heard something. They waited.

"Yelp!" they heard together.

Kiyo quickly looked left and right, and rapidly made a decision to lead them out of the water, over a grassy bank, across a bed of rocks and deep into a laurel thicket. They dismounted behind a field of giant granite boulders and tied off the horses. Taking their bows and quivers of arrows, he and Windtalker returned a few steps down the trail, but remained as quiet as possible.

Windtalker touched Kiyo's face to get his attention and pointed back to the stream. Kiyo turned in the direction and together they counted a dozen Shoshone warriors moving slowly through the stream to the north on horseback. Their weapons glistened with fresh blood still dripping to the ground. They were not hunters but full grown experienced warriors, and the sight of them nearly caused the lads to shake with fear. Kiyo and Windtalker almost held their breath while praying the men would fail to find their tracks. Suddenly, they all heard another yelp to the north.

The Indians began rapidly chattering at each other, and then suddenly they went out of the water on the eastern bank of the stream and galloped away. The young men had no idea what had spooked them, but they didn't wait around for their return. They led their horses through the thicket, crossed a second stream, and kept moving west for the rest of the day. They said little to each other while plodding along the animal trails, afraid someone would hear and attack. They communicated with hand gestures or knowing eyes, as they could almost read each other's mind. They continued for as long as possible, only stopping as darkness fell. At night, they planned strategies for defending an attack, and kept their weapons at the ready at all times. Fearing more Shoshone warriors, they began taking turns standing watch at night.

12

As they crossed the next big ridge, they realized they were now at least two moons away from the plains of the Blackfeet, and by air, they were over two hundred miles to the west. With the warmer weather, the tribes would have already left the safety for the mountains, and moved to the plains where they would follow the trails of the buffalo. This would put much more distance between them and the families they now feared. They felt like they might have crossed through the Shoshone area as well, but had no idea what tribe might be next. After resting a spell on the ridge after a hard climb, they suddenly heard a gunshot. Although there were no guns in their village, several were stolen from the explorers and hunters, and fired, so they knew the sound, but no one knew how to reload the weapons or make more bullets or gunpowder.

At first, they thought they should turn south and away from the gunfire, but that would put them back in Shoshone territory. If they could go north for a few more miles, they could turn west again across a long ridge, and in a few days be up and over the next big mountain. Reluctantly, they followed the ridge to the north, wondering what they might find. After a mile, they could smell gunpowder, and a half-mile later their nostrils inhaled the aroma of food on a campfire.

Carefully, they continued until they knew they were close. They tied off the horses and crept up the trail placing an arrow across their bows. At twenty yards away, but safely hidden by the laurel brush, they could see a campfire, the leg of a downed white man, an arm of an Indian, and away just a bit, a leg of another Indian. Blood marred the ground, but what stopped the Indians still in their tracks was a large dog resting on his belly next to the white man. He looked a bit bigger than a wolf but similar in structure.

Windtalker motioned to Kiyo that he was going into the camp so Kiyo prepared to cover him with his bow ready to fire. They saw no one else alive and nothing else moving. The man and the Indians had been without horses. The dog spotted Windtalker and snarled at him. Wisely, Windtalker retrieved a bit of jerky from his waist pouch and held it out for the dog to see. The dog stopped snarling and licked his lips. Windtalker moved closer and now could see two dead Shoshone hunters and the dead trapper. Windtalker tossed the dog another morsel. The dog caught it. Finally and bravely, he left a piece in his hand, stretched his hand forward, and went down on his knees to show he was both not afraid of the dog nor meaning the dog any harm. One paw at a time the dog slowly walked to him and took the meat from Windtalker's hand. Windtalker petted him, and gave him another bite of jerky from his left hand.

Carefully, he stood, and began searching the campsite. He waved for Kiyo to bring the horses. After Kiyo entered the camp, Windtalker said, "It looks like the white man shot one Indian and then the other two fought with knives and killed each other. The man and the Indians have supplies. Let's gather up what we can and get out of here, or we could be blamed for killing a white man or the Indians."

They rummaged through everything, keeping a rifle, pistol, knives, bows and arrows, gunpowder, cooking utensils, and supplies. There was a rabbit roasting over the fire. They retrieved and ate chunks of it while packing the things they found. Both fellows tossed the dogs chunks of meat as well. Once satisfied, they climbed aboard their horses and left the camp. The dog circled around the camp as if confused at his situation. His master lay dead. If he stayed he would starve. Reluctantly, the dog slowly trailed the riders, but cautiously remaining behind the young men a hundred yards and out of sight. His nose easily tracked their horses, so he could follow even during a sudden downpour. When they crossed a stream, he sniffed the far bank until he picked up the scent again, but smartly increased his speed fearing he might lose them.

Late in the afternoon, the Indians felt they had gone far enough to avoid any connection with the dead white hunter and the Indians. They found a good campsite near a smaller stream that was safely away from the river and far away from any trails. The skies were clear so they made camp in the open. Windtalker began making a fire so he could cook a hot meal for them while Kiyo went hunting.

Kiyo made his way across the stream and into a small plain where he spotted the tracks of a rabbit. He threaded his bow and carefully followed the trail. He had been on the track for a half hour when suddenly he saw it leap about thirty feet ahead of him. He knelt down and fired his arrow, but missed his target just slightly. Suddenly, the big dog that had been tracking him, leaped over him knocking him down, and sprinted after the rabbit. Kiyo sat there astonished, having failed to pick up the scent of the dog. Just as he got to his knees, the dog returned with the rabbit in his teeth. The big dog caught the fleet-footed rabbit, shook it harshly to kill it, and returned it to Kiyo. Gently, he laid it down at his feet and then backed up a few steps and sat down.

Kiyo smiled. "Good dog. That's the way to do it. Let's find another one." He petted the dog numerous times, gave him a bit of jerky from his waist pouch, and then tied a leather string around the hind paws of the rabbit and threw him over his shoulder. Together, he and the dog continued the hunt.

An hour later, Windtalker successfully cooked cornmeal bread cakes for them, as well as some wild carrots and potato roots still stewing in a pot. He heard the soft sound of a dove. He knew it was Kiyo and a signal they practiced since they were little boys. He looked up to see Kiyo coming into the camp with the dog.

"Where'd he come from?"

Kiyo grinned. "I think he must have tracked us, and he must be good at it as many times as we went in and out of the streams today." "How are we going to feed him?"

14

"He's feeding us," replied Kiyo with a grin as he removed the three rabbits hanging on his back. "Look at these rabbits. You won't find a single arrow wound. The dog tracked them, made the kill, and returned the game to me. I'd say he has earned his keep."

"We'll have to train him to be quiet on command or he could accidentally give us up."

Kiyo said, "I'll train him. I think he may be the smartest dog I've ever seen. Let's get these rabbits over the fire. I'm starved." They quickly skinned the rabbits, tossed a few morsels to the dog, ran skewer sticks through the torsos, and placed them high over the fire using two limbs with forks to hold them as they cooked. Windtalker turned the roasting rabbits from time to time until satisfied they were done. They pulled off pieces and began chewing the tender white meat. Kiyo threw more pieces to the dog. The dog never failed to catch and devour the morsels. They ate the stew and cornbread while tossing more chunks of meat to the dog, as three rabbits made quiet a feast. Windtalker added some meat to his stew, plus more water and some seasoning from a dry pouch, and left it near the edge of the fire to keep it warm for breakfast.

Afterwards, they stripped naked and walked to the stream to wash several days of grime away. The dog played in and around the stream, and then suddenly snatched a fish like a bear catching a salmon. They laughed at him as the dog sat down on a bed of rock and stripped away the meat and ate it all. The water was cold to their bare skin but it felt so good to wash. They scrubbed each other's back and then sat on the rocks to dry a bit before walking back to the fire to get warm. The sun dropped quickly behind the big mountain peaks. They laid out hides and Windtalker soon fell sound asleep as Kiyo and the dog took first watch. Now and then, he put another stick on the fire. He played with the dog by throwing a stick for him to retrieve for a spell before letting the dog settle down and sleep. It didn't take long until he noted the change in the dog's breathing as he slept soundly.

Kiyo looked up at stars and thought about the journey they had taken so far. Most of the tribe would assume they were dead or captured by enemy tribes and made slaves, but mostly, they would just accept the boys were gone. He no longer feared capture by the Blackfeet but he wondered about the tribes to the west that he had never seen before. He thought perhaps they could rest a day or two here in this valley, and perhaps scout about for a place to live. They were now in the section of what the explorers called the Glacier Mountains. It was beautiful country with spectacular views, clean cold water, plenty of game, and so far no sign of another human.

THREE

Kiyo, Windtalker, and the dog finally left their campground where they enjoyed several good days of rest, made repairs to their belongings, and taught the dog to stay, hunt, fetch, attack by both word commands and sign language. They named the dog Emita, which is the Blackfeet word for dog. They realized how smart the dog was as he picked up everything they taught him quickly. He loved to run the trail ahead of them, and often took off running as they climbed on their horses and rode across the next peak. They traveled over the rugged area for another week while searching for the right place to live. One morning they set out not long after dawn. Emita ran ahead as usual and had been out of sight for ten minutes or so when suddenly, they heard a yelp. They rose upwards on their horses and spotted the dog fleeing towards them at a rapid pace. They were confused as to what scared him until they spotted a big grizzly bear heading their way chasing the dog. It would be too slow to go back up the mountain, so they rapidly turned south and rode hard while calling for Emita. The terrified dog soon passed them as they galloped away from the grizzly.

They crossed a stream thinking the bear would slow down, but the giant beast sprinted through the water quickly. They came out of the water and into the forest after finding an animal trail, and rushed down it as fast as possible. The bear must have been hungry and wanted the dog or the horses, and maybe the Indians, so he continued his tenacious pursuit. Suddenly, they crossed what appeared to be a well-trodden road. They feared other Indians on the road so they rode straight across and down the hill through another forest. They came upon a second stream and followed it upriver and soon made many left and right turns before they saw a high ridge ahead of them. They assumed there was no exit so that left the fellows with no options. They were going to have to attempt to kill the bear. They heard a waterfall about a hundred yards ahead so they kicked their horses and rushed to it.

As they rounded a bend they could hardly talk as the loud roar of the huge waterfall overwhelmed them. They slid off their horses and tied them in a thicket near the base of the falls. The exhausted Emita drank some water and then sat down to rest. Windtalker and Kiyo grabbed their spears, bows and arrows, and climbed on top of a boulder. They could see the big bear coming up the trail. His chest was wet from the chase and he did appear to have slowed some. Suddenly, he saw them and charged with renewed energy. They hoped to kill or discourage him by firing their arrows. They put a couple of arrows in the bear but they failed to slow him down. He stood up on his hind legs, growled fiercely with an aggressive roar that was loud enough to hear him over the sound of the falls, and then swung his paws and claws back and forth in the air at them. They fired arrows again, this time hitting the softer underbelly. They each got an arrow in before the bear suddenly collapsed and

16

fell hard to the ground. One of the sharp arrowheads must have struck his heart. They waited a while before climbing off the boulder and walked down the trail with their weapons ready.

They found the bear bleeding out. They knelt and gave thanks to the bear for the food and warmth he would provide for them. Kiyo took his knife and cut the bear's throat. Emita ran up and barked at the dead bear. They laughed at him, calling him chicken, and teasing him.

They walked back up the trail to get their horses. Emita ran out ahead of them and wrongly assumed they were going up the trail and leaving the old bear behind. When he got to the waterfall, he smelled the trail of a deer, and began barking as he tracked it. The deer's tracks went to the left side of the falls and disappeared. The perplexed dog kept his nose to the ground and stuck it through a sheet of the water, and then went on through. Kiyo just got a glimpse of him before he disappeared.

"Where's that dog going?"

The Indians ran up to the falls. They could see the deer prints in some sand, and Emita's big paw prints, and both sets of tracks went straight through the edge of the water. Kiyo called the dog and Emita replied by barking loudly. The Indians heard him. Kiyo reached forward and stepped through the water quickly. Windtalker followed him. Their heads were instantly drenched by the clear cold water. They followed a dry path behind the falls. Emita ran to them wagging his tail excitedly. They feared he had found another bear. They entered a large cavern carved in the rock and underneath the waterfall. They looked behind them, and they could see daylight through the cascading water. They turned around and followed the dog. The natural tunnel curved slightly to the west. Forty yards later, they came through an opening, and stepped out of the cavern and into a huge valley. Before them was a large lake. They went a bit farther while thinking the view was completely spectacular and decided they would make camp there. They called Emita and began making their way back through the falls.

It took a bit of coaxing, but they got each horse through the waterfall and out the back and together, they rode to the mouth of the lake, crossed over to a stand of nice timber where they could hear just a slight roar of another waterfall deeper into the valley. They quickly set up camp, put away their gear, and took the packhorse back through the waterfall to retrieve the bear. It took several hours of work, but they fed the dog while working on skinning the bear. They kept some claws, some meat, and the big furry hide, and returned to the camp. They ate well that night, but after all the excitement of the bear chasing them, they realized they were exhausted and went to sleep early taking turns as lookouts as usual.

The next day, they ate leftovers for an early meal, left the packhorse on a long tether so he could eat the surrounding grass, and began to survey the valley. They turned north and up a steep slope. Once they got to the top, they found an unusually high mountain lake that was carved by a glacier many centuries ago, and so clear they could easily see big fish swimming about. To their right they could see where the lake led into a riverbed that fed the waterfall they went through into the cavern.

Across the lake was a steep incline that went right into the water with no shoreline and no access for anyone to hike or ride a horse around. They followed the lake until they came to another rock face and began following the bottom of it around until they came into the wide-open valley. It took several hours or so to get back to the waterfall entrance before they both started grinning.

"I don't think we could find anything more perfect for us," said Windtalker.

Kiyo responded, "The lush valley has a good open area for the horses to graze, maybe a bit of farming for us, a big lake that I bet has loads of fish in it, plenty of freshwater, and a stand of trees to protect us."

"We could build a log cabin, too."

"I think it is secure as the only entrance is the waterfall. If we hide our tracks leading to it, I doubt anyone would find it."

Windtalker interrupted him, "Unless they were chased by a grizzly!" They both laughed. Emita barked at the laughing Indians while wagging his tail rapidly. After almost two months of rugged mountain peaks, valleys, and swift streams, they escaped their Blackfeet homeland, and everyone they knew, and made an almost impossible journey to the west so they could live and love each other for the rest of their lives.

FOUR

It had a taken a week to kill two more deer, tan the hides in the sun, and sew them together along with the other deer hides they collected on their journey. With their small axes, they began trimming and shaping the poles, fabricated the frame, and staked out the bottom. They dug a trench around the tipi to drain away the rainwater and dew that would daily bounce and slide off the oily skins. Twice during construction they were drenched in a thunderstorm, but finally they made a smaller tipi about two-thirds the size of their family tipi to keep their belongings and themselves dry. This morning they set out with their horses and an almost empty packhorse, hoping to find more game outside their valley, and to explore the region around their new home.

Windtalker and Kiyo marveled at the beauty of their valley and lake along with the gorgeous mountains surrounding their new home. They made their way through the large cavern ending behind the waterfall. Emita barked as he beat them to the waterfall and without hesitation jumped through. They rode through quickly while catching a quick splash of cold water on their heads and back. Today they took time to survey the natural animal trail leading up to the waterfall. The trail bed mirrored the river channel with a large scattered spillage of broken rock, but worn smooth with years of washing and tumbling in the rapid stream, and perhaps molded by centuries of ice before that. The Indians possessed no knowledge to help them understand that many thousands of years ago, gigantic glaciers constantly constrained, squeezed, and forced their way down, across, and through the mountains of seemingly solid rock. However, the immense glaciers were more than strong enough to fracture the boulder and push them south carving big lakes and valleys with ease.

Straightaway they spotted their own hoof prints, so to lighten the load they slid off their horses and moved to their right to the grassy areas, creating a secret path to their home. After a hundred yards, they jumped on their horses and galloped across an open area. They turned to the north to explore the land they had not yet traveled after finding their valley. In an hour, they were overlooking the upper lake above the valley and studied the steep slope carved by a glacier. The drop from the ridge was over three hundred feet and covered with nothing but broken shale rock, the result of centuries of frost wedging when the temperatures dropped way below zero. If an enemy attempted to climb down, they would rapidly slide and crash into the big rocks at the bottom and certain death. If they fell in the water, there was no way to climb out. The Indians could not see the bottom of this five hundred feet deep lake, but in the ooze were thousands of bones and skeletons of some animals that no longer walked the face of the earth. Though ominous, it gave the Indians a great sense of security. They studied the acres of thick forest on the far shore, preventing anyone from standing where they were and seeing their beautiful valley. This new knowledge increased their confidence in finding a secure location.

They continued up the mountain while stopping now and then to see if they could catch a glimpse into the valley and they could not. They were also studying the mountains and the hills around them, memorizing key landscapes so they would always find their new home. They were enjoying the view when unexpectedly they heard repeated gunshots from a valley to the east. The Indians argued for and against an investigation for just a minute before finally agreeing they needed to know all about their surroundings and possible inhabitants.

They called Emita with a whistle as they changed directions and made their way along the eastern ridge searching for a way down. Finally, Emita found a seven foot wide animal trail, most likely worn down over the centuries, but they found no horse prints and continued down the trail. They heard additional gunshots from time to time like a beacon guiding their way. After they reached the bottom of the gentle sloping trail, they crossed what appeared to be a natural road. They got off their horses, giving the animals a bit of a rest, and checked out the various tracks they found. They saw unshod horse tracks, much like their own and counted a dozen horses. They also saw shod horses and carefully counted six riders and a packhorse that made far deeper and distinctive tracks. Finally and astonishingly, they saw the ruts of two wagons. They were surprised any wagons made it across the plains to the west considering the numerous battles the western tribes of Indians waged on them along the way.

They flung themselves on their horses after hearing another gunshot to the south. Kiyo called to Emita and they set out galloping towards the sound. Emita ran hard and soon out of sight ahead of them. They were almost to a bend in the road when they saw the big dog running towards them faster than his normal pace.

Kiyo and Windtalker pulled their horses to a halt. Their faces displayed a combination of fear and wonderment. Suddenly, they heard a yelp and a scream like their Indian brothers often did when going off to war. This instantly alarmed them so they quickly steered their horses off the road and behind a stand of rocks. Kiyo slid off his horse, handing the reins to Windtalker. Kiyo ran back to the road in time to call Emita to him. The sprinting dog quickly leaped off the road just as the approaching riders came around the bend.

Kiyo rushed back to Windtalker. "Riders coming. Stay quiet." He turned to Emita and said, "Stay. No bark."

Kiyo crept back to the road, hiding amongst the tall cedars so prevalent in these mountains, and remaining low to the ground. He heard more yelps and soon saw the dozen horses as they rode by. He saw blood on their weapons, a few wore captured soldier hats, and two men carried a string of scalps lying across the necks of their horses. He had never seen Indians like these before. He recognized none of the signs painted on neither the horses, nor the way they wore feathers in their hair. They carried bows and arrows, and large battle-axes made from iron. Kiyo had never seen such weapons before. At the rear of the riders were several horses carrying the bodies of their warriors killed in battle.

Kiyo watched as they continued in a northeast direction up the road and out of sight. He ran back to Windtalker and quickly described all he had seen. They sat there for a while until finally they decided to investigate the battle scene. Kiyo sent Emita ahead as usual. As they made their way down the road, around a few bends, the dog stopped in a slight fork off to the left. Kiyo and Windtalker noted numerous horse tracks and the now familiar wagon ruts. They slowed their horses as they took in the scene off the road to the left in the woods. Emita stopped at the edge of the apparent encampment, knowing something bad happened ahead of him.

They tied off their horses, kept their bows and arrows ready, and slowly scanned the camp. Scattered around the camp were the bodies of eight white men, two women, and three children. Blood covered the ground around their lifeless torsos. Many were cut brutally, the result of the battle-axes, and many had arrows in their bodies.

During the battle, the horses scattered, but they returned having no idea of where to go. Two pairs of horses were still wearing their wagon harnesses. The Indians walked quickly from body to body looking for any sign of life but found none. The sight of the bloody children sickened them. The rape of the women, and the cutting away of their clothes and body parts shamed them.

Windtalker spoke first, "What should we do?"

Kiyo thought a second. "I think we should quickly load one wagon with anything we can use and rush back to our valley. We do not want to be caught with this gear. Some of the men were soldiers so there must be a fort nearby." He stopped and pointed to a wagon already heading back towards the road. "We'll take that wagon. Go ahead and start loading the wagon and I'll try to figure out how to hitch these wagon horses up."

Kiyo walked softly towards their horses speaking to them gently until finally he could touch them and rub their heads. He led them back to the wagon. He studied the tack and finally realized the big hooks went in to rings along the rail and to the rear. Once he had them hitched, he untangled the reins and threw them up to the seat.

He then joined Kiyo, who loaded all the boxes of food and supplies from the other wagon into the hitched one. They gathered up all the rifles and pistols along with boxes of ammunition. They stowed cooking utensils, and to Kiyo's delight, they found two farm axes, and a long skinny piece of metal with sharp teeth and wooden handles on each end. They had no idea what it was but they took it as well. They removed gun belts, canteens, and clothes of the settlers, but took no uniforms from the soldiers. They also found several wide brim hats and threw them in the wagon as well. They collected money, gold, and a watch, thinking they would be of value for a trade. They also collected unbroken arrows, and found a battle-axe slightly under one of the bodies of a settler and missed by the warriors.

Once loaded, they checked out the rider horses, selected the best ones and tied their leads to the back of the wagon. They studied the saddles on the other horses, then removed the saddles and bridles, and put the tack in the other wagon with a canvas top to keep them out of the rain in case they had a chance to return. They encouraged the unselected horses to flee the area by throwing rocks at them. The small herd quickly darted down the trail.

Kiyo announced, "I'll attempt to steer the wagon. You get in front and maybe the wagon horses will follow you. We must make our way quickly back to the safety of the valley."

"We'll have to hide our tracks, too. After we get going, I'll ride ahead to make sure the way is clear."

"Send Emita out to scout, too. Let's get out of here. This place gives me the creeps."

The wagon horses instinctively followed Windtalker as he led them back to the road. Emita ran ahead as usual and soon they were back on the road. Kiyo had no idea how fast the wagon could travel but he tried to hurry. He was bouncing in the seat and twice nearly fell off. It took an hour to get back to where they had found the road. Windtalker and Emita waited for the wagon to catch up. Kiyo made the turn, drove the wagon down the smaller trail about a hundred feet and stopped. He figured out the pole coming up the side was a brake of sorts, so he pulled it and tied the reins to it.

He leaped off the wagon feeling thankful to be on solid ground again.

Windtalker laughed at him. "How was the ride?"

"I think my teeth were jarred loose. Come on, break some pine limbs and let's brush away our tracks."

They spent a half hour dragging the pines back and forth across the small but natural road after stomping in the wagon tracks. Once satisfied, they resumed their journey home. The smaller trail required a slower pace as the wagon bounced over rocks and logs down the hill. Two hours later, they made it to the fork leading to the stream and the waterfall. They stopped once more to remove ruts and tracks before proceeding.

When they reached the waterfall, they decided to walk their horses through first, then the rider horses, and finally the wagon team. The new horses shied from the waterfall, but they tugged and pulled until they came through. After the first one, the rest were a bit easier.

Using a long limb, he and Windtalker carefully measured the width of the cavern and determined it was indeed just wide enough for the wagon, and they hoped tall enough. Kiyo rested a while before climbing aboard the wagon, dreading the ride through the waterfall. Windtalker hooked two ropes to the bridles and led the horses to the waterfall. He ran quickly as they made their way over the field of rocks determined not to stop, but to race the horses through the falling water. He kept their heads low and almost before they knew it they had gone under, then they bolted slightly giving Kiyo a jerk and a big face full of water as they sprinted through.

Once through the cavern Kiyo sighed heavily, knowing their journey home had been a safe secret one, but they brought along numerous new possessions that would help them. He had no trouble fording the stream across to the stand of trees and their tipi. He pulled the wagon to halt in front of their campground, tied off the brake and the reins, and leaped out. Windtalker laughed as Kiyo rubbed his sore butt.

"That is one uncomfortable ride. I'm sure my butt has sores on it."

Windtalker slid off his horse, removed the reins from both of their horses, and let them loose so they could get water from the stream and head to the grassy fields. They unsaddled the rider horses, setting the saddles on the ground under the wagon to keep them out of possible rain. Finally, they studied the harness for the wagon horses so they would be able to reattach them if needed, then unhitched them, removed their bridles and set them free, too. They were confident the horses would not ford the stream or go through the waterfall if they didn't have to.

"I'm starved. Let's eat and then we'll sort through the stuff." They ate a meal of flat corn bread and beef jerky, along with fresh water. Emita was fed, too and quickly settled down for a much needed nap in the shade of the trees.

Windtalker said, "We can build a cabin now with the axes we found."

"What was that long metal thing with the sharp things on one edge?"

"I don't know. I'll look at it again."

"We'll have to leave a lot of the stuff in the wagon to keep it dry. Do you think we should go back for the second wagon?"

Windtalker replied, "Yes, I'm afraid so, or someone else will steal it from us. There are lots of supplies, saddles, and gear that we may not have a chance to obtain for years."

"So you're thinking we should go back tomorrow."

"Yep, the sooner the better. We'll take our horses and the two wagon horses and leave the rest here. The tack for the other wagon is still there."

"Okay, but you'll have to drive this time. My butt hurts."

Windtalker laughed. "It'll hurt even more after tonight."

Kiyo grinned slyly. "Okay, let's see what we brought home."

They both played with the battle-axe, realizing it was a formidable close-in battle weapon. They had seen the results at the site of the brief battle as each man hit with the axe died almost instantly. The blade almost severed heads, and they noted one man that was hit at the top of his shoulder with the sharp heavy blade. The blade continued downward shattering the bones, slicing through the heart and lungs, and stopping deep in the stomach. It was a gruesome example of the carnage this axe provided.

They counted eight rifles, ten pistols, and numerous gun belts. They tried them on and then lifted the guns. After their second trip for rest of the gear, they thought they would spend some time learning how to shoot the guns. They found a tin filled with small cakes and they devoured the sweet food. They counted four bags of flour, three bags of cornmeal, and big sacks of grain for the horses. They had an assortment of clothes, knives, boots, hats, pants, shirts, jackets, and coats, plus thick blankets.

They hunted later in the afternoon and with Emita's help they obtained a fresh rabbit for dinner. Windtalker knew how to make a biscuit like bread with a mix of the flour and cornmeal. They also cut off a slice of a smoked ham, heated it next to the fire in their new cast iron frying pan, fed some to Emita, and ate the rest.

They slept well after their first day of exploration and adventure, and they vowed to do more journeys, but first they wanted to build a cabin with their new tools. They found farm tools at the massacre but they left them in the other wagon. They would attempt to bring it all home tomorrow.

The adventure of the day tired the young men so after a bit of lovemaking, they went fast asleep cuddling together on the bearskin rug and pulled a settler blanket over their naked bodies.

FIVE

With a whistle, Kiyo called their horses to them at dawn the next morning. The other horses followed suit with a little help from Emita as he rounded them up like an untrained sheep dog. They tied off the wagon horses with a rope over their necks, bridled their own horses with their customary rope bridles, and led the horses back through the waterfall.

It took a few hours to reach the other wagon, but the site was even worst than the day before as the scavengers from the air and the ground were feeding on the dead. In another day, there would be no meat or flesh left, and the human bones would be scattered. With the stench infesting their nostrils, Kiyo and Windtalker wasted no time. Though they had to think a bit about what went where, they began hitching the wagon horses as quickly as possible. Between the two of them, they finally attached the harnesses correctly. They went through the camp, loading everything of value into the wagon, including the extra saddles, lots of farm tools, and with a careful eye, they found a few more scattered pistols, knives, another bow and quiver, and found a second battle axe almost completely covered in the grass.

Once satisfied, Windtalker tied off his horse to the rear of the wagon and climbed aboard, taking a grip on the reins with a bit of coaching from Kiyo. Emita led the way and Kiyo followed as they began scouting the trail ahead, then the road, and Windtalker came along as fast he could in the wagon. An hour into their journey, they suddenly saw Emita once again running rapidly towards Kiyo. Kiyo let out the sound of a hawk and began riding towards Windtalker, while searching the road for an exit.

Frantic, he finally found one and waved the wagon off the road and around the back of a thick stand of trees and some scattered giant granite boulders. Windtalker jumped out and went to settle down the wagon horses. Kiyo took care of their Indian horses and Emita. They heard the hooves of many horses as they watched the road through the limbs.

Soon they heard a yelp and saw the tribe of Indians that attacked yesterday sprinting by but in larger numbers. They guessed at twenty or more. They wore battle paint but their bodies were free of blood. They suspected they were looking for a fight and didn't notice their tracks. Kiyo sprinted to the road after they passed and watched until they were out of sight. He sent Emita in the direction they were heading while he ran back to help Windtalker turn the wagon around. He led the horses in a tight circle and soon they were back on the trail feeling very lucky.

Fearful of discovery, they almost spilled the wagon as they made their way up to the road, made a second hard turn, and began picking up speed. Emita soon disappeared out of sight, and Kiyo rode farther ahead in case he needed to warn Windtalker once more.

It was a long hour before they reached the western fork, and a half mile farther they pulled the wagon into the forest, stopped, and went back to wipe away ruts and tracks. Emita sat down to rest for a bit or at least until Kiyo sent him towards home as they once again began moving. After another hour or so, they began to relax, as they knew they were safely far away from the menacing band of warriors now seen twice in two days.

Kiyo saw the last fork ahead and grinned. He felt they had made it with more stuff and many reasons to celebrate, including avoiding the warriors twice. They stopped once more to wipe the trail clean, and made their way along the lake, crossed over the stream, passed the dried bones of the grizzly, and up the trail to the waterfall. Emita snagged a dry bear bone as he ran by and leaped through the waterfall. Kiyo slipped a rope over the heads of the wagon horses and led them quickly through the waterfall. Once through, they both sighed as they made their way along their lake, forded the stream, and pulled into the camp.

Kiyo removed the bridles from their horses and let them once again roam free, and then he and Windtalker removed the harness and bridles from the horses, and set them free as well. Kiyo asked, "How's your butt?"

"Sore as hell. I think the white men must have more padding than we do."

"Perhaps so. Let's eat. I'm starved and we need to make a plan."

Emita returned from a long drink in the stream and settled down next to Kiyo. The Indians took turns feeding the dog some jerky as they ate a late lunch. Soon Emita was sound asleep, a tempting thought for them as well, but they discussed plans and decided building a cabin had to be first on the list. They would hunt early in the mornings so they would have fresh food, and if they killed a deer or an elk, then they would have food for days so they could continue construction.

The cabin they discovered years ago became the model for their own. They selected a spot facing the lake and the entrance to the waterfall, in a stand of trees for shade, and on top of a slight knoll so rainwater would drain away from the cabin. They took out the farm tools and laid them side-by-side on the ground. They selected iron mallets and dug skinny ditches in long rows using a leather rope for measurement. They made the cabin a square of twenty feet.

There were a few trees in the middle of their future floor so they attacked them first using the new farm axes. The blades were sharp so they made quick work of learning how to use the blades to chop down the trees. After the tree fell, they chipped away the trunk until it was below the ground level. They took smaller axes from the second wagon to cut away the limbs close to the trunk. Using the leather rope, they measured the required length and cut away the excess. Using a selected measuring stick, they cut notches on both ends about a foot from the end. There was enough of the fallen tree left to make a second cabin log. They cut it for length and set it aside preferring thicker logs for the base. They downed each of the trees in the middle of the construction in the same fashion. By dark, they had the base set and surprisingly level by using only their eyes.

They were sore from their work, and very dirty from the digging and chopping, so they stripped naked, and swam in the stream to clean off. They ate deer steaks that night along with cornbread, and soon asleep.

They awoke the next morning with stiff muscles, but soon were back at work taking down the trees near the cabin. They only took the trees that were within twelve feet of the walls, preferring to maintain the shade. They knew from their childhood that the hot sun on the plains could easily heat their tipis. They preferred to keep the cabin cool and comfortable if possible.

At lunch, they discussed how to make a door and windows though their language lacked the words to describe such. In the dirt near their campfire, they drew out the front of the cabin, drawing in two windows and the door. They decided to cut the logs to the correct length to leave a gap for the door. They would do the same for the windows once they had the wall high enough. They had a stack of logs ready to go from their chopping in the cool of the morning.

All afternoon, they carefully chopped for length, as well as the connecting notches on the top and bottom of the logs near the end. Each log was fit to the base while carefully cutting until the log settled as level as possible. By dark the walls were four feet tall all the way around after clearing the land around the cabin and depleting their pile of logs. They returned from washing in the stream, feeling exhausted but happy with their progress.

They began discussing where to get the next logs and their years of living with the village came in handy. They recalled how each time the tribe moved, they sometimes took the poles for the tipis with them, but other times they cut new ones. These new poles were cut a fair distance from the new camp. The Indians left the nearby fallen dried limbs from ice storms and high winds alone for now, saving it for firewood. They decided to do the same. Kiyo came up with the idea of using the wagon horses with their harness to pull the logs to the cabin. Having never seen a horse drag a log, Windtalker laughed at him.

The next morning they hiked farther upstream and chopped down a few trees in the forest. After they downed six, they led the horses to the camp, put the harness on the wagon animals and led them to the first log. They found a big thick rope like those used on a ship in the second wagon and twenty feet of chain. They weren't sure what to do with the chain so they looped the end of the rope around the base of the downed tree, and tied the other end to the rear of the horse harness. Kiyo stood off to the side with the reins while Windtalker went in front to pull the horses. Together, they began pulling and in just a minute or two, they had the first log in front of the cabin.

Kiyo laughed. "I told you it would work. It would have taken you and me quite a while to roll that log to the cabin."

They repeated the process until all the logs were at the cabin. Inspired, they grabbed their axes and downed more trees and hauled them as well. By lunch, they had a pile of twenty-four logs laid out. After the first few trips with the rope on the logs, they realized the rocks were eating away at the rope so they switched to the chain with good success.

At lunch, they discussed how to get the logs in place as the walls became taller. Kiyo said, "We need a way to roll the log upwards to the top of the wall."

Like his grandmother, Windtalker possessed a bit of natural drawing talent and could see things as they are. He began drawing in the sand and soon had the wall of the cabin drawn and together they studied it. "What if we use lodge poles and roll the log up?"

Kiyo grinned. "Now that's an idea but the logs are pretty heavy."

"We'll need some stout poles to support the logs and then we could use short sticks to roll them."

Kiyo added, "So we notch them first, then roll them up and in place, work all the way around with that level and start again. Is that right?"

"I think that is our only choice."

Using the farm axes, they selected the first log and notched out the ends top and bottom, cut some long poles, and using the smaller axes, they removed the limbs, made the poles smooth on one side. They notched one end and set it against the top of the wall after stabbing the other end in the dirt. Using six foot sticks, they maneuvered the notched log in place, and using the sticks to stab and hold, they rolled the log up, carefully stopped at the top, and twisted it over and rolled it in place. Satisfied, they made their way around, but by late afternoon, the wall was taller than they could use the sticks to roll up the next log.

They returned to the forest and cut twelve more logs, and hauled them to the cabin. Done for the day, they washed, ate, and discussed how to get the last of the walls up by putting three more logs on top, and then how to make the roof. Windtalker drew many roofs in the sand, but with no knowledge of roofs in their villages, he didn't have a clue where to start.

After resting a while, they recalled the only cabin they had ever seen, but it didn't have the common pitched roofs like the homes in the colonies, but the back wall was taller than the front, crossed logs covered the roof slanting downward to the front, but he had trouble figuring out how the side walls could be closed in.

They knew the space between the logs would be packed with clay, and while hunting they found a clay pit next to the stream and only about a hundred yards upstream. He began drawing the sidewall with the roof slanting down, and suddenly it dawned on him they would continue going up with the back wall and the sides but each log of the sidewall would be cut a foot shorter. They had found some long big nails in the second wagon and would

28

use them to hold those logs in place since a notch wouldn't do.

The next morning they notched the back wall logs, and rolled the first one in place, but this time they were smarter. By using two rolls of rope, they looped it over the wall, down the rails, under the new log, and back over the wall, and tied it to the horse team. Kiyo carefully led the horses as Windtalker yelled instructions, and in a half-minute, they had the next log in place. As planned, they cut the side log a foot shorter and rolled them up as well. By lunch, the walls were done. After lunch, they cut thirty six-inch diameter logs but very long for the roof, notched the rear and measured carefully for the front by using a rope to measure the angle length to the front wall. They allowed the front length to go long for an overhang to keep the rain out of the cabin at the door.

By dark, the cabin was framed in and ready for windows to be cut, but they needed a roof on the framework and began thinking hard about how to do it. They felt they could put limbs on it, but it would leak and require constant replacement of the limbs as they lost their foliage. They decided to think a while and sleep on it, but still, a good solution remained elusive. As a desperate measure, they removed the canvas top of the second wagon and managed to cover the cabin. They drove in nails and tied it off all the way around. Now it would be dry. They moved the supplies and gear from that second wagon inside on the dirt floor. They would have to trim out the windows and a fire hole, plus figure out how to build doors and windows. For them, all of this construction required too much thinking.

Now that the new cabin had a roof to keep the rain out, they decided to take the day off, and go exploring and do some hunting. They left the valley on horseback, made their way back to the main road in a couple of hours and turned northwest watching for tracks. They sent Emita ahead and galloped for a couple of miles, stopping to enjoy the view over the next peak.

Windtalker noted a trail of smoke a few more miles ahead. They decided to continue down the road and discover the source of the fire. Forty minutes later, Emita came running around the bend rapidly. The Indians knew what that meant and searched for a place to hide. They veered off into a laurel thicket and waited for Emita to join them. Kiyo took the animals deeper into the forest while Windtalker stood guard waiting for the riders. Soon he saw a squad of twelve soldiers wearing their dark blue uniforms and tan hats. They rode by without noticing the tracks left by the Indians.

After they rode out of sight, they returned to the road and continued heading towards the smoke. They talked for a while and decided the soldiers were not pulling packhorses, nor did they carry cooking and tent gear, so they determined there had to be a fort to the northwest. After a few miles with more bends in the road, suddenly they could see the top of a fort off in the distance. Below in a small valley, they saw a settler farm, and the fire came from the settler's effort to clear away some debris so they could plant additional crops.

They had no intention of hurting the settlers or soldiers, and though the white men puzzled them, they did not believe in killing women and children. They continued cautiously, but were very curious about their cabin construction and their farm. They wished for a closer look that would solve their construction problems.

SIX

They left the road when they saw the clearing for the farm. It had been easy to find the settlement due to the smoke. They thought the settlers were crazy to advertise their location so boldly with so many fierce looking warriors riding about. The tribal warriors used a small amount of smoke for signals and cooking, but never a huge fire like this, as the smoke would be seen for miles. They made their way through the woods and continued until they were closer to the farmstead. They tied off the horses and told Emita to sit and stay. The anxious dog whimpered with a quiet sigh, as he stretched out to lie down, but ready to leap to action if required. The dog didn't much want to but obeyed as commanded. They took their bows and walked to the edge of the forest. They counted four, one adult man and woman, and an older boy with a younger sister. They had four horses, a wagon like the ones the young men recovered, and an open wagon with seats. They also had a fenced in corral for the horses and plowed fields with crops growing.

The dwellings on the property consisted of a cabin with four windows and a door, and Windtalker and Kiyo very much wanted to study the door and windows to figure out how to build similar ones. They also saw a roof that went half one-way and half in the opposite direction, peaking at the top. This fascinated them, as did the wood shakes on the roof to keep the water out. On the side of the house, they discovered a rock chimney, something they had forgotten about in the cabin they found in the woods. There was smoke coming from it. Windtalker sniffed the air. He thought someone was baking bread. He grinned, knowing these white settlers knew how to cook indoors, and therefore not as dumb as they were led to believe from their elders.

The men were working in the fields burning the debris away and nearly done. They had lots of corn and other vegetables growing. Windtalker studied the construction of the chimney while Kiyo looked at the other buildings. Across from the house they saw a cow come out of their barn, but noted a second small cabin with a small chimney near the house, and a very small cabin with no chimney behind the house.

They watched the settlers for almost an hour, when suddenly the men quit their work, hitched up the open wagon with four seats to two horses. The man grabbed his rifle and the four of them climbed aboard. They rode out on their small road to the main road on the other side of their farm, and away from Windtalker and Kiyo. They didn't take food, or belongings, so they suspected they would not be gone long.

"I want to see that cabin up close," began Windtalker. "We need to so we can copy it."

Kiyo nodded. "I agree and I want to see the other buildings, but if we get caught, they will think we're trying to steal from them."

31

Windtalker smiled. "Then we'd better not get caught. We go in fast, look at everything, and get the hell out of there."

They scanned the area carefully, and then ran to the next tree and the next, watching, listening, and running again. They looked at the crops of corn, squash, okra, tomatoes, grain, cucumbers, and other vegetables they had never seen. At the edge of the field they saw a weird piece of gear that set on a big blade, with two handles and hooks like those on the wagon. Kiyo caught on that the horses pulled it and Windtalker noted the furrows in the planted field. He realized it was used to turn the dirt over instead of doing it by hand. It amazed them. They ran to the barn and cautiously crept inside. They noted the various wooden stalls, and saw a horse in one and a new colt in another. They smelled the sacks and barrels of grain. They climbed a ladder and saw the straw and hay in the loft and more of it in the stalls below. They realized the settlers grew this weird grass, and fed it to the animals, most likely in the winter season when there was no grass. They saw chickens and eggs in a pen.

Quickly, they ran across the open area and into the house because it wasn't locked. They saw the kitchen, pots and pans, studied the cabinets, the table, and went over to the fireplace. They saw the iron racks for pots and baking things, and the rock fireplace that extended into the room, especially on the floor to keep the wood from burning the surrounding wood. They went to the adult bedroom and looked at the bed, lifted the blankets, and saw a rope crisscrossing from side to side. They saw a loft for the kids in the extra space from the split roof. They studied the windows, the leather hinges, and especially the door, and the interior sliding stick lock.

In the yard on the far side, they saw where they cut the firewood and stacked it against the cabin all the way around. Above, they realized the cabin roof extended over this stack of wood, keeping it dry and ready. Then they saw two sawhorses, holding a log, and the flat blade tool was stuck in the log. Beside it were slices of the log. They went over to it and it looked exactly like the one they now had. They pulled up on the handle, and sawdust fell to the ground. They pushed down, and it did it again. It was a cutting tool, they surmised. They looked at the boards, looked back at the doors and windows, and over to the barn, and the lumber cut was used for such things.

Inside Windtalker looked at the interior of the ceiling and found flat boards covering the roof. He went outside and climbed onto the roof, discovering foot long flat wood pieces cut for length by the saw and split into thinner slices by the axe. He smelled them and recognized the smell of cedar. The roof was made of boards and cedar shakes. It amazed him. He would like to see how it worked in the rain but he quickly climbed down.

They went to the next small house and immediately smelled meat. They opened the door and discovered a small fireplace that filled the room with smoke. Meat hung everywhere and it smelled very appetizing. They realized it was how they stored game for the winter.

They ran to the next smaller house but held their noses after opening the door, as it was an outhouse or privy. They laughed at the hole in the seat board that the white men sat on. They looked around the farm at the other tools, and then began making their way back to the field and on to the forest.

Not long after the trees and bushes safely hid them, they saw the buggy returning with big sacks on the back of the floorboard. The family went somewhere, mostly likely a fort, they assumed, traded for the sacks, and returned so apparently the fort could not be far away. They looked at the sky and realized they had but a few hours until dark so they slid onto their horses and with Emita in the lead they began making their way home as safely as possible.

Windtalker studied their cabin before sunset and in the light of the fire he drew out the settler cabin. "We must make a new roof tomorrow. I know it will be a pain, but if we do so, we'll be able to enjoy it for many moons."

"You are sure? That will be a lot of work."

"Yes, I'm sure, but it will be worth it. Their design keeps them dry with a good roof, their doors and windows keep them warm, the fireplace also heats them, but it allows them to cook in bad weather and all winter, and we'll learn how to use the tools in the process. We can do it."

Kiyo sighed. "Okay, but I'm going to bed."

"Not without me," teased Windtalker. "I'm horny."

"Well, don't go putting your 'horn' in me."

After a moment of silence, they both laughed, cuddling tighter together.

The day had been a long one. It began by taking the canvas off the cabin poles and returning it to the wagon. They began moving their belongings back into the wagon as well to keep them dry in case it rained. They removed the staggered wood on the sides so the walls were all the same height, at least for now. Using poles, they made a new frame with a tall centerboard, and poles cut at an angle on each end, attaching to the beam with notches and nails, and resting the other end on notches in the outer wall. Once they had it straight, they added more poles, nailing them in place and making the roof frame stronger with each addition.

They built sawhorses like the ones they saw at the settler farm with sticks, rope, and notches, and took turns pulling the saw back and forth through the wood. It took an hour for just four boards, but they kept at it. The next morning with twenty-four boards ready, and using a bucket of two inch nails, they laid the boards perpendicular across the framework, and starting at the outer edge, which now overhung to keep the firewood dry, they laid down a row of boards. The next row began with the bottom edge over the previous row. This would let the water that seeped through the shakes, drain off the house. When they ran out of boards, they began sawing again. It took two weeks to fully cover the new cabin. It was already dry, except for a few knotholes. They filled in the front and rear walls under the roof with logs cut exactly right, and nailed them in place with the big nails.

They cut down several cedar trees and using the horses, they pulled the logs to their work area. They had already cut several big oak logs about three feet in length, dug a twelve inch hole, inserted the logs vertically, and used those with their small axes to cut firewood. Using the saw they cut off a twelve-inch cedar log, and then with the small axe, they began making a pile of roof shakes. It took them ten days to make enough to cover the roof and nail them in place. Now they were dry.

They had seen a round wooden bucket at the settler farm, but had no idea how to make one. They used a sawed off piece of a log about an inch thick, cut thinner boards to curve around the bottom board, and used rawhide to wrap it tight to make it secure for holding water. They added a loop rope at the top to make a handle. They made a couple of the new buckets. They saw the farmer use a shovel by stepping on it so they used the tools to dig clay from the riverbank, and starting at the top of the walls, they packed the clay tightly into every crevice, crack, or hole until they sealed the entire cabin.

They made the doors and the windows like the ones at the settler farm. They installed the door first and then they trimmed out the holes for the windows. They framed the newly cut holes with freshly sawed boards. They began framing the floor and the front porch with stout logs for posts, and sawed timber for the rails, but it took two more weeks to cut the boards to cover them. They also cut boards to make a flat sled and nailed it on top of notched logs and nailed in another notched log to attach the chains. They used the horse team to pull the sled through the riverbed. They waded into the riverbed, while carefully selecting the flat rocks they would need to build the chimney. It took thirty trips to get enough rocks and placed the stones in sorted piles by size near the side of the cabin.

They stowed all their gear in the cabin and took down the tipi. They emptied the wagons and sorted the gear into various piles on their new floor. They loved the smell of the fresh cut wood. Once completed, they decided to take some time off, and head back to the settler farm for another glance at both the lock mechanism for the cabin door and the construction of the fireplace. For now, they leaned a stone against the door to keep it closed for the night. They took a packhorse with food in case they needed to wait a few days for the family to leave so they could study the cabin a bit more. They learned a lot from their previous trip, but in their young inexperienced minds, not nearly enough.

They made the trip in a half-day while searching for signs of horse or wagon tracks, and with Emita's help, they kept a sharp eye for both Indians and soldiers. On the way back, they planned to kill a deer providing food enough food for a week or so while they worked. They once again crept through the forest leading to the cleared land of the settler farm. They tied off the horses and turned towards the cook smoke they smelled.

Crack! The gunfire stunned the Indians. They knelt down fearing an attack, but no one came running towards them. Next they heard a man scream, and a boy cry, but not far away. They decided to investigate and turned west away from their trek to the farm. The boy continued to cry out leading the Indians to their position. Once they could see through the new spring leaves, they saw a man hobbled on the ground in great pain, as his foot remained pinched inside of a steel animal trap. A boy of about fourteen desperately tried to get it open, but couldn't. They saw the man's rifle off to the side. Smoke rose from the barrel from the accidental firing.

Kiyo and Windtalker were not sure if they should help or not. They studied the area but saw no one else. They smelled the air but found the forest clear of any other animals. The boy's pitiful pleas stirred their hearts. They cautiously moved forward until they reached the little clearing.

"We help," said Kiyo in his native tongue.

Windtalker laid his bow and arrows down, removed his new battle-axe from the sheath he carried at his back. The boy's eyes went wide but Windtalker smiled at him. Kiyo also set his weapons down and came over to help. They looked at the steel trap. They had seen some of these a few years ago when white hunters first came to their homeland. They hated the traps and often threw sticks or rocks to spring the contraptions before throwing the menacing devices away.

Windtalker carefully took the axe blade and inserted the edge between the steel jaws near the man's trapped foot. Kiyo took his knife and placed it on the other side of the man's foot. They placed a stone next to the trap.

Windtalker said, "Okay, I'll pull hard. Use your knife to help me, but once it is open, stuff that rock in the edge to hold it open. Watch your fingers."

The farmer and the boy sensed the Indians were there to help so they settled down and waited. Windtalker and Kiyo grunted hard, but managed to pull the rusty trap apart, wedge the rock in, and then gently pulled the poor man's foot out. Once they cleared his boot, Kiyo snatched out the rock and Windtalker slowly let the blades close. They spoke to the man gently, and then took off his boot as he grimaced at the pain while noting his blood filled sock.

Kiyo went to get the horses and Emita. The boy loved the dog as he licked his face, calming the boy down. They put the man on the packhorse. Windtalker and the boy got on his horse while Kiyo brought along the man's rifle. Together, they made their way through the forest to the edge of the fields. Kiyo studied the farm finding only the little girl playing on the porch. He looked back towards the road for Indians or soldiers but saw no one, so they made their way towards the cabin.

The little girl screamed when they came around the cornfield and pulled to a stop at the cabin. The mother came out of the cabin carrying a

Winchester rifle like the one Kiyo carried in his scabbard. She screamed at them but the wounded man called to her from the packhorse.

"Honey, these men saved me. I stepped on a trap and hurt my foot. They mean no harm."

Slowly, she lowered the rifle, placed it inside the door, and ran to her husband and looked at his bloody foot. "Oh my. We'd better get you inside."

The Indians slid off their horses, Windtalker helped the boy down, and Kiyo handed the boy the man's rifle, indicating they held no intentions of stealing. Together, they carried the man inside and set him on a bench on the far side of the table. The woman brought a pan of water and some cloth. Carefully, she pulled off the bloody sock and began cleaning the wound. Thought it hurt, it only broke the skin, and created a lot of swelling, but it did not break his foot. The man felt very lucky. She began dressing the wound with some white torn cloth.

He looked up at Kiyo and Windtalker. "Thank you. Thank you very much." He smiled at them.

They didn't understand his words, but they knew what he meant. They smiled back in return.

While repairing her husband's foot she asked the Indians, "Are you hungry?" She motioned with her hands the sign of lifting food to her mouth.

Kiyo grinned because he first misunderstood her and thought she meant for them to eat the poor man's foot. He just smiled while waiting for clarification.

She went to the sink area, selected two plates, and cut a piece of cornbread for each man. She brought it to the table where there was butter and honey. She poured two cups of fresh milk. She motioned for them to sit at the table on the other bench. They watched her as she sat down, buttered the cornbread, put some honey on it and pushed the plates to them. They sat down. Carefully, they brought the bread to their mouths, took a bite, smiled, and then chewed and swallowed. They soon ate every morsel so she gave the lads a second helping. They drank the milk, too and smiled with big white marks on their faces from the milk.

They nodded approvingly, stood up, and walked to the fireplace, studying the construction carefully, and then they did the same with the door lock, and slid the shaft in and out a few times until they understood. They went outside and eyed the chimney carefully. Once satisfied, they came back to their horses.

The man, with the help of his family, hobbled out to the porch and plopped down on a bench used for removing dirty farm boots. He smiled and spoke to them, "You're hunters, aren't you?"

They watched as he spoke and made motions with his hands. Windtalker took an arrow and sketched out a deer and two Indians shooting arrows at the deer. The man smiled and said, "Deer. That's a deer," he said as he pointed at the drawing. "You shoot the deer. My family needs meat."

36

He repeated each word as the Indians said them. They finally understood they needed food. They sat on the porch and conversed learning a few words here and there. Finally, Kiyo spoke to Windtalker, and they decided to go hunt a deer for them. They motioned once more while saying a few of the English words, slung up on their horses, and went across the back of the farm into the forest.

A few hours later, they came back with two deer across the back of the packhorse. The settlers were shocked to see their quick results as it often took the man several days to locate and kill game. They took one of the deer near the smokehouse where they found a rope overhanging from a limb. The boy helped them lift a carcass and tied off its hind legs. The boy hesitated as his dad had always skinned their game. Windtalker smiled, took his knife, quickly cut the head off, sliced away the hide, cleaned out the bad parts, and began slicing out good chunks of the meat. The boy took some to the smokehouse with Kiyo's help, giving him another view of the smokehouse. The boy sprinkled salt on the meat, hung it up, put a few logs on the smoldering fire, and closed the door. The Indians tasted the salt.

Windtalker took a roast to the cabin and gave it to the woman. She thanked them. After they finished their work on the deer, Windtalker washed up in their nearby creek, and then he and Kiyo walked over to the fields and studied the plants. She walked with them while picking vegetables for them and placing them in an empty grain sack. Windtalker drew seeds in the dirt. She caught on and they followed her to the barn.

They studied the barn once more while she filled a smaller sack of seed, and then handed both their food and seed sacks to them. They smiled and thanked her. She told them her name was Molly. Her husband was Samuel. The boy was Michael and the pretty girl Trisha. The lads said their Indian names in their native tongues.

They waved goodbye with the other deer still on their packhorse. They felt like they made friends with the white settlers and would visit again soon. They made good time coming home to their valley and ate deer steaks that night over the fire. The next morning they set about making the door and window latches, and began chopping away the hole for the fireplace. It took the rest of the week to complete the fireplace, using the flat rocks, and clay to pack it in tight. They used several flat stones on the floor extending out from the fireplace to keep from setting it on fire. They had seen smoke go up through the vent hole in the top of their tipis all of their lives, but it thrilled them when they built their first fire in their new fireplace inside their new cabin. They watched the smoke curl as it came out of the top of their new chimney.

They built their own smokehouse in just a week, but this time they built the fireplace as they went while making a good tight seal to the log walls. They put in exposed rafters and using a trick they learned from Samuel's work, they used deer antlers to hang their meat. They already had a pile of dried antlers from their previous kills. They planned to fill the smokehouse with game before winter. They would wait a while longer to build a privy. Their next goal was to build a barn, but they were anxious to get their new seeds in the ground. However, the clearing of the land became slow and difficult. They kept at it for a few days, but soon tired of the farming work and decided to make plans to go exploring.

Before sun down, they set up targets and began practicing with the rifles they found along with the wagons. They were experts with bows, learning to aim very well at a young age, but it took a while to relax with the rifle. An hour later, they were hitting a stump at fifty yards pretty well. They would keep practicing, but for now, they would leave the guns at home.

SEVEN

They packed for a longer journey, tied off the cabin door handle with a short looped rope over a nail, and took Emita, and three horses for the trip. They left the other horses in the pasture to fend for themselves, but spring grass was growing quickly so they would be fine. After leaving the valley through the waterfall, around the second lake, up the hill to the lightly used road, and on to the road to the settler farm, they turned north as if going there, but a few miles down took a right fork leading to a massive valley with huge mountain walls. They wanted to see where this road went and if there were other tribes or settlers in the area. They were more fretful of other tribes than of settlers.

They saw no one for two days, but noted plenty of horse tracks both shoed and shoeless, and there were too many to count. They guessed about a dozen shoed horses, maybe thirty or more Indian horses, and the ruts of three wagons. They also found the game in the area to be plentiful, but they shot by bow and arrow only small game for now as they planned to travel farther away from their home. They reached a low ridge between two mountains and the view on both sides amazed them. Far to the east, they noted beautiful green trees as far as they could see, and then turning west, they saw a lake, a waterfall, and more green trees. They looked towards a very tall mountain to the north, and though they were approaching summer, the mountaintop remained covered in snow.

Boom! Crack! The sound of rifle fire stunned them, but over the north side of the ridge somewhere down in the valley they heard the whoops and yelps of Indians mixed in with the rifle fire of the white men. They knew an attack was in progress.

Kiyo said, "Maybe we should turn back. There are at least thirty warriors."

"I agree, but if the settlers lose, we might be able to get more stuff."

"Okay, but we'd best be extremely careful when we get close."

"We'll send Emita ahead so we don't get caught in the open. Let's ride."

Emita gleefully ran ahead as they followed the road downward in a switchback fashion to make it easier for the wagons. Not long after they reached the bottom of the hill, Windtalker spotted Emita coming towards them fast. Windtalker quickly exclaimed, "Find a place to hide! Hurry!"

Kiyo rode a bit farther, turned off into the brush, and kept going until he was behind some gigantic rocks. They tied off the horses. Windtalker ran back to the road to wait for Emita. The dog panted hard as he leaped off the road and followed to their hiding place. They told him to sit and no bark and he instantly obeyed while attempting to cool down with his soft panting.

Kiyo and Windtalker climbed the big rocks and lay flat on top so they could see the road, but out of view of the riders. They began to hear yelps and knew immediately the approaching riders were the Indians. The scouts no longer wore anything distinguishing their appearance as Blackfeet Indians. They had long given up their traditional black moccasins but instead wore light brown deer hide ones. They wore no feathers, nor necklaces or beads. The only thing that would give them away was the language they spoke. They had discussed trying to learn more of the white man's tongue as they hoped to trade with them for supplies and knowledge of farming and construction.

Twenty or more riders came around the bend, but not as fast as before, because trailing them were ponies carrying the dead warriors. There were at least seven of those. The warriors carried things they stole including uniforms and waved a few rifles, but they did not have a wagon, or the means to carry more supplies. The scouts studied them, and thought they looked like Shoshone Indians. They thought they had already passed through Shoshone lands so this revelation worried them as the Blackfeet fought often with the Shoshone tribes. They were warriors that were very powerful in battle.

After the warriors were long out of sight, the scouts made their way back to the road, and turned right on the road that lead to where they thought the fight might have taken place. It took them almost two hours to get there as the road went up and down hills and around many bends, but also because they were being extremely heedful of danger. After their nostrils picked up the smell of gun smoke, they slowed down. After cautiously walking their horses another hundred yards, they could finally see the site of the fight.

There was blood everywhere. The Indians killed some of the horses, but the rest must have run away from the battle, but now hung around as if lost and wondering what to do. They led their horses off the road and behind a stand of trees. They each wore their battle-axes in a sheath on their back, their quivers remained full of arrows over their left shoulder, and they carried their bows in their left hand. Using their right hand, they retrieved an arrow from the quiver and threaded an arrow. Carefully, they crept closer while making Emita stay behind them.

The bloody scene nearly made them gag. They counted eleven dead soldiers, three women, four white men, and once again several children. They saw no sign of life, but as they approached the first wagon, they heard a twig snap behind them. Instantly, they both spun in opposite directions while moving away from each other, and automatically bringing their bows up and pulling back on the string.

Kiyo and Windtalker saw a soldier with an arrow in his right shoulder, blood splattered on the front of his uniform, and painful sweat dripping down his face, but slowly he began walking towards them with a pistol cocked and aiming back and forth between the scouts.

Kiyo realized he thought they were the Indians that attacked them. He spoke his thoughts to Windtalker. Windtalker paused while thinking, and then began speaking a few words of the English they learned from Molly. He said deer. The man stopped. Windtalker said peace. The man listened. He then said Molly and followed with Samuel.

The man smiled slightly though still in pain. He uncocked his pistol, and placed it in his holster. He said to them, "Molly is my sister. Samuel is her husband."

Kiyo added, "Trisha and Michael."

The man smiled again. "They are my niece and nephew. Please take me to them. I don't think I can get there by myself. I have bled too much." He sat down on the rump of a dead horse. "We need to take these bodies back to the fort. If you'll load them, I'll pay you well."

They didn't understand all his words, but with motions, they finally understood. Kiyo went to dress the wound of the man while Windtalker began gathering the horses and tying them off. Kiyo broke off the shaft just before it entered the man's chest. He put a stick in the man's mouth and told him to bite hard. He made motions with the stick and his own teeth until the man understood. He went around to the back, took a strong hold on the protruding arrow, and yanked hard and fast. The man shook as the pain rushed to his brain, but he didn't scream. Kiyo fetched cloth from the dress of a dead woman, cleaned the wound front and back, and then wrapped a long cloth around the man's chest to hold pads of folded cloth front and back to slow the bleeding.

They gave the man one of the canteens they found and told him to drink. Kiyo joined Windtalker and one by one they hitched up two wagons, and split the gear of the third wagon between the two. They made two long strings of horses and tied them behind the wagons. It took them an hour, but soon all the bodies were lying over a horse, some had two bodies, and they were tied with rope so they wouldn't fall off. They helped the soldier into the seat of the first wagon after they tied off their three horses behind the second wagon. Kiyo got up beside the man to drive the first wagon and Windtalker handled the second rig. They sent Emita ahead and they began the journey. They got to the top of the ridge by dark, but with the help of the full moon they kept going, stopping only to rest the horses for a while.

A few hours later, they reached the fork in the road, and turned right or northwest. By dawn, they reached the edge of the settler farm. Samuel was coming from the privy when he saw them coming. He ran to the house, woke his wife and kids, and came out with his rifle. Kiyo and Windtalker called to them, as did Molly's brother.

They turned into the settler farm and pulled the first wagon to a halt right in front of the cabin. Samuel put away the rifle after recognizing the scouts and his brother-in-law.

Samuel began helping the wounded man down. "Robert? What the hell happened to you?"

Robert grunted when he finally put his boots on the ground. "We were attacked by Shoshone, probably thirty of them. They killed eleven of my men, and three families of settlers. These Indians came along and saved me. They dressed my wound and brought the bodies back."

Molly had come out of the cabin and onto the porch. "Oh my lord," she screamed as she ran to her brother and tried to hug him.

Robert exclaimed, "Please don't. It will hurt like hell. Help me get my coat off, and let's patch up this old soldier one more time."

Molly looked into the face of her beloved older brother. She wiped some dirt and blood from his freckled face, pushed back some of his bright red hair, and smiled. "You'll live. Thank God, you'll live."

Robert looked up at Samuel. "I promised to pay them for bringing me here, along with the bodies. Can you lead them to the fort, and tell my quartermaster to pay them a hundred dollars apiece? They can have the settler wagons and what's in them, including the wagon horses. There are three brown horses that belonged to the settlers that you can have, but the rest of the horses belong to the army."

Molly then took him inside their cabin after waving and saying a few words to the fellows.

Samuel had been overlooking the string of dead bodies and felt great sadness, as he knew most of the men in his visits to the fort for supplies and to visit Robert. He and the fellows conversed as best they could. They weren't sure they should go to the fort, but Samuel assured them they would be fine.

They left the wagons with Michael who brought them water and grain. The horses stopped in a stream behind the barn and drank. Samuel saddled his horse, then divided up the horses carrying the dead bodies, and began walking their horses towards the fort.

After they went around a couple of bends, they reached a long flat area where they could see the fort. It was built in a typical stockade fashion, a square of hundred-foot walls made from twenty-foot tall poles, and they were sharpened at the top. There were two gates at the front and rear and a guard or watchtower on two corners. They soon noted a few other settler farms nearby and heard sounds from inside the fort as they approached.

An alarm went out, followed by the sound of a bugler. A group of soldiers with rifles walked out to the meet them. A major wearing a white hat soon followed them.

Samuel pulled his horse to a stop in front of the gate. "Howdy, Bill. I'm afraid I have bad news. Eleven of your men are dead. These are their bodies, along with the dead settler families, and some of the horses. The rest of the horses were killed. The tan horses are mine. Robert is the only one that lived. He is at the farm. He got shot with an arrow that went through his right upper shoulder. Molly is tending to him, but these Indian scouts saved his life and brought these bodies and horses back. I'd like for you to meet them. This is Kiyo and that is Windtalker. They are friendly. They also saved me when I stepped in a stupid old bear trap while hunting.

"My wife has been teaching them English. I think you can trust them.

42

I sure do. They could easily have scalped Michael and me, and killed the girls, but they didn't. They took nothing, but seem to want to learn how we built a cabin and English.

"Now that they saved my brother-in-law, for which I guess I should be thankful," he added with a slight grin even though the current situation appeared dire.

The major took in all that he heard. The scouts noted how tall the man was, taller than any white man they had seen, so they nodded in his direction, and then cautiously said hello in English. The major began thanking them for their help. He ordered his men to lower their rifles.

Samuel added, "Robert promised them a hundred dollars each for their trouble. He also gave them the settler wagons. He said your quartermaster would pay them."

"And that he will." He turned to his men and sent a private for the money. He ordered the others to form up a burying detail. They led the horses with the dead men inside the fort and began removing their personal gear before grabbing shovels. The dead soldiers were getting ripe in the sun. A sergeant began writing down the names of the dead.

Windtalker and Kiyo looked inside the fort. The major spoke again, "Come on inside, and let me get you something to drink. I'll need for you to sign for the money, regulations and all. A civilian witness is what we'll call you."

The scouts watched Samuel tie his horse up to the hitching post so they did the same and slid off. The major led them into his office and brought cool water for them to drink. The quartermaster came in with the money. The major thanked the Indians as best he could and gave them the money. After they said goodbye, Samuel took the scouts into the trading post and with hand gestures, and words, he showed the Indians what they could buy with the money.

They walked around the room and saw pots and pans for cooking as well as farm tools, which they had. They saw shelves of bullets, but they had boxes of those, too. They saw clothes and hats like Samuel wore and boots. They bought clothes, food, and sacks of seed, and then tied it all on Samuel's horses. They had over half of their money left and this pleased them.

As they unhitched their horses the major suddenly stepped out of his office, "Samuel. Do you think these scouts could track the men that did the killing?"

"I suppose, but Robert said they were on the northern trail. I think they call it Whitehall trail now. The attack was two days ago. They came back south and turned left down the Calvert road. There's a lot of tracks on that road."

"Okay. Maybe they can help us in the future. Why don't you teach them English because I'm too old to learn Indian?"

Samuel tipped his hat to him. "I'll try. I'm sorry this happened. We'll be leaving now."

"Thanks again," replied the major as he tipped his hat at Samuel and then nodded politely with a smile at the scouts.

After helping Robert, the Indians agreed to stay a few days at the farm so the Indians and the white folks could learn from each other. They would postpone their exploration trip for another time. The Indians helped with chores, watched Michael milk the cow, work in the garden, feed the animals, and they also took interest in watching Molly cook. The tribe taught the boys that squaws do the cooking, but the young men knew if they didn't want to starve, they would have to learn to do it themselves.

Samuel came in from the garden for lunch one day and found the fellows covered in flour as Molly attempted to teach them how to make biscuits. Samuel chuckled. Robert, healing but still bedridden, got a good laugh out of it, too. After their lunch of fried chicken, corn on the cob, green beans, and potatoes, and of course, their first batch of biscuits, the young men followed Michael to the stream behind the house and small cove to clean up. The white boy stripped naked and dove in. The Indians did the same. The cool water felt great in the middle of the summer and they returned to the farm fresh and clean from their biscuit making.

After Samuel explained the Indians might be a big help to all if they could just speak with them, Molly began teaching English as fast as she could. In the five days they remained at the farm, their vocabulary improved dramatically. The Indians also learned from Samuel as he taught them how to plant the seeds, feed the horses, and take care of the cow and chickens. They liked the taste of the milk and the eggs the animals provided. They learned quickly from Michael as well and enjoyed his teasing with Trisha who was a bit of a pretty tom-girl. The family also liked playing with Emita after declaring him the smartest dog in the world.

Every afternoon, the Indians taught Samuel and Michael how to shoot arrows with their bows and they taught Kiyo and Windtalker about their rifles and pistols. They told them they had similar guns they had found. The scouts were soon better shots than Samuel and Michael became with a bow.

One day, they showed them their battle-axes. Samuel had a grindstone wheel in the barn and showed the Indians how to sharpen their axes as well as the steel knives. He told them to bring their farm tools and he would sharpen them as well.

On the morning of the last day, they ate a big breakfast of grits, eggs, potatoes, and biscuits, and Molly loaded a sack of cooked food for them. They all fared well from the visit, Robert thanked them repeatedly for saving him, and they left for home.

EIGHT

Summer arrived at the fort but throughout the unseasonably hot warm season the attacks by Indians on the whites nearly doubled the previous year. Major Bill feared the fall would be just as bad as new arrivals reported a thousand people were heading west every week from Saint Louis. Most of them were heading to the northwest since Mexico still controlled much of the southwest and there were many problems with the Indian tribes in that region. He knew of the news of the many successful wagon trains that worked their way through the valleys in the Rocky Mountains, and the pass he guarded to the northwest would attract more families to bravely travel through the hostile country. His dispatches reported long hot meetings in Congress on what to do about the Indians with a common attitude from most politicians that only death would solve the problem. Major Bill felt sorry to admit that he once felt that way, too. However, after living in the west, and meeting Indian families from time to time, he hoped they could find a way to live peaceably together. However, Major Bill swore an oath to faithfully carry out his duties, so he would protect the settlers and the wagon trains as ordered.

In the Midwest, the Sioux and the Cheyenne tribes rebelled against the unpopular treaties the white soldiers insisted on, because so far the white man's government failed to keep a single one of written treaty promises. This caused even more conflict as the warriors stole horses when they could, murdered when it suited them, and took white slaves now and then to humiliate and breed fear amongst the whites. They took scalps and carried the bloody pieces around as a badge of honor around the necks of their horses.

In the far plains of Montana, the Blackfeet and Shoshone tribes were battling each other as well as the settlement in the southwest, but the Blackfeet also stole and fought with the Crows to their immediate east. To an outsider, it just seemed the Blackfeet warriors were never happy unless a battle was brewing with someone. As a rule, when it came to attacking the whites, they generally killed everyone, leaving not even a single witness. They kept slaves only for a while before quickly trading to other tribes for horses. They didn't want to feed the slaves in the winter, nor chance a sighting with them if the soldiers came.

Spotted Owl was the eldest son of his father, the chief of a large band of Blackfeet living on the eastern side of the Glacier Mountains in northwest Montana. Although he came from a long line of honorable warriors, as a young boy, his father often caught him stealing or lying, and punished him hard, but nothing would make a difference in Spotted Owl's character. His mother began calling him a bad seed that nothing good could grow from.

As a young warrior, he enjoyed spilling the blood of his enemy, and soon led a group of twenty similar in age warriors into his missions of plundering, stealing, and killing. By twenty-five, he had a pole stacked with over a hundred scalps. But while leading his men they also killed about sixty-five enemy Indian warriors and families, and murdered almost two hundred white settlers and soldiers.

As the days went by, he argued more and more with his father, and disobeyed by attacking a wagon train not far from the village. The soldiers traveling with the wagon train repelled the warriors, but the next day, they tracked Spotted Owl and his men back to the encampment. The revengeful soldiers murdered over half of the tribe in just fifteen minutes with their rifles while the rest escaped deep into the forest hiding from the tracking parties. The soldiers burned everything they owned including tipis, hides, blankets, and trampled their pottery and other cooking utensils. They rode their horses over their food supplies, stomping everything into the ground. The survivors found nothing of use.

When his father questioned his son's men, he knew Spotted Owl once again disobeyed and attacked too close to the village, and they were too lazy to make a wide winding trail while hiding their tracks in and out of rivers to prevent the soldiers from finding the tribe. He blamed his son for the massacre. Filled with rage and anger, he confronted his son; they fought with knives. Spotted Owl stabbed his father, but not mortally. His father banished his son and his warriors from the tribe. He told them he would send word to the other tribes warning them to avoid his group. He never wanted to see his son again, but he said if he did, he would shoot him down with a hundred arrows.

Spotted Owl cursed his father and the rest of the leaders. They left in the night with nearly nothing in the way of food, and made their way west to find a new hunting ground. They continued to dress like Blackfeet Warriors adding only a single white circle of war paint around the area of their heart as if daring anyone to attempt to kill them.

They set up camp deep in a gorge and learning from their mistakes, they made sure no one knew the location of their encampment, or how to get to it. They began by raiding small Shoshone tribes, but at the beginning of the summer, they went farther west and won many battles against the Yakima and the odd looking Flathead warriors. After winning bloody gruesome battles, they offered to let some warriors live if they joined him. He promised they would kill all the white settlers and soldiers. He now led an army of seventy-five renegade warriors that grew about a dozen or so every few weeks. It was some of his men that attacked Robert and his men on the Whitehall Trail.

On their return route to their village they stopped and studied the fort where Major Bill resided from a small mountain that overlooked the fort while swearing that one day soon they would burn it to the ground and kill everyone inside. He left a small group of scouts on the hill watching the fort around the clock in secret. If a squad went on patrol, a rider followed them, while a second rider galloped to the village to alert Spotted Owl. In many cases the military squad returned to the fort before Indian reinforcements could ambush and kill the smaller force. However, sometimes they were lucky as thirty or more of his men would catch a squad away from the fort and they would absolutely annihilate their enemy.

Spotted Owl made his own rules and customs, and particularly enjoyed torturing his captives, be it Indians or whites. He took pleasure in the bloodiest ideas from his comrades on more ways to create pain before death. He raped the women and made them watch as he strangled their children. Body parts were cut away and bones and skulls broken. Not a single enemy was allowed to die easily or with honor. To maintain absolute discipline, he would occasionally kill one of his own men that dared to cross or disobey him, or even sighed disapprovingly at him. He did this to make all his men fear him.

They had a hundred horses, stacks of hides, weapons, food, and stolen trinkets. He appointed a squad of twelve men as hunters for the entire village. They spent every day finding game to feed them all. He kept scouts posted on all the high rocks overlooking the trails and roads the settlers or soldiers used. When he could, he would wipe them out. If possible, he would burn the settler farms, hoping to starve them. He took great chances and cared little for how many men he lost, as he knew how to replace them.

A Blackfeet warrior often left an identifying mark on a victim of their slaughter to show how powerful they were. Spotted Owl embellished this practice in two ways; first they all pissed on the dead, and if they killed a soldier, they cut off their genitals and stuffed the appendages into the mouths of the victims. The discovery of these mutilated corpses always spilled the stomachs of the squad who found them. The soldiers desperately tried to find Spotted Owl and his warriors, but learning from his past, he never attacked unless he had two avenues of escape. He also made a habit of attacking only when his numbers were far greater, increasing the odds of success. After the attack, they always broke into smaller groups as they made their retreat, taking less used trails towards home. Although Spotted Owl always led an attack from the front, he had yet to receive even a scratch. He killed more men than anyone in his bloody band of warriors and he took great pride in victories and his accomplishments.

In one of the two wagons given to them by Robert, Kiyo and Windtalker discovered a plow. It was just like the one they found at Samuel's farm. It stirred a list of questions they planned to ask on their next visit. They also found many other useful things, including cooking utensils, a two by three foot mirror, weapons, bundles of cloth, and men's clothes. They began wearing boots instead of moccasins because they held up better when shoveling, and it didn't hurt as bad if a horse accidentally stepped on their foot. They also wore the new hats to keep the sun out of their eyes and the field dust out of their hair. In no time, the new store bought clothes looked broken in and no longer itched. The boots, on the other hand, caused a few blisters, but now they were almost as comfortable as a deerskin.

Learning from Samuel, they hooked up a team of horses to the plow, and soon managed the tilling of several acres. This inspired the Indians so they crisscrossed the fields several times until no grass remained. For now, they went around big rocks and trees, but later they planned to pull the objects out of their new gardens. They cut poles for fence posts, and then returned to the fort to buy spools of barbed wire to keep the horses out of their garden. The storekeeper ordered rolls of three-foot rabbit fence to keep small critters from eating their crops. It would be a month or more before it arrived, unless it was part of a shipment the storeowner previously ordered. They planted every single seed that Molly gave them as well as the bags of seed they bought at the fort. Samuel explained how to save the seeds when they harvested the crops and to let them dry for next year's planting so they would always have a supply of fresh new vegetables.

They also planted a lot of grain products to give the horses more to eat, especially for the upcoming winter. In the other wagons they found the tools to cut and bale the grass for winter. Samuel said for them to return in a month and he would show them how to use the new tools. Along with the fencing for the garden, they ordered rolls of barbed wire so they might keep the horses from eating the fields of grain.

Windtalker studied Samuel's barn, but felt the project too big for now, so he designed a smaller barn that could be added in the following spring. Their goal was to have a place to store the hay and grain, as well as their farm gear to keep the winter weather from rusting and ruining it.

They also began riding with saddles on their horses. At first the Indian horses rebelled, throwing Windtalker high into the air and dropping Kiyo into a stream, but soon the horses grew accustomed to the white man's saddles. However, the butts of the Indians remained sore for quite a while, but their lovemaking at night tended to either soothe the muscles or create unforgettable memories of pleasure.

They wanted to learn how to use the saddles so they could carry their rifles in a scabbard sleeve under one leg, and their bows and arrows in a similar device on the other side. They also wore a pistol on their gun belts, shooting right-handed, and put their hunting knife in a sheath on the left side. They preferred hunting by bow because it didn't disturb a whole valley by scaring away other game possibilities. If they used the rifle, they often were done for the day after the first shot. However, several times a week they practiced with pistols and rifles near the woodpile by starting close at thirty feet, and daily backing up another five feet. It didn't take long for their bow and arrow aiming skills to transfer to their new mechanical weapons.

After they finished the roof on the new barn, they finally built an outhouse, but they had yet to use it, thinking it would be best used in the winter. They loaded up a packhorse and with Emita running out front, they left their ranch through the waterfall, and made their way to the road. Carefully, they waited and watched until they were sure no one saw them. They rode quickly in the direction of the Samuel farm, but after a mile, they pulled off the road and retrieved their bows to begin hunting. They intended to kill several deer and planned to drop one off as a gift to their friends. The area they picked was a lucky one as they shot their bows seven times, killing three deer, and four rabbits in just a few hours. After tying off their game atop the packhorse, they set out for the Johnson farm. When they came out of the forest near Samuel's fields, they immediately felt something might be wrong as no one could be seen anywhere. Thinking the family must have gone to the fort for supplies, they rode by the garden and pulled up near the smokehouse. They called for the family as they were taking a deer over to the tree to skin it for them.

Suddenly, they heard Molly scream as she ran out the cabin door and over to them. She spoke too fast and they became confused with her new words, but they knew something must have happened. She held an arrow in her hand. She handed it to Windtalker. They recognized the handiwork of a Blackfeet arrow, but it didn't make sense that the Blackfeet were nearby as they thought they were too far away. They also knew the Blackfeet tribes would be far from the mountains and onto the plains to the east for the summer hunt for buffalo. She led them to the cabin where they found Samuel on his bed. An arrow shot him in his upper part of his thigh just inches from his hip, but Molly cleaned and dressed the wound and he was recovering, but too weak to stand.

She finally explained that six Indians had suddenly shown up and taken Trisha, and ridden to the south. Samuel desperately tried to stop them and they shot him. An Indian slapped Molly, knocking her to the ground. Just minutes before the attack, Michael walked two of their horses down to the stream to drink and remained hidden after discovering the Indians were next to his cabin. She said Michael didn't have a weapon on him and felt useless in not being able to save his sister. She sent him to the fort to fetch help.

Once the scouts understood, they assured the family they would find Trisha. As they came out of the cabin, Michael rode up with Robert and six soldiers. Now recovered from his wound, Robert swung down to hug his sister. "Don't you worry. We will find her and bring her back. How is Samuel?"

"He'll be okay. I was so scared. I thought they were going to kill all of us."

"They probably would have, but you're so close to the fort they most likely didn't want to attract attention." Robert turned to Kiyo and Windtalker. "Do you know who it was?"

Windtalker replied, "The arrow that shot Samuel is a Blackfeet arrow. I didn't think they were this far west. They usually stay in the plains east of the mountains and especially during the summer hunting season. It could have been a captured arrow."

"What?"

"When an Indian war party raids another group of Indians, they usually gather the arrows and bows of the fallen warriors for two reasons. Arrows are hard to make so it saves time, and if there are no arrows left, the wounded and survivors can't chase and attack them."

"I see. Do you think you could track them?"

Kiyo said, "Hold your men right where they are. I assume all your horses are shod?"

"Yes, they are."

Kiyo and Windtalker carefully began scanning the ground. Soon they counted six riders amongst the Indians. They studied the unshod hoof prints carefully, memorizing their unique shapes. Kiyo swung up on his horse, "Follow us."

Windtalker ran back to the cabin. "Please give me something that belongs to Molly."

Molly's face puzzled, but finally she understood. She brought Trisha's doll and gave it to him. Windtalker smiled, took it to Emita, and told him to smell it. The dog got a good whiff. In his native tongue Windtalker told the dog to find her. Emita began searching the area before running across the field towards the road. Windtalker swung up on his horse. They left their packhorse and the other deer with Michael and rode out quickly. The soldiers scampered to stay up with them, but often they slowed to study the ground until they found the tracks of the raiding party.

They rode hard all afternoon and finally stopped near dark. The soldiers were afraid to travel during the night. They made a cold camp with no fire, but Kiyo, Windtalker, and Emita continued on for a few more miles. Now that they were away from the soldiers and all the noise the galloping troopers made, they desperately tried to listen for any sound of the Indian warriors. Hearing none, they reluctantly returned to camp. They ate cold biscuits and with soldiers taking turns standing watch, the Indians slept hard and fast, as did Emita.

Without a timepiece, the scouts were somehow up long before dawn, and soon led the soldiers along the trail.

It was a long way to the village, but they were anxious to show Spotted Owl their new white slave. They would all have fun by raping her. They tore her dress and laughed at her flat chest, as she was still too young to have breasts. They had ridden far to get to the area of the fort. As they continued their second day of the journey the trail became more difficult as they climbed the steep mountain slopes.

As Kiyo and Windtalker topped a hill, they suddenly spotted Emita running towards them at a quick pace. At first the Indians thought someone was coming, but this time Emita swirled in circles, barked several times, and then took off back up the trail. They galloped to catch up with the tail-wagging dog as he led them to the Indian's stopover spot. They again counted six riders. They saddled up after Windtalker felt the still warm coals in the fire.

"We are close," he said as they took off again. "Good dog, Emita. Find Trisha!" The dog barked twice in reply and took off running just as the soldiers caught up with them. The scouts explained the finding of a campfire and then galloped up the trail.

They rode all day but Emita became more excited after finding fresh steaming mounds of horse dung just before dark. Again the soldiers set up a fireless camp and since they were close to the Indians, they posted several men on guard duty. Quietly, the Indians continued on in the dark. They whispered for Emita to stay close and quiet.

They stopped from time to time until finally they heard voices. They crept up the road a bit farther, and then down in the valley near a stream they saw the light of their fire through the trees. They gently walked their horses off the trail and tied them to tree limbs, and made a reluctant Emita stay with them. Taking only their bows and arrows, they crept forward until they spotted a scout keeping watch. They counted five riders in camp, but near the fire, they saw Trisha tied to a tree.

Instantly, they began thinking of ways to take out the six men and rescue her. There was a chance that if they didn't kill them all within seconds, one of them would slit the girl's throat before trying to escape. They whispered to each other ideas, but finally decided to return to the soldiers.

51

NINE

After they unsaddled their horses and tied them off, they sat down on a log and explained to Robert the situation. Robert lit a single candle. Windtalker drew in the dirt the setup of the Indian camp, marked where the girl remained tied, and the location of the scout on alert. Robert began thinking of a plan of his own, but Kiyo and Windtalker made a few suggestions.

Kiyo said, "We must kill them all at the same time, or one of them will take a knife to the girl."

Windtalker added, "I'll kill the scout with my bow."

Kiyo said, "I'll work my way close to the camp and kill the two men near her. We need for you to take out the other three men."

"Using our rifles?"

Windtalker replied, "Yes, but firing at the same time Kiyo fires the first arrow. Otherwise, they will scatter into the dark of the forest. We can't let any of them live because they'll return to their village and bring back many warriors."

Robert gulped. "Okay, show me again where the three are. I'm a good shot and so are Johnny and Sam."

Kiyo said, "You can't take a chance on missing. Try to get as close as you can without discovery. When you see the first man go down you must fire. Kiyo will work his way along the far side of the stream so I will wait until he is in position before I fire and kill the scout. I'll rush forward as a backup to kill any Indian that is still alive. Any questions?"

"Are we leaving the horses here?"

Windtalker nodded. "Your horses make too much noise." He sighed hard and grinned. "You make too much noise. Take off anything that clicks or jangles."

Robert smiled as they began removing belt buckles and such. "Okay when do we go?"

Kiyo smiled. "Now."

It took them two hours to get to the camp and slowly make their way to their hiding places. Windtalker went across the stream and made his way up the hill and behind the scout. The warrior on duty appeared to be lazy as he was sitting down. Kiyo went above the tribe on the road, then slowly made his way down the bank to the stream and came through the water towards the campfire. The sound of the water masked his movement. Robert and his two men carefully made their way to just fifty feet from their assigned kills. The other soldiers remained on the road but down the trail about thirty yards as a backup.

Kiyo looked up the hill until he found Windtalker. They both brought out two arrows from their quivers. They set one against a tree trunk, and threaded the second. Windtalker fired catching the scout in the throat so he couldn't scream, and his second shot pierced the man's heart from the front. The man instantly fell dead, but no one in the camp heard him fall. Windtalker began moving up the hill towards the camp while threading his bow.

Kiyo spotted the leader along with a second man stirring a pot over the fire. He fired and hit the leader dead center of his chest. The man stumbled backwards, but somehow managed to remain on his feet in spite of the intense pain the arrowhead made as it drilled deep inside his torso. Kiyo took the second shot and put it in the right eye of the man by the fire. He fell instantly to the ground. Robert and his men fired their rifles hitting all three of their targets. Before Kiyo could fire a third arrow, he saw the leader shutter from head to toe as he received one of Windtalker's arrows to the heart. He went down hard as his head bounced limply as it hit a rock.

Kiyo sprinted to the girl. Windtalker came down the hill. Robert and his men returned to the road as instructed. Kiyo smiled. "You're all right, little girl. Time to take you home."

Windtalker cut her feet loose. She gave both of them a hug. Kiyo took her up the trail passing Robert and his men as they came into the camp.

Robert said, "Way to go. Excellent plan."

"We must hurry. We need to take their bodies away from here. I'll go get the scout I shot. Can you get these dead men on their horses?"

"Yeah, sure, but why go to all the trouble?"

"If they are found with bullet holes, they will attack more settlers. If they can't find them, there's no one to blame."

Robert grinned. "You're good. You should have been a soldier."

Windtalker replied with a sly grin. "Better to be an Indian. We hunt and eat soldiers."

Robert laughed. "Okay, I know when someone is pulling my leg."

Windtalker grinned. "Hurry now. We need to get as far from here as fast as possible, and hope it rains."

"Rains?"

"We need for our tracks to wash away."

Robert shook his head in disbelief. "Right again. You're smart all right. Very smart."

He quickly organized his men and they led the horses up to the road with all the dead Indians tied onto their horses. Windtalker brought the other man across and tied him on the remaining horse. Kiyo placed the girl on the extra horse they brought along while the rest of the men saddled up. They rode hard heading south for a mile, but then Kiyo suddenly stopped and turned east.

"Hey, you're going the wrong way," protested Robert.

Windtalker grinned. "He's going to shake off any trackers. Trust us. Just follow."

They went down the bank and led the horses into the stream. They went down the stream until they found a large area of river rocks on the eastern bank. They came out of the stream leaving no tracks, went down about forty yards, and then back into the stream. They went another mile until he found a large bed of rocks on the western side. They exited once again and made their way back to the road.

A few hours later, they made it back to the fork in the main road, but once again Kiyo took them south for just a hundred yards before doubling back. He then sent them towards the farm as he and Windtalker cut limbs and wiped away their tracks. He knew a tracker would see the trail go south, he would then yell to the men to gallop ahead, and they would charge down the road and not realize the soldiers had doubled back. If they were suspicious, they would not find the tracks heading west to the farm.

They rode into the farm at daybreak. Molly ran out on the porch after she heard their horses. She was afraid of receiving bad news that their daughter had been killed. The moment she saw her daughter she ran out into the yard to greet her. Trisha slid off her horse and ran to her mother's beckoning arms. Tears streamed down their faces as they held each other tight.

Kiyo said to Robert, "Take these bodies to the far side of the fort area, find a gully way off the road and dump them. Scatter the Indian horses."

Robert reached out and shook their hands, "You fellows did a great job. Thank you so much."

They just nodded politely, unaccustomed to praise, and suddenly shy. They rode to the cabin and climbed off their horses. Michael hugged his sister, and showing his appreciation, he took their horses to the barn to be fed and gave the animals plenty of water.

The fellows went inside and saw Samuel hug his daughter as well. "Honey child," he began between sobs and tears, "I'm so sorry I couldn't stop them."

Trisha kissed him. "Nothing to be sorry for. There was six of them and just one of you. Daddy, you should have seen Kiyo and Windtalker. They were amazing. And Emita found me." She knelt down and called the dog. She gave him big hugs and kisses.

Molly dried her eyes and announced, "Well, I'd say it is time for a good breakfast. Come on to the table fellows. I'm going to cook you a big country feast to celebrate."

The Indians never left a morsel of food on their tin plate after one of Molly's meals. Samuel noted they seemed nonchalant about their chivalry and exhibition of their skills to track, and their ability to quickly put together a strategy and fight. He felt indebted to the young men for saving his daughter while making sure no revenge would ever seek his cabin in the night. He thanked them during the meal and several more times before they left for home.

Near midday and almost home, they heard a loud crack sound, followed by a big boom, and shortly thereafter the clouds let loose a heavy downpour of rain that continued all the way home. Kiyo and Windtalker were thankful for the rain to help their garden, but also because it would wash away all the horse tracks of the Indians they killed.

Captain Robert explained to his major how well the scouts worked together, and how smart they were in their abilities to track while using their scouting knowledge intuitively. He told him they formulated an attack plan, and implemented their scheme with perfect precision, while using quick brutal force, and wisely leaving no one alive. He explained how they acted after the battle, taking the dead Indians with them, working on and off the trail, in and out of streams, and doing all they could to prevent any blame coming to the fort or Samuel's family. He didn't mention it the first time through, but after thinking a spell, he recalled seeing Windtalker take his knife and dig the arrows and bullets out of his victims. He failed to catch on as to why until now. He explained this to the captain and they both surmised the scouts did not want anyone to know that a white man's gun killed these bad guys, nor did they want any Indian to know of their participation.

Major Bill wisely stored Captain Robert's report in his brain as well as in his journal, as he felt sure he would be able to use the scouts again to help stop the attacks on the settlements and on his men. He asked Robert where they lived or how they could find the scouts if they needed to. Robert had no idea, but promised to ask Samuel on a visit to the farm on Sunday for dinner.

TEN

Kiyo and Windtalker worked hard on the farm, trying to get the most out of their crops, while adding grain and corn to store in the barn, but taking Samuel's advice, they often spent several hours a day cutting down trees, dragging the trunks and big limbs back to the cabin with a horse team, and swinging their axes while creating lots of firewood. He showed them how to pick bad and crooked trees for firewood while saving the tall and straight trees for future lumber or posts. He also showed them how to avoid clearing out all the trees in an acre unless they were turning the ground into crops. They stacked the cut to same length logs next to the cabin all the way around as high as they could reach, and nearly finished a second row of firewood. They did the same with the smokehouse to keep the fire burning throughout the winter. They stored a huge pile of kindling by using a canvas cover to keep it dry with a log on top to keep it from blowing away. After studying Molly's kitchen area, they painstakingly cut long boards, made some primitive cabinets, and used a big pan for a sink. They were working on some high cabinets above the working counter, but lacked the hardware for hinges and handles so they used thick leather to make the hinges and pieces of rope with a knot for handle.

Their hunting skills came in handy as they loaded up the smokehouse with fresh game, and spent many hours cleaning and drying the hides. They kept stacks of hides in the corner of the cabin. They took very good care of their buffalo and bear hides so they would be warm this winter season. They hoped to build a bed soon, but they had been shy about asking Molly about the bed. They desperately wanted a second look at their cabin. Kiyo finally said he was going to ask Samuel how to make a bed frame the next time they visited.

Spotted Owl waited three days for his men to return from scouting the fort. When they failed to show up he sent six more men out to find them. They came back to the village a week later with absolutely nothing to report. They could not find any sign of them at all. They looked for their horses while they kept two men hidden in the trees near the fort watching to see if their men were captured. Several times, the scouts could see inside the fort, but their horses were nowhere to be found.

This puzzled Spotted Owl, but he decided they must have run off, or were captured by the Shoshone or Flathead warriors. He never gave the disappearance another thought.

The scouts did report that a wagon train made it to the fort with forty wagons and twenty head of ugly looking steers. Spotted Owl cursed numerous times because they missed an excellent opportunity to raid and plunder such a large group. By late summer, Spotted Owl and his men managed to kill six more soldiers and twenty settlers.

Major Bill felt sure that this wagon train would be the last to reach his fort until spring. He knew it would be suicide for anyone else to try as the snows came early in the glacier area. They quickly helped the settlers repair their wagons and supplies, and sent an escort with them to the west to continue their journey out of the mountains before the snow fell. He did not want to babysit such a large group all winter, and his supply officer assured him they did not have enough food to handle the wagon train as well.

Last summer when things were a bit calmer with the Indians, he took twenty men and over the course of a month they rode all the way to Canada, almost due north of the fort, but they traversed northwesterly to get around the steep mountains. He wondered if a pass could be found through them. He wrote a lengthy report requesting an expedition of explorers to find such a pass. He knew he wouldn't get an answer from his commander in Saint Louis until late spring, and it was just as well as no one could go anywhere during the numerous big snows of the winter season.

He spent most of his time training his men, sending out squads to watch for Indians and to help the settlers where possible. There were forty-two families and farms near the fort and all were doing well with their crops. The Army bought fresh food from the settlers, but often they were rewarded with a fine home cooked meal from time to time. Everything the farmers managed to produce tasted ten times better than army chow. He also made sure his men and the settlers put up plenty of firewood to see them through the winter.

By the first week of September, Kiyo and Windtalker put the last of the hay and straw in their new barn. They packed the small structure to the rafters. They bought a dozen sacks of grain at the fort and hauled it to the barn as well. They filled the smokehouse with excellent game and the cabinets were filled with vegetables. The nights were turning cooler and they guessed winter might be just four to six weeks away. They bought more supplies from the trading post inside the fort along with heavier coats for winter.

Two days ago, a squad of a dozen men found Indian pony tracks near the fork and they followed them up Whitehall Trail. When they didn't return the next day, Captain Robert took a second squad to find them. He had just reached the fork from Calvert Road to Whitehall Trail when he spotted Kiyo and Windtalker coming his way trailing two packhorses.

One of his new recruits drew his rifle and took aim, but Robert told him to put his gun down. The man called the Indians cursed heathens. Robert gave the man a stern look as Kiyo and Windtalker pulled their horses to a halt beside them. He quickly shook both their hands.

They talked about their farm and he asked if they were ready for winter. They replied yes but they were heading to the trading post with a load of hides to sell for more supplies. Robert explained the situation and asked for their help. The young lads would have done so for free, but Robert offered two hundreds dollars for their services, a figure the major already approved.

Kiyo said to the new recruit. "Give me your hat."

The belligerent hawkish man replied, "I will not."

Kiyo smiled. "I just need it for the scent." He pointed to Emita.

"I ain't giving my hat to no dog either."

Robert laughed. "Private, you're an idiot. The dog can track our men. The hat will give him a typical soldier scent to do so, although your stink may lead us to a bevy of skunks! Give him your hat and that's an order."

Kiyo smiled as he took the hat and said in perfect English, "Thank you. I will return it to you shortly." He walked over to Emita and knelt down, and spoke in his native tongue to the dog. He let him get a good whiff of the hat. The dog took off up the Whitehall Trail. Kiyo tossed the hat to the man and swung up into his saddle.

Windtalker said to Robert, "If you don't mind, get someone to pull our pack animals so we ride out ahead of you."

Robert's face puzzled as he asked, "How come?"

Windtalker grinned. "Because you still make too much noise. We heard you coming from over a mile away." He handed him the leads for the horses, spun his horse around and swiftly squeezed his legs into the ribs of his mount. The horse galloped to catch up with Kiyo. Emita reached the bend in the road ahead of them and gleefully kept on running. The only thing the dog loved more than big adventure was water. He would jump in a lake, river, stream, creek or mud hole, just for the fun of it. He also liked to eat, but he burned away the calories faster than a horse.

They rode the rest of the day, finding tracks, but no sign of Indians. They made cold camp near a stream away from the road. Captain Robert posted two sentries. Tired from the ride, the Indians fell asleep quickly, however, as usual they were up and ready to leave before dawn the next morning.

Finally, they found tracks that were not as old, but still a few days old. No sign of fresh horse dung, but they felt sure they were on the right track. They had never been this far to the north on the trail. They noted lots of gullies and much game, but they stuck to the mission of finding the lost soldiers.

Near the end of the day, Emita suddenly came running towards them as hard as he could.

Kiyo spoke rapidly, "Quick! We must get off the road. Riders coming."

Windtalker led them off into a stand of trees. Emita quickly followed until they were all out of sight. With weapons drawn, Robert stood between

Kiyo and Windtalker and waited. A single Indian rider galloped along failing to note their tracks or their location. He seemed to be in a hurry to get somewhere.

Robert asked, "Where do you think he is going?"

The Indians frowned while assessing the situation. Windtalker replied, "For more men. We must be close."

Robert again asked, "Is that good news?"

Kiyo swung up into his saddle, "It means your men must be alive and holding them off, but it also means more warriors will be coming. We should have killed that messenger. We must hurry."

He led them back to the road and sprinted behind Emita as they continued up a long hill. Near the top, they heard gunfire in the valley on the other side. The sun disappeared behind the big mountains to the west and soon it would be very dark until the moon moved high in the sky. They went about half way down the road and heard more gunshots from time to time. Windtalker told Robert to prepare his men for a fight but to wait here. He told Emita to stay with Robert. On foot, Kiyo and Windtalker made their way down the road.

Robert found a path behind a group of big rocks and led his men and their horses off the road in case another rider came their way. The dog obediently stayed by his side.

At the bottom, Kiyo and Windtalker discovered the situation. Off to the left of the road, the soldiers were trapped in a dry gully. They remained hidden behind a field of big rocks. Their horses were behind them. At least a dozen Indians were hidden behind the trees and rocks above them. There were no campfires so they could not see how many soldiers were alive, but from time to time, someone fired. They also heard the zip-zip of an arrow but no screams. They believed the Indians intended to either wait for dawn to attack, or for more of their warriors to arrive.

Carefully, they moved closer until they were higher than the Indians and behind them. They looked for firing positions and whispered information to each other. With great effort, they avoided stepping on a twig and snapping it with their new boots, and once far enough away, they sprinted back to Robert.

Kiyo reported, "Your men are caught in a trap in a gully. There's no way out. The Indians are on the rocks overlooking them and can easily fire down at their targets. I couldn't tell how many of your men are alive. The moon will be up in an hour. We must go quickly but silently."

Windtalker added, "Leave your horses. Take only your weapons. Cock them now. We must get up behind them before they discover us. We must kill them all quickly when the moon is up. Wait until I have counted how many Indians there are. No one must escape."

"We're ready," replied Robert.

Kiyo ordered, "Take your spurs off."

Robert gave the order. Kiyo and Windtalker went to their saddlebags and removed their moccasins. They took their own boots off and put on their well worn but quiet deerskin shoes. They put the boots in the bags, slipped a short rope over Emita's head, and led the men down the road. Near the bottom of the hill they left the trail and made their way around and up a hill.

Near the top, Kiyo whispered to Robert to stay put and out of sight. They gave him Emita's leash to hold. Cautiously, they climbed through the rocks until they were on top of the hill. Dropping to their knees, they crawled to the edge of a big rock just as the moon broke through the clouds. They spotted eleven Indians and they believed they saw eight soldiers.

Kiyo went back down to get Robert and his men, while Windtalker scouted around. When the men arrived, he carefully placed them in good firing positions. Kiyo brought Emita with him as he made his way around to the far right so that he would be closer to the road to prevent any escapes. Windtalker moved north for the same reason. They told Robert to hold fire until they were discovered. They planned to try and take out a few of the Indians before this happened. He took Emita off leash in case something happened to him but whispered to the dog to stay and he did.

Once into position, Windtalker threaded his bow, found a warrior away from the others and with a solid thud, the arrow went through the man's back and into his heart killing him instantly. Kiyo managed to take out a man on his side as well, but before they got another chance, they heard a war whoop, and they knew the surprise was over.

Robert and his men picked their targets. Kiyo and Windtalker managed to kill another man apiece and in just a few minutes, the battle appeared to be over. Robert called to his fellow soldiers, and they heard shouts of joy. Robert led his men down the hill as they began checking the bodies of the Indians to be sure they were dead, and then they carried them down to the road picking up their bows and arrows. Emita stayed close to Kiyo as he went to the nearest man. As he came around a rock, out of the dark, a warrior jumped him and nearly caught him with a knife. Kiyo managed to step back, but he fell after tripping on a rock in the dark.

The warrior took advantage, brought his knife up, flung his arm back with the sharp blade, but just as he started to dive on Kiyo, Emita leaped from behind him and began chomping down harshly on the man's wrist. The knife fell away as the man felt the dog's sharp teeth break bones and tendons. Kiyo got to his feet pulling his pistol and shot the man in the chest twice. He went down like a rock. Emita let go as he fell.

Kiyo holstered his pistol. "Good dog. You saved me." The killing became Kiyo's first with a gun instead of his bow, spear, battle-axe or knife.

Windtalker came up behind him. "You missed one."

Kiyo grinned. "He must have been behind that rock and underneath the ledge where I fired from."

"We must hurry. Our shots may have been heard, so we must get back to the fork in the road before dawn. Find Emita some water. We're going to need him on lookout once more."

Captain Robert found eight of the dozen soldiers alive. They quickly got the wounded taken care of and loaded up, and then tied the bodies of dead soldiers and Indians alike to their horses. Kiyo and Windtalker searched for the Indian weapons and flung them over a cliff to a deep gorge. Thirty minutes later, with Emita out front, they made their way up the hill and began hurrying down the road. They galloped for an hour, then walked the horses for a half hour, and galloped on.

The sun came up before they reached the fork but they could see it. Emita waited at the fork to see if they were going home or towards the settler farm. Kiyo and Windtalker turned their horses in circles at the fork to destroy tracks, and then galloped around the bend towards the fork. Once out of sight, Windtalker pulled his horse to a halt and began speaking to Robert.

"There may be Indian scouts watching the fort. There's a gully over there. Let's dump the bodies there."

"What about the horses?"

"We'll run them across the stream and down the ridge. We'll hope they'll keep on going."

"Okay," the captain replied as he began barking orders to his men. A half hour later and with the job done, they began making their way to the fort.

Kiyo and Windtalker placed their bows in the rifle sleeves on the left side of the saddle, switched their moccasins for their boots, and pulled their hats low on their heads. They wanted to look like white men as well.

After their arrival inside the fort, the wounded were hauled into a barracks where the army doctor began treating them. Captain Robert met the major outside his office. "We rescued eight, but sadly we lost four. All of my men are fine. Kiyo, Windtalker and Emita found them for us. That dog got just a brief scent from a private's hat and tracked them down. They were caught in a gully with the Indians firing down on them. They had been there for more than a day. We hid the bodies of the Indians in the gully near Raven Rock and scattered their horses across the river."

"Excellent job though we mourn the loss. I'm thankful you were able to save the rest."

Robert grinned. "I promised Kiyo and Windtalker a hundred dollars a piece for their trouble."

The major walked over to Kiyo and Windtalker as they got off their horses and tied them off. He shook their hands while thanking them. "I'd say a hundred for the lives of our men is the bargain of the year. Thank you. Come on in and we'll get you something to drink, and a chunk of meat for your tracking dog." He bent down and gave Emita's head a good rub.

They went into the trading post bringing their stack of hides from the packhorses. The quartermaster brought their cash to them. They traded for more supplies and bought a few things for the farm including more socks, new shirts, and a big pair of scissors. The store clerk explained how they were used. They also took care to load up sugar, salt, cornmeal, and flour.

The major asked if they would be willing to help from time to time by scouting for them and he asked if they had been north. He told the scouts of the expedition he hoped to lead in the spring. They promised to talk about it, but did not promise they would do it. He asked how his men could find them when they needed help.

Kiyo and Windtalker did not want to lie to the major. Neither did they want to explain where they lived. "We go deep in the mountains for the winter," began Kiyo, "but we'll check in from time to time."

Windtalker added, "We'd better get going if we're going to stop off and see Samuel and his family. Thank you, major."

The major smiled. "Oh, it is I that owes you a big a thanks. Have a safe journey."

After they stowed away their supplies on the packhorse and saddled up, the major spoke again, "Were the Indians Blackfeet?"

Windtalker paused while getting his English words in line, "Yes, they were, but I did not recognize the band or tribe they belonged to. They had no hunting tools."

"What does that mean?"

Kiyo smiled. "A hunter would have longer arrows, a bundle of carving knives, as well as hide scrapers. They would bring along a packhorse, and gear for making a travois."

"What's a travois?"

Windtalker answered, "Long poles tied on either side of a horse and dragged behind and a cloth or hide tied between the poles that would allow the dragging of the game back to their village."

The major thought for a second and then asked, "So what were they hunting?"

Kiyo and Windtalker smiled slyly. "You."

The major gulped at the thought, but waved as they rode out of the fort and made their way to the farm. Michael came running to them as they rode up to their cabin. Samuel, now healed from his wound, came out of the barn. Trisha and Molly came to greet them as well.

"Hello," they said in unison.

"Hello to you," laughed Molly. "Your English is improving."

"We're on the way home and wanted to see how you were doing."

Samuel smiled. "Thank you, we are doing fine. Did you find the soldiers?"

"Yes, but four died. We killed some warriors to save them."

"Thank you again. You fellows be careful going home."

"We will. See you next time."

ELEVEN

Spotted Owl thought long and hard about the second group of missing warriors because his closest friend and the leader of this group were boyhood friends. He doubted they deserted, but after losing two squads of scouts, he felt mystified that nothing could be found. They failed to find bodies, spilled blood, weapons, or horses. This left him greatly baffled, but with winter coming, he reluctantly doubled his hunters to fill the village with game for the winter, reducing his available warriors. He kept four separate attack squads in the fields searching for white men. Two groups were ordered to attack any last wagon trains, while others were to attack anyone that was seen leaving the fort, or any nearby settler farm. Over the next few weeks, the warriors were successful by killing three soldiers and fifteen settlers. They also burned two cabins to the ground, killing the families. The warriors mutilated the bodies and took no prisoners to avoid feeding slaves through the winter.

Daily the scouts sent riders back to the village to report on troop movements and wagon train arrivals. They saw no wagons, but almost every day a squad of a dozen soldiers went out on patrol. Another scout would trail the soldiers and report to Spotted Owl anything they thought would interest him. It appeared they, too, were looking for wagon trains. He also realized they were looking for him and his men, but laughed that they thought he and his warriors would stand on the road in plain sight and wait for them. He knew they were afraid to go into the mountains and search for the location of his new tribe of merciless butchers.

He put aside this problem for now and took a pretty slave recently captured from a Yakima village to his tent for brutal sexual use. The village heard her screams as he raped her with great fervor and intensity. They knew she would not last long, but if lucky, perhaps through the winter.

Unlike his boyhood tribe that roamed the plains during the summer before retreating to a gorge in the mountains to hide from the powerful winter, his new village remained hidden in the mountains from both man and nature year around. They had only to build up their winter stores, but they also piled rocks and wood around the outside of the tipis, and hung additional hides on the inside walls to protect them from the wind. They made piles of disorganized wood, as they would have to keep a fire burning inside the tipi from now until late spring to survive.

Spotted Owl hated winter as it left him feeling bored. He wanted to attack and kill the white men, but only a fool would venture far from the village as the temperatures went down, and soon the snow would begin endlessly falling. In his home village, every warrior possessed a wife that took care of foraging for food and wood, and made clothes for the winter. His band of warriors was not following traditional Indian marriage by raising families.

They were women in the camp, but they were kept busy on their backs. They cooked but had little time or interest in clothing the men who took advantage of them. His men were not as prepared for winter as they should be. This resulted in his warriors forced confinement in the tipis to stay warm.

On the first day of September, the soldiers celebrated the third anniversary of the building of the fort, with a big a feast for dinner, and the firing of their largest cannon. The settlers also came to the fort and joined in the celebration. Everyone held their ears as the big bore gun blew a big iron ball high into the air before falling near the road with a heavy thud. On a small mountain across from the fort sat the scouts watching the village. The watching warriors immediately sent a runner to Spotted Owl relaying news of this powerful weapon. They wondered what other weapons the white soldiers might use against them in battle.

Windtalker and Kiyo were swimming and washing in the river after working all day to bring in more of their crops. They soon planned to build a cellar in the cabin floor for storing their vegetables and to provide a hiding place if attacked. For now, they stored all of their food in an unused corner of their cabin.

They were just getting out of the water when they heard the big cannon from the direction of the fort. The unusual boom echoed through their valley. Like most Indians, new sounds were compared to what they knew, and this noise proved to be greater than the thunderous sound of a running herd of buffalo. They could not see the arch of the fireball with its long trail of sparks from their farm, nor the impact sound as it plowed into the ground, but they could definitely hear the boom as it exploded out of the cannon. The reverberation soon surrounded their hideaway in the valley. Suddenly, they didn't feel as isolated as they wished.

The Indians began experiencing several cold days for almost a week, forcing a change to long pants and shirts, and a lighter jackets. However, they enjoyed snuggling up close together on their recently constructed bed they made from logs they sawed up and framed with nails and pegs. They made a mesh area of rope across the flat area by weaving it back and forth, and added a stack of hides with the buffalo and bear robes at the foot for warmth when needed. Samuel showed them how to tighten the ropes with a short piece of a stick to get them as taut as possible. Samuel assumed they were making two single beds instead of the double bed. As close as they were as friends, the men kept their love for each other a secret.

They kept the door locked and slept naked as usual in each other's arms. Beside their bed they each kept a loaded rifle and pistol, and a battle-axe leaned against the wall just in case of a surprise attack. This is what they feared might happen if their secret farm were found. The waterfall remained cold in the midst of summer, so getting wet in the winter was not something most warriors would do. However, they hoped their horses would whinny and neigh at the sight of strangers. They were also confident that Emita would pick up the scent of an outsider and growl a warning to alert them of approaching danger, but they felt they needed something more. What exactly, they were not sure. They would have to think on it. Emita would sleep at the foot of the bed until the temperatures dropped before moving to a favorite spot near the fire that burned all winter to keep the cabin temperature above freezing.

The following week the weather surprisingly changed to mildly warm so they decided to make a trip to Samuel's family and the fort in case they needed something. In the past few months they led several search parties for the major and he rewarded their skills with cash, providing more money than they needed. Samuel told them to hide some of it and to never carry too much in case they were robbed. He also told them not to hide it in the cabin or barn as the Indians might burn those to the ground and the money would burn as well. They hid it under a flat rock behind the privy. He also warned the scouts not to speak of their money or to show they carried cash publicly as it would tempt those on hard times to rob and kill them.

They arrived to find Samuel and Michael working in the fields pulling out potatoes and carrots. He gave some to the fellows. When they got to the cabin, they found Molly washing some clothes in a tub of water with a washboard and soap. They smelled the water and watched her. She showed them how to take one of Michael's dirty shirts and scrub it clean. She hung the shirt on a clothesline using wooden pins so they dried in the sun.

Trisha was on the other end of the porch churning butter. They enjoyed butter often at Molly's table by putting it on cornbread, flapjacks, and biscuits, but didn't know how to make it. Trisha taught them, but they didn't have a cow. Molly laughed and explained a cow remained essential to the task plus it gave them milk to drink and buttermilk for her recipes. Samuel came up to see what they were laughing at and they explained.

Samuel said, "Well, purchase a churn and some molds at the store, some covered pails, and I'll give you some milk on your way home. It has to stay cold, but with winter coming, that won't be a problem." He took them around back of the cabin to the creek and over to an area he dug out and framed with rocks and put a board over it. The cool water kept everything in it cold. They saw buckets of stuff floating in the water.

The Indians thanked him for the offer, but they didn't want to take advantage, nor did they want to buy a cow as it required attending, as they planned to keep taking long explorations into the mountains in the north and through the valleys to the west. Windtalker replied, "Thank you for your kind offer, but we might want milk more often. I propose we buy some from time to time. This will help us and help you."

Samuel grinned. "You're right about that, but can you afford it."

Kiyo grinned. "The army pays us to scout and track for them. We pay you. How much?"

Samuel replied as they walked back to the front porch, "I think you'd better get some clay jugs with a cork stopper. This will keep it cold and it won't spill on your packhorse. How about twenty-five cents a jug?"

Windtalker smiled. "Very good. How much is that?" He held out a silver dollar coin.

Samuel replied, "Well, one jug is twenty-five cents or one fourth of this coin."

Kiyo frowned. "What means one fourth?"

Molly helped. She took a stick and drew a circle. "This circle is like one dollar." She then drew lines cutting into four quarters. She pointed to one, "This section is one fourth, so there are three fourths left." She tapped the other ones.

Windtalker and Kiyo nodded while seeming to understand, but Windtalker replied, "This hurts my head. We buy four fourths!" He handed Samuel the silver dollar.

They all laughed as Samuel said, "You drive a hard bargain, but when you get to the trading post buy four jugs and pack them well so they don't break against each other."

Kiyo politely asked if they needed anything at the fort.

Samuel said no. Molly added, "When you get back we'll have an early supper together. I hope you're hungry."

Both fellows always grinned when she said that. They loved her cooking. "Yes ma'am," they replied in unison.

Captain Robert spoke some instructions about his horse to the blacksmith and then looked up as Windtalker and Kiyo rode into the fort with a packhorse on a lead. They tied up at the trading post store. He smiled and waved at his friends, realizing in the months since meeting the Indian warriors, he noticed many changes in the way they dressed like white men, the saddles on their horses, the gun belts with pistols, and saddle scabbards for rifles and bows, and the hats on their heads. Most Indians didn't wear hats or boots. To most folks, they looked like white men with a nice tan. As the weeks went by, he noted their accomplishment in picking up the English language. The fellows had Molly to thank for that as she took every opportunity to help them learn to speak and read.

He called out to them as he came across the yard. "How goes it?"

Windtalker frowned. "Where does it go?"

Robert grinned. "I'm sorry. That was an improper sentence, but it means, how are you?"

Kiyo replied, "I are fine."

They all laughed as Robert corrected him. "No, you should say, I am fine."

Kiyo nodded. "So how am you?"

They all laughed again. Robert caught on. "You're pulling my leg, aren't you?"

Kiyo replied with a sly grin, "How can I do that? I'm standing six feet away and holding the reins to my horse."

They laughed again. "You are too smart for me. Come on in the store and let's see what you need."

The storekeeper liked the Indians, as they were always polite, they told him exactly what they wanted, and they bought a lot. The Indians liked looking at so many items they had never seen or touched before. They bought a washtub, washboard, soap, and four jugs with stoppers, a butter churn, butter molds, four sacks of flour, and a slab of bacon. On the counter they noted a new fifty-caliber Sharps rifle.

Kiyo picked it up. "What this gun for?"

Robert showed him the features of the gun. "It is a buffalo gun. It is very powerful and shoots a bullet a long, long way. You can fire it from way off so the sound will not scatter the herd." He showed them the large bullet for the gun. "Let's go outside and I'll show you."

He took a handful of cartridges and they went outside. He began looking around for something to shoot at. He didn't see what he wanted so he looked around the side of the trading post and saw a pile of tins. He asked a private to take a bag of tins to the far corner of the fort, climb the rail, and put a tin on the top of the post, and then back off a few steps.

Kiyo and Windtalker watched with great interest as Robert put a shell in the rifle, brought back the hammer to a cocked position, used the hitching post to steady the big gun, took aim, and fired. The noise was loud but the powerful shot hit the first can, sending it flying into the air. The private put another can on the post.

Windtalker said, "Let me try."

Robert asked, "You can shoot a rifle?"

Windtalker smiled slyly. "A little."

Robert handed him the rifle. Windtalker inspected the rifle carefully, before slowly lining up the shot with the barrel again resting on the hitching post. Slowly, he pulled the trigger. Boom! He hit the can dead center while knocking it far from the post.

Kiyo laughed. "Wow, it has huge power. May I try?"

Robert began to think they were better shots than he thought. "Okay, but let's make it harder." He turned around looking for something for him to shoot at. The gates were open. Across the road he could see a pitiful windblown tree. At the top, he spotted a short limb with a single pine cone hanging from it. He pointed and smiled. "Let's see you hit the pine cone at the top of that tree."

Kiyo spotted it as he took the rifle after Robert loaded a second shell.

67

Once again he followed Windtalker's pattern by inspecting the gun, feeling the weight and balance of it, and then he lined up the shot from the wooden post, took careful aim and fired. The pine cone disintegrated instantly.

Robert laughed aloud in amazement. So did the major walking up behind them. "That was an excellent shot. Where'd you learn to shoot like that?"

Kiyo handed Robert the rifle. "Samuel taught us."

Robert laughed again. "Samuel is not that good a shot."

Windtalker grinned and replied politely, "He is a better teacher. We already had the shooting skills from our training with a bow. Tell the private to put up another can."

As the soldier placed the can, Windtalker retrieved his bow, bent the bow to hook the string, tested it by pulling the string and letting go several times, selected an arrow, took aim at the can, held his breath as he slowly sighted down the shaft, exhaled gently, and fired. The arrow flew rapidly across the courtyard and hit the can dead center.

The major laughed. "You're right. You have excellent skills. I am very impressed."

Windtalker smiled. "Thanks. This gun is very powerful, but what gun did you shoot yesterday? We could hear it from our hunting place." He chose not to say home or settlement.

"We fired a cannon," he replied as he pointed to it near the front gate. They walked over to look at the gun.

Kiyo laughed. "You can kill many buffalo with this gun."

The major smiled and replied, "Twenty or more, but this gun is not used for hunting. We use it to attack or defend from an attack."

Windtalker sighed. "Too big for me."

The major smiled, but after thinking a second he asked, "You could hear the gun?"

"Yes, it produced a big boom and then echoed through the hills."

"I think we have found a way to summon your help. If we fire just one shot like you heard, it will mean we need your help. If we are practicing we'll fire two shots, wait a while, and fire two more. However, if you hear us fire three rapid shots, we're under attack and beg for your help. Will that work for you?"

Windtalker replied, "Yes, we'll try. Sometimes we are farther away while hunting and in the warmer months we like to explore."

"I'll remember that as I'm still hoping to win approval for an exploration team to move north. What do you know of the Flathead tribes?"

Kiyo frowned. "They are a fierce tribe, known for their excellent hunting skills, and they are brave in battle. They look weird."

"We have reports they are northwest of us and some of my men have seen them. They have not attempted to come here, but they have attacked smaller squads on patrol. What tribe are you from?"

Windtalker paused for a second while looking at Kiyo. Without talking they decided to trust the major. "We were members of the Blackfeet tribe. We left the tribe to live on our own as we did not agree with their attacks on the innocent women and children in the wagon trains." Kiyo knew he would not tell the soldiers the bigger reason, as they trusted no one with their feelings for each other.

Kiyo added, "We grew up as brothers and did the hunting for our families since we were half grown. We liked the freedom of hunting and going where we wanted to."

The major smiled. "You're very good at it. I'll see you next time."

Windtalker, Kiyo, and Robert returned to the trading post. Robert placed the Sharps gun on the counter. Windtalker asked, "How much for the gun?"

The trading post clerk looked at Robert for approval. Robert nodded yes. The man said, "Fifty dollars. A box of shells is five dollars."

Kiyo quickly replied, "But it is used and thus should be cheaper."

This caught both the storekeeper and Robert off guard at least until they saw the sly grin slowly forming on Kiyo's face.

"We'll take one, and four boxes of shells," replied Windtalker. The storekeeper laughed as he retrieved the shells.

Kiyo smiled. "We'd better get going."

Windtalker paid the man for all their supplies and the new gun. They loaded their packhorse with great care making sure the load remained balanced, and that their new empty jugs didn't break. They shook hands with Robert and left the fort. They pulled their hats down low as they rode out of the fort.

Across the road and hidden in the trees on a hill, two of Spotted Owl's men watched the lone riders leave the fort, but assumed they were settlers. They followed them to the Samuel farm. They cursed them as they did all white men. They vowed to take their scalps at the first opportunity. They had no idea they were Indians as well.

The fellows gave Molly a sack of flour as a gift for her help with the English and the good food she made for them, and set the jugs on the table for Michael to fill. They joined Samuel in the field and helped him pull some big rocks from his expanded garden. He told the fellows he spent much of the fall preparing for spring planting, but often hunting early in the morning filling their stock in the smokehouse. It took two teams of horses to pull the big stone free. He used the rock to dam up part of the creek that ran through their farm to provide a pool of water for their horses and cow to drink.

Samuel and Michael showed the fellows their new fenced in area for their animals to roam in. They divided the area into two parts. Samuel explained he would allow the animals in one side for a week before moving them to the second, and by doing so, the animals would not eat the roots of the wild grass. The grass on each side would have a chance to recover. Windtalker and Kiyo were pleased at the location of the fence after advising him not to put the horses too close to the woods because at night the Indians might attempt to steal them.

Michael showed off his bow and arrows that he practiced daily, but received some extra tips from the fellows. Samuel and Michel also practiced shooting with their rifles, as did Molly and Trisha. They also practiced with the pistols. They hoped to fend off any future attacks by the Indians.

The Indians ate a late lunch with the family before heading home. Not far to their cut off, Emita came running back as hard as he could. They quickly found a place to pull off, but hiding became difficult, as many of the leaves had fallen. They kept going deeper into the forest stopping only when they heard the horses. Windtalker crept back to the road to watch.

A few minutes later, a group of a ten warriors galloped by. He guessed they were Shoshone and they wore battle paint. After they passed and rounded the next bend out of sight, they returned to the road and made a hasty gallop towards home.

For several months, they began stopping in the woods near the waterfall, then hid behind a stand of boulders and waited. They wanted to be sure no one followed them. They took great care in covering up tracks, but a good hunter would most likely be able to find their tracks after they left the road. They marched through various streams and across beds of rock to make it as difficult as possible. Once satisfied, they made their way through the waterfall. Emita ran ahead to the farm while they kept a careful eye to be sure no one hid in ambush for them. Thankfully, Emita did not pick up the scent of a stranger. After failing to find any tracks, they rode to the cabin.

The spent the following week adding game to their smokehouse using the new Sharps fifty-caliber rifle to bring down a big moose at three hundred yards. The accuracy and distance amazed them, as did the big hole in the torso. They could only imagine what it might do to an enemy warrior. They had no idea how long until the first big snowstorm, but they knew it would come soon. The following day, the weather once again turned uncharacteristically warm. They felt they were well prepared for winter so they cut down trees, cut boards, and began building the next phase of their barn. They worked hard, but the days were shorter and it took them three days to frame the larger addition; another five days to put the roof and walls on, and eight more to put the cedar shakes on the roof.

Near the end of the exterior work on the barn the weather became much colder and the daytime temperatures barely reached fifty degrees, and the nighttime dropped below the freezing mark. They were dressed in their new long johns underwear that they purchased from the trading post and made fun of each other as they walked around the cabin. Kiyo somehow put his on backwards with the potty flap on the wrong side, so he quickly took them off and flipped them around before putting the cotton underwear back on again. They also wore long sleeve shirts, under thick brown jackets, as well as fur lined hats and gloves to protect their hands from the wind.

Quickly, they worked on the new doors for the barn and once completed, the wind could no longer race through the barn. They removed the former exterior wall of the old barn where the new section butted to it, and used the boards for a stall in the new section. They hauled in more trees, moved their sawing apparatus to the inside, as well as the rest of their cutting tools. Their hard woodworking efforts warmed their cold bodies, and after a few days, they floored the loft of the new section. They used some of the exterior walls to mount all their farm and construction tools as Samuel did inside his barn. He said it prevented rust, but he also gave them a jar of oil for rubbing on their metal pieces to protect them.

They hoped to build a chicken coop on the outside of the new section, but before they could finish framing in all the stalls and building a grain and feed room, the snow began to fall. For the next four days, it snowed continuously, but they worked anyhow until they had a stack of logs against the wall inside the barn so they could work on sawing and cutting. Two weeks later, they completed the inside of the barn, and began spreading the piles of wood chips on the floor of the stalls, and began moving the horses in and out of the stalls so they would be comfortable coming and going.

Their grain rooms were filled with feed for their horses as well as seed for spring. They cut enough hay to fill one loft, and next year they vowed to plant more hay and straw to fill the second as well.

The snow settled to just over a foot deep and they kept a packed path to the barn, privy, and smokehouse. With temperatures dropping, they worked mostly inside the cabin, building new shelves, and cabinets, and replaced the benches with four chairs. They used the benches on each side of the bed to help with dressing and a new bench at the door to get their muddy boots on and off. They kept a fire going all the time to keep the cabin warm, and though the wind howled continuously, they found no air leaks in their new cabin walls.

Twice a day they bundled up warmly, and trudged through the deepening snow to check on their horses. Wisely, the horses came inside for the night or during snowstorms, but went out for water and search for food. They fed the animals both grain and straw to keep their weight up. About once a week on a sunny day, they would saddle two horses, and with Emita attempting to run ahead in the deepening snow, they rode to the tunnel to check for signs of humans. They also rode around the valley, but always returned without signs of any humans about.

By late November, the snow reached three feet with drifts exceeding twelve feet. They worked daily on clearing the door and a path to the barn, smokehouse, and the privy. They decided to take on a bigger inside chore.

After cutting a two-foot square in the floor, they made a trap door. They attached store-bought hinges under the new door and attached them to the frame. When in place the floor remained flat and almost hidden. They covered it at night with a hide. Beneath their floor they began digging out a cellar. The first few inches or so were frozen and required the mallet, but as they dug deeper, the digging became easier. They hauled the dirt to the front door and threw it on their paths.

The digging kept them strong, but it took several weeks before they completed a twelve by twelve feet room. Not yet satisfied, they dug the floor down about six feet, boarded the walls right to the floor of the cabin to keep the wind and mice out, put in the cellar floor, and made shelving and cabinets for the walls. They hauled the empty barrels they bought from the trading post, placed them in the cellar, and filled the containers with bags of potatoes, carrots, and turnips. They also stored their extra weapons from the wagons they found including rifles, pistols, and ammunition. In the spring, they planned to find a place to store half of their cache of weapons in a location away from their cabin and barn as Samuel suggested.

By January, the daytime temperature never got above ten degrees and often remained in the single digits or worst. The side of the cabin farthest from the fire sometimes showed frost on the inside even though the cabin felt warm to them. The stream moved fast enough to prevent freezing so the animals could drink, but the animals wisely stayed in the barn most of the time. The warriors spent their time learning how to cook, and using the note cards Molly made for them, they practiced over and over making the recipes. They teased and laughed at each other, but in a month, they were making biscuits almost as well as she did, and they loved making cornbread. They missed her fried chicken, but made mashed potatoes and gravy, baked and grilled potatoes, roasted carrots, and ate venison of all varieties.

They loved their life together, especially at night when they could make love, while cuddling and buried under a mound of buffalo and bear hides, and sleeping as long as they wanted.

TWELVE

Though the days became longer, by late March the winter refused to go away. A blizzard blew for three straight days making even going to the privy and the barn almost impossible. They struggled in the high wind, making their way across the deep snow to the barn. Daily they shoveled snow away from the cabin and barn doors to make entry possible. They only opened the back of the barn to let the animals out for water in the mornings and before nightfall. Most of the time they were forced to keep the barn closed to protect the horses from the windchill.

They were anxious for the warm sun to return, the snow to melt, and the leaves and grass to turn green, so they could once again hunt for fresh game, as well as explore the vast mountain regions to the north and west of their new home.

They never allowed boredom to creep into their minds. They stayed warm in the cabin and used their idle time to make arrows and new bows, sharpen their knives and axes, and clean their rifles and pistols as Samuel taught them. They sometimes enjoyed sex in the middle of the day just because they could.

A few weeks later, the snow began to melt, and now their farm became a large mud squalor. The previously hard packed snow path to the barn made squishing sounds as they slogged their way to each of the outer buildings. The thick sludge desperately tried to pull their boots from their feet. When the snow rescinded to just a foot, the rains came. Sometimes it rained for hours, and a few times for days, and yet the air gradually became warmer.

By early May, they began plowing their garden and making it twice the previous size. They planted all of their seed, but ran out of fencing wire to encompass the new acreage. They cut poles and dug holes for the anticipated fencing, but once around the garden, they decided to travel to the fort for supplies.

They retrieved some of their cash from the root cellar, changed to cleaner clothes, saddled up their horses, and put the carriage racks on the two packhorses. Finally, they checked and loaded their weapons. With an anxious Emita, they made their way through the tunnel and ducked quickly through the cold waterfall for the first time since late last fall. The views were amazing as the leaves were still small, but produced a beautiful shade of green to the forest. The air smelled clean and fresh, and after a long cold winter inside the cabin, the sun on their faces felt bright, warm, and wonderful.

They rode first to Samuel's farm to check on the family. They were working the fields, preparing their crops as well. They sat on the porch talking with the entire family about how they fared during the blizzards, and how thankful they were that spring finally arrived. They told Molly their cooking improved over the winter and thanked her for the recipe cards. She noted improvement in their English as well. They forced themselves to speak only English throughout the winter, though they sometimes cursed in their native tongue, usually the result of missing a nail and finding their thumb instead.

They told Samuel about their additional garden area, and that they hoped to soon add a chicken coop to their barn so they could have eggs and fried chicken. Samuel warned them about reports of Indian trouble along the trail to the east and west of the fort, and encouraged them to be careful. They promised they would as they left the family for the fort.

They found the fort in a bevy of noise as workers were building a new addition to the fort. Much like their expanded barn, the new area would make the fort at least twice as large. With a few guards on duty, the rest of the soldiers were busy chopping down trees, flaying away limbs, sharpening points, digging holes, and erecting the twenty foot poles around the new perimeter. Cross boards were nailed from the inside, and new guard towers and interior walkways were also constructed.

Captain Robert saw the scouts and welcomed each with a hearty handshake. They talked about the winter and heard first hand reports of trouble with both the Blackfeet to the east and the Shoshone tribes to the south. They tied up their horses to the hitching posts in front of the trading post. They found the owner expanding his building as well. He made huge supply orders in the fall and expected delivery soon. He heard reports of over ten thousands settlers coming this year. This fact bewildered the Indians. They could not fathom so many people.

They bought lots of seed and grain, rolls of barbed wire for their new fence posts, and a new set of clothes. They were securing their stock to the packhorses when Major Bill walked up to greet them.

"It looks like you survived the winter and that is no easy accomplishment so I congratulate you. I have been looking forward to seeing you. I have received approval for an expedition to the north from two explorers carrying dispatches, and I want to hire you to lead us. We leave in two weeks and will be gone about a month. It pays three hundred each. Will you help us?"

Windtalker and Kiyo spoke quickly to each other. They didn't want to be away from the farm too much, but they knew they needed the money for additional purchases for the farm, so they replied they would accept his offer. This pleased the major very much.

After returning home, they unpacked their supplies, and while eating a late lunch, they took a piece of paper and wrote the numbers one to fourteen on it. They circled the first number so they could see how long before leaving on their journey. They spent the rest of that day and part of another fencing in the new garden, and building a gate for the entrance to their property.

In the coming days, they spent every waking moment working on their farm, making repairs, and planting every seed purchased. They also began riding their horses to build up their stamina, and to help shed some winter fat as well as fur from their coats.

On the fourteenth day, and long before dawn, they saddled up their horses, and one packhorse, loaded their weapons including their bows and arrows, a Winchester rifle on Kiyo's horse, and the new fifty-caliber Sharps buffalo gun on Windtalker's saddle. They also carried two pistols, knives, and their battle-axes. They prepared bedrolls and filled their saddlebags with extra rounds of ammunition and beef jerky.

The night before the upcoming journey, they took turns cutting their hair with their new scissors to make them look more like a white man and less like Indians. They pulled their hats down tight as always, flung upwards into the saddle, made a whistle for Emita, and off they went. With the grass in their valley rapidly growing, they no longer worried about feeding the remainder of their stock.

They stopped briefly to speak to Samuel before heading on to the fort. The major's men were completing their preparations as well. Soon the scouts rode alongside the major as they left the fort with a dozen soldiers and followed by a cook and his helper pulling a string of packhorses.

They followed the road as it made a winding path to the north for almost forty miles before turning westward. The major studied the mountains to the north and sought advice from Windtalker and Kiyo. They suggested following the riverbeds, but they rode out ahead of the soldiers while escaping the noise the squad produced. They chose a large stream and soon picked up a natural animal trail cascading downward from a large gorge.

They returned to the major with the suggestion, and he agreed and gave the orders for the men to leave the road as instructed. Windtalker told the major to send back two men armed with pine limbs to sweep away their tracks.

Upon hearing this, the major asked, "So you think there are Indians that might trail us?"

Windtalker smiled. "They saw us leave the fort this morning. I saw the sun sparkle off a knife or an axe on the small mountain across the field from your front gate."

The astonished major replied, "You saw them. Why didn't you say something?"

Kiyo grinned. "It's easier to catch a trailing bear than to chase one."

The major couldn't help but smile. "So we're going to wait for them to catch up?"

"No, you're going to follow the trail next to the stream and continue making all that noise your soldiers seem to be fond of. We'll wait for them and ambush them. I hope they'll miss where we turned off, but if they are as good as I suspect, they will find our trail."

"All that noise?"

Kiyo smiled again. "Sir, your men create a jingle and jangle noise with every step that can be heard for miles. Just hold still and listen as your men ride by."

Once the major's voice remained silent, he could not believe all he heard. "I see your point. I guess you can't sneak up on an enemy wearing a cowbell. Tonight, we'll attempt to remedy the noise, but for now, we'll proceed as requested. Do you need some of my men to help?"

"No, it will probably be just a few scouts. We'll handle it with our bows in case there are other Indians in the area. It will be a quiet kill."

"Good luck then and please be careful."

After the soldiers swept the trail and caught up with their troop, the scouts carefully followed looking for a good spot to hide. They split up amongst some large rocks with each scout on opposite sides of the trail. They would catch the scouts in crossfire should they need a second shot. They withdrew their bows and arrows and prepared to sit and wait. They told Emita to sit and stay. It didn't take long before they heard two riders. They signaled to each other. Windtalker would take the first man and Kiyo the second. They watched as the warriors studied the ground until they picked up the trail once more. They spoke rapidly to each other before digging in their heels and galloping towards them.

Windtalker and Kiyo threaded their bows while waiting patiently. At twenty yards, they fired their arrows. With the short range and powerful bows, the arrows went all the way through the chest of each scout. The intense pain made them fall off their horses to the ground in a limp tumble. The scouts ran to them and slit their throats to end their pain and their lives. It was then they realized one man was Blackfeet and the other Shoshone, and this astonished the scouts, as they had never known the two tribes to work together. They also noted that both warriors wore a white circle over their heart. This was not a familiar symbol to either Indian.

They retrieved their horses and tied them off. They loaded a body on each horse and used rags to tie the bodies by hands and feet to the other. They took the scout's weapons and went back for their own horses and Emita, and soon they led the ponies back to the main road, but this time they turned right, went about fifty yards, and let loose the ropes on the Indian ponies. They slapped their butts with sticks sending the frightened horses trotting to the northwest.

The scouts returned to the diversion trail, broke limbs and once again brushed away the tracks, and then galloped to catch up with the major. They showed him their captured weapons, and he marveled at how smart and clever they were. They made camp about an hour before dark, though they wished they could move farther away from any warriors in search of the scouts.

The major sipped his coffee after eating cornbread and beans, and asked them about the noise the soldiers made. Windtalker took his knife, walked over to a saddle, and tapped all the metal buckles and loops. He tapped the uniform of the cook and the spurs on their boots.

Kiyo pointed at the major's brass belt and brass plate on his hat, explaining the sun would reflect and make it easy for a good scout to spot them. He picked up the major's white hat and said, "Only a fool would wear this in battle. Your hat should be dark like the others. If you are the only soldier with a white hat they'll know who the leader is and you'll die first."

The major gulped. "Okay, I get the picture." He stood and turned to his men. "Come here. I want you to listen to these men. We're going to fix our gear so we can ride silently and safely. You'll do as they suggest because our lives may depend on our stealth."

For the next thirty minutes, they showed them what to fix while the major stowed his hat in his saddlebag, and pulled on a black cap he had worn most of the winter. The next morning, the Indians showed the cook how to wrap his pots and pans in cloth to keep them quiet.

As they saddled up the major asked, "Is there anything else we should do?"

Kiyo replied, "Your horses are fine for working near the fort, but the next time you go on a journey into hostile Indian Territory you should ride only unshod or Indian horses."

"Why is that?"

Windtalker answered, "If you are on ponies and your tracks are found, they'll think you're warriors and probably not follow. If they know you're soldiers, they will send a warrior for reinforcements and attack vigorously. Don't shout out your commands like you do in the fort. Use hand signals to direct your men as needed. Come on let's ride. We'll go ahead as before."

Everything the scouts told and showed the major were the result of many winter discussions they did in their cabin, inventing ways to protect the soldiers and settlers, and helping these men learn how to fight the greatest warriors of the west, the Blackfeet Indians.

The scouts knew they were climbing the entire day but not steeply. Steadily, the stream grew narrower and by nightfall it had become a creek. They suggested a campsite, and then they rode on alone looking for a way out of the back of this gorge. They failed to find a pass, so they would have to climb a steep hill to the ridge in the morning. Hearing and seeing nothing, they returned to camp.

"Heavy work in the morning," reported Kiyo, "but once on the ridge, we can make it up and around that mountain." He pointed to the north.

Windtalker sat down by the fire, "Major, tell me again what you're looking for?"

"I want to build a road to Canada. This road will increase trade with our neighbors. There's a big shipping port in Vancouver. I hear they have found a route from Winnipeg to the Pacific Ocean. If we can link up with it, we can get supplies to our system of forts from the west in weeks instead of waiting months for the same from Saint Louis."

Kiyo asked, "You're going to haul wagons?"

"Yes, of course," replied the major. "So we have to find a passage requiring the least amount of effort and road construction. If I find it, the government will send in engineers to build the road. Who knows, perhaps one day, tracks will be laid for a railroad."

Windtalker's faced puzzled. "What is a railroad?"

The major grinned. "It is a giant iron horse. It runs on steam and that makes the metal wheels turn and then it can haul both passenger and freight cars."

Windtalker asked, "Can you draw this railroad for me?"

The major took a stick from the fire and drew a rough sketch of the train. The scouts shook their heads in disbelief. The major smiled. "There's a whole lot of fascinating things back east that will gradually make their way to here. Settlers are going to love these beautiful mountains."

THIRTEEN

Spotted Owl fretted over the missing scouts, cursed some of his men, and wondered if they were captured or just run off. He sent men out to track them. They found tracks heading west, but lost the tracks on the road, and returned with news of their disappearance.

Meanwhile, another scout rode in from the east reporting a large wagon train coming their way. He forgot about the two men for now and made plans for a large force to attack the following day. They hustled about preparing their weapons.

The troop began the climb up the side of the mountain by traversing diagonally to the right, and then working back to the left, and so on. They hoped the zigzag pattern would prevent a horse from slipping and breaking a leg, or tumbling down the hill killing the rider as well. An hour into the climb, they reached an old well-worn narrow animal trail. The major assumed only deer or a mountain goat could ply their way safely along the precipice.

Kiyo and Windtalker rode ahead of the column where they took turns with the lead rider watching the trail for tracks, and the follower scanning the forest for any sign of movement by human or animal. Kiyo suddenly whispered, "Panther. A big one."

Windtalker responded, "How old are the tracks?"

"Not old at all. He's probably watching us."

"He'll have a cave nearby." Windtalker turned and whispered to the major to pass the word to keep their pistols ready.

The men were nervous and frightened, but they trudged along at a steady pace as they continued the slow climb up the mountain. Two hours later, Kiyo reached the top of the ridge. He climbed off his horse to allow the animal to rest after the long difficult climb. Windtalker did the same. The major told his men to dismount.

The major asked, "Any water for the horses?"

"Not this high up," replied Kiyo. "Let my horse rest a while and then I'll scout ahead. You have canteens, and we'll get more water soon, so let the men give water to their horses."

The major gave him a perplexed look, as he had never fed water to a horse from his canteen, but slowly nodded and gave the order. They didn't teach him to take care of their horses in this manner at the academy, but the simple wisdom from the scouts surprised him. The locals knew the value of a horse in this country, and he felt he should have as well.

The soldiers plopped down after taking care of their horses. Two of the men went back down the trail to take an urgent potty. One of the men stood over six feet tall and weighed at least two hundred forty pounds. The other man, a rookie of just six months, stood just five feet seven inches, and only a hundred and forty pounds. They both laid down the rifles and dropped their pants about a dozen feet from the other.

Kiyo, Windtalker, and the major walked ahead on the ridge while overlooking the valley below and to their west. The major brought along his binoculars and began scanning the terrain from the north to the west looking for a route. He pointed at several possible routes, but without the aid of the field glasses, the Indians used their sharp eyes and knowledge of the mountains to make alternate suggestions.

Suddenly, they heard the unmistakable sound of a growl from a large cat. Kiyo and Windtalker rapidly left the major running back to their horses. Kiyo pulled his bow while Windtalker snatched the Sharps rifle from his saddle scabbard. They ran through the soldiers in the direction of a human scream and a loud snarl. They were nearly run over by the hard charging bigger man as he ran towards them with his rifle in his hands, and too afraid to turn around and shoot.

They dodged around him and slowed as they could hear the sound of thrashing. Kiyo threaded an arrow and Windtalker loaded a shell in the Sharps. Carefully, they moved forward. In just a few minutes, they found the scene of the attack. They fingered the large paw prints. They saw the man's rifle and a large amount of spilled blood. They could see the trail that the cat left as it dragged its prey away. They quickly followed the bloody trail as the cat dragged the limp body up and over rocks.

"It must be a female. It is taking food to the litter."

"Then we have to watch for a male as well. We must hurry. An attack by another large cat is highly possible after seeing how easy their mate snatched this man."

They ran up the rocks, crossed over the blood trail, and went up a little higher so they were overlooking the bloody path. A few minutes later, they heard the gnashing of teeth. They found the cat. She struggled to pull the corpse up a section of loose shale. Kiyo brought his bow up and fired. Almost as soon as the first arrow struck the cat, he threaded a second and fired again. The wounded cat dropped the body, and charged at them. Windtalker brought the rifle up, cocked the hammer, and took aim. Kiyo never moved as he fired a third shot catching the cat in the left shoulder causing him to slow. A fourth arrow caught him in the eye, and then suddenly, he fell like a big rock.

Quickly, they scanned the area, anticipating an attacking of her mate, but they found nothing. They began carefully backtracking their way down the rocks and back to the scene of the attack. They picked up the rifle and returned to the terrified soldiers. They gave the rifle to the major.

Windtalker spoke first, "The big panther is dead, but I'm sorry to report so is your man. This is his rifle. Kiyo killed him with bow and arrows to avoid the sound of a gun."

The major's face displayed intense sorrow at the loss of his soldier, but thanked Windtalker and Kiyo for their skill and bravery. "Kiyo, how many

80

arrows to take him down?"

"Four."

Windtalker grinned. "I could have done it with one shot, but Kiyo must have been teasing him. The fourth arrow he shot right in the cat's eye. We must move on quickly, as it was a female. Her mate must be out on a hunt, and we do not want him hunting us."

The major gulped but turned to his men and said, "Saddle up fellows. We must move on."

A private asked, "What about burial?"

The major looked at Kiyo who replied, "I'm sorry, sir. That's not possible. Much of the man's body is gone, and the rest is on a slippery slope of shale and loose sediment. We must move on."

The major reluctantly nodded approvingly and they began moving. The packhorses were moved to the middle to protect their supplies, and the rear now protected by two men with rifles pulled and ready. For most of the day, they stayed on the ridge, and though the animal trail became a bit wider, the winding back and forth around the large boulders at the top slowed them down. Late in the day, they began a descent after hearing the sound of water. They made camp, fed and watered the horses, and posted guards while the cook began pulling supplies from the packhorse to go to work on supper. Three soldiers brought dried wood for the fire, but the scouts suggested moving their planned fire between some big boulders. The major asked why.

Kiyo smiled. "Smoke from a fire at night is not much of a problem unless the moon is full, but a bright fire can be seen for miles. Hiding the flame behind the rocks prevents our discovery."

"You think there are Indians nearby."

Windtalker responded, "I think we're in range of the Flathead Indians and maybe the Yakimas."

Kiyo added, "They are fierce tribes. I don't know how they feel about white men, but most tribes are afraid of strangers."

The major sat down on a log and smiled. "I read the accounts by explorers Lewis and Clark as well as numerous explorers. I don't know much about the Yakimas, but I recall they battled with the Flatheads after first trading with them."

Kiyo grinned. "It is an old Indian tactic to offer trade as a way of sizing up your enemy. My tribe would trade by giving the white men horses for blankets. The next day they would trail the white men all day and in the middle of the night, they'd steal their traded horses back. Near the end of the following day when the white men were tired, they would attack and kill them all."

Windtalker added, "That's why we didn't shoot my gun at the cat, and why we must hide our cook fire. If you want hot coffee in the morning, we must eat before sun up so the smoke will not be seen."

"Okay, you're right. Thanks."

Captain Robert led a group of twenty men on a three-day march from the fort to the east. Near the end of the first day, they came upon a lot of horse tracks and none were shod. He didn't have the skills to figure out how many horses, but he guessed at least sixty or more. He recalled that Windtalker and Kiyo studied horse dung like checking a watch. The dung he found still felt warm. He hurried his men along, but warned them to be on the alert with guns ready.

They made camp well off the trail after hiding their tracks and posting guards. They continued tracking the unshod horses the next day, but had yet to catch up. On the third day, they arrived at the last ridge overlooking the long valley to the east. He took out his field glasses after noting a trail of dust. He studied the terrain until finally he spotted the lead horses of the first wagon as it came over a knoll. "It's a large wagon train." He continued watching the train, but something caught his eye in the valley below them. He moved the binoculars and refocused the ring. "Oh my goodness. There's a force of about sixty Indians waiting to ambush. We have to stop them."

"We're only twenty men," protested a sergeant.

"But we're armed with rifles," he replied. "We must warn the train."

"How we going to do that?"

"I don't know. Saddle up. Let's ride fast."

Bob led his men along the ridge as fast he dared. Near the end, he saw the Indians suddenly gallop out across a small valley towards the train. He turned his horse around in a circle while pulling up his binoculars. No one on the wagon train could see the imminent attack just minutes away. Bob dismounted, pulled his new Sharps from the scabbard of his saddle, chambered a shell, laid down on the ground, using a rock to hold the barrel still, and looked for something to shoot at. He found nothing. He knew he must do something immediately. Reluctantly, he sighted in the lead horse of a group of three men guiding the train. He fired. Boom!

A second later, he saw the man's horse stumble and fall. At first, nothing happen, but then suddenly the alarm went out and the wagons began breaking into two groups creating a circle. They were well trained. Passengers disembarked and took cover. They brought out every rifle and pistol they could find and then they waited.

Robert pushed his rifle into the saddle scabbard. "Saddle up. We're going to attack the rear."

Spotted Owl and his men screamed as they rode their horses hard down the slopes of the valley anticipating a surprise attack. They failed to hear the boom of the Sharps. When they came over the knoll they saw the circled train. He should have pulled up, but he felt they were far superior to any white men. The wagon train captain told his people to hold their fire until they were closer. Just before the Indians could fire their bows the train opened fire. A dozen warriors went down on the first volley, but it did not deter Spotted Owl. He fired his bow repeatedly landing three of four shots. They began circling the wagons, but the Indians lost more men.

Insulted and aggravated, Spotted Owl charged his horse between the wagons and his men followed. Suddenly, they were inside the circle and firing into the backs of the white men. The surprised settlers began turning and firing. Spotted Owl lost a few more men, but took down a dozen settlers before leaping once more out of the circle. Realizing they must escape, he led the men in retreat towards the mountains, but just as they reached the rise of the first hill, Captain Robert and his soldiers opened fire as they galloped towards them.

Spotted Owl took a shot to his left arm, but managed to stay on his horse though he lost his bow. He yanked his horse in a hard right turn and sprinted for a grove of trees. Some of his men followed but another fourteen warriors were killed. The cavalry chased them to the woods before Bob called them back. They attended to their wounded, and then made their way to the wagon train. They began helping where they could, but forty men, women, and children were dead, and the settlers stood shell-shocked at the sudden attack. He spoke with the wagon train master, and gave him orders to prepare to leave. Rapidly they dug shallow graves and buried the dead, including some of the soldiers. Robert picked up an arrow, broke it in half, and put it in his saddlebag.

He knew the people were hurting, but to stay at the scene of the battle would allow the Indians a chance to regroup, bring in reinforcements, and seek revenge. He knew he must get them to the fort as soon as possible.

FOURTEEN

The scouts led the major and his men up and down the side of mountains, across steep ridges, and through cold, swift moving streams. Every time the scouts thought they found a pass through the maze of steep glacier carved mountains, they rounded a bend and ran into a thousand foot wall of jagged black rock. Reluctantly, they once again turned back, and made their way west once more before turning up the next large valley.

As the days ticked by, the major began to understand the glaciers of this northern area were most likely impassable by horse, but most certainly not by wagons. He also realized the mountains did not stop at the border, but mostly likely continued far into Canada. Frustrated, they moved farther west until the height of the mountains rescinded, and in the valley, they found a natural road most likely begun by the movement of animals centuries ago. Kiyo and Windtalker dismounted and studied the road carefully. They discovered unshod horse tracks, but none too recent. They relayed the news to the major that brought about a discussion before he decided to continue checking this westward path that might to the coast or did it turn back to the north and around the mountains.

Two days on the trail, it did indeed turn north. They were now making good time and averaging over ten miles a day. To their east, they could see the pinnacles of the big snow topped Glacier Mountains. The major realized, that the Indians were smarter than he by going around the impenetrable mountains. The major calculated that in just a few days they managed to move farther north than the hard weeks of traversing the mountains.

Reluctantly, he turned the explorers around because he knew they must turn their attention to the south and figure out a way to get back to the fort. If successful, he would return in a month taking the easier and more pliable route. They camped off the road in a valley, built a fire before sunset, and continued posting guards. Kiyo and Windtalker knew there were Indians in the vicinity, but where and whom, they did not know.

Several hours before dawn, Windtalker's eyes suddenly popped open, but he remained completely still. He didn't have to nudge Kiyo as he heard the faint sound as well. Windtalker sniffed the air. His brain broke apart the menagerie of scents his nostrils inhaled as his brain analyzed and placed each one as recognizable except the last.

He pretended to yawn and stretch as he slightly turned his head. His eyes caught Kiyo's and though dark, they knew Indians were about. Suddenly, they leaped up, calling the men to alarm. They grabbed their weapons and rushed behind rocks as a barrage of arrows began hitting the camp in the dark, but only two men were hit as they all took cover. The major was thankful the scouts insisted on dousing the fire with water before they went to sleep. The post sentry missed all the signals the Indians presented him, but especially his nostrils, as the warriors smelled of smoke, grease from cooking over the fire, and carried the scent of their horses on their bodies. The scouts knew they were after the horses, but losing the horses meant almost certain death for the soldiers as the walk home would be long and hard, and would leave them defenseless.

They picked four men with rifles and carefully they made there way from rock to rock until reaching the horses. Kiyo spotted the downed guard with his throat cut. Four Indians were untying the horses. The men took aim and instantly killed the four, but eight more immediately charged. Kiyo and Windtalker quickly turned and fired as did the soldiers, but behind them, another group attacked. They kept firing until their rifles and pistols were empty. Their numbers surprised the scouts, so as the remaining Indians made a final desperate assault on the group, Kiyo and Windtalker picked up their battle-axes, and bravely left the rocks running towards the advancing warriors, leaving the soldiers busy fixing their bayonets before joining in the hand-to-hand fight. With only a few shots left in his pistol, the major drew his sword and led his men into the battle.

The major watched in disbelief in this life or death battle as he picked off an Indian here and there with his pistol before receiving an arrow in the thigh. He marveled at the bravery of Kiyo and Windtalker, as the two lone Indians took on a force of at least eight or more warriors. While dodging an occasional arrow, the scouts swung the well-sharpened blades, catching arms and legs before adding a killing thrust to their enemies. Only two Indians survived as they scampered into the woods, but Kiyo and Windtalker began chasing them. Windtalker caught one man quickly and killed him with a quick thrust to the back. Kiyo chased the last man for a hundred yards, and the man almost escaped before Kiyo flung the big battle-axe at him. The blade spun end over end before impaling the man deep into his back. Kiyo ran up to him and pulled the blade out as the man died. Wisely, he quickly dropped down while turning in a circle, listening for any movement from the forest. Finding none, he returned to Windtalker who had run after him. Together, they made their way back to camp.

Windtalker announced, "We must go quickly. I think we got them all, but with the sound of the guns, others will come looking for them. We must hide the bodies."

They began pitching the bodies into a ravine, and began loading up their horses and returning to the road to head south. They rode hard for a few miles before settling down into a steady gallop. Emita ran out ahead as usual. They stopped from time to time, ate some beef jerky, drank water, took care of their horses by giving them grain bags, followed by water, and rode on. During one of their stops, Kiyo cut the arrow stick into, yanked it through the major's leg, and made a bandage for his wound.

They made no fire that night and returned to their journey the following day. On the third night, they finally made a fire, ate hot food, and let the horses rest for twelve hours. They stood watch, with Kiyo and Windtalker splitting the night into their own shifts, so that they obtained some sleep while the soldiers learned to listen and smell the air. Thankfully, the dawn arrived without attack. The major asked for the name of the tribe that attacked them, and Kiyo explained they were Flatheads.

Near the middle of the next day, Emita came running towards them at a fast pace from his point position ahead of the scouts. Kiyo urged the men to hide off the road. They scattered on both sides, dismounted, and waited.

They heard the horses before they could see them. It was at least twenty riders and they were Flathead warriors. Kiyo and Windtalker quickly noted they were returning from a battle as many had wounds, but they also carried Indian scalps. They rode quickly to the north and up the road. The scouts wondered if the warriors were being chased, so they waited a while longer before sending Emita running down the road once again.

They continued their journey for the rest of the day and hid a good hundred yards off the road to make camp. The Indians and the major rode up to a ridge to try and figure out where they were. They studied the terrain of the mountains to the east, and realized they would soon be out of the steep section of the Glacier Mountains. They decided to continue on the road the next day, hoping for a trail to the east, but very wary they might run into either more Flathead warriors, or the Indians they battled with yesterday.

After returning to the camp, the major unloaded his maps he carried in his saddlebag, and showed the scouts where he thought they were. If they traveled south for a day or two, then they should be due west of the fort, in say, twenty-five or thirty miles. They hoped his mathematics were correct. They posted guards and put out the fire after a hot supper.

The next morning they began riding before dawn, hoping to clear as much ground as possible while moving far away from the Flatheads. They were forced to do the killings to survive, but they knew a vengeful hunt for them would begin. The days were getting longer with summer coming so they continued their journey as long as they thought their horses could hold out. They had no idea they had been seen.

Spotted Owl's woman dug the bullet from his arm, and he cursed it and her for the pain she caused while knifing around for the slug. She pinned the skin together with small thorns, put medicinal herbs on the wound, and wrapped it tight with a cloth to keep the dirt out. He lost over forty of his men and it pissed him off greatly. This cut his numbers to just over fifty, forcing him to rest a spell before attacking again.

He spent his days planning ways to attack the fort and torture the soldiers that killed his men and nearly killed him. He continued keeping two teams of scouts watching the fort and told them to be careful. One of his men rode in every day and a fresh man with food rode out. This kept him in daily contact with the watchers.

He also had scouts watching for the next wagon train from the highest ridge on the eastern side of the Glacier Mountains nearest the plains. He knew that the first train arrived safely at the fort, and would most likely spend a few days there recovering from their journey before heading west and out of his territory. If he had the manpower, and no wounds, he would have chased the train and killed them all.

Chief Mad Wolf, of the Shoshone clan, lost a son today in a battle with the Flatheads. He had men on the watch to the northeast for Blackfeet warriors, but he never suspected the attack from the northwest by the gruesome Flatheads. They painted their noses black and drew red lines on their faces. They attacked just before dawn, but thankfully, they missed killing one of his scouts who yelled out an alarm before taking an axe to his neck. Ten of his men were killed including his son, but they won the battle, and sent the mangy Flatheads running north. He would go after them tomorrow, but today he would pay homage to his son, and comfort the boy's mother. His warriors numbered over a hundred and fifty, and they were itching for revenge. He sent scouts farther out than before to protect the village, and sent four men to trail the Flatheads.

The Shoshone scouts waited until long after the fire disappeared before creeping closer to take a look at the soldiers. Two of them wanted to steal horses, but the elder reminded them of their orders. Kiyo blinked his eyes open and smelled the air. Windtalker, sitting on a nearby log, made a small sound with his cheek to let Kiyo know he smelled them, too. They waited silently, but nothing happened, as they watched the changing of the guards. They could no longer smell the Indians, and wondered if they imagined it, or perhaps the Indians felt outnumbered and moved on.

The next morning they scouted the area looking for tracks, but failed to find a single one. Kiyo thought the Indians were either extremely good or wisely cautious. It puzzled them, but they saddled up and began riding once more.

The Flathead leader was Chief Talonga, and he became extremely angry as his warriors described their attack on the Shoshone tribe. He thought they should have won the battle and taken many scalps, but they came home without horses or slaves, hides or food, and only a few scalps. He scolded the survivors, and called for fifty of his men to prepare for war. The excited warriors began preparing their weapons, while the women bundled food for the journey, and then mixed paint color so they could paint the faces of their fathers, brothers, sons, and friends. The leftover paint they used to decorate their horses. All the warriors carried a bow as well as a quiver full of arrows and their hunting knives, but some also carried spears, pole knots, and a few battle-axes. Pole knots were three-foot long poles, and at one end, they fastened a round rock. They bored a hole through the other end of the shaft and threaded a strong leather rope through it and made a circle of about eighteen inches of the rope. The user put his hand through the rope and gripped the stick to prevent dropping and losing it during battle, but the rope also provided additional momentum when in tight battle quarters, allowing the warrior to swing it continuously by letting go the handle and swinging the pole knot rapidly around at head height. When swung against an enemy's head, the man's teeth, jaws, and skulls were quickly shattered. A hard swing to the back of a head and the warrior immediately fell to the ground as limp as a rag.

The chief chose White Eagle to lead his men on this second attack. Known for his clear battle judgment, as well as his ruthlessness, White Eagle's experience would give the Flathead warriors the upper hand. They rode around the village building courage by yelling and screaming. Their children and wives screamed as well. The medicine man blew spirit smoke from his pipe giving the warriors a feeling of great superiority. After a while, White Eagle waved his bow and the warriors began following him south out of the village.

FIFTEEN

The scouts and the soldiers managed twelve miles without discovery, but with the sun low on the horizon, they climbed a hill to the east, and found a creek overlooking a meadow on the other side of the road. Kiyo climbed atop a huge boulder, giving him a view of the road from the south and turning forty-five degrees, he could see the road to the north. He climbed down while suggesting to the major that he post a guard with field glasses on the rock.

Windtalker inspected their horses as well as the Calvary horses. Unfortunately, they were forced to ride the poor animals hard every day, and now they were in desperate need of day's rest, but knowing they were in enemy territory, and most likely outnumbered by far, he knew they would have to move on in the morning. He made sure they were well fed, and given a good long drink of water at the creek. He encouraged the men to check their animals for thorns or briars, check their hooves for sticks or stones, and then to rub the animals down. He politely reminded the men that their lives depended on the health of their horses.

A stack of firewood lay ready while they waited for darkness to avoid the detection of their smoke, and learning from experience, three huge boulders protected the view of the flame. After supper, the men settled down quickly, as the weeks of riding were taking a toll on them as well. The major once again discussed his feelings that they were not far from the fort and perhaps only a few mountains separated them.

Windtalker looked up at the big mountain behind them and smiled. "Oh, just a few mountains like that one?"

The major smiled at the sarcastic question. "Well, I was hoping for smaller ones to the south before we turn east." He showed them the map by the fire. "The trail from our fort to the west turns north before going westerly. We must be close to it. Do you think this road is it?"

Kiyo answered, "No, I did not see any wagon ruts."

Windtalker added, "They might be gone from the winter snows and the spring rains, or there could be a second road farther west than this one."

The major concurred about the possibility of another road but added, "It is too soon for the first train of the season to have reached here, but it is possible that the first train has reached the fort and heading this way soon. I must make an effort to get more information about the route to the west, and search for better maps before our next exploration."

The long night finally ended, so they ate a quick breakfast with hot coffee before the sun came over the mountains, and then they hastily put the fire out. They packed their gear, added water to their canteens, removed the hobbles from the legs of their horses, threw on their saddles, checked their weapons, and prepared to mount. Kiyo surveyed their sleeping area, wiped away tracks, and made sure not a scrap of paper or food indicating a white man could be found. Using a shovel, he carried the ashes from the fire and poured them in the stream, then scattered the remaining dirt.

The men were just about to mount up when the scout on the big rock whistled. He then crouched down and whispered, "About fifty Indians coming down the road from the north."

Kiyo and Windtalker knew they were too late. The Flatheads must have found the bodies, and were now searching for them. Thankfully, their encampment was well hidden from the road. The scouts began searching for a way across the creek, as they could no longer use the road. Before they could decide, a pebble fell in front of them. They looked at the motioning scout. He was urging them to come up there.

The major told his men to hold still and remain secluded from the road, and to keep their horses calm. He and the scouts cautiously climbed the rock and slid out on their bellies to avoid detection. The guard whispered, "The fifty from the north are near the bend, but look south."

They all turned their heads and discovered a similar force riding north. Windtalker spoke quickly, "Those are Shoshone warriors, and they are painted for battle."

Kiyo added, "The Flatheads from the north are also painted."

The major gulped. "You mean that both tribes are looking for us?"

The scouts thought for a second. Kiyo spoke first, "I doubt such a large force is looking for just us."

Windtalker added, "I think they are about to do battle with each other, and we're sitting almost in the middle of it."

The major asked, "What do we do? We can't fight two tribes at once with over a hundred and twenty warriors."

Windtalker said, "When the battle starts, they will be too busy to notice us. I think we should cross the creek, and work our way south through the woods. We can return to the road south of the Shoshone warriors, and then ride like the wind."

Kiyo added, "He's right. We must get to the road leading to the fort before their retreat towards home."

The major nodded, "That's about the only choice we do have."

Windtalker warned the major, "Sir, make sure your men do not fire their weapons as both tribes would hear it. If we are discovered by a few Indians, we must kill them with our bows and knives, but not gunfire."

"Okay, let's get ready."

The major went down with the scout to prepare the men as the Indians suggested. Kiyo and Windtalker remained alone on the rock deeply fascinated they could just sit and see the impending battle. Suddenly, the alarm went out, and the Shoshone warriors left the road and cut across the meadow, hoping to encircle their enemy, but were immediately met with the charging force of the Flatheads.

The scouts quickly climbed down and jumped into their saddles and led the men across the creek before turning south. They could hear the whoops and yells, and the occasional sounds of a crunch. They knew this meant heads were smashed, spilling the blood of many warriors across the meadow.

After they rode about a hundred yards, they reached a sandy area where the creek often spilled out after heavy rains. They picked up their speed for another hundred yards, and then made their way back to the road. Windtalker checked the road but found no one. He sent Emita south and waved to the major. Together, they galloped down the road as fast as they could, hoping to put as much distance between them and the Indians as possible.

White Eagle wisely did not send all his men into battle at once, but rather divided the group into three. The first group charged straight across the meadow and into the entire force of the Shoshone. Their leader failed to stay behind and watch, but instead chose to lead his men into battle. With great experience, White Eagle spread the remaining groups wide before signaling their charge from both sides of the meadow, effectively boxing in the Shoshone.

White Eagle watched as his men surprised their enemy, taking many down with their arrows as they rode swiftly into the battle. White Eagle then lifted his battle-axe, and rode straight into the fray, keeping his eye on the leader of the Shoshone. He rode like a god, swinging his axe back and forth like a machine, killing men with a single swipe, severing heads and limbs, and covering his horse in their blood, but he never changed course as he rode through the melee of the two tribes fighting it out in hand-to-hand warfare.

He spotted the leader as he killed one of the Flatheads with his glistening axe. He turned his horse slightly in the man's direction, squeezed his legs, swung back his battle-axe, and charged. The Shoshone warrior turned just in time to catch a glimpse of White Eagle. He jerked back his spear with his throwing arm, and on foot, he bravely ran to meet his enemy.

White Eagle swung hard and fast, but the warrior ducked while swinging up with his spear, cutting a nasty gash along the side of White Eagle's horse. The horse screamed out at the pain, and unexpectedly reared up, spilling White Eagle to the ground.

The Shoshone warrior seized the opportunity and began running to get to the Flathead leader, but White Eagle hit the ground, then rolled to break his fall, leaped to his feet, and spun around rapidly anticipating his enemy.

All around them, their warriors continued fighting, stabbing, and punching each other, but the two leaders never took their eyes off the other. Their faces revealed their hate and contempt for their enemy, but not a trace of fear. Suddenly, the Shoshone warrior charged with his spear held high and ready to put it deep into his enemy's heart.

White Eagle deftly deflected the blow with the shaft of his battle-axe, turned quickly in a tight circle with his axe hand extended, his speed accelerating, and then he swung it, catching the Shoshone man high on the leg. The cut went deep into the man's leg, spewing blood. The pain was immense, but he showed no sign of backing down, and lunged at White Eagle. He stabbed him in the left arm, twisted the spear to increase the size of the wound and amount of pain before yanking it back for a second blow.

White Eagle faked retreat. The Shoshone warrior took quick steps in hopes of stabbing the spear through the man's heart, but White Eagle dropped to his left knee, and spun around bringing the axe around as fast as he could. The Indian lunged with the spear just as the axe caught him just above the hip. The impact cut deep into the man's torso, knocking the spear from its target and his hand. The Shoshone's intestines spilled out as the blade continued cutting across his lower belly. The pain too massive to ignore, he fell to his knees, trying to hold his guts inside his torso, and attempting to hold on to his life.

White Eagle grinned as he stood and laughed at his enemy. The beaten warrior could do nothing to stop him. White Eagle spat at him before turning once more in a sudden fury, bringing the axe around, and severing the man's head from his body. He then screamed louder than the noise of the remaining warriors. On foot, he began cutting down every Shoshone warrior in sight. Twenty minutes later, the Shoshone's warriors were annihilated to the last man, but they managed to reduce White Eagle's force to just a dozen men, all wounded in some way.

Together, they brought up their horses, loaded and tied their dead warriors on them, while making sure not a single enemy breathed. Once they cleared the battle scene of their own dead, four of White Eagle's men rode their horses over and over the corpses, smashing and breaking bones, and spilling blood.

Wounded but victorious, they began their long journey home.

Near the end of the day, Windtalker and Kiyo rounded a bend and found Emita sitting in the middle of the road facing south. The dog wisely listened for any approaching riders while waiting for his masters. They were puzzled and a bit apprehensive, but as they rode up they realized Emita's dilemma. He found a fork in the road and didn't know which way they wanted to go.

The scouts were surveying the tracks on the roads at the intersection as the major and his men caught up with them.

Kiyo asked, "We found the fork, but which one is the correct one?"

Windtalker replied, "This one heads south and that is where the Shoshone warriors came from. Look at the numerous tracks heading towards the battle."

Kiyo stood on the other road, "This one has experienced some traffic, though nowhere near as much as the other road, but I did find this." He held up a short round piece of wood, obviously well carved with narrow ends."

The major took it from him and studied it. "Well, I'll be. It is a wagon wheel spoke. I say we take the road less traveled."

The scouts saddled up. "Let's ride away from here as the Shoshone could be right behind us. Let's hope they go home the way they came."

With the major away, Captain Robert found himself in quite a mess. He and his men safely escorted the wagon train through the mountains and to the fort. They made camp just outside the gate and his doctor tended to the wounded, while the blacksmith repaired wagons, replaced some shoes on a few horses, and even repaired some of their leather tack.

Robert felt obliged to help all he could, but the serenity of their fort quickly disappeared. The train brought along several wagonloads of supplies for the fort, successfully replenishing their stores after the long winter. The trading post also received wagonloads of his orders from last fall. After five days, the wagon master announced they would leave in the morning. Robert promised to escort them twenty miles, putting them hopefully out of the range of the Blackfeet and Shoshone warriors.

The major and his men rode into the fort late in the afternoon before the wagon train was scheduled to leave. He settled up with Kiyo and Windtalker and thanked them for more than once saving their lives, and patiently teaching him about the Indians he was ordered to control. He knew now that remained an impossible order with just the soldiers in his fort.

Kiyo and Windtalker bought a few things at the store, replaced their spent ammunition, and rode to Samuel's farm. Spotted Owl's men noticed them, but they were to find a way to attack the wagon train, but for now it was too close to the fort. They were continuing to send daily reports to Spotted Owl.

Trisha saw the Windtalker and Kiyo as they rode into their farm from the main road. Molly called to Samuel and Michael in the garden, and soon they were all sitting on the porch as the young men told tales of their adventure to the north.

"Sounds like we're better off staying right here," stated Samuel.

Molly laughed. "Oh sure, we're better off here. The Blackfeet are to the northeast, the Shoshone to the south, and the Flatheads to the northwest."

A silence momentarily fell over the group before Kiyo grinned slyly, "Well, it could be worse."

Molly quickly replied, "What could be worse?"

"Well, there are ten thousand Sioux to the east, but thankfully, they don't like our tall mountains, and they are afraid of the Blackfeet."

After a moment of stunned silence before Molly laughed. "Well, there you go. We at least don't have to worry about the Sioux."

Windtalker laughed. "You forgot about the Yakimas to the west."

Molly shot back, "Okay, forget it. Let's don't talk about it. How about a piece of pie for our friends."

Windtalker and Kiyo grinned. "I have been thinking of nothing else for a month."

Kiyo added, "Sounds good to me, too."

Arriving home just before dark, they were pleased to see their vegetable garden still intact, their horses well fed from the meadows of green grass, and their buildings still standing. They stowed their gear in the cabin, put the saddles and tack in the barn, fed their horses a good portion of grain, and set them free.

Emita walked with them to the garden as they inspected their crops. The corn was already four feet high, the potatoes and carrots looked fine after they pulled a few up from the dirt before putting them back in the ground, and together they walked back to the cabin, stripped out of their clothes, and walked to the stream to wash away the month of riding.

After putting on clean clothes, they made cornbread for supper, along with some potatoes from the root cellar, slices of venison, and ate every bite. They fed Emita a huge meal, and getting out of their clothes once more, they made their way to the bedroom. They missed being intimate on their journey, as well as holding hands, soft kisses, special squeezes in private places, and making love. They truly loved each other, and somehow their love grew with each day of their new life alone. They knew they were lucky to be together, and they were so happy to have a farm of their own.

SIXTEEN

The next morning, the major sent a squad of twenty men to the east to watch for the next wagon train. He would replace them in a week, but he hoped to prevent any future attacks by having a force present and ready. Robert led another group of twenty on an escort mission for the wagon train as they left at dawn to the west.

Spotted Owl's scouts took note of the two forces leaving the fort and one of them quickly rode to relay the news to their leader. A second man trailed the wagon train, and a third followed the squad to the east leaving only one man watching the fort.

The major spent most of the day working on reports of his trip to the north and other mundane reports of activity at the fort, requests for supplies, ammunitions, maps, and cash. He hoped to persuade someone in Washington to seek copies of maps from the British as to what roads and trails were north of the border on his side of the Glacier Mountains. He took a nap after lunch, the first in almost five weeks.

The Indians slept well and made a big breakfast with the eggs and ham Samuel gave them. They also made biscuits and ate every morsel of food except for a few bites for Emita. He did get a chunk of fresh venison to chew as well. They dressed in farm clothes, retrieved their long hoes from the nail racks inside the barn, and made their way to the garden. Shoots of wild grass and weeds crept in somehow and it took most of the day to clear them. They made piles of the grass on the edge of their garden, and later transplanted them in the dirt in front of the house, hoping it would grow well and cut down on the dust and mud.

Late in the afternoon, they rounded up the horses with Emita's help as he barked and chased them to the barn. They were brushed after an inspection found thorns, ticks, and other oddities, but then they took them to the stream for a swim. All were fed well and released as the Indians and Emita took their turn in the stream, before walking to the cabin to prepare supper.

They ate well the following morning before heading out for a hunt for fresh game and particularly for a rabbit, pheasant, or maybe a wild turkey. They made the sounds of the birds for Emita before the dog scampered ahead of them. They went to the west of their property before cautiously slipping into the forest. Emita picked up the scent of something as his tail wagged rapidly, and he quietly trailed the animal. In an hour, they managed to kill both a rabbit and a pheasant with their bows, but continued hunting for more game.

Spotted Owl, his wound mostly healed from the gunshot to his arm, fretted over the news from the fort. His village boasted eighty warriors, after picking up new recruits, but he did not want to divide his force. In the soft, well-trampled dirt inside his tipi, he drew the fort and the road leading to it from the east, and the road leading away from it to the west. He studied it for the better part of an hour before calling one of his scouts over to him. He began to question the man.

"How many men inside the fort?"

The man replied, "Until a few days ago, only sixty, but ten or so arrived from the west."

"How many went with the train?"

"Twenty."

"And to the east?"

"The same."

Spotted Owl grinned. "So there are only thirty soldiers left."

"Yes, sir. That's right."

"Very good. You may go."

He pondered his plans after sitting down and lighting his pipe. If he could take out the fort and kill all the soldiers, then it would be easy to take care of the other squads when they returned and found nothing to hide behind, and no way to obtain supplies or ammunition. Satisfied with his conclusion, he began to plan their attack.

Lieutenant James Johnson led the squad to the east. They were almost to the ridge that was north of the southern most tips of the mountains, where they could oversee the road and valley beyond. It had taken three days for them to get there, but so far, all had gone well. He knew the area well, and led his men off the main road and into a narrow valley where a stream provided fresh water for their encampment. He failed to notice the men hidden off the road to the west and watching them.

They set up camp while James and a sergeant rode up to the ridge. He removed his field glasses from his saddlebags, and scanned the terrain in the valley below.

The sergeant spoke first, "We should see their dust long before we can focus on a wagon."

"Ain't that the truth? We'll need a man here every day. I think we should post guards at all hours. The Indians are about, and the Blackfeet took quite a whipping after attacking the last train, so if we're spotted, I'm sure they'll attack. You and I will sleep in four-hour shifts. I need your leadership should we receive an attack."

"Yes, sir. Shall I post a guard up here now?"

"No, I don't see anything and we have only an hour or so before dark. We'll start the scouting at dawn. Let's go make sure we set up a good camp, secure the horses, and look for protection in case of attack."

"Yes, sir."

They rode back down the hill together.

The men called him captain, but Leroy Jones fled the army over four years ago after a conviction of raping a woman in Lexington. He escaped from the brig before transfer to a prison to serve a five-year term. His outfit of ragtag thug remained loyal to him and secured his escape. They fled to Saint Louis where they lost most of their army pay on whores, liquor, and gambling, though not necessarily in that order. Leroy refused to work for a living, he hated farming, after growing up on a poor one, hated government work and especially high and mighty officials, and now hated sheriffs and deputies that protected the towns and the citizens.

He studied the town's bank for several days before creating a plan to rob it. Using his army skills, he used four of his men to create a diversion by setting a house on fire at the entrance to the town. The remaining eight men waited at the rear of the bank as the town began ringing bells, and its fine citizens duly responded in full force with a bucket brigade from the creek as they made a futile failing attempt to save the house.

Leroy's men tied a rope to the back door of the bank, tied the other end to their saddle horn, and with a quick kick of the horse, they sprung the door free from the hinges. Using a stick of dynamite, they blew the safe, loaded up duffle bags with the cash, and escaped out the other end of town without a single person discovering their robbery.

Leroy remained smarter than most bank robbers by riding far from their hideout for a robbery, and remaining hidden there for up to three months before striking again. He never allowed his men to go into town, preferring to use other workers to fetch supplies and whores. He also left a town in the wrong direction, covered their tracks, and so far a posse remained perplexed as to who robbed their banks, and which way they went.

He demanded complete loyalty and if a man questioned his judgment, or sassed him in anyway, Leroy rapidly shot him right between the eyes. He didn't split the loot like other thieves, but chose to pay his men wages as if they were still in the army. He fed and clothed them, took care of their horses and ammunition, and gave absolute orders.

For almost four years things had gone exactly as planned, but though well paid, one of the whores told on them after Leroy's men killed her brother in a neighboring town while robbing a bank. No posse would tackle capturing them alone, so the state marshal called on the cavalry. The army surrounded his hideout before mounting a fierce battle, but Leroy trained his men on various escape routes. As darkness fell, the battle came to a temporary halt, but by dawn, not one of Leroy's men could be found. They had been on the run ever since until he grew tired of it, and decided they had but two choices, go south to Mexico or west to San Francisco. On one of his first military assignments, he stayed in San Antonio, Texas, and hated the heat and the Mexicans. He chose to go west.

Throughout Kansas and Missouri they attacked settler farms for food, killing all they found including children. He made sure there were no witnesses to testify should they become captured. With a force of ten, they followed the trail of a wagon train, pulling packhorses filled with stolen food and ammunition.

His scout heard the cavalry squad from Fort Green before they reached their planned site of encampment. Leroy and his men remained hidden in the brush on the far side of the road. Sorely tempted to rid them of their food, weapons, and horses, he thought it best to disappear from an army report announcing his whereabouts. He planned to change his name, get rid of his men, and live a better life off the gold hidden deep in his saddlebags.

He didn't know the lieutenant planned to stay there for a week by choosing to camp nearby, so he thought he should wait until after dark before sneaking away on the road heading around the bend at the bottom of the Glacier Mountains. They ate cold jerky with no fire while hiding just two hundred yards away.

At two in the morning, nature provided a path of escape. The soldiers heard the booming thunder to the north, saw the bright streaks of lightning race across the sky, and instantly the skies appeared to open up and throw the rain down on their tents with great intensity. The wind also picked up. The sentries cursed as the water dripped off their hats, and ran coldly down their backs soaking them to the skin in seconds. No one noticed the dark riders as they walked their horses down the road, and made their way north and away from the soldiers. The posted guards were huddled down low to the ground, hoping to avoid any chance of lightning striking them. They failed to detect the movement of Leroy's men, nor did they hear anything but thunder and rain.

By morning, the skies cleared, but not a track could be found from Leroy's horses as the rain had washed their path away. He sent a scout ahead as usual and the second day, he saw the man wave a warning before disappearing off the road. Leroy's men huddled their horses behind pine trees as a group of fifteen Blackfeet Indians rode south on the road. He had no intention of confronting these well-seasoned warriors, but he warned his men that if under attack, they were to fight quickly, and kill everyone with overpowering gunfire. Waste no time in the killing, he had warned, and let no one escape to run for reinforcements.

Spotted Owl listened to one of his scouts that just arrived from watching the plains. There was a small wagon train heading west about twenty miles out. He left another man watching the train to be sure they followed the usual path of circumnavigating around the foot of the Glacier Mountains. He went back inside his tipi to study his drawings of the fort, as well as the location of the wagon train, and the unknown location of the squad of men presumably sent to watch for the train. He drew in the mountain terrain near the plains and the expected path of the pioneers. He surmised the cavalry probably took a high lookout position to watch for the train.

He then looked to the west on his map, and so far with the squad continuing to head west, it left the fort at least forty men short. They would be too far to return to the fort if attacked. He decided the time to strike would be early in the morning. He selected ten men and told them to attack the small wagon train in hopes of attracting the cavalry out of hiding in the hills. His warriors were told to kill as many whites as possible, but if the cavalry attacked, they should lead them far to the north before escaping in the night to the mountains. They were to cover their tracks before returning to the hidden village.

The men prepared their weapons and two days of food, and left the village at midday, hoping to find a place near the edge of the mountains to make camp and prepare for an early morning attack.

Spotted Owl also called all his warriors together and told them the soldiers intended to take all their lands, and run them off their hunting grounds. He spoke in a voice, whipping them into a fit of anticipation and hatred. This sent the Indians into a frenzy of whoops and yells as they scattered to sharpen their knives and spears, paint their faces and horses, and prepare for the battle.

Captain Robert and his men found no signs of Indians during their escort duty. They were almost to the twenty-mile limit and tomorrow would see the train descend out of the mountains on their journey west. At that point, he and his men would return to the fort. Except for a settler receiving a tasty bite from a rattlesnake, the rest of the trip remained uneventful, and he felt happy for their success.

Major Bill received a report of an attack on a settler farm from a highly frightened, twelve year old boy arriving on horseback without a saddle, boots, or a shirt. The boy said the attackers where white men and the leader looked like a cavalry officer. The major didn't know what to make of that, so he led a group of a dozen men to investigate.

A scout watching from the hill sent a warrior in a hurry to Spotted Owl's camp. Spotted Owl laughed when he heard the news, realizing that now only thirty soldiers remained at the fort. He also knew he would attack these twelve soldiers after they took the fort, further reducing the enemy's numbers.

Lieutenant Johnson woke with the rest of his men before dawn so they could enjoy a hot breakfast and coffee before putting the fire out, preventing the detection of their smoke. He took a much-needed leak before climbing the hill with another soldier to replace the last sentry on duty. He took his field glasses with him. The hungry sentry gave his binoculars to the new lookout, and hustled back to camp for breakfast.

Johnson and his man scanned the horizon but saw nothing. Johnson decided to stay for a while, as it was cooler on top of the rock. Now and then he would pick up his field glasses and scan the terrain below. About an hour later, the sentry became excited.

"Sir, we have about a dozen riders heading east. I think they're Indians!"

The lieutenant picked up his glasses and stared off in the direction the scout pointed. He turned the focus ring until a clear view could be seen. "You're right, private. Excellent eyes. Way to go. You're right, but I count ten."

"Where are they headed? There's no town or settlement out there."

"I'm afraid they know more than we do. There must be a wagon train coming this way."

They continued staring west for twenty more minutes until the faint trail of dust could be seen to the east. The lieutenant broke the command of silence and yelled down to his men. "Sergeant! Quickly break camp, saddle the horses, and be ready to leave in ten minutes. Get your weapons ready and prepare your horses for a hard ride."

Both of the men on the rock continued scanning the east until finally they saw a few white men on horseback followed by the first wagon. "Let's go."

They scampered down the hill as fast as they could and began helping the men get their gear stowed. Minutes later, they made their way back to the road and began galloping east. It would take them an hour to round the southernmost point, and an hour or more to reach the train. He knew the Indians would attack long before they could get there.

Almost two hours later, two Indian scouts on a hill on the eastern side saw the lieutenant and his men galloping to the east. They smiled, though they wished they had a group of warriors to tail and kill them. One of the scouts flung himself on his horse, and galloped to get the news to Spotted Owl.

SEVENTEEN

This morning, the Indians deliberately slept in after a wonderful early night of making love to each other, and then sleeping hard. They felt secure and safe in their cabin in the middle of their farm, so they relaxed and forewent their natural vigilance with Emita on guard dog duty, and together they enjoyed a good, deep sleep. After their slow start in the morning, they ate a big breakfast, and set about catching up on the work around the farm. They kept ongoing lists to practice their handwriting skills, but it was also a long list, one in which they might never get to the bottom of, as daily, they added more ideas about as fast as they finished one.

For the next few days, they followed a similar pattern by spending the early part of their mornings tending to crops, pulling weeds, and picking some of the recently ripened vegetables, and putting them in safe storage away from their animals, other wild animals, and field mice.

Afterwards, they put on their already well-worn nail aprons with the various pouches for different nail sizes, as well as a loop for their hammers, and went to work on the exposed side of the original barn where they were constructing a chicken coop. On the ground lay several rolls of what the trading post owner called chicken wire, designed for keeping the chickens inside the fenced area, and the wolves and other predators out. The trader gave the scouts a few tips on installation, including digging a trench to bury the bottom edge of the fence, then packing it tightly with dirt, and covering it with heavy rocks. On the outside, they were to lay long poles and stake them in tight to the fence. This would prevent animals from digging under the fence to get to the chickens, or pushing in on the fence to break it loose from the dirt. The posts were placed close together at four-foot intervals to maintain support and strength. He told them wild animals would go to almost any length to get a fat chicken.

After several days of working on the project, it began to look similar to Samuel's coop. They finished the fencing, and began constructing the wooden and wire gate. They put the gate on the side of the coop across from the house so they could see that the gate remained closed. They used their new store-bought door hooks to keep the gate locked.

After lunch, they planned to start building the roost or housing section for the chickens they planned to buy. Their mouths watered as they began thinking about all the things they could make with the eggs, including hatching some chickens for more eggs and eventually fried chicken like Molly made. After they finished their farm chores for the day, the Indians walked naked to the creek to wash up, towel off, and make dinner. They loved the routine of working on various things during the day, and then enjoying there evenings together.

Major Bill and his men galloped quickly and arrived to find the entire settler family killed. What disturbed him most was the fact that they were not killed by arrows, but by white men with guns. He thought he already had enough trouble with the various tribes of Indians, but now he had to find a gang of bad white men. Everywhere he looked about the farm, he saw death. They found the father in the dirt near the cabin, a small boy on the porch, a young girl not far away, and an obliviously raped mother and as she lay naked on the bed with many bruises including a bloody nose and busted lips. Once they were finished with her, the bad men killed her with a single shot between the eyes. They wanted no witnesses, but failed to see the older boy slip out of the privy, run to the pasture, and ride his horse bareback to the fort. There was blood everywhere, including the barnyard, the steps and porch, on the door, across the floor, and on to the bed where she died. He thought it was a sorry sight for anyone to have to see. He hoped they could catch the killers. As acting judge and jury, he'd make sure there was a rope waiting for their necks for sure.

The cavalry quickly buried the family, hitched up the man's wagon, loaded all their valuables and supplies, plus their livestock, and locked the cabin door, while the major began following the trail until it reached the gorge leading into the higher mountains. Bill counted the various tracks as best he could, estimating a force of twenty, and riding shod horses. He knew they were outnumbered so he turned back as they began the trek to the fort. Not a single man spoke a word on the way. The horrific tragedy instantly changed the hardened soldiers. They were used to seeing dead Indians and somewhat used to seeing dead soldiers, but they would never get used to seeing murdered women and children.

One of Spotted Owl's remaining scouts watched the major ride into the fort with his soldiers, but with orders not to leave his post, he had no way of warning Spotted Owl. His chief assumed the major and his men would be away for days, but though only taking a few men with him, he felt the major was their leader and the one with most experience. The scout debated on leaving his position, but Spotted Owl gave strict orders that at least one man was to remain on duty at all times while keeping up with troop movements.

After arriving at the fort, the major requested a head count because he knew his force remained low in number until Captain Robert returned, but he could not let these killers of the settler family go free. He feared they would attack other farms as well.

"Fire a single cannon shot," he ordered with a sudden loud shout.

"Just one?" asked the sergeant

"Yes, I am signaling Windtalker and Kiyo that we need their help. Tell the gunnery crew to aim just this side of the ridge of that small mountain across from our gate. Prepare a squad of twelve men that are well armed and ready to ride when the scouts get here."

"Yes, sir," responded the sergeant with a quick salute. He retreated from the major's office and yelled for the gunnery soldiers to prepare the cannon. He explained the major's instructions. A few minutes later, they fired the shot.

Leroy and his troop of former soldiers, now murderers and thieves, retreated to a new encampment back in a small gorge on the western side of the Glacier Mountains. From the settler farm, they secured enough food and supplies from the raid to last a few weeks or so, and before heading west, he planned to hide in the forest until things cooled down.

The Indian scout on the small mountain across from the fort nearly wet his pants when he heard the boom of the cannon, and stood there wondering what the heck was going on. He failed to see the arc of the black ball fired from the big muzzle as it sailed high into the sky before returning to earth and racing towards the ground near him with a streaking, squealing, whistling sound. It slammed into the soil just a few feet away from his hideout. The explosion knocked him backwards and into a rock that split his skull, and left his limp body heavily marked with blazing hot shrapnel that smoldered into his flesh.

The scouts heard the cannon and waited to see if there would be more. It was the first time they heard the summoning signal. They frowned at the interruption but ran back into the cabin and began changing clothes. Minutes later, they came out wearing their trail clothes, including the buckskins they made over the winter, and new boots. They carried their weapons to the porch and ran to saddle up two horses. Emita knew something exciting must have happened, so he began barking and running in circles in anticipation of a trail run.

They loaded their bows and arrows in the new hand stitched, leather sleeves that went under their left leg and attached to the saddle, and on the other side of the horse, they carried the Winchester on Kiyo's horse and the Sharps buffalo gun on Windtalker's. They wore pistols on their right hip and long hunting knives on the left. They also carried a shorter knife hidden in their boot with a short leather sheaf to protect their leg.

Throughout the many days of snow captivity in the cabin during the winter, they practiced rapidly drawing pistols, knives, and retrieving the boot knives as well. They also wrestled to stay fit and also for fun. They attached a two-foot squared board to the wall, and entertained themselves by throwing their knives with amazing accuracy. Outside, they learned to throw the battle-axes into a tree trunk with a slow spin that seemed to gain momentum before digging deep into the practice tree. They could only imagine what the weapon would do to an enemy. They could throw it about thirty yards with deadly accuracy.

On their backs they hung a leather pouch to carry the battle-axes so they could be drawn quickly if needed. They filled the saddlebags with extra ammunition. They carried no food supplies, as they didn't know if this was a single event or not, and if the summons required a longer journey they knew the soldiers would load food on packhorses for them.

With a quick yell to Emita, they rode out the trail to the tunnel, dashed through the waterfall, followed the stream bed for a while, then crossed over, and skirted up the hill to the small road leading to the bigger one. They galloped towards the fort while wondering if the fort were under attack.

Thirty minutes later, they rounded the bend and felt immediate relief in seeing Samuel and Michael working in their fields. They stopped briefly to see if they knew what happened, but they knew nothing. Windtalker told them to keep rifles handy just to be safe.

They sprinted once more towards the fort, unsure of what they might find, but to their surprise the gate remained open, and they noted a guard in the tower. The guard hollered down to alert the major. They rode in quickly and tied off their horses as the major came out to greet them.

"Thank God, you heard the cannon shot."

"We heard it loud and clear. Are you okay?"

"I have grim news." He looked around to be sure the boy, the only survivor, was out of earshot. He had already been told his family had passed on, and they put him on a bunk in the ammunition shed to let him rest for a while. The major continued. "The Miller family was all killed last night except the twelve year old boy that escaped and rode his horse here to warn us. We got there as quick as we could but we were too late. They raped the mother and then killed her. They also killed her husband James and his children."

Kiyo asked, "Indians?"

"No, at least I don't think so. They used guns to kill them, no throats were slit, and I didn't find a single arrow. I also tracked about twenty riders and they were all riding shod horses. The boy said they looked white, but dirty. He said a man led them wearing a soldier's uniform. We must find and arrest them because I fear they will attack another farm. We're short handed at the moment. I sent Robert and twenty men to escort a wagon train to the western edge of the glaciers. I sent Lieutenant Johnson with twelve men to the eastern ridge to watch and escort the next train in, so I only have about forty men here."

"What do you want us to do?" Windtalker knew the answer to the question, at least for their part, but he waited for the major's strategy to be told.

"I'm sending ten men to find them, but I need for you to track them down, and help my men arrest them."

104

"Arrest? We may have to kill them," warned Kiyo.

"You do what you have to and be careful, as we already know they are not only killers, they are merciless. They've killed the parents and their children, and stole from them. If you have to kill them, so be it. They sealed their own fate by this act. I wish I had a telegraph out here so I could see if there were any reports on these men. I think the wire only goes as far as Saint Louis from Washington. Sergeant Buck Henry will lead the squad. He's a good man and he'll listen to you. Ride quickly."

Kiyo and Windtalker saddled up, waited for the sergeant to order his men to mount, and soon they were led out of the fort. They galloped for forty minutes to reach the section of the road where the major saw the tracks. Windtalker dismounted and began counting the tracks as they both studied the shoe markings so they could recognize them. Windtalker called Emita to him and urged the dog to smell the tracks. He knew it would be tough to trail horses that ate the same food, but Emita knew to follow their trail. He barked and took off running off the road and up a smaller animal trail. The scouts and the soldiers took up the pursuit.

Kiyo told the sergeant they would ride on ahead to avoid being ambushed as a group. He also wanted to get ahead of the noise ten soldiers make. Windtalker already made them silence some of their gear, and intended to talk to the major about teaching all his men to ride with less things jangling.

They rode for about an hour when Emita sat down and waited for them. Kiyo and Windtalker rode up carefully while looking in all directions.

Kiyo whispered, "What is it boy?"

Windtalker smelled the air. "He smells bacon cooking."

Kiyo gave Emita a good rub after climbing off his horse. "That's a smart boy." Together, they walked their horses quietly until they could pinpoint the direction of the campfire.

Windtalker whispered, "Here. Tie off my horse, and keep Emita with you. I'll scout out the situation. You wait and keep the soldiers quiet when they arrive."

Lieutenant Johnson's horses were nearly exhausted by the time they reached the wagon train. The settler group had circled and the Indians rode around it, but stayed pretty far out. A few settlers were wounded from their arrows, but not a single Indian had been shot.

His men came charging in by firing their rifles, but the Indians quickly scattered into a nearby grove of trees. The men charged into the forest and one of them received an arrow to an arm, but the Indians escaped out the other side, and galloped north as planned.

The major gave chase for almost a mile, but soon realized pursuit to the north would leave him far from the security of the fort, and his post as lookout, and felt he must return to the wagon train and escort them to the fort. Reluctantly, he led his men back.

The wagon master came out to meet him. He was a feisty fifty-year-old man with a black handlebar mustache, green eyes, and appeared to be in excellent shape for his age. He left Ireland ten years ago, made America his home, but fled the big cities to live on the plains. This marked his tenth trip across the plains and each one endured an attack or two by the Indians.

The lieutenant asked, "Anybody hurt?"

"Just a few arrow wounds. Looks like one of your fellows caught one as well. Bring him on down. We have a doctor so he'll dig it out and patch him up for you. Thanks for scaring the bastards away."

"Thank goodness they were a small group. We have heard of attacks by as many as forty or so. We'll escort you towards the fort. You can rest there and regroup."

"How far?"

"I'd say twenty miles."

"We won't make it today. Maybe we can get half way."

"Okay. We will let the doctor attend to the wounded and set out. We have six hours of daylight left and might as well get as far from here as possible in case those ten return with more warriors."

Spotted Owl led his group towards the fort. He would attack at nightfall, making it tougher for the soldiers to shoot them. He continued making mental plans of the assault he planned. They rode quietly through the forest hoping to keep their location a secret until they were ready to attack.

Captain Robert pulled his men to a halt as they reached the long down slope to the plains to the west. He wished their leader and families a safe journey. He watched for a while so their horses could rest before turning back. It would take at least a day and a half for them to make the fort.

Windtalker crept quietly and cautiously as he approached the camp of the white men. He spotted two men on lookout duty across opposite sides of the small valley. The rest of the men were in the bottom of the valley near a stream. He began counting until he knew they were a force of twenty men.

He spotted a man in a worn cavalry uniform barking orders at his men, but they didn't look like the soldiers they were accustomed to. Most only wore pieces of uniforms. They were unkempt, dirty, and took poor care of their horses. He also noted they were not hunters, as he spotted no sign of game cooking over a fire, or a deer hanging by its hoofs. He saw a pile of loot they must have taken from the settlers. He surveyed the terrain carefully. They were well armed with every man wearing a pistol with a rifle nearby.

Windtalker began making his way back to Kiyo and the soldiers.

Kiyo asked, "How many?"

"Twenty. They are well armed. I think they are former soldiers as only the leader has a full uniform. The rest of the men are poorly dressed, and

I think they have been on the run for a while. They carry both pistols and rifles."

The sergeant spoke, "So we're outnumbered, and unequal in power."

Kiyo grinned. "But they don't have two fierce warriors on their side."

Windtalker smiled. "And they don't know we're here. I think we should wait until dark so they are all in camp, except for the two guards I spotted."

Kiyo, let's find a place to hide our horses so we're not heard or found until then. They rode back down the trail about a hundred yards before pulling off behind some big rocks. They told the soldiers to rest, as well as water and feed their horses, eat some grub, and get their weapons ready.

Windtalker spoke first as he drew out their foe's campground in the dirt with a stick. I think Kiyo and I can take out the guards with bows. I also think we should take out as many sleeping men with arrows as well. We need to try and equal the number of men against men before they awake and begin shooting at us.

Kiyo said, "I guess once we're discovered, we'll open fire with our rifles."

"Right," replied Windtalker. "I think we should split our force, putting a group on the opposite hill and the second group on this side. I don't know what lies farther into the canyon, so we should try and divert them all here."

The sergeant replied, "I guess asking them to give up is out of the question."

Windtalker frowned. "I think if we try to do that first, we'll have twenty experienced soldiers firing a barrage of lead right at us. Some of your men will surely die. What do you want to do?"

"I was with the major when we went to the farm. They treated the woman savagely, and I still can't believe they would kill children. I think I should protect my men as well as prevent them from inflicting harm to others."

Kiyo grinned. "Don't worry about us. We can dodge bullets. However, you make a very good target in your blue uniforms and hats. I'd leave the hats here, and after dark, your uniforms will help you disappear from their rifle sights. We'll rest our horses and be ready for the fight."

"Okay. Just let me know if there's anything else you think will help."

Kiyo and Windtalker walked down to the creek to let their horses and Emita drink. A couple of the soldiers played with the dog, giving him a good rub. Kiyo waited until they were out of earshot of the soldiers, "So what do you really think?"

"Just as I said. We can take them unless we're discovered. I think we have a chance of killing them all, or maybe a few will surrender if we kill most of them, but these men sound like they are killers."

"I guess we should be prepared to ride away quickly if the attack fails."

Windtalker grinned. "We'd better ride like the wind and plan another attack to finish them off."

EIGHTEEN

Major Bill ate his supper with a bit of anxiety for his men on duty away the fort. A group to the west, another to the east, and now the sergeant with the scouts were chasing after killers in the middle. He knew they were vulnerable in the fort, but so far, not a single tribe dared to attack. However, he was a soldier of the old guard, so he called the lieutenant who told him to lock the gate very securely, and to double the guard and the lookouts. He ordered the cannon prepared and their rifles ready.

Spotted Owl and his men arrived in the valley behind the knoll where his scouts made their camp. He followed one of the scouts up the hill on foot to see the encampment with his own eyes. The scout made the soft sound of an owl as he approached, so the scout watching would not fire his bow at them. They heard nothing in reply. He made the sound again. Fearful, he pulled his knife, and led the chief to their hiding spot.

When they got to the top, the sun was almost down, putting an orange glow all around them, but they had never seen such destruction. The exploding cannonball shredded their man, his hides, and even the bushes around him. They saw bits of metal everywhere they walked. When they found the body, his face looked like a thousand knives had cut him. The body reeked from baking in the sun.

Spotted Owl moved about twenty yards away from the stench as he stared at the fort between the limbs of the bushes he hid behind. A lookout at the fort stared in his direction, but couldn't see him. He felt his men could loop ropes on the poles and pull a section of the fence down, but he decided a fire would not only be easier, it would require the attention of the soldiers while his warriors attacked.

He planned to take out the guards in the towers with arrows, and quietly set numerous fires outside the wall. If necessary, he would burn the place to the ground. It made for a clever plan, because a fire on the inside might be extinguished, but the soldiers had no means for putting out a fire on the outside without leaving the fort to do so. Spotted Owl hoped they were foolish enough to open the gate to do just that, and if so, he would charge right through it.

He returned to his men, drew out the fort in the dirt, and divided his men into five groups. He kept twenty men with him, and the rest were divided equally. They were to prepare torches and brush to haul to the fort walls to set them on fire. He picked six of his best archers for his group. They were ordered to make arrows with torch materials tied with rawhide on the end. Their job would be to take out the lookouts and wait for the fire on the wall to be discovered. To distract them, they would fire flaming arrows over the wall hoping to catch some of the buildings on fire. While the soldiers attempted to put those out, the outside fires would burn and grow until they engulfed the fort.

He sent the men to get ready. He told them to wait until the moon reached high over their heads. He hoped the soldiers would be asleep when they attacked.

With the moon almost to the high point, Windtalker wished a cloud would sail by and hide the glow of the moon from the ground below. Carefully, he led five soldiers down the hill, across the stream, and up the other side. He took his time as the soldiers often tripped over rocks with their boots. Kiyo and Windtalker wore their moccasins in preparation for the attack.

Kiyo led the sergeant and the remaining men up the road and got as close as they dared, knowing a scout remained posted just fifty yards away. Kiyo left them hiding there as he silently made his way around the scout. He prepared for the attack when he was about halfway between the scout and camp. He would fire and kill the guard first. He would then send Emita back to the sergeant to lead them up to him. He looked around the encampment for targets.

Lieutenant James and his men ate well in the safety of the circled wagon train, and amongst some women who could really cook. They ate until full, posted sentries, and slept better than on post in the mountains. He stared at the moon for a while as it climbed upwards. He could not fathom what made it glow as it did, but he closed his eyes, and slept well.

There were two men in the guard tower on duty. One of them lit a cigar. It was the last thing he ever did. Spotted Owl's best archer shot an arrow deep into his heart. A second arrow struck his face before he could drop to the floor, sending the man tumbling over the wall to the ground. At the same time, a second archer struck the other man in the back, and also followed with a second shot to the back of his head. The man hit the ground with a quiet thud. The four groups of warriors were only twenty yards away in the brush. Quickly, they began moving piles of brush and debris, putting it against the outside of the four walls. Once completed, they used their flints to light their torches and lit the mounds of dry limbs. They caught quickly. The Indians retreated and prepared for their assault.

Spotted Owl's remaining four archers made a similar small fire behind some rocks, but easily within range of the fort. They laid out their bows with the torch material tied to the end and waited for the fort to discover the wall fires.

A small breeze removed the stench of the fort for a while and the major finally slept well. Near midnight, his nostrils picked up the scent of the smoke. He assumed the watch fires in the center of the fort were lit, and perhaps the wind changed direction, but as it so happened, his bunk was against an outside wall. The wall became hot, and dried pine began to heat up and pop. He opened his eyes in time to see smoke bellowing into his sleeping area.

Bill rolled out of bed, looked around, and knew instantly something was wrong. He called out an alarm as he pulled his pants on, stepped into his boots, fastened his jacket, put on his holster, grabbed his hat and rifle, and ran out into the courtyard.

"Guards, what do you see?" He got no reply. He yelled again, but nothing. He called for the bugler to sound. The soldiers came running out of their barracks half dressed and sleepy. The major began yelling orders as he ran to the guard tower to find out the direction of the fire. Before he got there, he saw numerous flaming arrows sailing through the sky and landing on rooftops. He stopped and yelled at his men to quickly grab the arrows and put out the fires and prepare for battle. He made it to the tower. He saw another barrage of flaming arrows coming right for him. Quickly, he looked over to the wall to his right, then left, and saw that the walls were on fire. In the firelight, he got a quick glimpse of a dead soldier.

Suddenly, an arrow whizzed by his ear. He dove before a second one struck the post behind him. He knew they couldn't open the gates, as he had no idea the size of the force attacking them. He tried to recall his army training, but could think of no immediate tactic for a fort on fire. He climbed off the platform and ordered twenty of his men to the wall, but with orders to keep their heads down.

He sent other men to move their ammunition and other supplies away from the outside wall. He told the cannon squad to aim the cannon up and over the wall and to load it and wait for his orders. He sent men to put extra support on the gate. For now they kept their horses in and around the blacksmith shop, but he stopped moving when he heard the whoops and yells outside the wall.

He ran back to the wall and carefully looked over the top. His eyes saw twenty or thirty men shooting at them. He quickly ducked down as five arrows sailed over the wall near him. He moved down the wall again and popped his head up. He saw about twenty more men coming from the road on horseback.

Spotted Owl grinned as the first phase of the attack was going perfectly. Four fires were burning. A few soldiers shot some of his men, but they in turn caught a few of white men with arrows. They continued firing torch arrows inside the fort to keep them busy putting out the fires. He spread his men out and began firing their arrows at the wall while some of his men prepared ropes for pulling the gates apart if the fire didn't burn a wall down first.

On the mountain ridge, Windtalker gave the sound of a hawk and fired his arrows into the posted sentry. The sentry dropped to the ground silently. Kiyo did the same to his man. He sent Emita for the soldiers. He waited a few minutes for Windtalker to move a bit closer to the camp. They each selected targets from opposite sides of the camp and killed two men asleep with silent arrows before the alarm went out.

Kiyo yelled, "Fire!" and the sergeant and his men opened up. They killed a few more men before they scattered, but Leroy ran to a darkened corner of the camp area and removed a tarp covering a prized Gatling gun. He stole the gun from a group of soldiers in Kansas. His men had killed everyone so the army didn't know he had the gun. He hauled it all the way across the country as his secret weapon. One packhorse carried nothing but the gun, while another hauled the ammunition.

He began rapidly turning the crank first in Windtalker's direction, and hit one of the soldiers, then turned and swung the gun around to the other side. They were quickly forced to take cover.

The sergeant said, "I think we're outgunned. That's a Gatling gun. It can fire fifty shots for each one of ours. I saw one in Philadelphia at a show. I've never seen one out here until now."

"Wait," said Kiyo while thinking hard. "How long before he has to reload it?"

The sergeant replied, "I think the belt holds a hundred rounds. Oh, I get it, we wait until he reloads..."

Kiyo cut him off, "And then we fire with everything we have. I'll aim for the man running the big gun."

Leroy held up his fire realizing he had no targets. Windtalker and Kiyo kept jumping in and out of various places, and Leroy would fire for a while at them. Windtalker fired an arrow off that bounced off the gun. Bravely, Leroy ignored the arrow, turned the barrel in Windtalker's direction and ran off more shots but Windtalker already moved to his next position. Leroy began yelling at his men to take up offensive positions. They began slowly working their way up the hill.

The sergeant said to Kiyo, "I am not sure we can wait. They are just forty yards from us."

Kiyo sized up the situation and agreed. They were a smaller force and outgunned. He gave a whistle to Windtalker who quickly led his men back to the trail. Once safe on the other side, they all retreated down the road. Kiyo and Windtalker talked about attacking again, but they would have to wait a day or so. They asked about the gun, and could it be used when they were moving. The sergeant said no. This gave them a direction to think about. Instead of attacking at night, they would catch them on the road.

Just as they got to their horses, they heard not one, but several cannon ball shots. Windtalker spoke up first, "I think the fort is under attack." Sergeant agreed. "Saddle up men. Let's ride. We must help them."

Kiyo and Windtalker waited a second as they hated to let the bad men escape, but they also doubted the major would fire the cannon unless it was a serious attack. They saddled up and began riding hard, passing the men with Emita out front, who helped lead them in the light of the moon.

NINETEEN

Captain Robert's sentry remained high on the mountain overlooking the road. He called down to wake the captain. Robert scampered up the hill in the dark, until he reached the sentry. "What is it?"

"Something is wrong due south. I think it may be the fort. Here, use the glasses. I heard a small boom sound as it echoed through the mountains."

Just as Robert lifted the glasses to his eyes, he saw the streak of cannonball going up in the sky with sparks trailing it. A few seconds later, he heard the boom, too. "I think you're right. The major is under attack. We must hurry to help. Come on." He began sliding down the embankment. "Break camp fast. The fort is under attack. We must hurry."

Ten minutes later, they were galloping down the road with the help of the moonlight.

Their quick departure surprised the lone Spotted Owl scout trailing and keeping an eye on them. They were now between him and Spotted Owl in an area where getting around them would be next to impossible unless they camped again. He heard the boom and wondered if that is what sent the captain and his men scrabbling in the middle of the night.

One of Lieutenant Johnson's sentries shook him lightly to awaken him. "What is it private?"

"I just heard a boom off to the northwest."

"A boom?" The lieutenant stood up just as they both heard a second one. "That's in the direction of the fort. Oh gees, the major is under attack. Assemble the men fast."

As his men prepared to leave, James went to the wagon master, woke him, and explained they would hasten to the fort to help and return to escort them. He told him they should follow the road and take the left fork to go the fort. They saddled up and began riding hard down the road.

In the fort they were constantly putting out fires from the arrows, while the men on the banquette were firing back at the Indians. Twice the men at the gate fired through portholes with their rifles as several Indians tried to attach a rope to the gate. Once they tried to bring torches to the gate, but every warrior that approached the gate was shot.

Spotted Owl watched their attempts and finally realized they should not approach the gate from the front, but from the sides. He sent out new orders.

Flames began licking up the sides of the walls forcing the guards to move away from that area as they popped up to shoot and ducked down to avoid an arrow to the face. Four of the soldiers had been shot and one of them fell backwards breaking his neck in the fall.

The major ordered the cannon shots hoping Captain Robert and Lieutenant James would come to their aid. He also hoped the sergeant with Kiyo and Windtalker would arrive as well.

Spotted Owl jumped back at the first firing of the cannonball as it sailed over his head. He watched it streak over the sky before exploding on impact. He wondered what else the soldiers might offer in response to his attack, but he did not back down.

He watched as the men made their way along the side of the walls. The major saw a loop of rope flip over the top of the snagging on a pole. "Shoot that Indian at the gate now!" he ordered as he lifted his own rifle and fired at the gate. A bullet went through a crevice and caught the warrior in the chest killing him instantly. The major quickly rushed to the wood pile, found a long narrow stick, sharpened it with his knife, took it to the gate, and gave it to one of the privates guarding the gate. "If you see a rope come over the top, flip it off with this stick and do it quickly, or they are liable to pull the gates down."

He rushed up the steps to the railing. "Sergeant," he called, "shoot any horses that get near the gate. They're trying to pull the gate down with rope."

"Yes, sir!"

The major rushed down to the ground and ordered the cannon to the middle of the yard. Then he and two other men pushed wagons on both sides of the cannon, and began moving empty crates to create a barricade in case the gate did come down.

He ran back up the steps. "Sergeant, do you see a group of Indians waiting to attack?"

The sergeant quickly took a look and ducked down. "Sir, there's a group of twenty or thirty about sixty yards off to the right of the gate."

The major replied, "We're going to fire a cannon shot at them. Give us some directions as to short or far, left or right."

"Yes sir!"

The cannon master quickly did some calculations for a shot sixty yards away. He aimed it slightly to the right of the gate, locked in the sighting, and lit the fuse. The cannon roared and shook as it exploded a cannonball high into the air.

Spotted Owl watched with amazement, while wondering if the arching, flaming ball were some kind of signal, but his curiosity turned to fear when he realized it was roaring back to earth in their direction. He quickly kicked his horse as the ball exploded just behind his men.

The shrapnel killed two men, wounded several others, and frightened his men, but he gave orders to stand ready to charge the gate. He could see several of his men attempting to hook a rope to the posts.

Inside, the major suddenly leaped to his left to avoid a flaming arrow coming right at him. On the ground, he could see under the gate and he saw feet. He ran to the gate, and he and a private knelt down and opened fire.

The Indians at the gate fell to the ground as the pain of the leg shots stunned them, but once they fell back, the soldiers at the portholes shot them in the chest.

Spotted Owl cursed at this new discovery. He gathered his men around them and prepared to tell them to charge the gate. Before he could finish, a second cannon shot rang out. Seeing the fireball streaking through the sky scared his men, and they scattered before he could yell charge. He, too, made a dash away as the ball slammed into the ground. Hot pieces of metal flew into his back knocking him from his poor horse that received the worst of it. The right rear leg of his mount broke, and the terrified animal began violently thrashing about the ground, unable to get to its feet and run away.

Spotted Owl cursed as he grabbed a nearby horse from one of his warriors that was also killed in the blast. He yelled at his men to charge the gate. They ran up with ropes, many were killed, but they finally got a rope on the top. Just as they started to pull, Spotted Owl looked away from the fort at the charging group of twelve men. They were spread out side-by-side and firing as they charged.

He called for his men to run, and they turned south and rode about fifty yards before they saw a larger wall of men led by Lieutenant Johnson. Their bugler sounded the charge. They, too, were firing as they rode.

Spotted Owl yelled for all his men, and they turned north. Some of the cavalry shots were catching the rear of his men as they sprinted south, but as they cleared a knoll, they ran head on into Captain Robert's charging men, with their bugler announcing their charge as well. More of the remaining warriors were killed as Spotted Owl circled before finally dashing west into the forest. Then he looped around the back of the fort, and then turned south to make his way back into the mountains.

Captain Robert's men gave chase for a while, but in the forest at night, they could easily become ambushed, so they were called back. They all rode up to the fort together and called for the major.

The major heard the buglers but he was still lying in the dirt, ready to shoot more feet when he heard Captain Robert's voice. He leaped up with great joy. His men stopped firing. "Open the gate lads. We have fires to put out."

As the gates were opened, he ran out and began shaking the hands of his officers, including Robert, James, his sergeant, and the scouts. "Take your men and surround the fort about forty yards out while we put these fires out."

A bucket brigade went to work and in a few hours, all the fires were out. Dawn arrived so they could survey the damage. They ate breakfast quickly, the doctor attended to the wounded, a squad buried the dead, and crews set about making repairs to the fort fearing a second attack.

Captain Robert reported the wagon train made it to the west unharmed. The lieutenant reported he left his group about ten miles away. The major immediately sent the lieutenant and his men to escort them in. The sergeant reported on finding the ex-soldiers with the Gatling gun.

"A real Gatling gun. My goodness. I sure would like to have used it last night."

Windtalker spoke up, "They used it on us, pinning us down quickly. I think we killed about six of his men, but none of ours were hurt. I suspect they will head north since we were in the south, but I doubt they know the terrain."

"Do you think you could find them?"

"Yes. They are using twenty horses and that gun must be on one of the mounts. They make lots of tracks."

The major thought for a second. "They are going to kill again. They have a taste for it." He turned to the captain, "Robert, reorganize your ammunition and supplies, take packhorses, as you may be gone a while, and extra horses, then Kiyo and Windtalker will go after them. At the worst, come back with the Gatling gun, and the ammunition. At best, arrest them, but it sounds like you will have to kill them. Proceed with all haste."

The major turned to the scouts. "I'll double your usual rate if you'll help Robert and his men."

Kiyo and Windtalker spoke in their native tongue for a moment before finally smiling and agreeing to help. They all set about loading supplies and getting more ammunition, and left within the hour.

Spotted Owl and his men, many of whom were wounded, made their way back to the camp. He seethed with anger, and spoke to no one as they made their way down secret trails to the village. His enemy defeated him once more, but soon, he vowed, he would avenge his dead and his honor.

TWENTY

Emita ran hard and far ahead of the scouts, along with Captain Robert and his soldiers as they rode back to the site of the attack on the ridge the night before. They found only debris, and the hasty burial in shallow graves of some of Leroy's men. Robert showed the scouts the piles of spent casings where the Gatling gun was set up.

Robert said, "That deadly machine fired over a hundred shells in just a few minutes. We were lucky we escaped its devastation."

Kiyo spotted a piece of torn clothing with blood on it, perhaps from a wounded soldier, so he let Emita smell it and the dog soon led them back to the road, and then they continued their ride tracking Leroy and his men.

Windtalker searched the ground for tracks, and noted with a keen eye that there only fourteen horses with riders, and five packhorses. He knew the gun was on the second packhorse as those hoofs went deeper in the dirt and mud due to the weight. The size of the shoes for this animal were larger than the other horses, so they wisely put the big gun on the back of their largest horse.

As Leroy continued up the trail, he felt both anger and confusion at the attack on them. It began like an Indian attack with flying arrows, arrows that killed not only his sentries, but also two of his men as they slept. Soon, however, the onslaught of rifle fire began, and he felt certain, without the advantage of the Gatling gun, they would have been captured or killed. Only once did he actually see a uniform of his enemy in the shadows due to the moonlight, but seeing a man with a bow, but dressed like a white man, puzzled him greatly. He assumed they were probably Indian scouts, working for the army.

There were two wounded men in line behind him, and they removed an arrow from the shoulder of one, a bullet from the other, and bandaged their wounds. He forced them into the saddle. He also threatened if they complained too much he would shoot them, because he knew if the group last night continued to chase them, he might need as many men as he could get. However, he would stop for the wounded, as they must all hurry to flee from these soldiers.

Leroy's military training did not include leading a force of thieves over such steep terrain. He hoped the same applied to the soldiers in pursuit, and perhaps they would not continue tracking them. He had outwitted and outrun several posses, and felt determined to do it again. He also knew, if given the chance, he would kill all the men that attacked them. That was the only way, he thought, to be sure that none pursued him to the west. He didn't wish to be forevermore looking over his shoulder.

After they reached the end of the next valley, they took an animal trail leading up the side of a small mountain, and another trail that went upwards towards a larger one. They climbed for an hour to reach the ridge of the first hill. He checked the sky to guess at the weather, and decided to rest the horses for a while after checking his watch. He allowed his men a chance to get something to eat, and from the advantage of the ridge, he knew he could see the enemy if they were coming.

An hour later, they continued their journey with the captain now feeling a bit more confident, as he saw no sign of soldiers following them. They walked their horses along the ridge, thankful for the animal trail, but nervous as the hoofs of the horses were very close to the edge. After a perilous trek, they made their way down five hundred yards, before following the back and forth trail up the largest mountain any of them had ever seen. The men thought the giant mountain looked impossible, foreboding, and treacherous, but they trudged along as they did all the way across the country with endless walks into the western sun.

Emita reached the end of a natural road and waited for Windtalker and Kiyo to catch up to him.

Windtalker asked as he pulled his horse to a stop, "What is it boy?"

Emita ran in circles and then darted up the animal trail of the first mountain.

"They went that way, huh. I wonder how long." He got off his horse and kicked at some animal dung that was still soft. He knew they were not far behind.

Kiyo told Captain Robert, "It looks like they are heading up the mountain. I suggest your men secure their saddles, and check the packhorses. It'll be going up there."

"You should consider untying the string of packhorses," began Windtalker, "and assign each horse to a man. Otherwise, if one falls, they all could."

Robert nodded his understanding of the suggestion, told his men to dismount and get to work on their saddles, and to prepare the packhorses as described. He then walked up to Windtalker and Kiyo to speak privately with them.

"How far ahead of us are they?"

Windtalker replied, "A few hours or so. They will have to go slower than our group as they are carrying a heavy load, and at least one or two are bleeding."

Robert asked, "You saw blood on the trail? I saw nothing."

"Just a drop or two now and then." Windtalker paused as he pointed up the hill to the bigger mountain. "I suspect they are forced to climb the larger mountain as there must be no escape over this hill."

Kiyo added, "They could decide not to climb the big mountain, preferring to ambush and kill us so they can go back the way we came."

Robert sighed. "I guess we are vulnerable on the ridge."

"Exactly," replied Windtalker, "so we must spread out to make targets more difficult. Emita will let us know if they are nearby. We might also smell them if the wind is blowing towards us."

Robert looked puzzled. "You can smell them?"

Kiyo grinned. "We can smell you, too."

Robert grinned. "I'm smart enough not to ask what we smell like, but what scents do you pick up from them?"

Windtalker replied, "They have been riding a long time without a bath. Their horses have traveled far, but they, too, haven't been in a stream for a long time. There's a new scent, too."

Robert asked, "What's that?"

"The scent of fear. They wouldn't climb that big hill unless they feared for their lives. However, make no mistake, if they killed a family including women and children, they are bloodthirsty. We should be very careful to avoid becoming one of their victims."

Robert gulped. "We will do all you suggested, but please be careful, too. I want all of us to return to the fort alive and well."

Kiyo grinned. "Let's get on with it."

They saddled up after giving Emita a command to track, and followed him up the animal trail. On the ridge, Kiyo told the captain to tell his men to let go of their reins and let the horse choose their own path. It was difficult for the soldiers to do, as holding the reins reflected their feeling of being in control, but in this case, a horse would take the safer route, and yanking his head could either confuse the horse, frustrate him, or cause him to lose his balance. If that happened, rider and horse alike were intertwined, and could tumble over and over down the mountain and certain death.

With the attention to safety, and slow going, they made it along the first ridge without an accident, but Kiyo and Windtalker began to worry about the next big mountain for two reasons. First, for the safety of the men and horses on the treacherous trail, but secondly, they were fearful because they would be exposed to an ambush from the advantage the men they chased would have while firing down at them.

During a brief rest stop for the horses, Windtalker reminded Robert to keep his men spread out, to avoid easy targeting. He also suggested that he, Kiyo and Emita move out about a hundred yards ahead of them. He suggested they might be able to hear the men they tracked before they could see them. Robert just shook his head in amazement at the ideas the scouts thought of, and watched as they began the more difficult climb up the tall mountain and the beginning of countless switchbacks.

Leroy's men steadily continued their desperate climb up the steep mountain that went higher than any they had seen since crossing the northern plains. As they ascended, they occasionally saw brief distant views. His ears popped several times from the difference in atmosphere pressure as oxygen began thinning. The back of his shirt and underarms were wet from nervous sweat. His horse panted hard for breath as it struggled to haul the weight he carried on his back. Steam eerily rose off their horses, and sweat rolled down their legs in steady streams. Leroy knew they would have to stop soon to allow the horses to rest, and he wondered if they should dismount and pull the animals along, but he feared the weary horses might rebel and bolt away.

Just a hundred yards from the top, one of the wounded men must have died or passed out as he began falling off his horse on the downhill side. The sudden movement caused his horse to lose its footing. As the animal tried to regain control, the falling soldier's foot twisted in the stirrup, breaking his ankle as his body twisted, but the now hanging limp body offset the balance that the horse desperately tried to stabilize on the narrow uneven path.

The men began yelling at someone to do something. Leroy yelled as well, but there was nothing that could be done. There was not even room to get off their horses, and no way to get to the horse to help. Tragically, they could nothing but watch the horrific scene play out.

Eventually, the frantic horse could not hold that feeble position, so it began shaking while trying to free himself of the dead man as his body already hung over the precipice. Suddenly, the struggling horse took a misstep off the edge, and in a flash, man and horse began tumbling over each other down the side of the mountain, bouncing off rocks bigger than stagecoaches, with the full weight of the horse falling on top of the man, breaking nearly every bone, but also breaking the legs and ribs of the horse as well. The men above watched in horror as animal and man continued tumbling farther down the mountain. The gruesome scene brought instant fear into all of Leroy's riders. One of the men threw up the contents of his stomach onto the side of his horse and saddle, while still clinging tightly to his horse.

From a thousand feet below, Emita heard the noise from high above the trail, saw the horse falling, and quickly scampered, trying to get away, and barked at the scouts. They looked up, and instantly kicked their horses to move away from the path of the falling debris. They called back to Captain Robert to warn him. His men began to scatter than best they could on the narrow trail, both forward and back while trying to leave an opening. In a sudden flash, the two lifeless bodies of the man and the horse sailed between them, still gaining speed. They saw a flash of the horse, its saddle, and only the remains of a foot and boot in the stirrup, with the leg broken away on the first impact, and blood falling about them like a sudden rain. Finally, the man and horse crashed on a giant boulder near the bottom of the mountain in a gut wrenching, dreadful, gruesome sounding thud.

In the silence that followed, everyone stood still, calming their horses while trying to absorb the near catastrophic accident, and the realization of what could happen to them as well. They were lucky, as the horse and rider, or even some of the larger rolling rocks, could easily have swept them over the side as well. They waited for the sliding stones to settle down and a few minutes later, the debris stopped falling.

Kiyo called for Emita to stop barking. They were sure the riders they chased heard the dog or their yell to Robert, but it couldn't be helped. "Windtalker worried their position might have been revealed, resulting in a hail of gunfire." might cause a hail of gunfire. His eyes strained upward, but they could not see the killers though they knew they were there. He hoped they could not see their position as well.

Leroy heard the bark of the dog, and the voice of a man with an odd accent, but for now, he feared losing either himself or another of his men, so he ordered the group to keep moving upward. He called to them, "We only have fifty more yards. Be careful and keep moving."

Kiyo heard the echo of Leroy's voice and the temperament of his tone displayed fear, an element his grandfather told him he must overcome to be an exceptional warrior. They, too, urged the soldiers to continue, but to prevent assassination, they were told to dismount and lead their horses with thirty feet between each man to prevent an uphill horse from stepping on the man following him.

With no rider in the saddle, they hoped to avoid a lucky shot from the trail above. The men and horses struggled with the climb, but they could only imagine how tough it must be for the men they chased, as they were carrying perhaps too much weight on their supply horses, but certainly too much for the horse carrying the prized Gatling gun.

Leroy reached the top and found a small area of semi-level ground. He urged his men to climb off their horses so they could rest for a bit. He took his rifle, walked back to the edge of the mountain, and leaned out searching for his target, but the terrain conveniently hid the men below. He moved left and right, searching between the limbs and bushes that hugged the mountain, searching for sunlight to enhance their growth, but he could not see any movement anywhere. Frustrated, he turned around and searched for another way to slow them down, or better, to deter them completely.

Frantically, he walked in circles, looking up and down at the mountain wall above the trail, until finally, he spotted opportunity in the form of a large boulder precariously perched near the last switchback, but frozen in its spot for centuries. He ran to a packhorse, removed the lid of a box, and pulled out a stick of dynamite and a fuse. He nearly forgot about them, as there were no safes from the Midwest to the Glaciers.

"You men follow the trail over that crest and go down the other side. Take my horse and stop about fifty yards. Hold tight to your horses. I'm going to blast these men right off the mountain."

The exhausted, frightened men did as they were told and moved along quickly.

Leroy ran to the base of the boulder on the high side, used his knife to clear some debris, and buried the stick of dynamite with just the tip showing. He inserted the fuse, removed a match from his pocket, and struck it. He paused for second as a slow, wicked smile formed on his lips. He reached a bit further and lit the fuse. "Take that you bastards. I hope this rock knocks you to hell!" He then took off running to catch up with his men.

Kiyo rounded the next turn where he saw Emita sitting and puffing hard. "What is it boy? Are they close?"

Emita whined a little.

Kiyo looked up and then said to the dog, "Just two more switchbacks. We'll make it. Come on, old boy."

Boom!

Kiyo, Windtalker, Captain Robert and his men, all ducked down thinking it must have been cannon fire, but Kiyo looked up the mountain, and instantly, he sighed hard and screamed an alarm. He couldn't think of the right word in English fast enough. He yelled the Indian word, and then finally he said, "Rock!" From the intensity of his voice everyone knew something bad occurred.

Leroy thought the dynamite failed to move the boulder at first, but the slight shift in weight caused the crumbling of the smaller rocks below it to give way, and slowly the twenty-ton boulder began rolling downward across their trail and over the edge.

"Emita come!" exclaimed Kiyo, and then to the men, "Move ahead quickly! A big rock is coming!" he yelled as he dragged his horse along the trail to the far side, and beckoning Emita to come to him, as the ground beneath began to shake with each spin of the big lopsided boulder.

Windtalker also ran and pulled his horse up behind Kiyo. Captain Robert relayed the message, but the men were confused, as they quickly tried to clear the center of the trail. Those in the middle moved towards the scouts at the switchback, while Robert had the others back up to his switchback. Everyone needed to move to safety in a short window of just a few seconds.

Windtalker made it and yelled at the two men and horses behind, "Hurry! Pull them! Hurry!"

Robert yelled in a loud voice, "Move, move, move!"

It had been easier to pull the horses than to back up, but the frightened horses responded without direction in an attempt to move away from the ground that shook with each roll of the giant rock.

The boulder slammed into the other end of the trail where the fellows

123

huddled, while holding tightly to the reins of their horses. The rock continued over the side, missing the captain and the men near them, but kept on rolling down the traverse of the long trail. The rock slammed with great force into a soldier and his horse, instantly wiping them away like they were made of paper, ending their lives in a flash. The men below continued to rush to get out of the path and somehow managed to just barely do so. They watched as the big rock picked up more speed before slamming into the large boulders below.

Leroy ran back and smiled when he saw the pitiful remains of a man's leg and the crushed head of a horse on the big boulder. He ran back and climbed aboard his horse, and began the journey down the other side of the big mountain.

TWENTY-ONE

Robert dropped his gaze to the ground, while feeling sick that he lost one of his men. He felt helpless. The tragedy shook him into a mild stage of shock. However, after the earth stopped shaking, and the debris slowed, Windtalker called to Robert, "Come on, just a few more turns, and we'll reach the top. We're going ahead to secure the area. We are vulnerable here. We must move to safety."

Robert wiped his wet eyes, regained his composure, and took charge once again. "Thanks," managed a very frightened Robert as he began crossing over the path where the rock had swept by so quickly, but gathering courage he said, "Come on men. We can do this. We have to do this."

Emita began once more moving up the trail with Kiyo right behind him, and followed by Windtalker as they pulled their horses along. As they made the last turn, they pulled their pistols, anticipating an attack. They moved from one boulder to the next, but sighed with relief when they found no one with a rifle pointed at them.

Kiyo called down to Robert, "It's clear to the top. Keep coming."

It took another half hour to get all the men and horses onto the safe ground at the top. Meanwhile, Windtalker and Kiyo tied off their horses, pulled rifles from the protective saddle scabbards, and hurriedly ran to the other side of the mountain ridge. They leaped from rock to rock and then climbed to the top of a boulder and leaned over the edge.

Kiyo exclaimed, "I see them!"

They quickly took aim and fired. Kiyo hit the last man using the Sharps 50-caliber rifle, knocking him violently from his horse. Windtalker aimed his Winchester rifle, and hit the next one. The man fell forward as the shell shattered his spine, flattening the lead before tumbling through his chest creating massive internal injuries. His frightened horse instantly trampled him, as did the packhorse still tied to the rider's saddle horn.

Leroy urged his men forward as he tried to find someone to shoot at with his pistol. Finally, in desperation, he fired his pistol towards the top of the mountain, but it was too far for accuracy and he failed to find a target.

After he stopped firing, the scouts leaned back around the edge of the boulder while searching for a shot at Leroy and his men. But he and his men had entered a stand of trees and remained out of their sight. The scouts gave up and went back to meet Robert.

"We got two. They're just about two hundred yards ahead of us."

"So we must hurry after them," replied Robert.

Windtalker said, "No, not yet. Your men and our horses are exhausted. If we push them, they could lose their balance and fall, killing maybe another man and our horses. We must let them rest and then we'll continue."

125

Kiyo added, "Don't worry, we're closing in on the riders, and we'll get them."

Robert sighed, as he ordered his men to rest their horses and themselves. He sat down as the adrenaline slipped away, feeling exhausted and angry at the loss of one of his men. He let the men retrieve some food to eat and grain for their horses. They drank from their canteens and then gave the rest of their water to the horses.

In the valley on the northern side, a group of Shoshone hunters heard the explosion of the dynamite and the gunfire that followed. They sent one of their men back to the village to tell their chief, but the rest began making their way along well-known hunting trails. They made their way across the valley and looked upward at the mountain, trying to spot movement. Several minutes later, they saw a man on horseback pulling a packhorse. Excited, they began running to another trail, crossed a stream, and followed it upwards towards the area where the mountain the men were on ended and the next began. They knew the men would reach a cross trail of sorts, leading south or turning north. They hoped to reach the men before they could choose a path.

Leroy pulled the pocket watch stolen from a dead banker's pocket in a small forgotten town in Missouri, and noted the time was late in the afternoon. He wound the stem while thinking. He spoke to one of his men. "We must get off this damn mountain and find water soon. We have three hours until sunset. Watch for a stream or a pool of rainwater," he ordered.

They continued along looking left and right when a vista opened up, making it easier for them to see the views. They continued searching for the water they needed, while hoping for a chance for a hot meal. The men knew they must also find a way to attack the posse following them.

After they saddled up and began their trek across the ridge that gradually went downward, Kiyo spotted the men from time to time, but only briefly. Emita stayed nearby as they could see steam from the horse dung they found, meaning the bad guys were very close. The scouts didn't want to take a chance on Emita getting shot and killed. Windtalker took the lead for a while, and it wasn't long until he spotted a drop of blood. "Ah, one of them is still wounded and bleeding."

Kiyo replied, "I hope we can catch them and end this before the sun goes down. They need water and so do we."

"We'll get them," replied Windtalker, fully accepting the challenge of catching a powerful and smart enemy soldier that carried unusual weapons in the form of the Gatling gun and sticks of dynamite.

While resting, Robert told the scouts all he could about dynamite, how it was used, and the danger involved. Kiyo asked if they carried it on a packhorse.

Robert replied, "Yeah they probably felt safer with it away from their saddle."

Windtalker asked, "Would it explode if they shot it?"

Robert grinned and nodded his head. "The problem would be which horse carried the dynamite." Robert also reminded them that the major wanted the Gatling gun and ammo retained if at all possible.

A few hours later, Kiyo came around a bend and found Windtalker and Emita on a big boulder looking down. "Do you see them?"

Windtalker replied, "Only briefly, but I have bad news."

Kiyo came over to him. "What is it?"

Windtalker pointed to the valley below. Kiyo stared until he could see about fifteen Shoshone warriors rapidly running across the valley and towards the mountain they were standing on.

Kiyo said, "I guess they heard the gunfire." Looking at the terrain, he added, "They can't come straight up the mountain at this point." He turned his head to the northwest, "They'll attack as we come off this mountain."

Windtalker said, "The question is will they get there in time to attack the men in front of us or wait for us to arrive?"

Captain Robert caught up and they explained the situation to them. "Well, I think this is what they call between a rock and a hard place." The scouts didn't understand his statement. Robert smiled and continued, "If we're sort of lucky, the Indians will drive the men ahead back into us, putting the enemy in a pickle. They'll have to choose to charge forward into the warriors with their bows and arrows, or retreat and face our rifles."

Windtalker said, "I think we'll need more than luck. We'll have to kill those bad men we're after and maybe the Shoshone as well. They are fierce warriors, but we are stronger and more powerful with our rifles."

Kiyo said solemnly, "Let's get it done. The sun will set in a few hours and I don't want to fight them at night on a mountain."

They agreed and set out once more.

The Shoshone warriors crossed the stream, and began following the warrior, searching and tracking his fellow hunters. They pushed their ponies across the valley as hard they could towards the mountain. They were more experienced with the mountain terrain, so they began to slow their descent, allowing their animals to choose good spots for their hooves. They watched the stream near the trail diminish slightly every hundred yards or so. They knew the source of the stream and the forest around this section of the mountains very well. The history of their tribe went back centuries when their ancestors descended from the north into the fertile valleys. They were a proud people, fearing no one, but loathed the Blackfeet warriors most of all. Their medicine men warned of the white men approaching in large quantities with plans to steal their land and drive them off. They were friendly to early explorers, but when some of their men were killed in an attempt to steal the horses of the white men, they took revenge and slaughtered the rest of the explorers with great anger while mutilating the bodies. They became a vicious enemy of the white men, vowing to kill them to protect their families, their leaders, and their heritage.

The hours passed quickly and Leroy could see the merging of more than one mountain ridge about five hundred yards ahead of them. He began thinking about which way to go, though he knew he might have to just follow a trail, but he wondered what if he came to a fork and had to choose a trail? He hoped to move a bit southwest and back to his plan of finding the road leading to the Pacific Ocean. He had little desire to remain a man on the run in hostile territory with a squad of soldiers on his tail for very long. With luck, he thought, he would make it out of these gigantic mountains, and find his way to San Francisco, disposing of his men as needed along the way. From the newspaper articles he read about the early explorers, he knew the Glacier Mountains were supposed to be the last of the big mountains before reaching the ocean to the west.

Kiyo saw movement a few hundreds yards below his location, but somewhat ahead of him on the northern side. He caught a glimpse of a warrior, but then suddenly he saw the head of a white pony belonging to the Shoshone they spotted in the valley. He passed the word along quietly.

Less than an hour before the sun would disappear over the western mountains, Leroy rounded a bend, and heard movement ahead. Though exhausted, he managed to somehow shift his body quickly as a spear was rapidly thrown directly at his chest. He drew his pistol and fired hitting the thrower in the face. Quickly, he and his men dismounted. A few men held the horses while the rest of the men came forward with rifles pulled.

Kiyo heard the pistol shot and said, "I suspect the attack has begun. Should we continue to move forward or wait?"
Windtalker replied, "Let's use this chance to close in on them. I say move forward a few hundred yards, and then we'll leave our horses and Emita, and walk in."

Leroy's men found positions behind rocks just seconds before a flurry of arrows swarmed at them. They returned fire as two brave warriors ran up the trail with spears in hand. Leroy shot the first and his old sergeant got the second.
However, this did little to deter the Shoshone warriors as they charged forward once more, keeping the white men pinned down with volleys of arrows and threats of spears. The captain moved his men back to several

128

new positions, but the Indians continued their pursuit.

"We can't go back much further," protested his sergeant. "There are armed riders behind us."

Leroy scowled. "Hell, I know that! We have to kill these sons of bitches right now. How many do you think?"

"Twelve or more, I reckon. I've sent that many at least."

Leroy set his rifle down, pulled his pistol and reloaded it. "Load your pistols. We're going to have to charge and end this fast. Pick three more men and get ready."

Leroy ran to a packhorse while dodging from rock to rock, hoping to avoid an arrow in the back. He got another stick of dynamite out, put a fuse in and lit it. He calmly walked forward. "After it blows we'll charge. Are you ready?"

"Yes sir!" exclaimed the frightened men while looking at Leroy holding the spewing, ignited fuse.

Leroy held the dynamite until he thought the stuff would explode in about five seconds. Quickly, he threw it hard down the trail and into the midst of warriors. They looked at the smoking stick with great curiosity. One of them bent down to pick it up.

Boom!

Instantly, the blast ripped apart the warrior, while knocking the remaining warriors backwards and off the trail. Leroy and his men ran with pistols in each hand and shot anything that moved. In less than a minute, they killed all the warriors on the trail, but failed to note a few men holding the horses in a stand of trees about a hundred yards away. Quickly, the Indians saddled up, and galloped for reinforcements.

Kiyo ducked at the sound of the blast, thinking they might be throwing dynamite at them, but realized this happened about two hundred yards ahead of their position. "I think he threw it at the Indians. Let's move up quickly."

With pistols ready in their belts, Kiyo ratcheted a shell into the Winchester, while Windtalker put one of the big shells into the Sharps rifle. The soldiers did the same, then closed ranks, and moved rapidly up behind the scouts.

"Hurry men," called Leroy as they spotted a fork in the trail. "We're taking the trail to the left and hopefully away from these bastards and this damn mountain."

He ran back to his horse and began leading his men forward through the blast zone and carnage. Seeing no hope of going straight up the next ridge leading towards the steep mountain ahead of them, when he got to the fork, he turned left and hurried as fast as he could, though careful not to let his horse slip. After fifty yards, the trail leveled a bit, then became steep again, and finally leveled for far longer so they picked up some distance.

Emita hung tight at Kiyo's side as they reached the gruesome bodies of the warriors. Windtalker took a look and said, "We must hurry or any Shoshone will think we did this. We're close. Hurry!"

Windtalker took the lead guiding his horse down the trail carefully. He glanced at the sun because it was quickly disappearing behind the highest peaks to the west. As his adjusted his eyes, he used the last of the remaining light to follow the path for a bit longer.

Leroy continued downward until they reached a stream. He crossed over, stopping briefly so the horses could take in a little water, bounded up the far shore, and turned southwest with the intention of following the stream until they found a road or better path to the west and out of the mountains.

They road about two miles until he knew it would be foolish to continue in the dark. They stopped, took the horses to the river to drink, refilled canteens, and set up defensive positions. He knew either the posse or the Indians would be hot on their trail. He hoped the Indians took care of the posse. He sent a man back about two hundred yards with instructions to wait until he could hear riders before running to warn them.

They pulled out rations and ate quickly, as they were bone tired from the journey up and over the mountains, as well as exhausted and fearful.

Leroy sensed this and laughed. "Well, fellows, you are really something. You have killed several of the soldiers, and all the Indians, and this time tomorrow we should be out of these mountains. I'm going to follow the stream, which will keep us on better terrain, and we'll pick up time. If we have to we'll set a trap for these bastards and kill them all. Soon we'll be drinking beer and champagne in San Francisco." He laughed again at his lie, as he had no intention of sharing the gold he carried with anyone. He was ready to part with the past and that included getting rid of his men.

The men were glad to hear and feel their captain's confidence. Some of the exhausted men slept immediately while others stood guard. No one mentioned the name of the man they lost today.

Windtalker stopped at the river and waited for the rest to catch up. "I think we should stop here. We have just minutes of daylight, and we need water and food. I'm sure they are doing the same because they are less experienced than we are in the woods so they'll hunker down."

Kiyo agreed, as did Robert. They watered their horses, filled all their canteens, and then moved back away from the river, and behind a stand of trees and big boulders. They made camp, built a fire hidden behind the rocks, and soon ate some hot food. They would keep sentries posted as they slept. As soon as all were fed, Windtalker and Kiyo moved the fire next to the stream, put more wood on it, and went back to the campsite, allowing their eyes to adjust to the darken sky.

"Why'd you move the fire?"

Windtalker grinned. "Indians know that white men are lazy. They'll assume we bedded down next to the stream, and the fire will encourage that mistake. If we're lucky they'll charge the empty camp and then we'll fire from behind them."

It was going to be a long, fearful night. Most likely the Shoshone were behind them, and the bad men were ahead of them. Though fearful, nonetheless, they fell asleep quickly.

TWENTY-TWO

Windtalker woke before dawn and while taking a leak in the dark, he wondered if he should scout ahead before sunrise and locate the enemy. However, he nodded at the nearest sentry, and decided to play it safe. He felt confident they would get another chance to catch them tomorrow. He returned to his bedroll for a last hour of sleep.

Leroy, weary from travel, sore from the effort, and completely exhausted, forced his mind to wake up. He went around kicking the boots of his men until all were on their feet. The moon fell across the horizon, and he knew a hint of daylight could come in the next thirty minutes. "Saddle up, men. Our enemy will be doing the same. We must take advantage of the easier terrain and ride hard. We leave in five minutes."

Every one took a bite of hard tack or beef jerky, took a leak, tied their bedrolls to their saddles, prepared their horses, and slid up into the saddle. Immediately, they felt the sore spots on their butts and inside of their thighs from the long, unusual climb up the mountains.

The captain led them off at a slight trot to warm up the horses before picking up speed, as the valley lit up from an early hint of the sun. A half hour later, he squeezed his horse with his legs and rode at a gallop for close to an hour before slowing to a walk to rest the horses. He used his riding time to think about strategy, and he felt his best option might be in watching for the right place to trap his opponents and kill them with the Gatling gun and dynamite if necessary.

He knew if he found the right place for an ambush, they would need twenty or thirty minutes to unpack the gun, haul it up a hill, scatter his men in a circle and wait for the posse to ride into the trap. He felt confident this idea remained their best chance, but wondered how far would they have to ride to find such a spot. The riverbed remained thankfully flat for a quicker ride, but there were too many river birch trees in the way for a commanding attack.

He shook his head to wipe the sweat from his face and charged on. He had given Big Red, the name for the horse carrying the Gatling gun cylinders, an extra portion of grain last night, and time for a good drink before they left. He would need the horse to be sharp and true of step as they did their best to escape.

Windtalker and Kiyo woke the men before Robert could check his watch. He had no idea how they knew the time, but he trusted their instincts, as well as their judgment. They ate quickly and then packed the camp gear away. Meanwhile the scouts went from horse to horse checking the tack and gear, trying to keep them as quiet as possible. They talked with Robert as they warmed up the horses, warning him they must ride fast today, but be prepared to stop quickly.

Windtalker said, "If you were trailing me, I'd be tired of it and lay a trap for you. The trick is finding the right spot."

Robert asked, "How will we know where they'll attempt it?"

Kiyo replied, "We'll know. We just have to remain alert to see the signs. I'll take the lead with Emita. Watch for any change in the way I ride. If I slow, you slow down. If I speed up, you do the same. If I put my hand out to the right, spread out and take cover. If I put palm down, stop immediately and draw your weapons."

Windtalker said, "Yeah, we'll do that, but you better not get shot."

Kiyo grinned. "They can't shoot me. I'm invisible!" He squeezed the ribs of his horse with his thighs and began to gallop, putting space between him and the men. Emita ran out ahead of the group.

Windtalker laughed at Kiyo's response.

Robert asked, "What did he mean by invisible?"

"It was a game we played as children. We'd take turns pretending we were invisible and tapping the other on the head."

"But you could see him."

"We closed our eyes. It taught us to listen and smell, and just use all our senses to the highest power. You would be amazed as to how smart you are without your eyes. Let's ride."

They picked up their speed as well.

Leroy reached a peninsula between two rivers and instantly realized, one way or the other they were going to have to ford the river. He studied the mountains to his right and saw another big valley heading west. He decided to head for it and began looking for a place to cross before they ran out of land. Fifty yards later he led his horse down the bank and splashed into the water. Thankfully, it was only three feet deep, but the horses couldn't run, and it wasn't deep enough for them to swim. He was thankful for the latter, as the packhorses would have sunk to the bottom.

Painfully slow, the entire group began making their way across. Leroy's horse slipped in the mud clay on the far bank and began sliding back into the river. Fearful, the horse suddenly leaped up to dry land. The lunge by the big horse nearly threw Leroy off and into the river. Leroy urged his men on as he began circling on the shore and looking at the terrain. There were no big rocks to hide behind, but lots of fallen logs. Should they attack here, he wondered? He knew the men tracking them would also have to cross the stream, but as the last of his men made it ashore, he decided to ride on because the area might also leave them trapped with no escape.

"Let's go!" he urged as he kicked his horse into a trot and began making his way through the forest towards the valley.

They rode at a trot through the thick foliage before reaching yet another stream. Thankfully, it was not as deep, so they crossed quickly. Leroy decided the stream led off in the direction he wanted to go, so he began following as it slowly turned west.

Kiyo slowed his horse, and Windtalker and the men slowed as well. He had been following the river for several miles, but now he could see the approaching river to his right, and it appeared the two rivers would soon come together. He waved for Windtalker to come forward. Kiyo turned his horse in a slow circle looking at the land, as well as studying the opportunity for a trap.

"There's another river paralleling us over to the right," began Kiyo, "and the land we're on is narrowing."

"So they're coming together. They would have crossed left or right, but which one?"

Kiyo replied, "I doubt they would turn east or even south, as that would eventually lead back to the fort. They arrived in the Glacier Mountains from the east, and I bet they never planned to live here. They are heading west. I think I should cross over now before the land narrows, because if I were them, that's where I would attack. Listen for the sound of the hawk, and if you hear me, take cover quickly."

"I'll lead the men and continue following the track just to be sure they turned west. Be careful."

Kiyo nodded, but Windtalker knew he felt a bit of apprehension and trepidation. Windtalker waved for Robert and the men to move up to him. He explained the situation, told them to spread out to avoid a full frontal assault by the Gatling gun, and to be prepared for anything. Windtalker moved forward, while watching both the ground and the terrain ahead.

Kiyo crossed over the river, but never took his eyes off the shore on the other side. He searched the ground and his eyes went wide after discovering the tracks of a large grizzly and her cub. He slowly moved downstream, now alert for most anything. He kept a hand on his pistol, but as he approached the last fifty yards before the two streams merged, he decided to avoid riding directly into a possible trap by turning west through the trees, and began slowly making his way deeper into the forest. He wound his way gently to his left with the intention of coming up behind the assassins if they were there and setting a trap.

He soon found the next stream and decided not to cross, but continued his turn to where he thought the men might be. His eyes took a quick scan of the ground, and then the terrain, before moving a bit farther down the shore. Thirty yards later, he spotted the tracks of the entire group as they led into the next stream, and he could see where they crossed and turned west. The far bank led to thick foliage, but no rocks or boulders to hide behind.

He turned around and followed the tracks back to the second stream. He gave the sound of the hawk. Minutes later he saw Windtalker coming through the brush. He called to them, "They crossed another stream and appear to be heading west. Come on across." Kiyo turned back west and began trailing the tracks farther into the forest. He found a tributary of the stream coming from the north, and turned to follow it expecting the men to use the stream to cover their tracks. He had gone but fifty yards when Emita abruptly lifted his nose from the tracks to high in the air.

"What is it boy? " whispered Kiyo as he studied the dog's reactions. He could plainly see the tracks of the group, but the dog's attention turned elsewhere. Carefully, Kiyo crept forward with the hair standing and bristling on the back of his neck. He again put his hand to his pistol. Emita took slow steady steps before sniffing the air once more.

Startlingly, the sudden growl off to his right scared him as well as his horse and Emita. He fought to hold the horse still and Emita wisely held his ground, though he began a low growl. Between the foliage, Kiyo moved his horse just a step or two until, through the brush, he saw the big grizzly and her cub feeding on a fish, with blood on their faces, and instantly knew the loud growl to be a defensive one to protect her cub and her food.

Slowly, he turned his horse around, while bravely putting his back to the big bear, then whispered to Emita to follow, and together, they began walking back to the original stream where he met Windtalker coming out of the river.

Windtalker gave him a hard look and said, "You look pale. What's wrong?"

"Emita and I found a very large grizzly bear and her cub. She gave us a warning while protecting her cub and eating a fish. I think we should move this way quickly."

They explained Kiyo's discovery to Robert, so they continued on for a half-mile before stopping to let the horses get some water, while the men took a leak.

Windtalker smiled at him. "I'll take the lead for a while. You did a great job back there. Way to keep your wits about you." He then grinned and elbowed Kiyo playfully. "You looked like you were about to wet your pants."

"You know how I hate grizzlies."

"But we could use another grizzly hide this winter."

Kiyo laughed. "You're crazy. Absolutely crazy."

Windtalker winked at him. "Come on. Let's catch some bad guys and go home. I've missed Molly's fried chicken."

Kiyo grinned and added, "And her pies. Yum, yum."

TWENTY-THREE

Spotted Owl continued to fume over his failure to take the fort. He visited several Blackfeet villages and began talking to the younger warriors, doing his best to convince them to join his efforts to stop the white settlers. He spent a week stirring up the anger amongst the tribes and returned to his village with a new force of eighty warriors.

He sent new scouts to watch the fort, and men to the east to watch for the next train. For now he decided to put on hold an attack on the fort, and step up the attacks on the trains and settler farms, forcing the soldiers to leave the fort to protect these people. In every plan he prepared numerous traps. He started by sending a force of twenty men farther to the east on the plains to daily attack the wagon trains as it continued trying to move west. They would strike, kill a few, and disappear, while remaining ten miles from the mountains. He sent a second force of twenty men about twenty miles from the mountains, and farther than he supposed a military lookout could see.

Each group of warriors was divided into smaller groups. By coordinating their attacks, they waited until the train stretched out for another day's journey and abruptly attacked from the front and rear at the same time. They swarmed through the train and began shooting not only civilians, but also at least one horse amongst the teams pulling the wagon. With a dead horse, the wagons could go nowhere. They couldn't circle so the settlers leaped out and hid under the wagons. This was a distinctive change by Spotted Owl than the usual high value the Indians placed on horses, but an excellent strategy for taking on the settlers in the wagon trains. So far, the white men had failed to overcome this new tactic.

The Indians attacked the stranded wagons swiftly before disappearing. They waited for the folks to come out of hiding and then attacked again. In two hours, they killed fifteen or so settlers. They continued their assaults and by noon, all the whites were dead, their wagons pilfered, and all their guns and ammunition taken. They rounded up their horses, and set the wagons on fire so they could never be used again.

Part of the group returned the spoils of victory to the village, while another group prepared for the next assault. Spotted Owl kept a team of men watching from the mountains with orders to trail any squads that left the fort. So far, the fort didn't know about the slaughter of the stranded wagons. Neither did the next train coming along a few days later.

With his new victories, Spotted Owl again visited Blackfeet villages, boasting of his successes, and recruited more men to fight, as well as women to help keep everyone fed. He organized his camp and men, adding more hunters for food, and spending time training his warriors in the art of gruesome killings. They always savagely tortured the victims even after death by taking scalps, cutting away ears as well as a person's nose. They stripped the men and women, mutilating their private parts, and bodies were trampled by the horses and left rotting in the sun. The vultures were kept busy for days picking the meat clean from so many bodies.

The next train began seeing graves on the left and right of the trail long before they reached the scene of the last major attack. It left the entire train shaken, and they held a meeting to vote on continuing or turning back. They made the fateful decision to continue their dream of moving west. Two days later, a small group of warriors began attacking by finding their scouts that were riding sometimes miles ahead of the train looking for the next campsite. They charged these men from both sides, killing them all, but in this case, they stole their weapons and horses, hid the bodies, and did their best to make it look like the men just disappeared.

A few days later, the small wagon train began crossing the next river. Spotted Owl placed groups on both sides of the river and they waited until the middle of the train reached the river before attacking. They attacked swiftly killing the men as fast they could, killing lead horses for the trains, and sending victims scattering into the thin trees and brush to hide. The frantic horses overturned the wagons, spilling women and children into the river where they drowned. Unable to circle, the settlers that manage to cross were quickly killed. Those in the river, were shot and killed, and only those on the far bank remained alive a while longer before Spotted Owl and his men savagely attacked them as well.

The plains were just as the name implied...plain. You could ride for miles seeing nothing but grasslands until finally a small creek became a stream and the trees actually grew right beside these sources of water, but nowhere else. There were no rocks, boulders, or giant fallen tree trunks to hide behind. Due to the high wind blowing down from the arctic region in the winter, it froze nearly everything, so not a single tree stood more than twenty feet tall.

Feeling confident, the warriors unloaded the wagons, unharnessed the horses, and turned them into packhorses. They loaded food, pots and pans, some clothes, weapons and ammunition, and then set everything left behind on fire. After a group led the supplies and horses on their journey to their hidden village, the remaining warriors turned to searching for those settlers hiding in the brush. They killed them with arrows, affording a slow death. Often mother, daughter and son, died side by side. A few children lived by hiding like a rabbit in a hole or in the tall grass.

As they had done last year, Spotted Owl told his men to begin leaving an older boy alive, putting him on a horse, and sending him east to tell the gruesome story. He thought this old tactic would scare off more trains. It did work to some extent, but like the rest of the tribes, he under underestimated the resolve of the settlers to take the land and the government supporting them. Wagon trains began leaving St. Louis loaded with more weapons, with one comprised of new soldiers.

Meanwhile, Spotted Owl sent a force of fifteen to take out a settler farm located the farthest from the fort. They waited until the scouts reported a large squad headed east to watch for trains. With the group two days away, they attacked the farm in the night, killing all, plundering, and burning everything to the ground. They even trampled the crops and shot their dog. The attack sent a message to the fort that they could not stop Spotted Owl, no matter how hard they tried.

The men trailing the squad of soldiers to the east methodically took out the last man with a single arrow and then they disappeared. A day later, they did it again. They never attacked the soldiers in a battle, but continued these new guerilla style assaults, reducing both the number of soldiers and also the amount of sleep they obtained. With each killing, the warriors smiled at their victory.

Major Bill had no idea if his government was sending reinforcements or not, but he hoped they would not forget his outpost in the middle of Indian territory, and he began to wonder if he would be able to hold on until new men arrived, with a lot more weapons and ammunition. For all of his life, he read his Bible and prayed every night, but his prayers became longer and more fervent since the attack on the fort.

Leroy and his men were tired of everything. They were tired of the trail that, if not steep and rocky, became flat and muddy, with giant, annoying horse and deer flies by day and hungry mosquitoes at night. No one got more than thirty minutes sleep at a time. Without soap and a hot bath, their skin displayed rashes in bad, tender places, bug bites that were bright red and swollen, and finally their food began to run out.

Every day they did the exact same things. They rose early with a cold breakfast of just some jerky, rode all day while straining their necks to look behind them for the posse, and rarely ate anything for lunch. They hadn't enjoyed a hot meal since leaving the settler farm. They each lost ten pounds, as did their horses, and these were pounds they could not afford to shed. Leroy thought he left the mountains behind him, but instead he left only the giant Glacier Mountains, as there were still smaller mountains ahead to find their way to the west. The men groaned at the hills before them, but near the end of the day, they made a discovery.

Leroy rode in front as usual, but after he crossed a small stream, climbed up the muddy bank, and rode about fifty feet farther, he suddenly came out of the brush and onto a small road, a road with wagon tracks. His spirits immediately lifted, knowing they could now move farther and faster. He called to the men. "We made it! We made it! We're out of the wilderness.

We could be in California in a week, and to the ocean in a month. Come on men, let's ride!"

They quickly picked up their pace and rode hard for almost an hour before finding a spot to camp. They slept better that night, not because of a good meal, or less bugs, but because for the first time in weeks, they felt a measure of hope.

Captain Robert remained steadfast to his duty, as he had for his eighteen-year career in the army, but the days on the road hunting for these murderers took quite a toll on him and his men. However, he marveled at the tenacity of Kiyo and Windtalker, as well as Emita. They seemed stronger than his men, on the outside as well as on the inside. He wondered if their life as nomadic Blackfeet children gave them such an amazing drive and easy comfort to the difficulties created by the journey. They adapted to rivers, bugs, bears, and rain without a hint of whining, as did most of his men. He admired them and continued to learn from the scouts every day. He longed to join them on a hunt for deer or elk and they promised to take him after they returned home.

About every third night, after finding a campsite, Kiyo and Windtalker would scout ahead to be sure the bad guys were not close enough to attack. Once they felt secure that the area remained free of bad white men, feisty Indians, or hungry bears, they found a place to lie down and make love before the bugs ate them alive. They kissed passionately, groping and feeling, and sometimes mounting. In less than an hour, they did their best to make up for missing their nightly fun in the cabin.

The scouts wished they knew the territory so they could take a shortcut and get ahead of the men they tracked, but they were gaining on them. They expected to overtake them tomorrow, but they were wrong. After reaching the road, they inspected the horse dung, and knew the men had a good jump on them and wondered if their horses would hold out.

They waited for Robert to catch up, and then they pointed west and said they were probably eight miles ahead of them now that their pace could be hastened. Robert thought hard, as turning left would take them home, but turning right would take them farther from the fort. However, thanks to Windtalker and Kiyo, they were in better shape than the men they hunted. Every night the scouts would shoot a rabbit or two. Twice they brought down a deer and the men devoured the food. They brought in piles of wild berries and dug roots and made root bread. They were resourceful and every man respected them immensely.

Robert gathered up a second wind and said loudly, "Let's ride. I want to catch these murderers in the next few days. We'll push harder than ever before."

Windtalker thought for a second. "I think you can track them as well as we can on the road. Would you feel comfortable with Kiyo and I riding faster than you can with the packhorses, and doing all we can to catch up and begin attacking Indian style, taking out a man or horse at a time? This would force them to slow down to defend themselves."

Robert grinned. "In favor of such action? Are you crazy? I'm thrilled with the plan. Go for it, but please be careful. They wouldn't hesitate to kill you, so remain alert and kill them at the first opportunity. Ride like wind!" he yelled.

Kiyo, Windtalker, and Emita took off at full gallop for close to an hour, then walked to rest the horses and their dog, and then resumed galloping as they continued. During the slower walks, they checked the horse dung repeatedly, and near the end of the day, they saw steam rise off a new pile. They were close.

They left the road, found a good campsite with fresh water, killed a rabbit, ate, and though they made out from time to time, they took turns standing watch.

TWENTY-FOUR

Spotted Owl's men decimated another settler farm creating the same vicious mayhem as before by killing a family of six, taking food and livestock, and burning the cabin and barn to the ground. This frustrated Major Bill immensely because his orders called for him to protect the settlers. He studied the map he drew last summer of the acreage in the valley surrounding the fort, and with the help of a sergeant, he marked all the settler farms on the map. They wrote the family names by their location markers, and then marked the ones burned by the Indians and instantly discovered that the warrior chief was far smarter than Bill anticipated. They were attacking the farms farthest from the fort, so reinforcements could not reach them in time. They also attacked during the night to protect them from discovery, as the soldiers rarely left the fort after dark. Even if he could justify giving chase the following morning by attacking after dark, they afforded themselves at least an eight to ten hour head start. He sighed heavily after realizing without Windtalker and Kiyo, tracking these murderers into the northern mountains would be suicidal. He knew that neither he nor his men possessed the tracking skills to find these warriors, and certainly not the real fighting skills to take on an unknown possible large force.

He continued to study his map and recalled something the scouts told him last year. They said the fort remained under the watch of Spotted Owl's scouts, and they were most likely located across from the fort on a small mountain. He decided an enemy without eyes would be far less successful.

He began to devise a plan or a strategy to outsmart Spotted Owl. It began with a force of sixteen men leaving the fort on a typical run to the plains to watch for wagon trains. They would follow the road south until it turned west around the southernmost point of the Glacier Mountains, and then head east to the plains. He told them after they rounded the small mountain across from the fort they were to allow eight of his men to break off from the squad to the left of the road, and work their way to the back of the mountain where he thought the scouts might be. He suggested their approach and technique for the possible attack. The soldiers did as told and when they reached the mountain, they tied off their horses, ratcheted their rifles, and began carefully sneaking up the back of the mountain.

They took their time, spreading in a wide line, moving carefully to avoid detection, and within the hour, they found pony tracks leading upwards toward the ridge of the hill. They didn't follow the trail, but stayed far left and right of it while continuing to climb as the major instructed.

At the top, they spotted two horses. They expected their horses to pick up their scent, but the major began phase two of his plan by sending most of the men out and performing maneuvers as if in training for a big event. This kept the attention of the scouts focused on the fort, while trying to figure out what they were doing. It also created some additional noise.

Cautiously, and very slowly, two of the soldiers made their way around the horses and kept climbing until they saw the two scouts sitting on a rock with a perfect view of the fort and the grounds below. They were chatting back and forth with no thought of discovery. The two soldiers aimed their already cocked rifles and shot them in the back simultaneously.

They listened to see if anyone else might be on the mountain, but finding only the two horses and two men, this led them to believe they were alone. Following the example of Windtalker and Kiyo, they carefully removed the bodies, carrying them to the back of the mountain, but mindful to stay off the horse trail as instructed by the major, thus avoiding leaving tracks or blood droplets. Another soldier released the horses and scattered them. One soldier doubled with another so they could load both bodies on his horse. They took the bodies to a ravine about a mile away and dumped them.

They returned to the fort reporting their success to the major. For the first time, Bill felt a moment of satisfaction, but he wasted no time in preparing for the next step. With no Indians watching his fort, he sent squads of four men to the settler farms farthest from the fort. Their orders were to hide their horses in the barn, as well as themselves, and to remain there throughout the day. They took plenty of supplies, were not allowed to build a fire, or exit to take a leak. He warned that if the settlers brought them anything, be it water or food, they were to deliver it toting it in a bucket so it would appear they were just doing their chores. At night, they were to be on high alert, so they slept during the day.

He told them the Indians would most likely attack after dark and take on the cabin first. The families were told to act as normal as possible. They were well armed and ready. Every bucket remained filled with water in case of flaming arrows.

Daily, the major sent the same squad of eight on a fake mission to the east, but they followed the same drill as they looked for new scouts. It was a few days later before the next team appeared.

Spotted Owl could make no sense for his missing reports from the scouts watching the fort, but he had no time to worry about it. Scouts to the east reported the dust of a new train could be seen. He began making preparations to use the same strategy of attack and run on the train, while the largest group of warriors prepared to ambush and annihilate the entire train. Before making his final decisions, he studied the sand drawing of the fort and settler farms in his tipi, then sent ten men to raid again that night.

Major Bill gave simple orders to his soldiers hiding at the settler farms. They should kill without mercy any and all Indians attacking the farms. He made sure they understood not one should live or escape. They were to saddle their horses before dark, so if forced to give chase they could.

That night, sergeant Frank Travis and his men prepared their horses as ordered, ate a cold supper, and he assigned two of his men to watch out the back of the barn, while he and another soldier focused their attention on the front of the cabin through an open hay loft door, but they remained out of sight in the shadows behind bales of a hay at all times.

They waited several hours before a private in the rear whispered, "I see eight, no, make that ten Indians on horseback approaching the farm."

Frank whispered his reply, "Okay, men. Ratchet your rifles so you're ready to fire. Remember, no one escapes, so take out the men away from the cabin first. Let them begin their attack so they'll be looking only at the cabin, and then we'll open fire. I'll fire first. If they don't come in the barn from the rear, you men move to the big front doors and prepare to fire. Quiet. No more talking."

The soldiers were nervous, but so was the family acting as the unfortunate bait. The father and his eldest son kept their guns ready and lying on the table. Everyone older than twelve had a pistol.

When the Indians reached fifty yards, they sat quiet for a long while. The sergeant knew they were listening and being cautious, but hearing nothing, they suddenly let out a whoop, kicked the ribs of their horses, and galloped into the farmyard.

The sergeant gulped knowing they were four to their ten, but he knew the soldiers had fire power and surprise on their side. He waited until they were all in front of the cabin. Just as the leader leaped off his horse to run to the door, the sergeant fired, killing the man to the rear as he was dismounting. His men opened fire as well, killing three more. The surprised Indians turned towards the barn as the soldiers shot the next four. The cabin door opened and the father shot the leader in the face nearly taking his head off, and his son shot the stunned warrior behind him in the chest.

In less than a minute, they were all dead. The nervous ponies scattered for a minute or two before slowly returning. The farmer told his wife to keep the younger kids inside. The sergeant and his men cautiously came out of the barn, but failing to see any signs of other Indians, they gathered the ponies and tied the bodies on top as the major instructed. Then they brought out their own horses and began leading the ponies with the bodies away. The sergeant told the father they would be back soon.

Under orders from the major, they dropped the bodies in a ravine they chose on the way to the farm, then scattered the ponies, and rode hard to the fort. After reporting the news to the excited major, they gathered supplies and ammunition, and returned to the farm while still under the cover of darkness.

Spotted Owl left early with his men the following morning with no thoughts about the missing attack squad. He did order another ten men to investigate the farm, and then he left after pumping his warriors up with a fiery speech about the white men taking their homelands. They were a force of sixty as they left the village heading southeast.

When they reached the plains, one of the hidden army scouts saw them from a ridge in the Glacier Mountains, so he sent his partner to the fort with great haste. A single Indian watching the army scouts gave chase, but the army rider grew up in Kentucky as the son of a horse breeder. He rode faster than the Indian could catch him and dodged several arrows, but as he rounded a bend, he jerked his horse off the road, pulled his rifle up, and as the Indian rounded the bend, he shot him in the face, knocking him from his horse.

He wasted no time with the body, but continued his gallop to warn the major of the large group heading east. Major Bill reacted by sending a force of thirty men at full speed to the east after confirming from an earlier patrol there were no scouts on the mountain to see them leave.

The alerting scout returned to his post after stopping to hide the body that he shot and scattered the horse as instructed.

The wagon train topped a hill and began crossing the valley. Lying on their stomachs, the Indian's attack and pester squad studied the train. At sixty wagons, it easily became the largest to cross the plains, and most certainly the largest any of the warriors had ever seen. Their immediate concern was that in front of this group road a squad of ten soldiers and three scouts. This caused some conversation amongst them. They decided a daytime attack would be suicidal. They would attack under the cover of darkness and began making their plans. They failed to note that ten of the wagons placed in the middle of the long line of sixty were pulling the leads of two riderless army horses.

This new tactic for protecting the wagon trains began with a letter and report from Major Bill the previous fall, but also from an experienced early frontier explorer in the general's employ as an adviser. The plan remained simple. A show of force might deter attack, but an equally hidden force might assure victory in killing as many Indian warriors as possible.

The scouts rode out ahead and soon picked up the tracks of the Indians, but acted like they didn't see them. An hour later, they reported their findings, alerting all they were being watched. Before the train reached the next slight hill, a single scout would ride out and stand watch on the hill. When the soldiers took his place, they rode on to the next one preventing any frontal surprise attacks. This leapfrog strategy prevented a large force from suddenly appearing out of nowhere.

At the rear of the train rode ten settlers who were armed and watchful for a possible rear attack. With its military escort, the general planned for this wagon train to make it to the west safely. Their orders were simply to stop the Indian attacks by killing any attempts to harm the settlers. After the completion of their mission, they were to join the ranks of Fort Green until further notice.

After dark, the Indians crept closer to the wagon train. From the glow of the firelight, they discovered a new strategy by the white men. Instead of a big circle of sixty wagons, they somehow created a column of two and together they circled, creating both an inner and outer circle. The tighter double walled group would make it tough for an effective attack. The inner ring staggered the outer one, thus eliminating any opportunity for a pony to leap through the rings to the center of the camp. It also provided protection from the rear should there be a breech. No one slept in the outer wagons. In fact, only the women and children and half the men and soldiers slept. Everybody else remained on four-hour watches every night no matter what. The soldiers dug two latrines between the rows of wagons near the rear, one for men and the other for women and children, and hung blankets for privacy. They didn't want anyone in the woods at night. So far on their journey from Saint Louis, not one person died from an arrow as result of the new security techniques.

Feeling far superior to the wimpy whites, the warriors threw caution aside, flung themselves onto the backs of their ponies, gave a yelp to their companions, and rode hard to the wagons. As they drew back their bows for what they thought would be a surprise vicious attack, they were met with a large volley of gunfire killing them all instantly. Not a single arrow made it to the side of a wagon and all inside remained safe.

Satisfied, they were dead, the soldiers pulled the bodies to a grove of trees, scattered their horses, and remained on the guard for the rest of the night. The wagon train left at dawn, but with a heighten sense of alertness.

Leroy groaned from the sore muscles from the fast ride on the road west. As he woke his men, he heard their whimpers, moans, and grumbling as well, but with a stern look from Leroy, they managed to get out of their warm bedrolls. A half hour later, they were on the road again.

An hour later, Windtalker put his hand above the ashes of Leroy's cook fire that they allowed to burn itself out in the night. It was still warm. He relayed the news and saddled up. "Let's ride. They are close."

They rode hard for an hour, walked the horses to rest, and then rode again. By midday, they caught sight of the last packhorse.

Kiyo asked, "What should we do? We might can get closer before discovery or there could be men with rifles waiting over the next hill."

Windtalker said, "I think if they approach a hill, then we should take out a man or two or even a horse with the Sharps buffalo gun. That'll force them to gallop away. If not, then once they make camp, we should fire from various positions, and scatter their horses where possible. Come on, let's ride!"

They galloped earnestly having now seen the men they tracked for the first time in weeks. They closed to just a half mile when they reached a down slope and for just a moment they saw the string of men and packhorses ahead. Beyond them they saw a river.

Kiyo looked up to the sky. "Just a few hours of daylight left."

"If they try to cross before dark, we might take out one or two in the river."

They crept up to the slight ridge on foot and watched the rough riders disappear into a stand of trees alongside the road that continued a downward direction to the river. Anticipating an ambush, the scouts returned to their horses. They left the road veering north before making their way through the trees until they reached the water, and began moving south, while carefully staying out of sight in the sparse forest.

TWENTY-FIVE

Leroy made it across the stream, as did the second man pulling the Gatling gun. Three more went in the river pulling packhorses, and two more men were about to enter the water.

Windtalker spotted them at just a hundred and fifty yards. He gave Kiyo the reins to his horse, leaped off, and pulled out the Sharps rifle from the leather scabbard. He then ran to a rock, went down on his belly, inserted a shell, and began making adjustments to his ladder sight. Once satisfied with the range adjustment, he took aim at the last of the three men in the water.

Boom!

The shot instantly dug through the man's right arm, and then powered straight through his chest, heart and exited out the left side. He died on impact, and began falling from his horse, as the sound of the shot finally reached the ears of thieves. They all turned to the north as Windtalker took a second sighting. The other two men in the river hustled up the bank, as the last two entered the stream. Windtalker took out the first one. The packhorses pulled by the victim rapidly scattered. Leroy and his men hustled from the open riverbed and into the trees.

The lone remaining rider got off his horse and walked it across while remaining on the southern side. The act by the man impressed the scouts. Windtalker could have shot the horse, but decided to wait. The scouts cautiously crossed the river one at a time, while the other held a rifle in defense. Leroy wisely galloped away.

The sun seemed to set faster, as thunderstorms rolled in, covering the rising moon. The valley ahead became dark, slowing Leroy, as well as Windtalker and Kiyo.

Captain Robert heard the shots and did his best to hurry his men along. They found the dead men caught against a rock down stream, while their horses remained grazing near by. His men shortened the reins of the horses, but did not add them to their horse's leads. They could follow or graze as they wished. They were forced to make camp on the other side as they could see the storm rolling in. He knew they were about to get wet, so he wanted to try and feed his men and horses before the downpour began. They made a fire, cooked more beans and ate quickly. They also fed and watered the horses so they would be ready to ride at dawn. He posted sentries as usual.

When he found a grove of trees, Leroy decided to stay for the night, as they couldn't see, and he didn't want to chance breaking the legs of his remaining horses. The men ate what they could, and then Leroy scattered the men ten feet apart, and out of sight in the ravine.

Windtalker, Kiyo, and Emita crept along cautiously. They first noticed the stand of trees in a flash of lightning. They talked it over and decided if they were Leroy, that's where they would stop to rest and perhaps attack. They left the road to the north once more where they noted more trees. They memorized the nearby terrain with each bolt of lightning and then proceeded ahead. Emita could see better than they could, so they followed his white tail when possible.

They reached the trees about two hundred yards north of the road and decided to wait out the storm there. They watered their horses in the creek, fed them grain from a saddlebag and hobbled them. They fed Emita some jerky and they ate the same along with freshwater from their canteens. They knew they were about to get wet, so they put on their jackets, pulled the strings on their hats to keep them from becoming lost in the wind, and waited.

Twenty minutes later, the skies finally let loose, but not with the anticipated rain, but abruptly they were pelted with hailstones of various sizes. They knew since childhood the ice tasted good, so they ate some, but their horses were frightened, so they ran to calm them down. Losing a horse in a storm might be fatal for the rider, as it was a long walk to anywhere and no way to run should an enemy come after you on horseback.

Leroy could not remember being so miserable. He broke into a sweat on the long gallop away from the shooters, but now that the hail pelted their heads, followed by a huge downpour and some wind, he began shivering while feeling the cold all the way to his bones. A packhorse broke free from the lead line and they could not find him in the rain. They were afraid to go too far. Leroy hoped for the moon to rise after the storm passed so they could escape in the night.

Just a rifle shot away from the gang, the men hoped the rain stopped soon, too. If the clouds passed and the moon returned, they might be able to shoot another man or two before they could ride again. They had no doubt the men would ride again if the moonlight helped them see the road.

Captain Robert and his men didn't make it to the trees. They hunkered down between their horses on the open plains, and did their best to keep the animals calm. They chewed jerky when they could, fed grain to the horses, and waited.

About three in the morning, the rains finally stopped, but the moon remained covered by the clouds. Frustrated, Leroy wanted to leave, but he could not even see the road. He flinched at every shadow made by the trees from the distant bolts of lightning streaking across the eastern sky.

Kiyo and Windtalker removed the hobbles on their horses,

148

anticipating the clouds would soon move away to the east. Suddenly, Emita barked loudly while looking north at the creek. The scouts turned their heads trying to pick up what the dog heard. They knew the bad men were to the south, at least they hoped, but what could be from the north? They silently wondered if warriors were about.

At the first sound of water, Kiyo shrieked. "Flood!"

The scouts swung up in the saddle, turned east, and galloped out of the woods to higher ground with Emita chasing them. Mere seconds later, a wall of water over ten feet high slammed through their temporary camp, destroying everything in its path. The surging flash flood moved mud, sticks, logs, and rocks over and over in tumbling chaotic piles, while gaining more strength and power every ten yards. There was nothing in the ravine to slow down the rapidly growing wall of water.

Kiyo's voice carried in the wind. Leroy stood up and heard the water. He, too, yelled at his men, so they darted across the creek to the other side, and up a hill, but two of the packhorses and another man didn't make it, and instantly they were swept away in the flood. The legs of the horses were broken, causing loud shrieks from the animals, and the man's head cracked as it slammed into a hidden underwater rock. He slipped beneath the water and drowned.

The scouts stood in their saddles on the eastern side just as the moon began peeking through. They saw Leroy and his men on the other side just as they disappeared over the hill out of sight. The scouts waited an hour for the rainwater to retreat. Captain Robert and his men caught up with them, so they brought him up to date. At sunlight, they shot the wounded horses and found the dead man. Robert sent two soldiers to bury him.

Kiyo and Windtalker crossed the stream and began their chase once more. There were only six men left and they knew the thieves were exhausted, dirty, and most likely hungry. They were also fearful and the scouts would catch them soon enough.

Spotted Owl arrived at the plains and immediately sent scouts out in various directions to find his men. Meanwhile, he led a force of sixty seasoned warriors as they moved east in anticipation of intersecting the large wagon train. They rode for several hours, but as his scouts returned, not one could find the previous attack squad. Greatly puzzled and somewhat angry at the squad's poor performance, he worried little and sent the scouts out to locate the wagons. They returned within the hour, reporting the wagon train only a few miles to the east.

Spotted Owl rode out with some of his leaders and one of his scouts to see this big train. They left their horses on the backside of a hill, walked up slowly, and finally crawled to the ridge to avoid detection. The sheer size of

TJ Johnson

the large wagon train pissed him off. He felt he had done enough already to discourage more settlers from coming, but even if he killed every white person on the wagon trains, they were still sending more. He couldn't fathom how many white people were still waiting to leave the Mississippi River and head east. Perhaps the young surviving white boys he sent east weren't making it, he thought. He suspected that leaving only one alive might not be enough. This time he would leave five alive, but first they would be forced to watch the most horrible torture he could think of. He wanted the killings to be gruesome and sickening for the witnesses to describe. Spotted Owl planned to begin hanging bodies from the trees as a warning to any more wagon trains.

He studied the group of scouts and soldiers up front. He decided to hide twenty men on the ground as the terrain made it's way around a steep hill and towards a stream. He would divide the rest of his force in half and would place them on hills overlooking the left and right of the train. He gave orders to charge hard and fast. He told the men to shoot the lead horses to prevent the wagons from circling.

The teams of warriors divided and carefully made their way to their attack positions. The first group left their horses in a stand of trees near the creek. The men scattered, with some hiding behind rocks and logs, and others almost buried themselves in brush, as they began their long wait. Lying in the dirt, with the sun beating down on them, deer flies buzzed around their ears, and ants began crawling on their arms and legs, but nothing made the warriors waver from having the chance to make the first kill.

They could hear and feel the wagons long before they arrived. The ground appeared to shake, but the noise they produced was unlike anything they had ever heard. When their tribes moved, the travois rarely made a sound unless the poles were pulled across stretches of solid rock, but nothing of theirs ever clinked and jingled as they moved. Every rider, horse, and wagon made noise. They could see the scouts and soldiers in the lead and Spotted Owl expected his warriors to kill every one of them quickly.

The wagon train remained on high alert after the previous attack and every soul kept their guns handy. The men up front rode with rifles lying across their saddles that were already cocked and ready to fire. The men hidden in the wagons were ready as well. The wagon drivers kept a rifle at their side and many wives kept a pistol handy. The children were trained to remain flat on the wagon floor if the Indians attacked. The wagon master felt they were as prepared as possible, but he said his prayers and asked others to do the same as well.

As the scouts reached the top of the hill, a couple of their horses picked up the scent of the Indians and snorted. The scouts sighed and the hair stood up on their necks. The scouts scanned the horizon and just as they picked up signs of the Indians, the attack began.

A warrior fired an arrow from his hiding spot and let out a loud

150

whoop as he shot the lead scout in the chest. Suddenly, all of the hidden warriors were attacking, first by arrows and then by charging the group. The white men managed to kill a few warriors, but the ambush killed most of them before they could turn and run.

Immediately, after hearing yelps of the Indians, the wagons began circling. Spotted Owl let out a big whoop and the left and right flanks of his warriors began galloping in. Pandemonium erupted as they shot some of the horses, making it difficult for them to get a full circle, but the passengers ran to the center as rehearsed. As the warriors reached the train, they managed to kill or wound at least twenty people, but suddenly, the settlers opened up with a huge barrage of rifle fire. The hidden soldiers accompanied them, and together, they killed at least thirty warriors, or nearly half of Spotted Owl's men.

Some of the Indians broke through the circle and managed to shoot a few women and children before a soldier shot them down. Seeing the tide turning, Spotted Owl charged in with the rest of his men. On the rear section, they managed to overwhelm the settlers and soldiers, killing most of them.

With the circle defense compromised, the settlers hid behind anything they could find between the wagons as they fired at the circling Indians attacking from the rear.

Spotted Owl could taste victory and urged his men on. Half the hidden soldiers were dead, scalps were taken, settlers were shot, but the setters continued to fire their rifles, killing a warrior with about every third shot.

Suddenly, they heard the sound of a bugle coming from a hill to the west. The remaining soldiers recognized the sound of the bugle and began grinning, as they knew the horn announced the charging cavalry coming to their rescue.

Spotted Owl looked up and saw the thirty men charging towards them at full speed. He called to his men to charge in return.

With attention of the Indians turned to the cavalry, the settlers managed to kill a few more of Spotted Owl's men. The cavalry pulled up their rifles and began firing as they advanced on their horses. They shot and killed the first ten warriors, but in seconds, they were all intertwined like a battle in Roman times. The settlers fired at the warriors when they could get a clear shot.

The soldiers fought by first shooting, then swinging their rifles. Some were pulled off their mounts and knifed by Indians, but they fought with great tenacity. Several of the settlers left their hiding places and ran to the battle to pick off the Indians.

Spotted Owl suddenly realized they were outnumbered and outgunned. In a matter of minutes, there were only ten warriors left standing. He called to them and they galloped to the north. The cavalry gave chase, firing their rifles at the rear line of warriors, killing horses and men when they could, but soon the Indians were gone.

The cavalry horses were exhausted after riding hard all the way from the fort, and then galloping the last couple of miles on the plains to save the settlers. They had little strength left for a long chase, so reluctantly the men turned them back in a slow trot.

Though in tears from the loss of so many, the remaining settlers gave the soldiers a hearty cheer. The wounded were quickly attended to, while the remaining settlers began swapping parts and pieces from a broken wagon to fix another, and two hours later, they were back on the trail again. They left behind the quickly dug graves of the dead, as the soldiers urged them to move along, fearing Indian reprisals. Each person handled their grief in their own way as the wagons rolled west. They would have to camp at least once more before they could reach the fort.

Wisely, the lieutenant in charge kept his men scouting out the area as they moved along, while searching for any signs of any future attacks.

Spotted Owl seethed with anger all the way back to his village. He heard grumblings amongst his men, so he kept them filled with hatred and promises of bigger battles yet to be won.

TWENTY-SIX

It took Windtalker and Kiyo most of the day to catch up to Leroy and his gang. His men were hungry, his animals exhausted, and he knew he would soon have to make a stand. He desperately wanted to kill the posse and take all of their supplies, and for hours his mind raced for ways to accomplish this imposing task. With his eyes weary from trail dust and fatigue, he continually searched the terrain for possible spots for an ambush, but the plains in this area consisted of one easy rolling grassy area after the other, like small waves on a lake, affording little high ground to take the advantage and bushwhack the determined posse.

At the top of yet another knoll, he stopped and lifted his well worn field glasses to his eyes and spotted only the two men trailing them, but after watching a bit longer, he noticed behind the apparent scouts was another group of soldiers hot on their trail. He sighed greatly because taking out one group in their miserable condition would be hard enough, but ambushing two groups remained impossible, unless, he thought, he could set up the Gatling gun after they killed the two outriders, and use the big gun for a final fight with the soldiers. He rode on, thinking while searching for the right terrain to make a stand.

Late in the afternoon, the scouts were but two hundred yards behind the men. Windtalker called to Kiyo, "I think at the next hill, I should take out another man or two with the Sharps."

"I think not," replied Kiyo.

Puzzled, Windtalker asked, "And why not?"

Kiyo grinned. "Because it is my turn. I am as good a shot as you are."

Windtalker laughed. "Indeed you are. Okay, at the next hill, be ready as we may only have a few seconds for a shot or two."

Their horses finally reached the hill before them so they galloped up quickly to the crest. Kiyo dismounted and handed the reins of his horse to Windtalker. He pulled out the Sharps, inserted a cartridge, and then spun around to find his target.

The last man of Leroy's group struggled to pull the exhausted packhorses. Kiyo sighted quickly, while mentally estimating the rider's forward movement, and the time of the bullet to reach the target. He aimed just a little ahead of his target and pulled the trigger.

Boom! Smack!

Leroy heard the thud and turned as the sound of the shell reached his ears. The chest of the man in the rear exploded outward and towards the next man who turned to see what was going on. The dead man fell from his horse.

153

The next man grabbed the reins of his horse to lead them, but the frightened packhorses gathered on each side of him preventing a quick escape. Just as he cleared the animals, he heard a thud, felt the impact, and his ears heard the boom. His chest wall exploded, blowing him off his horse. He was dead as he hit the ground. The terrified horses reared and began circling.

"Ride quick men! Ride now!" Leroy dug in his heels to quickly catch up with his men.

"Good shots!" exclaimed Windtalker. "That's two more. Only four left and we can go home."

Kiyo stuffed the still smoking gun in the scabbard and climbed aboard his horse. With a big grin he said, "Let's ride. There's a little daylight left. We might be able to get another one."

Leroy's men galloped as hard as they dared, but their horses were spent and stumbling. He came upon a ravine, crossed over, allowed the horses a much-needed drink, and then made his way over to the opposite bank.

This will have to do, he thought. They found a place to tie off their horses, grabbed their rifles and ran back to the top of the ravine. Leroy scattered his men along the edge and told them to wait until he fired. He also told them to remain hidden.

Kiyo called, "I'll shoot again."

Windtalker laughed. "To hell you say. It's my turn."

"We'll see," teased Kiyo.

They rode on for a mile and began to note the shorter distance between the horse tracks. They knew the horses belonging to the men they chased were exhausted. As they topped a hill, they noted the gully ahead.

Windtalker pulled up and stopped. "Whoa."

Kiyo asked, "What's wrong?"

"I don't see them in the distance."

"Maybe they're galloping away."

Windtalker said, "I think their horses are spent. The gulch would make a good trap. We must proceed with caution."

They each pulled a pistol and trotted forward, searching the terrain. At fifty yards, Kiyo noted slight movement behind a bush. He whispered to Windtalker. "They're here. Let's…"

Boom!

Before Kiyo could tell Windtalker to gallop away, Leroy fired his rifle, catching Kiyo slightly in the outer part of his left arm, but the shock of it sent him flying to the ground. Windtalker leaped off his horse and began pulling their horses down into the ditch as more shots hit the ground all around them.

Windtalker ran to him. "Are you okay?"

154

Kiyo cursed. "Yeah. Just barely nicked me. Give me a piece of cloth to tie it off."

Windtalker quickly made a bandage and wrapped it around Kiyo's arm and tied it. He then ran to their horses while dodging some bullets, and grabbed the Sharps and the Winchester. The horses were safe behind a hill, though Leroy was desperately trying to kill them or their horses.

"Can you handle the Sharps?"

Kiyo thought for a second. "No, it's too heavy. You use it and give me the Winchester. We should scatter out. I'll keep them busy from the front while you move around to their side."

"How about I get up that little hill and see if I can get a shot at them?"

"Okay, but be careful."

Windtalker took off on a run back across the road, bringing about a few more shots and disappeared in the brush on the other side. Kiyo watched where the shots were coming from and fired. He caught one of the soldiers in the arm. When the man twisted from the impact of the shot, Windtalker caught him in the back of the head with the Sharps.

Windtalker said, "Three to go."

Leroy cursed. He fired his rifle in the direction of Windtalker, but wisely, the Indian had taken his shot and then moved again, working his way up the hill. Kiyo fired at Leroy.

Captain Robert heard the gunshots and called for his men to gallop. They were only two miles away and anxious to end this hunt as well. Their horses were also tired, but he felt they could make up the distance in a few minutes as he urged his men on.

Leroy ran to his saddlebag and retrieved a stick of dynamite and a fuse, as well as a box of rifle shells, and ran back to the gully. He prepared the dynamite, but with no boulders to topple, he did not yet have a means of escape in mind. He fired at Kiyo's position, only to realize that while he fetched the dynamite, the wounded boy smartly moved to a new hiding spot. He soon found out where.

Ping!

Leroy's hat sailed into the air. Though wounded, Kiyo managed to shoot it right off his head. He would later admit aiming at the man's skull, not his hat, but grinned just the same. He moved again.

Windtalker managed to flank the man on the left and watched him as he fired at Kiyo. Windtalker took aim, waiting for the man to show himself just enough. Kiyo ran to the next tree as all three men began firing at him. The man that Windtalker was sighting turned his body against a tree. Windtalker knew he could wound him, but instead he sighted him carefully and lined up his shot with a hole in the dead tree and pulled the trigger.

Boom!

The powerful shell raced across the ravine, hit the tree right in the hole, and plowed through the tree, hitting the man dead center in the side of his head. The man's limp body slammed to the ground, and slid down the embankment, kicking up a bit of dust as it settled to the bottom. There were now just two to go.

Leroy cursed again, but the other man panicked and began yelling. "We give up. Don't shoot. You can take us prisoner."

Windtalker laughed and replied loudly, "Indian's don't take prisoners."

The scared man's face puzzled as he repeated, "Indians?"

Kiyo called out, "You can give up, but we'll carve your skin off your bones while you're still alive. We'll gut your intestines to the ground. You'll die a horrible death!"

The frightened man began firing wildly at Windtalker, and then twice at Kiyo. Kiyo got him in his sights and when the man turned to fire once more at Windtalker, he took the shot.

Boom!

He caught the man in the right upper shoulder, knocking his rifle to the ground. The pain seared through the man's body. In shock, he unknowingly stood up. Windtalker shot him dead in the heart and he fell to the ground with a hard thud.

Windtalker said, "One to go."

Windtalker and Kiyo turned their attention to where they last saw Leroy, but the man didn't fire at them. Kiyo reached the edge of the ravine, but he knew he couldn't cross without being in the open. He waited for Windtalker to force the man out.

Windtalker moved around to the rear. He found their horses and began moving back to the gulch on the far side, hoping to come up behind the man, but as soon as he got there, he could not find him. Just as he started to call out...

Boom!

Leroy lit the dynamite, held it until the fuse burned down a bit, and then threw it at the last second across the gully at Kiyo. Amazingly, Leroy darted across the ravine at the very moment the dynamite blew up, knocking Kiyo backwards, covering him in dirt, stunning him while knocking the breath out of him, but otherwise not hurting him. Leroy sprinted to him and kicked the boy's rifle away, and put his pistol to Kiyo's head and lifted him up.

"Now call off your friend or you're dead," he demanded as he poked Kiyo's head with the tip of his gun. "Do it now!"

Kiyo spoke in Blackfeet to Windtalker. Windtalker heard him as he ran to the gully, but remained hidden by a bush. He pushed the barrel of the

Sharps through the bush and took aim.

Leroy tapped Kiyo's head with his pistol once more. "Tell him, I'll shoot you right now if he doesn't give up."

Using his Blackfeet language, Kiyo bravely told Windtalker the man smelled really bad and should be put out of his misery. Finally, he told Windtalker to take the shot.

Leroy cocked the pistol. Windtalker heard it. Kiyo counted to three in his language and dropped limp to the ground. Leroy struggled to hang on to him and hesitated just a slight second.

Boom!

Windtalker's shot took Leroy's head clean off. It entered the skull near the eye with such an amazing force and an impact strong enough to pull down a huge buffalo. In a flash of a second, the man's head went to the right and the body fell limp to the ground.

Windtalker asked, "Are you all right?"

Kiyo stood up and grinned. "I about wet my pants. What the hell took you so long?"

"I had to take a piss," he lied. "That's all of them. Come help me gather the horses."

"You're forgetting my arm."

"Okay, you sissy. Stay there and watch the dead. I'll be there in a minute."

Captain Robert rode up with his men. "Are there any left?"

Kiyo grinned. "Nope, that one there was the leader and the last of them. I got nicked, but I'll live. Windtalker is gathering their horses. Can we go home now?"

Captain Robert grinned and laughed. "Yes, we can. Thanks to the two of you."

Windtalker led the horses across the ravine and up to the captain. Robert quickly undid the tarp on the big horse and inspected the Gatling gun. "This might come in handy with our battles with the Indians." He put the cover back on. "You have earned some big cash rewards, but I'll also give you two horses." He picked out what he thought were the best saddled horses. One of them was Leroy's. "These two horses are yours. Thank you for a job well done."

Windtalker said, "Thanks and the gift is much appreciated. Since skinny boy is wounded and most likely whimpering, and it is only a few hours until dark, I suggest we camp here. There is water in the bottom of the gulch. Their horses are exhausted and need to be fed."

"I agree," replied Robert as he spoke a few orders to his men to set up camp. "How far to home do you reckon?"

Windtalker studied the mountains back to the east. "Probably five to seven days. We've never been this far west, but we should make good time on the road."

"Very well. Let's get a hot meal going."

"I'll go see if I can kill us a few rabbits."

Kiyo grinned. "Don't use that Sharps or there won't be any meat left to eat! That shell blew this man's head off."

TWENTY-SEVEN

The next afternoon, the wagon train rolled into the area in front of the fort and for the first time in weeks, the survivors felt safe and secure. They didn't know the fort endured a big attack by the Indians and none of the soldiers told them. The burned out perimeter posts were already replaced, and the scorched roofs were repaired with new cedar shakes. Major Bill gave each a hearty handshake while expressing sorrow for their losses. He assured the wagon master a squad of his men would escort them to the western plains and out of the mountains so they could continue their journey. He didn't encourage anyone to stay in his community. He felt it too dangerous for new settlers until they could conquer the Indians for, hopefully, the last time. His men started fixing their wagons, shoeing their horses, and his doctor assisted the wagon train's doctor in a host of maladies, including a woman about to give birth. They planned a big dinner together inside the fort, but to be safe, Major Bill kept forty men stationed a hundred feet outside the wagon train circle.

Though anxious to return to their home, Windtalker and Kiyo galloped for an hour, and then walked the horses for thirty minutes before galloping again. Emita also knew they were heading home as he wagged his tail furiously and took off for another run. The Indians knew the captured horses were still in bad shape, so the animals were given double portions of grain to build up their strength, and they lightened their load of the gear they had been hauling. The Indians just abandoned the junk at the ravine because they valued a good horse far more. The fellows brushed their new horses with great care while speaking to them, and saddled each one carefully before the day's journey.

They camped again for two more nights before finally arriving to the piedmont area that led to the Glacier Mountains. With Emita ahead of him, Windtalker rode out front of the group while scouting and looking for any sign of trouble. On their fourth day, he slowed his horse to a walk and got off to study the ground. Disappointed at his findings, he waited for Captain Robert and his men to catch up.

Kiyo asked, "What's up?"

Windtalker sighed. "There are at least a dozen Indian pony tracks here."

Robert asked, "Heading back towards the mountains?"

"Well, now they are. They were heading west, but stopped here."

Kiyo asked, "How long ago?"

Windtalker replied, "Maybe an hour or two."

Kiyo said, "So they saw us and turned around."

Robert added, "So that's good, right? They are heading back to their homes and away from us."

Windtalker shook his head no. "I wish it was so, but I suspect they fled back to avoid us seeing them. They'll probably set up an ambush and wait for us to ride into the trap."

Kiyo grinned slyly as he spoke to Windtalker. "Well, then, you go on ahead of us and when you see them, just give us a yell and we'll ride up and help you fight them."

Windtalker gave him a dirty look. "I was thinking it was your turn to take the lead."

"And I was thinking my arm hurt. I am wounded."

Robert grinned. "Do you want me to take the point?"

Windtalker replied, "No, you make too much noise. Let me get about a hundred yards ahead of you. Hopefully, I can hear or smell them before I see them or they shoot at me."

"We'll keep our guns ready."

Kiyo turned serious. "I think I should go with you."

"No, one horse is risky enough. You just watch me and read my signals."

Windtalker didn't wait to argue, but turned his horse and sprinted down the road. They rode on for a mile when, for the first time in days, they began to see trees along the side of the road. Gradually, the forest thickened, and soon Windtalker could not see deep into the woods, and that scared him.

They made camp in a midst of the forest near a spring. Windtalker used his bow to kill a couple of rabbits, and then fed and watered the horses. The soldiers posted sentries and hobbled their horses. After supper, the men put out the fire and went to sleep. The fellows took turns sleeping so they could listen and smell for attackers.

They were actually surprised when dawn arrived and no attack took place. They began following the winding road as it hugged the base of the mountains before climbing upwards and going through a pass and down the other side. They rode all day and made camp once more off the road, posting sentries as before.

At dawn, they set out again, but just as they reached a bend in the road, they were met with yelps and whoops as a force of twenty-five Shoshones attacked. Windtalker beat a hasty retreat along with Emita. Captain Robert took his men off the road behind some large boulders, dismounted and tied off their horses, and then hustled back to return fire. Windtalker sprinted past them as the soldiers and Kiyo opened fire.

Immediately, one of Robert's men took an arrow to the chest, but Kiyo killed two Indians, Robert shot one, and a few more by his soldiers. Windtalker ran up with the Sharps rife, and began taking aim, looking for the leader.

Kiyo killed another before looking over at Windtalker. "Why haven't you fired?"

Windtalker kept sighting in targets. "I'm looking to kill the leader. If I get him, maybe the rest will run."

Arrows buzzed all around him, but Windtalker kept a steady hand and eye as he worked his way through the encircling Indians until he found the leader on a slight rise near the rear, urging his men on. Windtalker sighted carefully, and pulled the trigger.

Boom!

He didn't wait for the reaction, but darted down and came up on the other side of the boulder he fired from. He saw the chief holding his chest, and then falling to the ground. He took aim at the warrior nearest the chief and fired again. Kiyo fired his Winchester repeatedly killing three. Robert encouraged his men and they took out six.

Suddenly, the fight ended with the last of the warriors hauling the body of their chief onto a horse and retreating. Windtalker waited a bit before saddling up. "Emita, stay."

Kiyo grabbed the dog as Windtalker checked out their trail. He returned to report. "They've made a hasty retreat. I think we should get the hell out of here in case they bring back more warriors."

"I heartily agree," replied Robert. They buried the dead soldier quickly, loaded up, and Windtalker and Emita once again took the lead.

They made camp that night worried and nerve weary, but nothing happened. Two days later, they finally arrived into the valley leading to the fort. The fort appeared to be under siege with forty wagons now circling the fort, the rest abandoned in the battle with Spotted Owl on the plains.

As they dismounted at the trading post, Major Bill came out to see them. "Greetings and welcome home. I take it your mission was successful."

Captain Robert saluted him and gave him a quick synopsis of the journey. Major Bill congratulated them. He ordered the paymaster to give the scouts a thousand dollars for their brave and hard work.

"Fellows, I have news. This wagon train not only brought the payroll and much needed supplies for the fort, but I have been granted an expedition for a journey to the north. There is a report that a British trapper made it down through the mountains on a possible road. I have his map and I once again want to give it a try. I'll be in touch when I have my plans ironed out."

Robert asked, "But what about the Indians?"

"These settlers, their escort soldiers, and our men, gave the Indians quite a thrashing. They killed over eighty percent of their men. I doubt they will be much harm, at least for a while."

"Very well," replied Windtalker. "If there's nothing more, we'd like to go attend to our farm."

"Yes indeed," said the major as he heartily shook their hands. "Thank you many times over. I have no doubt you saved many of my men's lives and

161

the settlers' lives as well. Thank you, fellows."

The Indians stopped briefly to visit Samuel and his family, but wanted to get home before dark. They didn't relax until they crossed through the tunnel leading to home. Emita ran ahead and barked at the horses in the pasture, and soon they dismounted in front of the cabin and began unloading their gear and weapons. They took the saddlebags and rifles off the two horses Robert gave them and set them on the porch.

They led all their horses into the barn, put away the saddles and bridles, and led them to stalls where they fed them lots of grain. While they ate, they brushed them down, and then let them wander down to the stream to drink and run free.

They returned to the cabin and opened doors and windows to air it out a bit. They hauled everything from the porch into the cabin. Kiyo went to the smokehouse and returned with a chunk of meat. Windtalker went to the garden, and picked buckets of corn and other vegetables. They stripped naked and went to the stream to wash, and returned to start on supper. They cooked the meat a bit more in a frying pan, made biscuits, cut strips of carrots and potatoes and put them in a pot. Thirty minutes later, they began eating every single morsel of food they cooked, except for the extra rations they gave Emita.

Afterwards, they stowed away their weapons, their saddlebags, and finally, they decided to put away the saddlebags from Leroy's horse. Inside the bags, they found what they expected on top, including shaving stuff, a brush, a shirt, and a belt, but the bag felt heavier than they thought it should be. After removing a few more clothes from both sides, they pulled out four heavy sacks of gold coins.

They poured them out on the table and placed them in stacks and counted them. They were rare hundred dollar gold coins and the total came to a thousand gold coins. They felt rich, though they didn't have an idea as to what they could do with it. They took it down to the root cellar and buried it.

Soon they were in bed, with the light of the dying fire creating a soft glow across the cabin floor and onto the naked muscular bodies of Windtalker and Kiyo. They took turns rubbing sore muscles and especially weary butts, but in spite of exhaustion, they managed to make love by taking turns at being tops and bottoms. Emita slept on guard duty at the door. The Indian would sleep late tomorrow for the first time in a long while.

TWENTY-EIGHT

Major Bill and Captain Robert spent most of the next week assembling and cleaning the dust out of the Gatling gun. They also completed an inventory on the ammunition and found it lacking. After the wagon train moved on, they tested the gun several times to the marvel of everyone in the fort. It performed as expected, but it took some practice to aim correctly. However, the shells were powerful and deadly.

Major Bill pronounced the gun fit and ready, and sent dispatches with the wagon train heading west, and with another wagon master and his scouts heading east. He requested thousands of rounds for the gun as well as more inventory for the fort. He hoped at least one of his messages would get through soon.

There were no reports of Indian raids, so Major Bill took the opportunity to once again expand the fort. He put everyone to work on the project to help keep his men fit while building stamina. They began making a new wall sixty feet out from the first one. Every day the men cut the forest down near the fort creating a larger kill zone, and making it more difficult for the Indians to shoot their arrows accurately from the farther distance. The wall would take a month to build, but it would increase their security.

Bill also devised several new designs for the new wall. The new gate became recessed into the fort by six feet. On the short walls coming inside and butting up to the gate, he created high and low gun holes. This would allow his men to shoot attackers attempting to put ropes over the top of the gate. If they were trying to place brush at the bottom for a fire, they could be shot as well. Above the gate, he stored barrels of water on the framework in case they needed to douse a fire at the gate.

He also had the men frame the gate at the top and bottom so there were no pointed tops for a rope to slip over. The blacksmith nailed in flat iron to make the gate stronger. The guard towers were enhanced with new higher six-foot walls to protect the sentries when under attack. They also had gun ports to shoot and look out from in times of battle, but for normal sentry duty, they created a three-foot square box that stood two feet tall. The men stood on it to see over the wall to protect the fort.

Major Bill rebuilt all the roofs inside the original fort, making each one very steep and less likely to catch on fire. In case a flaming arrow did stick, he made long lightweight rakes his men could quickly use to pull the arrow off the roof before the roof caught fire.

They also made many buckets and filled them with sand to put fires out, and he drilled the men on fire procedures. After the completion of the new walls and gates, as well as four towers in each corner, they began the construction of new firing platforms behind the walls and instead of cumbersome steps, they built long ramps so the men could run up to the platforms.

Major Bill then had his men dig a large hole in the ground that went down twelve feet. They built a roof over the structure with thick sturdy logs. The roof stood only two feet above the base of the fort. They covered the roof with dirt from the hole making it fireproof. They created a wooden floor, a ramp, and a door to keep the rain out. He also knew if all the fire prevention failed, he and his men could take cover inside. In fact, with all the extra dirt from the hole, they began building an edge to the roofs of their buildings and adding dirt as well.

Windtalker and Kiyo became farmers again and they loved it. Every day, they worked on their crops, pulling weeds, and picking vegetables and digging up carrots, potatoes, and onions. They also worked hard on new fields for hay and straw and made their first cuttings, putting away many bales of hay. They used some of their cash to buy a manual baler from a settler packing and moving west with the wagon train. He hoped to move far away from the Blackfeet and other Indians.

They also bought all the farmer's livestock, including chickens, pigs, and a milk cow. The settler got quite a kick out of teaching the Indians how to milk and care for a cow. He also taught them how to take care of their chickens, explaining that he used some for eggs, and other for creating more chickens. He also explained the roosters couldn't lay eggs. They laughed when they realized a rooster was a male chicken.

They made the deal with the settler, and returned the next day with two of their wagons. They loaded up almost anything the settler could not take with him, and they paid him in cash for extra grain and feed, as well as the straw and hay in his barn. They paid him more than it was worth, and the settler and his family were so thankful that they prepared a feast for the Indian before they left.

Returning home took a long time with all the animal squawking, mooing, and grunting. They didn't like being on the main road at the slow pace, but they kept their rifles handy. Emita rode in the wagon for a while, but was too excited to stay there. He leaped out and ran around the back of the wagons and barked at the cow and pigs.

They expected great difficulty at the waterfall, so they tied off the cow and pigs, and took the wagons on through the water and then went back to maneuver the animals through. Kiyo pulled the cow while Windtalker pushed and swatted until the big cow went through the tunnel.

Getting the pigs through the waterfall proved difficult at best. They pulled together until finally, they got each one through, but they were covered in mud. After tying the animals to the wagon, they went back through the tunnel and found a mess of tracks leading to the waterfall. They broke pine limbs and swiped back and forth for forty minutes until the trail looked almost normal, but they would have to return with shovels to put more small rocks over the trail to prevent tracks leading to the waterfall.

After arriving at the barn, they moved the pigs to their new pen, filled a trough with grain, and the pigs soon found the creek winding through the back of their pen so they could get water at will. They promptly flopped into the mud and seemed happy as they Indians went back for the cow.

They fed the cow in the barn to get her use to coming there for more food, but let her go into the pasture behind the barn. She, too, made her way to the creek for water.

Finally, they put the crate of chickens in the big coop with the divider in the middle, putting the egg layers up front. They also put a rooster on each side to keep them from fighting each other. They placed scattered seed for the chickens to peck for on the dirt of both pens.

After they removed the grain sacks and stored them in the grain room, they put away the bales of hay and straw by stacking them in the lofts, they stowed away the extra garden tools they bought. They were also pleased with the new grinding stone they bought for sharpening knives, axes, and garden tools.

They pulled the wagons back to their parking spot, unhitched the horses, and began studying the side of their barn. They had liked the extended roof they saw on the settler's barn that stretched out from the outside wall, covering the yard tools and wagons to keep them dry. They had studied the structure and now thought they might do the same.

They brought the small stuff into the cabin including some new utensils for food preparation and cooking. They particular liked a small grinding wheel for busting corn to create grits and flour, a butter churn, and butter molds. They were also excited about the new bread loaf pans that allowed them to make bread over the fire like Molly did.

After lunch, they took the hay baler to the field and set it up. They brought along a wagon and a horse team and spent the afternoon cutting hay, raking it with the big rakes, and cramming it inside the baler. The settler gave them a big roll of twine to tie off the new bales, but they planned to buy more at the fort.

By the end of the day, the loft now held another fifteen bales of hay. It proved to be hard work, but with Leroy's horses and the cow, they would need all the extra hay and straw they could put away for the winter. Windtalker sat on the fence of the horse corral looking at the back of the barn.

Kiyo brushed his pants with his gloves to remove the loose straw, took off his gloves and came out to join him. "What are you looking at?"

Windtalker replied stoically, "The barn."

Kiyo grinned. "You must have gotten some of the hay between the ears. It looks the same as it did yesterday and the day before."

"Perhaps, but I was just thinking. We like the new farm, the vegetables we grow, we now have milk and eggs, but all that is going to tie us down a bit from our work and hunting."

165

"Our work?"

Windtalker grinned. "You know, helping out Major Bill and the soldiers, protecting the settlers and such."

"Does it ever bother you that we sometimes have to kill Indians?"

Windtalker's smile left his face. "Yeah, but for the most part, they were either bad renegade Indians like Spotted Owl's men, or other tribes just trying to kill us. We don't have much choice if they are doing that. I don't plan to raid and kill harmless Indians like they kill settlers on their farms or on the wagon trains."

Kiyo didn't reply for a minute or so, but finally asked, "So why are you staring at the barn?"

"Oh, I think we should create or invent ways for the animals to get fed when we're not here."

Kiyo laughed. "And how are we going to do that?"

"Well, we figured out how to get them water by diverting the creek through their pens, so we can check that off our list. I though that perhaps we could build a narrow ramp with walls hugging the back of the barn wall from the loft to the ground. That would be about twenty feet of ramp."

"Are the horses going to walk up it to get fed?"

Windtalker laughed. "You've been in the sun too long. I think we could slide bales down the ramp until they fill the ramp. The horses and the cow could feed from the bottom. As they eat, the bales would gradually push downward. This could last them a couple of weeks."

Kiyo grinned. "That's clever. How about the pigs?"

"I haven't thought on that one yet."

"Well, you'd better add the chickens to your list, too."

Windtalker grinned. "Yeah, I guess you're right. I'm itching from the hay. Let's go for a swim."

They stripped at the cabin, grabbed their pistols, and walked to the stream and dove in. They left the pistols on the shore by their moccasins and took turns ducking each other before using the soap and brush to wash each other.

They devoured a dinner of venison, grilled potatoes, fresh corn, and cornbread made from newly ground cornmeal in their new grinder. Emita loved the meat and the leftovers they gave him. After dinner, they took a while to clean their guns so they would be ready for their next trip.

A few days later, they rode to Samuel's farm, and ate lunch with them. They asked Molly to show them once again what they needed to wash their clothes. They made a list of the supplies she suggested. They told Samuel about their baler and how the farm was doing. They asked for his ideas on feeding the chickens and pigs while they were away, but he never thought about it. Since childhood, he always worked on the farm and someone did the feeding every day.

166

Samuel took them around the back of the cabin near the creek and showed them a new spring cooler he built to make the milk and butter last longer. The young men thanked him for the tip and planned to do the same at their place.

They spent some time with Michael and Trisha, challenging them to a shooting contest with bows and arrows. Michael displayed much improvement, but Trisha remained a pretty good shot as well.

After thanking the family for the meal, they made their way to the fort. They were shocked when they came around the bend, seeing the new larger and better-built fort. They noted the expanded kill zone, the new towers and that now there were four of them. There were a few wagons outside from a supplier and his men who bravely made the journey alone. They were under contract from the government to deliver to the fort.

Some of his men were sitting on the porch outside the trading post and noted the young men were, in fact, Indians when they climbed off their horses, and tied up their packhorses.

Ernie, a big man from Ireland with bright red hair and mustache, gave the scouts a hard stare. As they turned to go inside the trading post, he suddenly stood up. "Where the hell do you think you're going? You don't belong here. You murdering thieves should get the hell out of this fort!"

Windtalker nearly lost his temper, but he politely smiled and replied in his best English, "We work for the major."

That didn't satisfy Ernie, who suddenly pushed Windtalker back and into Kiyo. Kiyo caught Windtalker, but now he became angry, but before they could react, Captain Robert intervened.

"Hey there. Keep your hands off our scouts. These are good men and they have saved me and my men many times."

"They are Indians."

Windtalker replied, "Yes we are and you're a stupid white man."

This pissed off Ernie, but Robert said, "I'm afraid he's right. There are good white men and bad ones. The same applies for Indians. These young men are good Indians."

Pissed, Ernie shot back, "I'll kill them the first chance I get."

Kiyo replied, "That'll never happen."

Captain Robert added, "You're right about that. Fellows, let's go into the trading post." Once inside, Robert added, "Don't worry about that stupid hauler. He ain't nothing and knows even less. He'll learn. You are leaders and heroes to the men in this fort and everyone outside. How's the farm coming?"

Kiyo smiled. "Very well. Even when the work is hard, it is easier than climbing those Glacier Mountains or chasing those bad men."

"I suspect it is, but after a week in the fort, I'm always volunteering to go out on a mission. I wasn't built to sit around."

The trading post clerk came inside his store. "Oh, howdy fellows. How are my best customers?"

"We have a list," began Windtalker with a sly grin, as they always had a list when they arrived. "But you may have to order a few things."

"Okay, well, let's see what you need." The man began studying the list. "I'll give you all the nails I have, but I'll have to order more. I have some rope, but will order more of that as well. These haulers are leaving tomorrow so we'll have more supplies in a month. I have the stuff you need to wash clothes, and the clay jars you need for storing. Sounds like you are building a spring cooler. That's smart. I heard you have a cow now. Good for you. I'll have to order a galvanized bathtub. I guess you're getting tired of washing in the stream."

Kiyo grinned. "It's a little cold in the winter."

The trading post manager and Robert laughed. "Yes, I suppose it is."

They bought some canned goods and ammunition, and they ordered a new long saw for cutting planks, and a hand saw for short ones. They bought more plates and utensils, as well as some candy. While they were loading their purchases onto their packhorses, Major Bill came out to chat with them.

"I suspect you're bored with farm life," he began.

Kiyo replied, "Not yet."

Windtalker added, "Has there been a raid?"

"No there hasn't—not even an attack on the wagon trains, at least not after they passed through Sioux country. That's why I think now would be a good time for another expedition. Can I show you the map I have obtained?"

He laid the map over the canvas cover of the packhorse. He pointed out where they were and where he thought the pass might be. The scouts showed him the road to the west and where they came down from the high mountains to follow the stream west while chasing Leroy and his men. They also told him the Shoshone warriors in that area attacked them. They realized that somewhere past the point where they found the road and began the rapid chase to the west, was a fork to the right leading around the mountain to the north. That road is the one the major wanted to find.

Windtalker asked, "When do you want to leave?"

The major asked, "How about a week from today?"

Windtalker nodded to Kiyo so Kiyo replied, "Okay, we'll be here before sun up."

"Very good. My men and I will be ready."

Windtalker asked, "How many men are you taking?"

"I think a dozen or so, but not too large a group. I don't want to appear like we're going to attack the Indians."

The scouts shook the major's hand. Kiyo said, "We'll see you then."

"Have a good week and thanks."

The young men nodded at the major and waved at Robert, but noted the stern look on Ernie's face as they slid onto their saddles. They hoped to never see him again.

TWENTY-NINE

They talked about the trip on the way home and for a few minutes they wished they had declined, as they felt there were plenty of chores for them to do, but they knew the summer would soon be over, and opportunities on the trail would be gone for the winter. As much as they loved their cabin and farm, they felt they were hunters at heart, and sitting still too long bored them.

However, with only a week before time to leave, they rose early and went to work on the farm. They built the bale ramp in one day and tested it and, for the most part, it worked, but sometimes, due to friction, a bale refused to slide down the ramp. They greased the board with animal fat and that helped, but finally they placed a round river rock behind the top bale and this extra weight solved the problem by pushing the bales downward into each other. They let the horses discover the hay feeder on their own.

They also planted more seed, especially corn for a second harvest, and did the same for the ground vegetables. They took turns milking the cow and soon enjoyed not only fresh milk, but butter for grits, biscuits, and cornbread. They drank milk for all three meals. They also enjoyed a feast of fresh eggs and were delighted they now had four baby chicks running about. Their first attempt at making Molly's fried chicken was messy but good. They would practice and continue improving their cooking skills.

They could not invent a chicken feeder, so they buried strips of seed so the chicken would have to scratch and dig their way to the food. The pigs were a different matter because they believed they were too lazy to dig for food, but in desperation, they buried buckets of seeds and hoped they would. They built an adjacent pen for the pigs filled with lots of fresh growing grass. They were going to open the gate between their pens so they could eat grass as well.

Every night they cooked big meals with fresh food and made big breakfast meals as well. They often ate five eggs apiece. They would miss the fresh food on their journey. They spent the last two days cutting hay and straw, and baling it before loading into the loft. They also finished the roof on the new patio shed covering the wagons and tools. They were already making plans to build another barn to store more hay and straw, and hoped to start on it when they got home.

They prepared their weapons the night before, and laid out their supplies and bedrolls, making sure they carried everything. This included their moccasins and bows and arrows, but also the Sharps buffalo gun, the Winchester rifle, and two pistols. They wore long hunting knives on their gun belts, and still kept the secret knife in their trail boots.

They rose hours before dawn, saddled the riding horses, and placed the supply saddle on the packhorse. They loaded everything and went back inside to make sure they didn't miss anything. They stirred the fire and let it burn out. They gave Emita a good rub as the dog ran amongst them, anxious to hit the trail as well. Emita barked at the chickens and pigs as they rode past on their way to the stream, the tunnel, and the waterfall. They turned around for a last look at their farm and beamed with pride at all they had accomplished. Windtalker pointed at the bale slide and hoped it worked. Kiyo said he hoped all their new animals fared well, and then together they moved to the tunnel and felt the cold waterfall hit their faces as they rushed through. It felt like they washed off their role as farmers, and returned to their heritage as hunters. As hard as the trail might be, whether crossing over a new mountain, or working their way around a bend, they continued to be in awe of the new lakes, waterfalls, or giant rock formations they saw. Even when it rained for days, or Indian warriors flung their arrows at them from all directions, they were always eager for a new experience. They were living their life with a heightened sense of wonder and adventure, and they loved every minute of it.

They arrived at the fort and found the major as excited as they were. His ten soldiers were packed and ready to go. The soldiers pulled four packhorses, plus the one for the scouts so they could ride out ahead and scout for the trail and Indians. Most of the men were on the last expedition and maintained a high respect for the scouts. Word spread amongst the rest of the troops, so they were known as experts in their field of tracking and hunting, phenomenal in the feats of bravery and fighting skills, and amazing marksmen with bows or guns.

The first few days were uneventful as they followed the same route the wagons did as they worked their way around the Glacier Mountains, but on a day when they hoped to find a fork to the right or the north, they ran into something quite different.

Emita ran most of the morning ahead of the scouts and far ahead of the soldiers. Kiyo spotted the hesitation in the dog's steps and immediately pulled up his horse. Windtalker did the same, but quickly noted the dog turned and ran hard and fast towards them. They knew what this meant so they turned and galloped back to the major, and quickly led everyone off the road into a thicket of Fraser firs not far from the road. The scouts cut limbs from the evergreens and raked the road as best they could. The panting dog ran to them and they led him to the hiding place, and then rubbed him vigorously while whispering, "Good dog."

They didn't have to wait long as they could hear the hoofs of the approaching horses. The ground began to shake and seconds later, they saw the beginning of a large group of warriors, dressed for battle, and armed with bows, spears, clubs, and knives. The first thirty of the group were Flatheads, the next group where Shoshone, and the last section were Yakimas. There were at least a hundred warriors in all, astonishing the scouts at the vast number, but also amazed because these three tribes were the sworn enemies of each other. What caused them to join forces? Why were they riding together? Where were they heading?

The major feared they were heading to the fort, but the scouts studied the rear of the force as it moved by, and noted there were no packhorses, no women for cooking, and no travois for supplies. The group consisted only of male warriors, but at the very end of the group he saw the beaten face of a Blackfeet warrior with a rope around his neck, his hands tied behind his back, and he had been stripped naked. His back was a mess of dried blood from cuts and whips. They didn't recognize him, but felt sure he and his men must have done something to these tribes and they wanted revenge on the Blackfeet.

After they rode out of sight, the major began with his anxious questions. "Are they attacking white settlers?"

Windtalker replied, "I don't think so, but they could. Did you see the prisoner in the rear? He is a Blackfeet warrior. I think he and his men did something to them."

The major then asked, "So, they are planning on attacking a group of Blackfeet?"

Kiyo said, "I think so, too, but there are puzzles. We are on the western side of the Glacier Mountains, and traditionally, the Blackfeet stay on the eastern side, though they often hunt through most of the mountains. Windtalker and I did the same as boys, but we never came this far to the west. The Shoshone normally live in the middle southern area of the mountains. The Flatheads to the north, and the Yakimas on the western side and out to the western plains. These tribes hate each other and have for centuries."

Windtalker broke in, "Long before horses arrived from the south, these warriors would march for weeks to make an attack on the other. Once the horses arrived, they began stealing the animals from each other, but the horses allowed them to fight more often. I have never seen three tribes together, but I can remember when the Blackfeet joined the Sioux to fight an attachment of British soldiers coming down from the north and invading our lands. The white soldiers were massacred to the last man. They were too far from their forts for help to arrive. There were no retaliations for the defeat."

The major said while thinking aloud, "Perhaps that is why the British stayed to the north."

Kiyo said as he walked his horse back to the road, "I wish we knew what trails the tribe took to get from the various sides of these mountains."

"Ah," the major said, "that is something we must find out and update the maps. Shall we continue?"

Windtalker answered, "Yeah, I doubt we'll see any of these tribes for a while, but we mustn't run into this pack of warriors on our way back." He then spoke to Emita, "Emita! Lead boy, lead!"

Delighted to be on the journey again, Emita sprinted past the scouts and continued his run ahead as they followed him, and then a few hundred yards back were the soldiers.

A day later, they studied the mountains and felt like they were at least half way around the giant ridges. Yesterday, the main road turned west as expected, but they took a smaller right fork in the road after studying horse tracks along the trail and decided this might be a trail to the north and began following it. They closed ranks on this narrow winding trail to avoid losing eye contact with the soldiers. Emita continued to lead the way.

Three days up the new trail, they reached another fork and stopped to make the decision on which path to take. The scouts split and rode a ways up each trail and found more horse tracks to the west. Windtalker thought the trail to the east might lead right into the high country of the glaciers. The major knew from his compass that both trails actually went northwest, but at least they didn't go due west. After much discussion, they took the left fork and hoped it would continue on a northern track, but not lead back into the mountains.

At times, the trail turned due east leading into the high country, but upon reaching a stream, the trail would turn due north, and a mile or two later they were heading west. They were winding in and out of the edge of the mountains. Giant trees, spectacular views, and occasional large waterfalls surrounded them, but so far the major felt confident the trail could be widened into a road with only a few short bridges to construct. He could not imagine where they would cross into Canada, and what they would find when they did.

The major continued updating his maps as they went, and guessed they were one hundred and twenty miles north of the fort. Three days later, the trail turned slightly northwest as it followed a stream leading from the Glacier Mountains to the west. The stream went from deep, as the water bounced from one boulder to the next, to a wider shallower section. The trail remained on the southern side and though still in a forest, they were no longer adjacent to the mountains.

That night they camped alongside the river in a beautiful location. The men could fish and wash their bodies in the cold clear stream. The scouts went away from the men and began fishing with their bows and arrows. The fish were plentiful, and as they stood on a boulder overlooking a pool of water, they estimated several thousand fish swam below them, and in twenty minutes, they shot and hauled in thirty fish. They gave Emita one and took the rest back to the camp for the men to cook.

As darkness came, the scouts urged the major to put the sentries away from the stream, as the noise of the rushing water could easily mask the approach of a stealth warrior. The major followed their advice and placed three men fifty yards out from the campsite so they could hear. They were encouraged to hide in the trees or bushes and remain out of sight. The scouts taught the soldiers to pick two places to hide. The first was used before dark, so if enemies were watching they could see where the sentries stood. After dark, they should quietly move to their second spot. If an enemy attacked, he would approach the first spot, allowing the sentries to see and kill them, or if there were too many warriors, he could sound the alarm and run like hell back to the camp. The major marveled at their clever and ingenious tactical thinking.

With the moon high in the clear blue sky, the group suddenly heard a deep growl coming from the water. They reached for their rifles as they heard thrashing in the water. The scouts came forward and smelled the air.

"It's a bear," whispered Windtalker.

"I bet he smelled the grilled fish," added Kiyo.

Windtalker said, "Kiyo, take the men to the top of those boulders. I'll stand watch and try to discourage him."

Kiyo grinned. "How are you going to do that…breathe on him with your horse breath?"

Windtalker smiled. "I will think of something."

Kiyo and the men left the camp and moved up on the big rocks. Windtalker moved near the fire and put more wood on to build it up. He then took a burning stick and held it so he could see. The bear soon came out of the water and growled at Windtalker. The hunter stood his ground and waved the burning stick at the bear.

The bear swung clawed paws like a boxer, threatening attack with each thrust, but Windtalker moved a step towards him, and began speaking to him in his native tongue. The men cocked their weapons, but Kiyo urged them to hold their fire. He told them a wounded bear became more dangerous than a hungry one.

The major whispered, "Maybe we should feed him?"

"He'd just come back for more and might even trail us." Kiyo grinned. "Besides we might be feeding him Windtalker. One taste of that boy, and the bear will go back to eating bugs, berries and fish."

The men grinned, but their eyes remained locked on the massive bear as Windtalker took another step forward while he waved the torch and spoke to the bear. At ten feet away, Windtalker stopped, and stared the bear in the eye while continuing to speak to him.

The bear growled a few more times, and then suddenly, he raised up on his hind legs and stood two feet taller than Windtalker, and to the major, the boy looked as if he might be facing Goliath. The bear swung his mighty paws with his sharp claws left and right, but soon tired of the stand, and began a retreat back into the stream. Windtalker followed him and raised his torch until he saw the bear snatch a fish from the water and go up the far bank to eat.

Kiyo and the soldiers returned to the camp as Windtalker placed the burning stick back into the fire. The major went up and shook his hand. "That was the bravest thing I have ever seen. What in the world were you saying to him?"

Windtalker grinned slyly as he returned to his bedroll. "I told him that although I smelled sweet and most likely tasty, the men on the rock smelled bad and tasted sour. I told him the fish were good and plentiful, and suggested he give them a try."

The men laughed as they settled down once more to try and sleep. Windtalker fell asleep in a matter of minutes, as if nothing had happened at all.

THIRTY

The scouts watched as the warriors continued riding south, but failed to notice that two of the warriors in the midst of the hundred didn't look like the rest of the three tribes. They descendants of their Blackfeet ancestors, but they were not part of the Blackfeet Nation. They were from the renegade group led by Spotted Owl. He sent two of his men to meet with the tribes and told them more wagon trains were coming from the east, bringing thousands of settlers to their lands. He asked them to join him in the fight to stop the whites from killing the buffalo and stealing their land. The two warriors were good speakers, and they were older, giving an appearance of wisdom. They met with each tribe and managed to fire up their warriors in a common hatred for the white. They rode under a banner of peace to the next tribe, and so on, until the force that was prepared to fight numbered just over a hundred.

The Blackfeet prisoner attacked the Shoshone while hunting the mountains, killing the chief's son. Spotted Owl's men suggested they give the warrior a chance to fight for them or die now. The man chose to fight, but still remained marked by riding naked so he would remember the pain the chief felt over the loss of his son.

A day later, they met in a hidden valley along a stream with Spotted Owl. He brought his women from his village and sent out his best hunters. They prepared a big feast for the approaching army. Tipis were set up around the edge of the valley so the men could rest and prepare their weapons. The leaders were given tipis away from the group, but next to Spotted Owl's. They began meeting under the shade of the trees as the hot summer sun warmed up the high humidity in the valley, but the nights remained cool, as a breeze blew off the stream.

The talks continued for several days with Spotted Owl providing a map he drew in the sand and the reports achieved by his scouts. He began with a report on the fort with estimated force of seventy or more. He knew of the expansion of the fort and still cursed his failure at burning the structure down.

He put a big X at the locations of the settler farms and then drew the road around the southern end of the Glacier Mountains and turned to the west. He showed the common routes of the wagon trains as they arrived from the east. He said they used the peaks of the big mountains as a guide to the southern road.

He explained his forces attacked many trains on the plains, winning many victories. However, he realized his warriors would be more effective to setting a trap on the road around the mountains. He said a surprise attack could wipe out a wagon train of a hundred or more settlers in a matter of minutes.

He also told them they must kill the settlers in a brutal fashion, setting a horrific example and warning to future wagon trains. He said they abused the land and the wildlife. They killed buffalo for skins, leaving the meat needed by the Indian families to rot in the sun. He said their animals eat all the grass and their wagon wheels were scarring their land. He said his shamans warned of a large army of white ants marching by the thousands from the east to the west, devouring the vegetation and wildlife, and pushing all the tribes into the sea to the west.

This prophecy echoed the same visions the other tribes experienced. One by the one the chiefs spoke, each one angry at the whites for their presence in their lands, and feeding the fires of war.

After a while, Spotted Owl spoke in a softer tone, admitting the earlier defeat on the fort, but said it remained a good lesson for him by teaching him he could defeat the numerous white men by himself. He felt he must have help from the fellow tribes if the fight was to be won by the Indians.

Spotted Owl spent the past few weeks visiting Blackfeet villages and recruiting more warriors. His numbers reached near eighty and they joined in with the other tribes. The event turned into a festival of sorts, with each challenging the other in arrow shooting, spear throwing, and wrestling. They also put together horse races. Spotted Owl felt these events kept his men sharp and ready for war.

They planned to discuss battle plans tomorrow, and this pleased Spotted Owl, as he expected at least twenty more men from a Blackfeet tribe that was way to the east for the summer, and he hoped they arrived in time. He had sent three warriors to speak to the tribe and beg for warriors. They were told to avoid his home tribes or even those bands close to them. He knew there would be no support for him there.

Windtalker, Kiyo, and the soldiers continued following the stream and the trail for almost a week until the river widened, and they reached an area with thousands of small rocks leading into the water. Windtalker crossed first and found the footing in the riverbed for a crossing, but upon reaching the other bank, he found many horse tracks, so he waved for the group to follow him and Emita. The tracks were from unshod horses. This put the group on high alert.

They spent two days across the stream and after midday, with Kiyo in the lead, he rounded a bend and found Emita sitting calmly in the middle of the trail. Kiyo knew this meant the dog found something, but nothing to fear.

He rode up and smelled smoke as he did. He slid off his horse and petted Emita. "Good dog. I wonder where the smoke is coming from." He waited on Windtalker and the rest of the men to catch up to him. "Do you smell it?"

Windtalker sniffed the air and picked up the smoke. So did the major and the men. The major said, "I smell smoke. Which direction?"

176

Kiyo replied, "Ahead on the right. I think I smell bacon."

Windtalker sniffed some more. "You're right."

The major asked, "What do we do?"

"We'll go ahead slowly and check out the situation. Stay here and stay quiet. It could be an Indian village, a cabin, or hunters camping out. I don't want to go charging in until we see what we're up against. Move over there in that stand of trees in case a hunter comes this way. I'll whistle if all is well so you can move up to join us, but if I give the sound of a hawk, draw your weapons and charge."

The major led his men off the road taking Windtalker and Kiyo's horses into the woods. The Indians told Emita to stay and remain quiet. Together, they walked along the road, made a turn or two, then slowed as they left the road for the forest, until finally, they could see the chimney of a cabin. They moved a little closer and stopped in a thicket of laurel bushes. They could see plowed fields, a pen of pigs, another of chickens, and the cabin off to the right that was about the same size as theirs. They saw a barn and off to the left they saw what appeared to be another barn, but from it they heard a combination of a grinding sound and the sound of a small waterfall.

A door opened on the extra building as a big white man came out toting sacks of grain or flour. Way off to the left they saw fields of corn, hay, and a different type of hay that appeared to have huge clusters of seed at the top. They watched the man, who wore a pistol. When he got to the cabin, his wife stepped out and she was an Indian. Two children came out as well. The scouts listened until they picked up the sound of English, but with a different tone than that of the soldiers.

The scouts decided to reveal themselves, so they went back around and followed the road to the property. Now they could see tall grass with beads at the top, but they continued on until the man on the porch of his cabin saw them.

"Hello!" called Windtalker as he waved and smiled.

Using his best English, Kiyo asked, "How are you?"

The man reached inside the door of the cabin and pulled out a shotgun. Automatically, he cocked the weapon. The man asked in return, "Are you alone?"

Windtalker took the honest route. "No, we are not, but I didn't want to scare you. We are scouting for Major Bill and ten of his soldiers from Fort Green on the southwest side of the Glacier Mountains. We are on an expedition looking for a road to the north. We come in peace."

Kiyo studied the man. He was over six feet four inches tall, bright blue eyes, long blond hair, freckles on his face, and a small knife scar just below his left eye. He had big broad shoulders with strong powerful arms, and he wore buckskins with tall boots. He wore a holster for his pistol and knife on his belt. The scouts kept their rifles loose in their left hand. When they reached him, the scouts stuck out their hands to shake.

The man studied them carefully, and then took their smaller hands into his powerful mitt. "I'm Daniel Fuller. You're Indian aren't you, but you speak excellent English."

Windtalker replied, "We're former Blackfeet. We have been living with the whites for a few years. We have a farm much like yours in the south. Your wife is Indian. What tribe?"

"She is Yakima. I sailed from Ireland to Vancouver over ten years ago with a milling stone. I planned to build a grinding mill in the western area, but after meeting and falling in love, well, we tried a town or two, but the locals were not very nice to my wife, so we left and moved here. The Indians are fine with us being here. I am a miller. They bring their corn and I grind it for free. They often bring game as a trade. Tell your major to move up."

Kiyo gave a long whistle and a relieved major led his men from the woods and made their way to the farm. Daniel waited for them.

Windtalker did the honors. "Major Bill, this is Daniel Fuller. He's from Ireland. He is a miller." The scouts didn't know what exactly a miller could do.

"I'm pleased to meet you," began the major as he climbed off his horse and shook hands with Daniel. You have a beautiful place here. How long have you been here?"

"About nine years. My wife is Yakima, but we didn't fit in with the village lifestyle, and the western white women were not so friendly to my wife. We decided to live on our own. The various Indian tribes treat us well, as I grind their corn for them."

The major could not resist asking, "Where does this road lead?"

"It goes to Smithfield. It is about twenty miles, and then on to Horace, Mekon, and then across the mountains and into Vancouver."

"How far to the ocean?"

"About two weeks journey."

The major paused then asked, "How about to the east? Is there a road north that intersects to the east?"

"Yes, about two miles past my farm, take the right fork and go north about one hundred miles, and that intersects to a road going west and another to the east. Why don't you take your horses to the stream just past the waterwheel? The water is good. Would you like to camp here tonight?"

"Yes we would. If you don't mind, I have much I wish to learn from you. We must update our maps."

"Very well. Tell your men there is a meadow about forty yards down the stream, soft grass and tall shady trees. It is a good place to camp."

"Thank you," replied the major before turning and issuing the orders to his men.

Kiyo couldn't resist asking, "I'm sorry Daniel. We don't know what a miller does or what a waterwheel is. Could you tell us?"

178

Daniel grinned. "I'd be happy to." Along with the major, they began walking to the grinding building. "Milling has been in my family for centuries. I did the same in Boston before loading up a ship and making my way to Vancouver." They walked to the right of the building and up a hill. He pointed into a forest. "The stream comes along up there and goes down a small waterfall. I dug a ditch by myself through the forest, and piled up rocks to force part of the water from the stream to come my way."

The scouts studied the structure leading from the ditch. It had a bottom about two feet wide with one foot boards on each side, and they noted water continually dripping through the cracks in the boards as it left the ground instead of going down the hill.

Daniel continued, "The water goes down this trough and over to the top of the waterwheel." He led them under the trough and around to the back of the building. The huge waterwheel was turning and spilling water along the way. Daniel kept walking while the scouts and the major looked up at the big wheel. When he got on the far side, he showed the scouts how the water came from the trough to just pass the midpoint at the top of the wheel. He pointed to the pockets in the wheel that filled quickly with water, making the wheel heavy on one side and the weight of the water forced it to turn.

The astonished scouts followed Daniel across a footbridge and around to the front of the building. He swung open the big barn doors and the scouts stared at a huge stone on the bottom of a shaft and a second stone on top of it. On the side were shelves that caught the flour. There were huge leather belts attached to the shaft that crossed the room to pulleys and more belts that fed down to the big shaft attached to the waterwheel.

Daniel explained the water turned the wheel on the outside, which turned the shaft on the inside, and the belts around the shaft made the top stone turn. He showed them how he poured in the corn and the stone crushed it into corn meal or grits, and told them he could mill grain into flour.

While Windtalker studied the operation carefully, Kiyo asked, "What is the crop in the fields with the beady top?"

Daniel laughed. "That is grain." He reached over into a bin and pulled out a handful. This is what flour comes from. I grow it out there and grind it down in here until it is as soft and fine as flour."

"We use flour for biscuits."

"And flapjacks," added Windtalker.

"That's right."

They went outside and Daniel closed the doors so they could hear again. They walked to his porch and introduced his beautiful wife. Her English name was Martha, after Daniel's mother, but her Indian name was Running Bird because she ran everywhere as a child. Though a bit shy, she did join in with the conversation.

The major retrieved his maps and on the floor of the porch he modified it with Dan's knowledge of the roads beyond his cabin. His mission now complete, he felt excited and could not wait to send his report to Washington. Daniel told him they were in Canada at this point, but just barely, or least that is what an English surveyor told him a few years back.

After a while, Beth called them inside for dinner. They met two well-scrubbed and well-mannered little boys and a beautiful girl. Windtalker and Kiyo were astonished at how beautiful the cabin appeared on the inside. Daniel must have been a master carpenter as well. He made furniture with carved designs, including a beautiful table and chairs, and a big rocking chair. They sat down and ate. The major began telling him about the large group of Indians they passed on the way here.

Daniel became a bit upset. "A week or so ago, two Blackfeet met with the Yakimas and told them thousands of whites were marching across the plains and they needed their help in stopping them. I told my Yakima friends not to get involved, but the young ones would not listen. I was told these men already had a commitment from the Flatheads and the Shoshones. I'm afraid they mean to bring war on the whites."

The major became alarmed and announced they must rush back to the fort in the morning. He asked if a message could be sent west and left one with Daniel in case someone came through. Windtalker and Kiyo returned to the mill before dark to study it once more. Daniel showed them how it fit together and explained he built the floor on solid ground, and using block and tackle from a sailing ship, he moved the stones in place, and then built the waterwheel on the shaft, then finishing the job by constructing the building around it all. He showed him the chisels he used to round the stone and how he fastened the wheel and catch panels. Daniel became impressed with Windtalker's ability to grasp the assembly while asking good design questions. Windtalker borrowed paper, and made notes and drawings. Daniel thought he drew better than he did.

He also taught him about the operation, as well as how a block and tackle are used and applied. Then they shifted gears when Daniel saw the Sharps buffalo gun and that piqued his curiosity. Windtalker explained that it was accurate to five or six hundred yards and knocked a powerful wallop into whatever it hit. They offered to demonstrate the amazing rifle. They set up some targets at the back of the cornfield and began shooting from the porch. Daniel hit one target on the second try with his Winchester, but Windtalker hit the next target on the first try with the Sharps rifle and sent the target flying high into the air. The soldiers watching were impressed as well.

At a closer target, the scouts showed him their pistol skills, and just for fun, Kiyo took his bow and hit the same targets with his arrows. Daniel wanted to learn how to use a bow, so they showed him how to make one. Daniel showed him some arrows he made with metal tips instead of stone. This impressed the Indians, as the arrows were lighter and flew faster. The tips were similar to the end of a bullet by being conical in shape, but a dull point.

On his second attempt, Kiyo hit an ear of corn at eighty yards.

Windtalker studied Daniel's arrows carefully and learned they were actually made with a bullet press.

Before they retired for bed, Daniel showed him his small, but efficient blacksmith shop where he could make iron pieces to fit any project he might be working on. The scouts and the major thanked him and Martha for their hospitality, and begged them to visit, so they could return the favor when the Indian wars died down. Daniel told them to be careful, as the Yakimas were very skillful with their bows, and vicious in close battle with their clubs and battle-axes.

THIRTY-ONE

They left early the next morning for home with the major exuberant as ever about his findings of the roads north, to the west, and then the east and west route north of Daniel's home. However, the boys only talked about the waterwheel and the metal arrow tips. At night they talked about the Indian situation and the major took out the map of the mountain and the plains, and they showed him where the tribes lived and their winter quarters.

The major said, "I just don't understand why we can't all just live and enjoy this land together."

Kiyo smiled. "The Indians believe they were already doing that before you showed up. Now they are worried about what is next. After you run out of whites, will there be green or purple settlers coming next?"

The major laughed at him. "No, no green or purple men, but the tribes weren't really living in peace. They were fighting and stealing horses, and making slaves when they could."

Windtalker said, "You're right, but part of that is tradition. It is the way the Indian warriors stay sharp and battle ready. They test themselves by stealing horses, but some go too far."

Kiyo said, "They don't use the word steal. It is like a game. I steal from you and pretty soon you steal from me. It is like proving we are both battle ready. However, some warriors are selfish and take too much by killing women and children and burning villages, as well as taking slaves. Sometimes the slaves are replacements for the women killed in their village, so they can have new families. The women don't remain slaves. Eventually, they accept their fate and most fall in love with the warrior they live with. The mixing of the bloods from one tribe to the next makes us stronger."

Windtalker added, "One of the reasons we left our tribe is because the leaders became obsessed with killing all whites, innocent whites, and yes, women and children. They slaughtered and mutilated them. We were taught to be good stewards of the land, never killing anything we didn't plan to eat with our families. We never wasted an arrow. We never left a buffalo rotting on the ground. White hunters kill buffalo only for hide and horn. We killed buffalo for survival."

The major sighed and pointed to his map. "What if we said the Indians have this section and we have that section? Wouldn't that be fair?"

Windtalker laughed. "Not if it was all yours to start with. That's like saying you're going to keep your pants, but you're giving me your shirt. You wouldn't like that."

"No, I wouldn't, but I'd buy you another shirt to keep peace."

"You can't buy the Indians another homeland. This is their homeland. Their ancestors are buried here. Would you like it if someone stole your cemeteries?"

182

"Good points, but we must find some way to stop the killing of innocents."

Kiyo replied, "There are bad Indians just as there are bad white men. Together, we must stop them. Daniel told us about two Blackfeet warriors visiting tribes, and they succeeded in stirring the Yakimas. He said a Blackfeet chief named Spotted Owl sent them. I have never heard of this man, so I don't think he is a real chief."

The major asked, "Why do you say that?"

Windtalker answered, "Because if he were a real Blackfeet chief, he would order all the Blackfeet tribes to send warriors and over ten thousand warriors would attack your fort. They would never ask the Shoshone or Yakima warriors to join them."

The major thought about this and said, "So who or what is he, and why is he making this bargain with his enemies?"

Kiyo replied, "I think he a bad Indian, much like the white men we chased to the west with Captain Robert. I bet he was kicked out of a tribe and to save face, he's trying to prove that his army of warriors is greater than those in his home tribe."

Windtalker added, "We've killed a lot of his men. Your soldiers have killed a lot, so he had to recruit more, and apparently, he couldn't go back to the big chiefs of the Blackfeet, so he went to other tribes."

"We must capture him."

Kiyo shook his head. "That'll never happen. He'd rather die than be captured."

Windtalker said, "His warriors would capture ten settlers and demand his release. They'd torture these people until you released him. Better to kill him."

The major once again thought for a while before asking, "How could we do that? Could you get close enough to kill him?"

Windtalker laughed. "Perhaps by pretending we're with him, but once we killed him, we'd never get away." He added with a sly smile, "I've grown fond of living and eating."

The major smiled. "Me, too."

Kiyo said, "I think if we see him in battle, we should try to shoot him. Then he would not be a martyr and there would be no revenge."

The major stood. "So the next time we're attacked by Spotted Owl, one of us should ignore everything else and shoot him."

Windtalker added, "You make that sound so easy."

The major replied as he stood to walk to his bedroll, "I wish. Sleep well boys. We've got another long ride tomorrow."

Spotted Owl tried keeping his temper in check, but he felt the other tribes talked too much, and could not yet agree to their plan of attack. After a few days, he suggested a new plan to them. He said, "Forty warriors must go to the plains in secret and out of view of the fort. Half of the remaining warriors would work their way to the back of the fort, but way out of the range of discovery. The remaining force would divide in thirds, with a one third heading east, but off the road, another to the west, and the latter third across from the entrance of the fort, but again well hidden." They would build logs with handles to bust open the gates, and also make a fire to burn down the fences.

He next told them they would wait to attack when the number of the soldiers decreased. He said, "The warriors on the plains will show themselves. The army scouts will ride to the fort and the big chief there would send more soldiers to protect the wagon trains. We must also attack farms east and west of the road. Their leader will have to send more men there.

"We'll attack these smaller groups and torture the victims within earshot of the fort. This would force the white chief to send someone to help. We'll kill them, too. We'll capture women and children from the farms and torture them as well.

"When the group rushes to the plains to help, we'll ambush them on the road and kill them all. We'll keep attacking until the number of soldiers is greatly reduced, and then we'll be ready to attack the fort."

The chiefs thought long and hard on his plan and they liked it. The risk of losing a warrior would be far less, the reward greater, and the chance of success possible, but still it took two more days until Spotted Owl became the war chief in charge of battle plans. The forty warriors left the meadow the following morning in route to the plains, but it would take days for them to get through the mountains, as they must ride through a secret passage in the Glaciers to avoid detection on the road.

He sent scouts to find the soldiers in the mountains and watch them. He explained his plan, and how the soldiers would run to the fort and call for reinforcements. He also sent men to watch the east and west roads, with orders to report any movement by the whites.

He picked group leaders to command the warriors, and moved the forty to the rear as planned. They would spend their time building ladders and logs with attached handles to break down the fort while preparing their weapons. They would also keep a team of scouts watching the rear of the fort.

He used his own men for the attack on the front of the fort, dividing the rest of the warriors as planned. The big chiefs went with him to a spot on a larger hill looking down on the fort, so they could see the entire fort and the surrounding area. He kept a large group of scouts and message bearers there as well. Though he never commanded such a large group, he felt it his destiny to do so. He would kill all whites until they refused to come to their homeland ever again.

A week of quick travel by the boys and the soldiers nearly wore Emita out. The boys took turns carrying him from time to time, but he didn't

184

really like riding on a horse. After a bit of rest, he'd leap off and run ahead once more. The men were wearing down as well, with every soldier falling asleep quickly in their makeshift camps, but rising with stiff and sore muscles in the morning.

The major allowed an early stop tonight so the boys could hunt fresh game as the men grew weary of no lunch, cold breakfast, and poor thin soup for supper. The boys brought back six rabbits for the feast. Emita chewed down hard on the morsels tossed his way and chewed the bones dry.

After a few more days, they felt they were within fifty miles of the fort. The major wrote in great detail into his journal at night, while marking rivers and streams onto the map to become guideposts for future travel on this western route. He also began writing his report while resting until the light from the fire faded and he fell fast asleep.

Every day began the same, a cup of coffee, dried biscuit or hard tack, the breaking of camp, the relieving of bladders, and then they were off. Emita took the lead, followed by Kiyo and Windtalker, and then the major and his soldiers.

Not long after a stop for lunch, the boys were on a long straightaway, but they could not see Emita as he disappeared around the next bend. Fifty yards later, they suddenly saw him high-tailing it back towards them. The boys stopped and turned to wave at the major, but before he reacted, they turned again as they heard the sounds of yelps and whoops. They could not believe their bad luck.

Before them galloped at least thirty warriors, and they would be upon the soldiers in minutes. Emita dodged several arrows and knew he could not reach the boys in time, so he darted off the road and down into a ravine before paralleling the road.

The boys turned in circles looking for the best spot to defend themselves, but after spotting a stand of boulders and forest, they rode back towards the major while screaming for him to gallop up. They met about half the distance and fled off the road to the boulders. Horses were quickly tied, weapons prepared, and the boys and the soldiers ran to the tops of the rocks and spread out.

They quickly abandoned hope that the Indians might just gallop past them. The warriors spread out on the road, dismounted, and began advancing in their direction.

Windtalker whispered to the major, "Sir, they have us at least three to one. We will not win a hand-to-hand fight. We must kill as many as we can now."

The major gulped, but agreed with the assessment and told the men to pick targets and fire. Windtalker took out the first man with the foreboding Sharps, hoping to scare them off. He hit a warrior in the face as he came up and over a tall boulder. The powerful shot slammed the man backwards off the rock, while spinning him head over heels before crashing to the ground in a gruesome, bone-crunching thud.

This infuriated the warriors who screamed out an Indian version of charge. Kiyo grinned and said to Windtalker, "Now you went and made them mad."

Windtalker exclaimed, "I think we'd better make them dead!"

The boys and the soldiers began firing random shots as the warriors exposed their positions while attempting to move closer. The Indians began firing their bows. One of the men carried a stolen gun, but his poor aim did little harm. Two of the soldiers received arrows to their limbs, but continued firing.

Sensing that a frontal assault would be impossible, the Indians temporarily disappeared from sight as they began circling the group. Kiyo realized their intent as he fired at a man to his far right. "We must circle our men and kill the warriors before they charge."

Windtalker and Kiyo removed their battle-axes from the pouch they wore on their backs and laid them on the ground next to them. The men changed positions as the major issued instructions. A whoop came from the right as four warriors charged. Windtalker took out the first man, the major a second.

Kiyo saw the charge on his side and killed another with his rifle. He noted an Indian trying to steal their horses and killed the man. The major put two soldiers facing the rear, protecting their horses, but even though they were killing warriors, it was not enough.

They were down to a group of maybe twenty warriors when suddenly everything stopped. The major whispered, "What are they doing?"

Windtalker looked at the major and shook his head. "They're getting ready to charge. We must shoot until no bullets are left, and then fight with our knives and axes."

The major told his men to fix bayonets and reload their rifles, and just as he finished, they heard a big scream. Suddenly, the Indians charged from all directions at once. Windtalker fired the Sharps and killed a warrior, but there was no time to reload. He picked up his pistol and fired, using all six shots catching two more. Kiyo did the same by emptying his Winchester and then his pistol before finally picking up the battle-axe. The soldiers began battling the Indians with the butt of their rifles or the bayonets. Two soldiers were stabbed with spears and another two men were shot with arrows. The major took a grazing shot to his left arm, but managed to fire the last of the bullets from his pistol.

Windtalker stood up as a warrior leaped at him. Windtalker side stepped the man and swung his blade sharp and true, catching the man in the side of the neck while the man flew through the air. He fell dead as a stone to the ground. Windtalker ran to the major and killed a second man charging with a spear towards them.

Kiyo swung his axe hard and low over the ground as he ducked a spear and took a warrior legs off at the thigh, sending the man careening to the ground screaming. His blood spurted from his stumps, and he quickly bled out. More soldiers were killed, but the boys kept swinging their axes and the major using the butt of his rifle for a while before drawing his rarely used sword.

Windtalker caught another man in the side, but a warrior jumped on his back before he could swing again. He dropped to one knee while grabbing the man's hair and flung him over his shoulder, a trick he once did to Kiyo. Before the man could get up, Windtalker brought his blood-dripping axe down hard into the man's chest.

Kiyo tripped on a rock as a warrior dove at him. The swing of his axe missed. Kiyo put his hand onto the man's knife wielding arm, and with all the strength he could muster, he stopped the knife from landing in his chest. They fell to the ground and rolled over a time or two, but Kiyo didn't think he could hold off the man much longer, as he was far bigger. Suddenly, he let go with one hand, snatched his knife from his belt sheath, and stabbed the man hard in the stomach and then yanked upwards, ripping the man's guts open and ending with a cut to his heart. The man fell away as he quickly bled out. Kiyo rolled to his feet, secured his knife, and retrieved his battle-axe.

Two more soldiers were killed, but six Indians remained alive. Windtalker killed two more in succession. The major hit one in the face with his rifle stock, then stabbed him with his sword. Kiyo ran across the way and sliced a man running with a spear towards Windtalker's back. Another warrior leaped off a rock and knocked the major down, but as he came up to stab the major, Windtalker took the man's head clean off with a fast swing. The major's eyes went wide with fear.

The last Indian leaped off a lower rock and ran for his horse to warn Spotted Owl. The boys did not want the man to bring reinforcements. Windtalker tossed his axe to Kiyo, picked up the Sharps rifle, calmly loaded a shell, laid down on the rock and took aim as the Indian galloped hard. Windtalker judged the speed of the horse, led just a little, and fired. They all watched as a half second later, the big bullet struck the man in the back and sent him flying over the horse's head. The frightened and terrified horse pummeled the body as he ran over him.

Suddenly, all was quiet. They reloaded their rifles and pistols, and then began checking to be sure the Indians were dead. Emita came running up and leaped into Kiyo's arms. "Good boy. Good boy!" He began rapidly rubbing and petting the dog.

Windtalker said, "Major, it is possible other warriors heard our gunfire. We must leave this scene immediately."

"Let's load up our dead and wounded and be gone."

Quickly, they put the two wounded soldiers on horses. Both men received arrow wounds, so the boys yanked the arrows through, and tied bandages to stop the bleeding. They tied off the bodies of their dead soldiers to their horses and created three long lead lines for the major, Kiyo and Windtalker. They sent Emita ahead as usual and galloped east.

Windtalker knew they couldn't make the distance to the fort in just a day, and besides, they were already half through this one. He wished they could have hid the bodies of the warriors, but instead they rode hard. By nightfall, they pulled off the road into a ravine to hide, and then covered their tracks on the road.

The major agreed his men must be buried, as they were rank with the smell of death. They dug a deep grave in the dark and buried all eight men in it. Words were said, but exhaustion remained, so each man took a turn at watch, and they hit the road the next morning.

THIRTY-TWO

The scouts from the fort grew weary of their secret post and longed for a bath and hot meal. The two weeks on the mountain began an adventure, but as the days of seeing nothing marched by, their boredom grew obvious. They expected replacements soon. About an hour after dawn, the sergeant with the binoculars called his lieutenant to his viewing spot atop a big rock. The officer made his way to him, saw where he pointed, retrieved the field glasses from the sergeant and searched the area. In a few moments, he found a group of forty warriors charging hard to the east. The lieutenant looked beyond them as far as he could, but he could not see a wagon train.

"I don't know where they are going and I don't a see a train or even a dust cloud."

The sergeant said, "They have to be after one. They don't need forty men wearing paint to hunt buffalo."

"Paint?" The lieutenant focused the glasses until he saw the paint on the men's faces and even their horses. "Good eyes, sergeant. They're out for blood." Without removing the glasses he made an order. "Sergeant. Get your horse and ride to the fort with your find. We'd better get a few squads out there soon or the settlers on the wagon train are going to die. Be quick about it." He looked at the sergeant.

The sergeant saluted and replied. "Yes, sir. I'll be there in an hour."

The lieutenant watched as the sergeant mounted his horse and took off on a run. He watched him from the rock until he could no longer see him through the trees. He turned back to the plains and watched the Indians ride over a hill and out of sight.

The Indians climbed off their horses and walked them down to a creek. The gallop had been long and hard, and they hoped it worked. The leader for this group carefully went back to the edge of the trees and stared back at the mountain. He soon saw the flash of the sun on his friend's knife. He grinned. An army scout took the bait.

He told the men to settle down and rest, as they would not ride again until dark.

From the group watching the army scouts, a smaller group of three Indians sent a messenger to Spotted Owl. This warrior arrived at about the same time the sergeant arrived at the fort. Spotted Owl walked to the edge of the rocks while being careful to remain hidden in the leaves, but thankful for clear skies, he waited to see what the army chief would do.

Second in command, Captain Robert received a shout from a sentry post with the news of a rider coming in fast. The gate opened after they could see the sergeant's face through their binoculars. Robert met him just inside the gate.

"Whoa boy!" said the sergeant to his horse as he pulled up to a quick stop and slipped off to the ground. He let the horse loose so he could find water as he had ridden long and hard to get there.

"What is it sergeant?"

"Sir, the lieutenant sent me. I spotted forty warriors riding east this morning at a full gallop."

"Forty? My goodness. Did you spot a train?"

"No sir, but we think they did."

"Why so?"

"Sir, the Indians and their horses were wearing paint and they were heavily armed."

"Jeez," replied Robert while sizing up the situation. He knew he must do something or another train would surely be massacred. Forty warriors could easily wipe out a group of settlers, and he didn't know if soldiers were escorting the train. He called for a group of twenty to mount up quickly and follow the sergeant back to the base of the mountains. He told the sergeant to report back to his lieutenant and to remain on duty. He told another lieutenant to lead this force.

Captain Robert stood in the sentry tower and watched his men ride out along the road, and then around the bend and out of sight.

Spotted Owl grinned. He looked up at the sun and knew they could ride for about a half day. He drew out the road in the dirt and counted off the distance. They would attack before dawn. He sent a messenger to the plains and another to the thirty warriors heading to the east. He sent similar messages, but the closer one was told to wipe out the scouts in the mountains first.

Spotted Owl sent messengers to the rear of the fort and to the west to keep them posted. He laughed at how easy it was to fool the white men.

Emita sensed a need for high alertness after the battle with the Indians, but the dog was glad to be back on the run again. He worked his way around the bend while smelling the air. The sun began the downward side of its arc, so it was hot. The dog stopped to get a direction on the scent he just picked up.

Zip!

Suddenly, an arrow hit the ground just in front of his rear legs. The dog immediately leaped back, spun, and took off running. Usually Emita ran silently to warn the boys of approaching riders, but the frightened dog barked loud and repeatedly.

Windtalker and Kiyo pulled up their horses while deciding whether to abandon the road and hide in the woods. They had never seen Emita do this

190

before. Windtalker dismounted as Emita ran and leaped into his arms.

"Something is very wrong," said Kiyo.

Windtalker spun while hugging the dog and knelt to set him down. Emita barked again and then licked Windtalker's face. He took off a few steps back down the road and then returned barking again. "I guess we're supposed to follow him."

Kiyo stated solemnly, "I don't have a good feeling about this."

The major caught up with them. "What's wrong?"

Windtalker replied, "Emita detected trouble, but we don't think it is someone riding towards us, however, something really set him off."

"What do we do?"

"We'll ride up and take a look. Stay back about fifty yards and draw your weapons."

"You boys be careful."

"Yes sir. We intend to."

Kiyo said, "I think I should fake having to pee and leave the road on the right and come down the road in the forest."

"Okay. Leave your horse with the major, but take your rifle."

Windtalker waited while Kiyo made a show of holding his crotch and running for the woods. Once out of sight, he rapidly began making his way forward, while frantically trying to see through the forest and running from one tree or rock to the next.

Windtalker pulled his Sharps from the saddle scabbard and put in a shell. He checked his pistol, and together, he and Emita moved forward while pulling his horse. After fifty yards, he saw the arrow in the dirt on the road. He walked up to it and immediately realized it looked like a Blackfeet arrow. They walked a bit farther before Windtalker noted the hair standing up on the back of Emita's neck. He had never seen this before on the dog.

He scanned the terrain on the left side of the road and saw nothing. He felt sure the arrow came from the right side. Zip!

The sudden sound caused Windtalker to roll as the arrow just missed his chest. Rolling to his feet he began running off to the right side of the road with Emita right behind him. He just reached the trunk of a tree when he heard yet another arrow. Zip!

He dropped down just as the arrow hit the tree with a thud and quivered. Windtalker leaned out to his left and then right trying to guess where the arrow came from. He ran to the next tree. Zip!

This arrow just missed him as he fell flat to the ground. He made Emita stay, fearing the dog would be shot. He crawled forward, but again he heard an arrow. Zip! Quickly, he rolled to his left, and the arrow struck right behind where he landed. He brought his rifle up, realizing the man must be atop a boulder, due to the angle of the arrow. He took quick aim.

Boom!

An Indian scout screamed. Boom! The Indian stood up and

Windtalker saw him, but before he could aim and fire. Boom! The Indian face exploded outward as the bullet entered his skull from the rear.

Windtalker waited until he saw Kiyo step up on the rock. He gave his hawk sound. Windtalker stood up. Kiyo said, "All clear. Just one scout, I guess. Only one horse and tracks."

"That was close. He nearly got me."

Kiyo came down to the road as Windtalker came back out of the woods. The major and his men came up bringing Kiyo's horse.

Kiyo smiled. "Looks like Emita saved us again."

Windtalker gave Emita a good rub. "Good dog. Way to go, boy."

Emita barked loudly while wagging his tail feverishly and ran in a couple of circles before running back for another hug and rub. He was glad to be alive, too.

They saddled up and took off on a gallop again.

The army scouts on the hill woke up to what they thought would be another boring day on the mountain overlooking the plains. The soldier on the rock came down for breakfast while the well-fed guy went up. He had just pulled the field glasses to his eyes and began scanning the plains when he heard and felt the pain of the arrows.

Zip! Zip!

The soldier dropped the field glasses and looked down at his chest as he saw the bloody points of the two arrows that had penetrated his back, coming out mid-chest. He dropped to his knees with a thud, and then as his heart beat for the last time, his eyes rolled up in his head, and he fell backwards, bouncing off the boulder and landing half on top of the previous scout eating his breakfast, and partially in the fire, sending sparks and shards that scattered the rest of the men out of the way.

When they saw the two arrows sticking out of their friend's body, they stepped quickly to pick up their rifles, but at the same time, fifteen warriors charged their camp. The soldiers only managed to get off a couple of shots before their bodies were riddled with arrows and then rapidly hacked with clubs and battle-axes. In less than five minutes, there were no sounds in the camp at all. Quickly, the warriors stripped the bodies of pistols and ammunition, picked up rifles, and stole their horses. With more time, they would have mutilated the bodies, but they quickly rode to prepare their ambush and attack on the road.

After they reached the road, they were met by the forty warriors from the plains arriving after their all night ride around the southern tip of the Glacier Mountains. The leaders made quick decisions and rode as a small army in the direction they expected the rescuing soldiers to arrive. A few hours later, they were met by two rapidly riding scouts, relaying the soldiers were but a mile behind them.

Quickly, they divided forces and moved north and south of the road, hid their horses, prepared their weapons, and hunkered down out of sight.

The lieutenant leading the force didn't know how to determine the difference in hoof tracks on the road. If he had, he would have found very few shoed tracks and lots of unshod Indian horse and pony tracks. He looked up at the sun and hoped to make the plains before late afternoon and perhaps in time to stop the attack on the plains.

Just as he wiped the sweat from his brow, an arrow hit him hard in the chest. His horse didn't know of the attack just yet and kept galloping even after the officer let go of the reins and tumbled out of his saddle. Inadvertently, the soldiers rapidly following him, trampled over his body, but they heard the whoops and cries, and instantly more soldiers were shot. Suddenly, they were enveloped in a mass of confusion and pain, as the warriors attacked with bows before charging.

The wounded soldiers were yanked off their horses and chopped with battle-axes, and once again, in a matter of minutes, the fight ended. The warriors shouted triumphantly, thrusting bloody spears and dripping axes into the air. Horses and weapons were taken, the bodies tossed aside, and the Indians mounted and began their ride to join up with Spotted Owl.

THIRTY-THREE

Just a mile from the fort Windtalker called to Emita and waved for him to stop. The sun disappeared behind the big mountains to the west, but there remained enough light to see. Kiyo, the major, and two wounded men caught up with him and pulled their horses to a halt.

Kiyo asked, "What's the matter?"

Windtalker replied, "I was just thinking a bit. We saw the force of Indians heading this way just before we arrived at Daniel's farm. Then we were attacked by part of that force on the way here."

Kiyo asked, "And?"

"Well, I'd just like to know where the rest of those warriors are. I think they may be waiting for us or anyone else that might be heading to the fort."

The major replied, "You may be right. Do you think another scout may have reported our arrival?"

Windtalker said, "Yes, I do, although I saw no smoke signals, or sun reflections off of any pieces of glass, mirrors, or knives. It is just a feeling I have."

Kiyo grinned. "I'm only feeling hungry and tired. So what do you want to do?"

"I think we should pull off the road and hide. After it gets dark, we'll ride in slowly and quietly, and make our way to the gate. Major, we'll need you to call out to sentries so they can open the gate as we get there."

"Okay," replied the major. "I agree. We've come far and should be careful for whatever the Indians are planning."

They led the horses off the road, then moved parallel to it, but remained hidden by the forest until they found a good hiding place. They took care of the wounded, giving the men food and water, and fed the horses the last of their stores of grain. They took turns standing watch. Two hours later, they checked their weapons once more, saddled up, and began moving out.

They continued walking their mounts through the forest as quietly as possible. It was only a mile, but the quiet, gentle pace took nearly an hour. Near the western corner, they came out of the forest with the major in the lead.

Spotted Owl drew out a partial map in the sand using a torch to see. He felt confident his force killed the men arriving from the west and his warriors would soon arrive to join the battle. He still had the men in the rear of the fort, and the warriors arriving from the plains on the road ready to charge. He also made ready his force in the front. He sent messengers to tell each group the battle would begin at dawn. He then sent twenty men out to attack two settler farms with orders to capture a few women and kill everyone else. They were to bring the women to him.

Although there were soldiers hiding in barns, they were overwhelmed and soon killed. Farms began burning and the men were killed, as were the children. Weapons were snatched, including farm tools and a few ladders. Spotted Owl asked for several wagons, so they were brought to his staging ground just over the rise and out of sight of the fort. The wagons were loaded with bales of hay and stacks of wood.

As the women began arriving, his warriors put ropes around their necks and tied them to limbs to prevent escape. Spotted Owl looked at them with disgust, but went about planning his battle.

"Captain Robert! Come quick. There's a fire!" The sentry yelled as loud as he could. Robert stopped from changing his clothes to go to sleep and rushed out the door. He ran up the new ramp, and in a few seconds he took the field glasses the private handed him and looked at where he pointed. Soon, he focused on a growing fire.

The private suddenly said, "Sir, look to the right. There's another fire."

"Oh no," began Robert. "That's the McClain and Smithfield farms."

"What do we do?"

Robert thought for a second. "We're already short handed. I'm not sure if we should ride out as it could be a trap."

"The settlers could be killed."

"Son, I'm afraid if there is a fire, they are already dead."

A voice suddenly came from the ground below him and outside the fence. "Robert, it's the major. Open the gate quietly and with no light and do it now. I have two wounded men."

Recognizing the major's voice, Robert smiled. "Yes, sir." Robert called down quietly for the lower guards to put out the lights and then open the gate. He ran down the ramp and got there in time to realize their group consisted only of the major, two wounded soldiers, Windtalker, and Kiyo along with their packhorses. His delight in his seeing his commander fell away as he discerned the rest of the soldiers were dead.

"Sir?" he began. "Are you all right?"

"We're glad to be back. A force of Indians attacked us about twenty miles west of here, and they killed most of my men. Get someone to get these two men to the doctor. Are you okay?"

Robert sighed. "Let me give you a quick report. Of immediate nature, there are two settler farms on fire right now. It's the McClain and Smithfield farms. Our scout group reported a large force of forty warriors charging across the plains that we assume are in preparation to attack the next wagon train. I sent twenty men to stop them. I haven't received a report back from the scout team so I am a little worried."

The major sighed. "You have reason to be more than a little worried.

We saw a force of about eighty to one hundred warriors heading this way a week ago. Part of the force on the plains may have been them, but where did the rest of the force go? I think part of them attacked us. We killed them all, but they wiped out most of us. I'm afraid the burning of the settler farms means our men in the barns are dead and so are the families."

The major paused while thinking. "We saw evidence that at least three more tribes have perhaps joined the renegade group that we are dealing with. This larger group will most likely attack us. Please have someone water and feed our horses. We also need to eat and rest a while." He turned to Windtalker and Kiyo and said, "Fellows, I don't think you should go home tonight. We may need your help tomorrow. I'll settle up with you in the morning. Sleep well, my friends, and thank you for saving the lives of my men and myself several times."

The horses were fed and watered, Kiyo and Windtalker ate heated leftovers provided by the camp cook, Emita a half bucket of food, but the Indians didn't much want to sleep in the barracks with a bunch of snoring men, so they settled outside, leaning against the trading post wall and out of the firelight. The stars were out so they felt sure a sudden downpour wouldn't drench them.

Windtalker said, "I think we're in the middle of a mess."

Kiyo sighed. "Yeah, I get that feeling, too. I'm worried about Samuel, Molly and the kids."

"Yeah, I know. If the major is right, all the farms will be hit tonight. With that many warriors, they don't have a chance."

Kiyo stood up. Windtalker looked up at him with a puzzled expression. "Where are you going?"

"I think we should go get them."

Windtalker grinned. "I knew you were going to say that, but tonight in the dark could be dangerous."

"Yeah, but they might not make it until morning. We'll have the advantage of the cover of darkness."

They began saddling up their horses. "The moon is shining bright."

Kiyo smiled. "There's always the shadows."

They went to see the major and knocked on the door to his quarters. Unable to sleep either, he called from his desk, "Come in."

Inside, they found Captain Robert and the major looking over his map of the area. "Sir," began Kiyo. "We're worried about Samuel and his family. We are going to get them."

The major sat back in his chair and let out a slow breath. "I'm afraid they are not the only ones in danger. We have five more families to worry about. Robert and I were just trying to figure out what to do."

Windtalker replied, "We figure tomorrow there could be Indians everywhere attacking the settlers and then finally us. They will be whooping it up tonight, building courage and spirit, so it would be better to get the settlers out now. We'll go to each farm, one family at a time, but we'll need a white soldier with us, as the rest of the families might not know or recognize us."

The major asked, "Why not send a squad of men?"

Windtalker grinned. "Because your soldiers still make too much noise. We need to get them in secret. The Indians will still have scouts on the hill."

"Okay, you're right."

Robert spoke up. "Sir, why don't I go with them? I can convince the families to come."

The major hated the thought of losing his second in command, as well as Windtalker and Kiyo, but after a long pause of silence, he reluctantly agreed.

Kiyo said to Robert, "Put on dark clothes and a dark hat. No white gloves. No spurs, and no noise."

Spotted Owl taunted his captives for a while and then began pumping up the warriors with talk of the white settlers trying to steal their hunting lands. Over and over, he continued speaking until they were excited about the attack at dawn, then he went back to his staging area to study his map. He could still feel the sting of previous defeats, and wanted to make sure his men eliminated every possible option and defense the fort might use.

His men burned two of the farms, but were told to leave the others alone until near dawn to once again try and draw out the soldiers.

The Indians and Robert walked their horses out slowly, but turned right hugging the fence, then immediately began heading for the woods. The Indians smelled the air, but did not pick up the scent of horses, Indians, or campfires. They whispered to Emita to remain close. Windtalker led them off the road and then deep into the forest. Robert caught on that he wanted to stay away from the road, as Indian scouts were most likely watching for movement.

It took about forty minutes to make their way through the brush before finally reaching the Samuel farm.

As they climbed off their horses, the door opened and Samuel came out pointing the loaded and cocked shotgun at them. Windtalker whispered, "Samuel? It is Windtalker, Kiyo and Captain Robert."

"Oh jeez, I almost shot you. What the hell are doing out here at this time of night?"

"Can we come inside?"

"Sure, I'm sorry. Come on in. I'll light a lantern."

Kiyo replied, "It would be better if you don't. Someone could be watching."

After they shut the door, Robert brought the family up to date. They were told to dress, grab weapons, and get ready to ride. Samuel asked while he was changing his clothes, "You think they would come here?"

Robert replied, "They've already burned two farms. The major lost most of his men in a battle with a group of warriors from the west."

Windtalker added, "We saw a force of about eighty and they were Flathead, Shoshone, and Blackfeet warriors. The tribes are joining forces. The best place to remain safe is in the fort."

"But they'll destroy our farm."

Kiyo said, "Sir, you can't fight a force this large. If you're not here, perhaps they will move on. There are other families to fetch. We must go now."

The Indians, along with Samuel, hustled to the barn, saddled horses for the family of four, and brought them to the door as they all came out and saddled up.

Windtalker whispered, "Please don't talk and stay as quiet as possible."

Emita took the lead, followed by Windtalker, Robert, and Samuel and his family. Kiyo brought up the rear while listening and watching for a rear attack. They were lucky, saw and heard nothing, and soon arrived at the fort. The family entered the fort, but Robert and Windtalker followed Kiyo as he took the lead with the dog as they moved through the woods to the Ferguson farm. They were the farthest out, so they were very cautious. Forty minutes later, Captain Robert woke up the family, the Indians saddled the horses, and this time, the younger kids rode with their parents alongside their older brothers.

Kiyo studied the sky on their return, and knew they were running out of time. They dropped off this group and made their way to the next farm. They returned an hour later, and set out again. Two hours before dawn, they prepared to leave the last farm on their return. Windtalker led the group into the woods as quietly as possible.

Zip!

The father took an arrow in the chest from a lone Indian watching the farm, while waiting for his fellow warriors to arrive for the first attack. Windtalker did not want to use his noisy gun, so he leaped off the horse, dodged a hastily fired second arrow, and ran hard into the man, knocking him backwards with great velocity, and Windtalker diving on top of him with his knife already pulled. Before the man could react, scream or yell, Windtalker brought the knife up and plunged the sharp blade deep into the man's chest with great force, stopping only when he felt sure the tip of the blade penetrated the pulsing heart. He didn't wait for the man to bleed out. He feared another attack. He ran back to his horse, and beckoned the group. He tried not to rush, but as quietly as possible, they made their way without further incident and arrived about an hour before dawn.

Exhausted, the Indians watered their horses once more, gave them more grain, and returned to their bedrolls for a much needed nap. Robert met with the major while giving him the details of their rescues, and relaying that an Indian was indeed watching the last farm.

THIRTY-FOUR

Spotted Owl sent word for his men to attack the next two farms, but an hour later he received word they were all empty. This puzzled him until the last group returned with the body of the Indian scout killed by Windtalker. This pissed him off. He cursed and made lots of angry noise to his men, but inside, he feared his plan might have been discovered.

"Set those two farms on fire!" he ordered. Quickly a group flung themselves on their horses and were handed burning torches. Spotted Owl watched as the warriors rode off to follow his orders.

He turned to another man and said, "Bring the women that we captured and let's move closer to the fort."

The late shift sentries on the four corner towers knew the time without checking a pocket watch. At this time of the year the last stage of night began when the moon disappeared beyond the horizon. However, for another half hour the sun remained far to the east, but with hints of arriving soon to brighten the day. The sudden startling sound of a woman shrieking rattled their bones. They cocked their rifles and brought their attention around to the front of the fort. They could see nothing. One of them called down and alerted a lieutenant who woke up the major. Windtalker and Kiyo heard the noise, as well as Emita. They didn't like the sound they heard. Though still exhausted with only a few hours of sleep, they quickly got up, put on their gun belts, retrieved their rifles, and followed the major and Robert up the ramp. They all stared into the distance, but with no moon or sun, they failed to see anything.

Windtalker suddenly pointed. He whispered, "There is movement just over that rise, near the big oak tree."

They all stared while the major used his field glasses.

The scream came again and they all did their best to focus on the direction of the sound.

Spotted Owl nodded again to his man inflicting the pain on their captive. The woman hung from a big limb of an oak tree by a rawhide rope around her neck, with just the tips of her feet touching the ground. Her hands were tied around her back. Her clothing hung loosely around her waist after fast swipes of the torturer's well sharpened, knife blade. So far, he just cut her now and then to make her scream. Spotted Owl felt he now had the fort's attention. He gave a nod to the man with the knife so he began a step up in the pain level.

The warrior came up behind the woman. She could hear him moving, but could not sense his plan. She swung her eyes frantically left and right. She tried to turn. Her peripheral vision caught just a glimpse of the large blade near her head as the man swung the knife and in a flash, her ear fell to the ground. The pain seared her brain and her soul as she let out a guttural scream that made Spotted Owl and his men laugh with delight. The torturer stabbed the ear and lifted it from the ground to show the woman what he was doing. Horrified, she screamed once more as loud as possible.

The major asked, "What the hell are they doing?"

Robert added, "I can't see anything."

The scouts stared intently, but more importantly, they listened. They heard the warriors laughing. Windtalker stated the obvious, "They are torturing a woman."

The major angrily snapped. "How in the hell do you know that?"

Kiyo sighed, "Sir, be quiet and listen. We hear the warriors laughing. They are cutting her. They'll take her ears and fingers, perhaps her teats."

"Why on God's earth would they do that?"

"To get you to attempt to rescue her. If you open the gate, the nearby warriors will swarm us."

Robert stated solemnly as the realization took hold, "So there's nothing we can do."

Windtalker said plainly, "It would be better for her to die. The pain is going to get worst. A whole lot worst."

"Oh my god," replied the major with great disgust. There must be something we can do."

Kiyo said, "Time to get ready for the attack, sir. They didn't come here just to torture a woman. They intend to kill us all."

The major eyes went wide with fear, but then he gathered his wits about him as he nodded in agreement. Suddenly, the woman let out another scream as she lost the other ear. The major ran down the ramp while yelling for the sergeant to assemble the men. He gave the soldiers a quick update and then began barking orders rapidly. Minutes later, they were dismissed and urgently following his instructions. Weapons and ammunition were brought out, water buckets were filled, the doctor and his aide prepared for the inevitable wounded, and the cook quickly fixed breakfast. In shifts, the men ate quickly, followed by the settlers, and finally the major, and his captain, along with Windtalker and Kiyo. It might be their last meal of the day, but for some it would be their last meal forever.

Over the next twenty minutes, the warrior cut her fingers, her breasts, and added awful gashes across her face, before finally ripping her gut and allowing her intestines to spill out. She screamed continuously for a full two minutes before finally bleeding out.

Spotted Owl ordered her replaced. The next woman could see the scene as they hauled her to the tree. She wet her drawers making the men laugh all the more. The torture began right away as a hint of orange could now be seen through the trees on the ridges to the east.

The soldiers reinforced the gate with the large prepared posts that went under installed steel brackets at the top, and then the posts were angled down and away from the gate to the ground and up against buried posts. This provided extra strength and support to the gate. They filled numerous water buckets to top off the barrels of water over the gate.

Windtalker and Kiyo stared across the open field as the light slowly came across the mountain behind Spotted Owl and his men. The Indians remained out of rifle range. Sentries began reporting movement in the woods from all four corners. Robert ran left and right, as did the major. Windtalker and Kiyo studied the forest until they could finally see they were completely surrounded by warriors wearing paint and brandishing their weapons in the air.

"Robert!" exclaimed the major. "Get four men to help and bring the Gatling gun up to the front sentry post and two cases of ammo. Do it quick."

Robert saluted. "Yes, sir. On the double, sir." Robert took off on a run, while barking orders to four of his men. Meanwhile, the cannon crew prepared their first shot. Robert's group brought out the Gatling gun with two men carrying it up the ramp. Another carried the tripod mount the gun set on, allowing it to easily swivel left and right as well as up and down. They all ran back to carry the heavy wooden boxes filled with the ammo belts that rapidly ran through the gun when fired.

The major ordered the bugler to play for the raising of their flag. As Bill and his men stopped to salute the flag, he hoped the drilling they practiced would pay off. Just as the bugler finished, they heard another blood curdling scream. The major brought his field classes up as a warrior cut the woman's teats off, put them on a spear and raised them into the air while laughing.

"Damn!" exclaimed the major. "There's nothing we can do to stop them! Even the Gatling gun will not reach them."

Windtalker sighed, and said softly to the major, "If I were her, I'd prefer to die quickly." He paused to let the thought settle into the major's mind. "Sir, I can kill her quick with the Sharps, if you ask me to."

The major's face went white, but as the woman screamed again, he shook his head back and forth in disbelief as to the decision he knew he must make. Finally, with building anger, he said, "Windtalker, kill the woman now. Please stop her pain."

Windtalker replied as he chambered a shell, "Sir, after I kill her, I can get the man doing the carving."

The major replied quickly, "I wish you would. The bastards are crazy."

As Windtalker prepared to fire, Kiyo asked to borrow the field glasses. He brought them up to his eyes and said to Windtalker, "I'm ready, go ahead."

The major called for another pair of binoculars so he could watch as well, but as he brought them up to his eyes, Kiyo said, "Sir, don't watch the woman, help me spot which warrior issues the next order. That's who we should be after. We need to kill their leaders." The major nodded his understanding and approval while marveling at how easily the young men understood the techniques of battle.

Windtalker suddenly fired. Boom! The Indians saw the flash. The shell hit the woman solid in the heart killing her instantly, but her body flew back knocking several Indians down at the same time. Windtalker quickly chambered another shell and took aim.

The man doing the carving turned to face the fort and brought his knife up defiantly. Just as he started to scream, Windtalker fired. Boom!

The shell hit the man square in the face, exploding his head like a pumpkin, and spraying brain matter all over everyone standing near him.

Kiyo said, "I see a man on a gray horse to the right of the tree that appears to be issuing orders."

"I see a man on a white horse," added the major, "and he's shaking his fist and yelling."

Windtalker lined up on the white horse because he could see it better. Boom! The shell hit the man in the chest and it was the man sitting on his horse right next to Spotted Owl. The man's blood splattered Spotted Owl and his horse. The sun continued climbing while gradually bringing more light to the valley.

On a black horse, Spotted Owl gave another order, but he made no hand gestures. Showing no fear, they moved slightly closer so the soldiers could hear better and dragged another woman to the next tree. He was tempting a rescue party that would force them to open the gates.

The major looked to the sentry station and noted Robert almost had the Gatling gun ready. The upper sides of the sentry stations were in place to make it hard for the Indians to shoot the soldiers. Rifles were now pointed out from every possible port, including the men guarding the new gate. Over the past few weeks, along the top of the fence wall, they cut narrow slits so they could shoot out while protecting their head and body from arrows.

Another man came to cut the girl, but Windtalker shot him in the back as he turned to face the girl with his knife held high. In retaliation, a warrior angrily fired an arrow into her back wounding her, but Windtalker took aim and shot the woman in the heart, depriving the warriors of their fun.

Kiyo noted the long line of warriors as they came up and over the knoll. He said, "I think they are going to charge. Tell the men to watch for the leaders in the woods opposite each wall. We need to kill them quickly. They're going to charge soon."

Windtalker looked up to see the sun peel over the mountain, lighting the fort up in the early sunlight. "Get ready."

Kiyo remained like a statue until finally he realized the man on the gray horse was not the leader, but instead he saw Spotted Owl on a black horse lift his arm and let out a war whoop. Flaming arrows were fired into the sky from all around the fort. The charge began, but Kiyo yelled to Windtalker, "It's the man on black horse, with a white band of cloth on his head, and a dozen feathers in his hair."

Windtalker saw the throngs of horses closing in on the fort from all around them, but he took aim at the chief, while realizing that most of the warrior's men had charged, but his messengers and the other leaders remained with him. Just as Windtalker fired, Spotted Owl kicked his horse to move closer to the fort. Boom!

The sudden movement saved his life, but not his earlobe. Windtalker took the bottom of the man's ear completely off, and the shell burrowed through the neck of the chief behind him, while nearly severing his head. The blood squirted into the air as the horses danced around in fear. The shot to the ear knocked Spotted Owl off his horse. He was now out of sight behind the horses. With blood oozing down his neck, he bravely flung his body back on the horse, and made a hasty gallop to a stand of trees closer to the fort.

Windtalker realized for now he had better targets. He ran to the left tower and began watching the woods. Kiyo remained a step or two behind, brought the binoculars up and scanned the woods, too. Thanks to the larger kill zone due to the expansion of the fort, it was more difficult for the Indian archers to reach the center of the fort. Arrows began hitting the protective cover at the sentry post, but some went over the fence and into the courtyard hitting no one. The horses instinctively hugged the sheds under the gantry way where they were tied off.

"There!" yelled Kiyo. "The pinto in the edge of the woods."

Windtalker saw him and recognized the Flathead warrior. The man began waving his arms at a messenger as he galloped off. Boom! Windtalker hit the leader in the chest blowing him backwards into the trees. Quickly, Windtalker loaded another shell, followed the messenger and just as he approached the road, he pulled the trigger. Boom! He hit the man in the shoulder with the lead power driving deep into his chest. It blew him ten feet to the other side. The man would never see the sun again.

"Fire!" yelled the major as he swung his sword down so his officers could see him from all around the fort. The officers echoed his command to their men on the ramps at their stations.

The soldiers fired a volley of rifle fire cutting down ten men or more on each side. They took aim again and fired, but the Indians kept coming. Soon the major saw the torches and yelled to Robert. "Don't let them burn our walls. Open fire with the Gatling gun."

Robert swung the gun towards the warriors charging with the torches and with the spin of the crank wheel, he began mowing down men and horses alike, but in a few minutes the last of the cartridge belt fell to the floor.

Quickly, he began reloading by feeding a new belt through the machine.

Windtalker saw men at the rear with torches approaching the wall. "Kiyo!" he called. "Help."

Kiyo ran up as Windtalker fired. Boom! He took down the lead runner. Kiyo brought up his Winchester and shot two more. Windtalker fired again. Boom! He took down another and the remaining men dropped the torches and ran for the cover of the trees.

Windtalker and Kiyo ran to the next corner and again shot anyone with a torch. They sprinted towards the next post. The soldiers were doing well by shooting through the new portholes, then dropping down a bit and moving to another spot. However, the sentry posts were manned by the best shooters in the fort, and hidden behind the new barricades, they fired repeatedly, averaging well over fifty percent kills.

THIRTY-FIVE

Spotted Owl cursed as the new rapid-firing weapon at the fort cut down his men. He called for the wagon loaded with wood and covered by dry hay. Behind a stand of trees, his men lit the rear of the wagon on fire. There were men riding on the team of horses pulling the wagon and a driver in the seat holding the reins. As the blaze grew, the men kicked the horses and they took off. The soldiers saw the wagon and immediately began firing at the warriors. One of the riders took a shot to his arm, but desperately hung on. They were steering for the gate.

"Windtalker!" yelled the major.
Windtalker and Kiyo sprinted to the front while loading shells. They wasted no time in lining up their shots and pulling their triggers.

Spotted Owl grinned as the wagon reached just fifty yards with orders to roll the wagon over at the gate and burn it down. He yelled for the wagon crew to ride swiftly.

Windtalker took aim and shot the driver, knocking him backwards over the seat and into the flaming bales of hay. As his body fell out the back of the wagon it dragged some of the burning bales and wood with him. The riding wounded warrior suddenly collapsed and fell between the horses, and was trampled and then run over by the wagon. Only one Indian remained, but he wisely leaped to the outside horse and then leaned down the left side like he might do on a buffalo hunt.
Windtalker took aim, but could not get a clear shot with just thirty yards to go. "Dang!" he exclaimed as he pulled the trigger. Boom! The shot hit the lead horse that the warrior was riding. It hit the horse so hard in the chest that it abruptly dropped it to his knees like a buffalo on the plains, sending the warrior sprawling hard to the ground, hitting his chin and snapping his neck. The falling horse caused the wagon to flip as it ran up and over the dead animal and warrior. The wagon could have continued rolling until it reached the fort, but the dead weight of the mortally wounded horse still strapped to the wagon brought the fire filled wagon to a grinding halt just fifteen yards short of the gate. The remaining terrified horses pulled hard until they broke free from the harness and sprinted away from the flames.

This unanticipated outcome brought the attack to a halt with the Indian warriors making a hasty retreat. The remaining leaders made their way around the fort, and met Spotted Owl in a ravine. Some wanted to quit, but Spotted Owl yelled at them and called them cowards.
"It's not our heritage to run from a fight! We'll wait a while and let

them think we're gone, and then we'll strike the rear corner, away from the big gun. We'll use our ladders to get up and over the wall, and kill every one of them." He began drawing in the sand, showing how a small force would fake an attack at the front, while the main force hit the rear. The leaders agreed to try one more time, so they prepared for the next wave of warriors to make a run for the fort.

After they left, Spotted Owl ordered the four remaining women to be brought to the front. Their hands were tied to the next one and so on, and then they were beaten and made to bleed about the face. He then marched them to the edge of the woods and told them to run to the fort though still tied to each other.

When he saw the soldiers pointing at the women, he gave the signal for the rear attack, followed by his men to the front. The terrified women began running as hard as they could towards the gate. Spotted Owl waited patiently until the women were close to the fort. He then took his bow and shot the woman nearest him in the back. She fell hard to the ground, causing the other fettered women to trip and fall as well. He laughed at their sprawling onto the ground.

Quickly, they stood and began trying to drag the dead woman, making little progress. They were horrified and panicking at their predicament. Spotted Owl had his archers standing by with their arrows on their bows. He hoped the gate would open and a man would come to rescue the women.

The soldiers yelled for the other women to pick up the body of the dead woman and run. Finally, they began to life her, just as the warriors at the rear of the fort ran through the forest with their ladders, others were rapidly firing one arrow after another. The rear sentry called for help as they began firing. The major sent some of the front garrison to help the rear guard.

Windtalker and Kiyo kept looking for a way to shoot the man that had shot the woman. The major remained quiet and still as he watched the struggling women.

"Come on. Lift her. Run!" he suddenly exclaimed to them. Then he turned and looked down at the soldiers manning the gate. "Get the gate ready for quick entry," he ordered down below.

Windtalker and Kiyo didn't think opening the gate was a good idea, but they understood the major must try something to save them.

After the three terrified women managed to pick up the lifeless, limp dead body of their companion, they turned to make their way to the fort again. They got but five yards when Spotted Owl fired his arrow into the back of another woman. The entire group fell hard to the ground once more. Two were dead, and two remained alive but frustratingly tethered to the bodies on the ground.

Angry, the major began running down the ramp. He called Robert. "Cover me." The major asked for volunteers and three men quickly joined him. They set their weapons down as the major looked up at Robert and got a thumb up from him. He nodded to the gatekeeper who unlocked the gate. The four men began to run.

Spotted Owl saw them and whistled to his men. A squad of six began galloping towards the women at great speed. Spotted Owl began firing his bow at the running soldiers.

Windtalker and Kiyo saw the chief on the black horse at the edge of the forest issuing orders. Quickly, he sighted his target between the trees and limbs, but a split second before he pulled the trigger Robert once again opened fire with the Gatling gun. He sprayed the six riders, killed four men, and a few horses, while sending the survivors scattering. He quickly turned the gun towards the Indians at the edge of the forest. Just as Windtalker fired, Spotted Owl reacted to the Gatling gun by diving to the brush. Windtalker missed him.

The major used his knife to quickly cut the line between the women. His men picked up the remaining women and began the run to the gate. Two of the soldiers were hit with arrows in their backs or shoulders, but somehow they managed to get to the gate. Other men came out to help and soon the gate closed, as Spotted Owl cursed and slammed his fist into the ground.

However, a messenger reported that not all was lost. During the diversion at the gate, the ladders went up in the rear, in spite of the soldiers killing ten of their warriors, but a lucky arrow caught the fort's best shooter, killing him. The warriors were making headway in the rear.

One of the men screamed for help. "Major! Help! They're breaching the wall!"

The major and his men set down the women, picked up their weapons and ran to the rear. Soldiers also ran down the wallboards just as the Indians were coming over the top, firing bows, swinging battle-axes and clubs, and thrusting spears. Windtalker and Kiyo stopped twenty yards away and began taking aim, killing two out of five, but the warriors kept coming. Some of them managed to pick up the rifles of those they killed, and they began firing at the soldiers and killing several.

Windtalker and Kiyo moved back a bit but kept firing. The bodies began to pile before falling to the ground below. Ropes were put around the top of the fort's fence posts and dropped to waiting horses. The Indians leaned out and shot at the men, but they quickly moved around the corner and out of their fire. The horses tugged hard, but so far, the wall remained steadfast.

Windtalker set down his Sharps, removed his battle-axe from the sheath at his back, and charged the siege of warriors. Kiyo finished the last of his rounds in his rifle, put down his gun, and did the same by removing his battle-axe. They began hacking and killing every warrior they could. They were punched and shot at, but they kept swinging. Instantly, they were sprayed with blood until their clothes dripped with blood and brain matter.

For a while, Spotted Owl thought his men would succeed as he saw them going over the wall, but what he could not see were the heroic hand-to-hand battles his men were fighting on the inside. Twenty made it inside, but in eight minutes they were all defeated, but not without killing at least a dozen soldiers.

Windtalker and Kiyo were covered in blood after the last warrior was killed, but mostly not their own. They were cut on the shoulders and arms by the spears and blades of the warriors, but they managed to repel the Indians, cut away the ropes, and pull the ladders inside the fort. The Indians on the ground retreated rapidly to the woods as the soldiers fired at them.

The Indians put away their axes, picked up their rifles and reloaded. They ran back to the front. Kiyo picked up the field glasses and studied the woods. "I see the man we tried to kill earlier. He has to be the chief because he is berating his men."

"I doubt they have any more prisoners. The rescued women said they were the last they saw captured," began the exhausted major, as he came up to the walk boards to the front of the fort. "So what will they do next?"

Kiyo and Windtalker looked at each other, and Windtalker replied, "Indians begin a fight to simply win, but as the battle progresses and their friends are killed, they begin fighting for revenge, and that is when they are the most dangerous."

Kiyo added, "That's when they are at their best, or their worst, depending on which side you are on. They'll want revenge for their dead and wounded, and for the shame put upon them so far."

Windtalker added as he sat down on an ammo box to rest, "Get water and ammo to your men and prepare for another assault."

The major did as suggested, but wondered how much more they could take.

Spotted Owl met with the remaining chiefs and the twenty-five men left to fight. As they argued behind a stand of trees, Kiyo watched them through the field glasses, trying to find a good target, when suddenly he grinned as an idea came to him.

"Major," he began. "Do you think you can land a cannon shot in that stand of trees?" Kiyo pointed as to where he could see movement.

The major asked, "How far is that? Three hundred yards?"

Kiyo scanned sections of ground and replied, "I'd say about three hundred twenty yards." Robert tried to teach them about yards on their last trip together. They just memorized how far fifty yards was and then used that as a guide for longer distances.

"Right," grinned the major as he ran down the ramp and called to the cannon crew.

Windtalker decided to move to the next corner and out of the firing range of the cannon, and with Kiyo's help it was steered and carefully aligned towards the target. The major and the sergeant in charge discussed the distance, made adjustments several times, and then they all stood back as the sergeant lit the fuse.

Boom!

The entire fort flinched at the explosion. Windtalker and Kiyo stood there amazed at the powerful gun. They watched the arch of the spewing cannonball as the men prepared for a second shot. Kiyo lifted his field glasses and looked out at the stand of trees.

Spotted Owl heard the cannon and momentarily paused in his rapid-fire speech to his men. They heard a whistling sound, but before they could react, the shell exploded as it hit the ground, killing six men, wounding eight more, and knocking the entire group to the ground. Spotted Owl took a piece of shrapnel to his forehead, sending a stream of blood down his face. He quickly blotted it, but the remaining men thought he was dead, and began scattering and running for their horses.

Spotted Owl leaped to his feet and managed to wrangle six of his men.

Boom! The cannon fired again after Kiyo told them to add twenty yards. The shell hit the ground again, killing two more of his men and blew Spotted Owl back into a tree. He felt the sizzling shards of hot metal in his back and neck. Once he got to his feet, he called after the remaining four men as they sprinted away. Spotted Owl swung up on his terrified horse and began galloping after them. Kiyo saw him run.

"Come on!" he called to Windtalker. "Emita!" The dog leaped up from his hiding place in the trading post where they had left him during the battle. He quickly ran out and circled with excitement.

They ran down the ramp while calling to the major to open the gates. They flung themselves on their horses after stowing their rifles in the saddle scabbards. They began a gallop towards the gate that opened at the last second as they sprinted out, beginning the chase across the field, and soon caught sight of Spotted Owl and his four men on the run.

Kiyo said, "If we don't catch him, he'll build another army and sooner or later, he'll try again to take out the fort."

"I know, but we're two against five," protested Windtalker.

"It's only two and half a piece," shouted Kiyo.

Windtalker laughed. "You're crazy. You're going to get us killed."

"No," replied Kiyo strongly. "We're trying to keep us all safe." He paused as they topped a hill, before adding with a sly grin, "Okay, I'll kill three and you get the other two."

Windtalker laughed again. "Gee, thanks. Okay, let's get it done."

Spotted Owl didn't know they were chasing him until he reached the ridge of the hill far in front of the fort. He circled his horse, stared at the riders, and wondered what they thought they could do. He vowed he would take out his revenge on them. He galloped down the other side of the hill and into the forest. He rode for a mile before finding a spot he liked. He stopped and yelled for his men to split up and hide while preparing for an ambush.

Emita ran out front and picked up the scent of the riders, but didn't need instructions to give a chase and track them down. He topped the hill and waited briefly for the Indians to catch up. Down the other side they went and entered the forest. The Indians watched the tracks carefully, discerning the confirmation of five riders, but also memorizing the distinctive prints of each horse.

They made their way through the forest, but Kiyo noted the change in the stride of the horses. He whistled. Emita stopped and came back to them. Kiyo whispered, "I think they have slowed."

"It could be a trap. Let's leave the trail to the right."

They moved their horses to a walk and made their way away from the trail and around to the far side. A few minutes later…

Zip!

The arrow luckily grazed the edge of a tree limb, deflecting the aim and missed Windtalker by inches. They quickly dismounted and retrieved their rifles. Using hand signals, they instructed Emita to stay close. They spread out, and began a circle route in the direction of where they thought the arrow might have come. Emita walked beside Kiyo as they began carefully moving through the forest.

Kiyo kept his eyes looking forward while scanning a bit left and right, and then inhaling through his nostrils. Finally, he smelled the smoke on the warrior's hair. He stopped while listening intently, and then suddenly saw the warrior rise up and draw his bow to fire at Windtalker.

Boom! Kiyo shot him in the chest. Windtalker nodded at Kiyo as they continued making their way through the forest. Emita drifted towards the center between the Indians, but after forty yards, the dog suddenly froze. Kiyo crouched down and moved a bit to his right behind a big tree. He faked starting out the other side and quickly stepped back. Zip! Thud! The arrow remained vibrating in the tree trunk he hid behind.

The arrow hit the tree about the same height as his head. Anticipating the shot, Kiyo dropped low, came from behind the tree, and saw the tip of the bow in the midst of the bushes. He took quick aim and fired.

Boom! The man dropped the bow, clutched his chest, and fell dead through the bushes to the ground.

Kiyo sighed with relief, and as he checked to make sure Windtalker was okay, he smiled slightly, then held up two fingers and pointed to his chest with his thumb, and then held up the sign for zero by touching index finger to thumb tip and pointed to Windtalker.

Windtalker grinned while rolling his eyes at him and slowly shaking his head. They began moving once more, while carefully searching the terrain for another warrior. As they reached a small hill, they heard the feet of several men running. They began running after them. They followed the men back to the road, but sighed heavily as they heard the sound of horses. They stepped out on the road and saw the three men galloping away on their horses. Kiyo and Windtalker both fired their rifles, but one shot missed. The rear rider received a shot to his left shoulder forcing him to drop his bow. Somehow, he managed to hang on as they galloped around a bend and out of sight.

Kiyo quickly said to Windtalker, "Go get the horses."

Windtalker started to run before suddenly asking, "What are you going to do?"

Kiyo deadpanned, "I'm going to sit down and rest. So far, I've been doing all the work. I killed two, probably wounded a third—what did you do?"

Windtalker laughed. "You're crazy. Come on!"

They trotted back to the horses and began galloping up the trail with Emita out front as usual. They reached a river and stopped because it looked like the perfect place for an ambush. They could see the tracks leading down into the water, as well as the tracks on the other side, so the men were in too much of a hurry to hide their tracks.

Windtalker said, "This could be a trap. They may have left the tracks to encourage us to gallop across. I'll go first and you cover me."

Kiyo pulled his rifle up and began scanning the far shore, but found nothing. Windtalker gulped as he kicked his horse, leaned low on his neck, and darted across with Emita right behind him. Once safely on the other shore, Windtalker pulled up his loaded Sharps, and began covering Kiyo as he galloped over. They studied the ground while noting the riders had turned north. The Indians began following the trail as Emita sniffed the ground, picked up the scent, and took off running.

THIRTY-SIX

Spotted Owl watched the killing of two of his warriors in the forest, and he knew Flying Bird's blood loss would most likely kill him as well. However, he feared for his own life, but remained intensely angry at the defeat at the fort. There were forty warriors guarding his camp, so as he attempted to lose the hunters, he mentally planned the quickest route to his village. This included going through a very tight, deep ravine, one in which he usually had to walk his horse, as the area frightened the animal.

He called to his men to hurry along, but Flying Bird no longer could keep up. With each mile, he fell behind another fifty yards until Spotted Owl could no longer see him.

Windtalker and Kiyo followed the trail and watched Emita pause briefly as he continued sniffing the drops of blood. They knew they were close, so they continued rushing along while keeping a watchful eye. As they came around the next bend, they saw Emita stop, so they quickly yanked their horses to a halt and slid off to make their bodies harder to shoot.

Emita sniffed off the trail and into a small clearing. The dog stopped when he saw a horse. Windtalker whispered, "Good boy. Stay."

The scouts moved apart as they approached the horse. Windtalker spotted the man on the ground but saw no movement. He signaled to Kiyo to cover him as he sniffed the air, scanned the area with his eyes, and stepped cautiously into the clearing.

He poked the body with his boot, but the man did not move. He leaned down and placed his palm on the man's neck and felt nothing. He grabbed a wrist and pulled the man onto his back. He had bled out. Windtalker searched the ground finding no hoof or moccasin tracks. He returned to the woods.

Windtalker said, "That was the one I shot."

Kiyo teased back. "I don't think so. I shot him. You saw the hole in his back. It was small and not large like the Sharps."

Windtalker knew it to be true, but he grinned. "I only used half a shell. The other half went on to the next man."

Kiyo laughed. "You must have hit your head on a limb. That's three for me and zip for you."

Windtalker smiled. "Come on, let's ride."

Spotted Owl went down into a stream, but this time, instead of hurrying to the far bank, he turned upstream in hopes of losing the hunters. The lone warrior followed him, though he constantly turned to see if the riders were close. Spotted Owl didn't have a clue as to who they were because they didn't wear the usual blue soldier uniforms. He knew they were good shooters, so he took no chances.

He went about a mile in the stream before coming out of the water and on to a spread of flat river rocks. He picked up speed once more, working his way deeper into the valley and still heading north.

After traveling a mile or so, he began noting the closing in of the valley walls, the stream became a creek, and his horse had to step around large rocks that had fallen centuries ago from the peaks of the mountains on both sides of the trail. He stopped and turned his horse around to scan the land behind them, but he saw no signs of movement.

He turned his horse north once more, and from where he stood, it appeared the trail would soon end as the two ridges of the mountains merged. The trail continued to become narrow, and more than once, he had to kick his skittish horse forward. At the base of the mountains, he got off his horse and began leading it through a stand of big rocks. The other side looked like an above ground cave or tunnel, barely wide enough for the horse and only seven feet tall.

The horse pulled at Spotted Owl, and even though he had been through the pass before, it still scared the animal. Spotted Owl cursed his mount and yelled at the warrior behind to hurry along. About half way through, a squirrel leaped from a limb to the rock face, breaking a pebble loose from high up the wall that began cascading downward, and knocking other rubble free like loose marbles. As it fell to the backside of the horses, the jittery animals rebelled, and nearly ran over the two warriors before they managed to settle the horses down.

After twenty minutes on the worst of the path, it suddenly began to widen to the great relief of both man and animal. Soon, Spotted Owl and his last man could swing up onto their horses and make their way deep into the forest on the other side.

Emita struggled through the water for a while as the scouts moved upstream, carefully watching the banks for the exit of the warriors. They assumed they would continue heading north, and after some discussion, they guessed the men were heading back to their village for reinforcements. They decided they must catch them before they got there.

Now and then Kiyo would threaten to turn back, stating he had already killed his three men, that surely Windtalker could handle the remaining two by himself. Windtalker would laugh at him for a moment and then go back to concentrating on watching the forest for any movement.

Windtalker saw the wet hoof prints on the rocks and came out of the stream with Emita right behind him. Once on shore, the dog began sniffing excitedly, and soon ran to the trail where the warriors had gone. Windtalker waited for Kiyo to exit the water.

"It looks like they are continuing north."

Kiyo replied, "The mountains left and right of us are closing in."

"So they could be trapped with no exit."

"Yes, but that means they will ambush us because they are not going to just give up."

"Well, let's get this over with so we can go home."

"You be careful. These men could be like a trapped mountain lion."

"Oh good, I was worried. I was afraid it would be like facing another grizzly bear."

They rode about a mile or two while watching the trail and constantly scanning the terrain ahead for movement. The valley diminished as the sides of the canyon crept inward.

When they reached the apparent dead end, they studied the ground, picking up an occasional hoof print, though the ground consisted of mostly broken rocks. They wound around the big boulders and reached the narrow pass.

Windtalker dismounted and whispered back to Kiyo. "I saw moccasin prints. They had to walk the animals through."

"Boy, this would be a great place to attack us."

Windtalker sighed. "Pull your rifle up and keep your pistol handy. As we walk through, don't follow too close to my horse in case he rears or kicks."

"Tell him to behave."

Windtalker grinned. "Right. That doesn't work when I tell you to behave." He paused and sighed. "Okay, let's go and be careful."

Kiyo replied, "I'm safe. They always shoot the guy leading the posse first. It was good knowing you."

Windtalker didn't reply, but shook his head smiling. He began pulling his horse through, and thankfully, the training their animals had going through the waterfall and tunnel at home helped.

Once on the other side, they mounted again after seeing the shape of the hoof prints change to a trotting stride, followed by galloping. They rode quickly through the forest. An hour later, they saw a steaming pile of dung on the trail, and knew they were very close.

They pulled up their rifles and galloped forward.

They reached a strange looking part of the valley where giant boulders and trees intermingled, giving it an eerie feel. The hair stood up on Windtalker's neck as he rushed along the trail. All of a sudden, he caught sight of one of the warriors. Windtalker brought his rifle up and fired.

Boom!

The Sharps projectile caught the man in the left shoulder, flinging him from his horse. The man screamed at the pain, but Spotted Owl took only a quick look backward before kicking his horse hard to try and escape. Windtalker galloped to the spot where the man fell and brought his horse to a quick stop. He saw the man's bow on the trail. He guided his horse to it so the animal would step on it and break the bow. He saw the trail of blood and could see where the man had crawled.

Windtalker whispered to Kiyo. "You track this one and I'll go after the last man, the chief." This time he didn't wait for a smart sharp reply, but kicked his horse down the trail.

Kiyo swung off his horse as he ratcheted a shell into his Winchester. He saw the broken bow, then scanned across the trail on the opposite side, and then he, too, saw the blood. At first, he thought he would just follow the trail, but then he thought better of it, and went back down the trail about ten yards before stepping into the forest. Systematically, he cautiously made his way from tree to rock to tree again. He listened for movement. He smelled the air. He wished he had Emita with him, but the dog had taken off after the last warrior with Windtalker.

Kiyo listened intently and finally heard slight movement ahead about twenty feet. He continued making slow steps before finally seeing the foot of the Indian through the bushes. Fresh blood covered the toe of the moccasin. Kiyo moved carefully as he realized the warrior was watching the trail while expecting him. He came around the back of the rock and decided to climb the twelve-foot boulder. At the top of the rock, he peered over.

He spotted the warrior holding a battle-axe in his right hand, while his left shoulder remained bleeding and useless. He could have waited until the man bled out, but he knew Windtalker might need his help with the last man. After making his decision, he brought his rifle up and shot the man in the head, ending his life and the pain instantly.

Kiyo leaped to the ground, made his way quickly to the trail, saddled up and galloped after Windtalker.

Spotted Owl heard Windtalker's shot, and then later, he heard Kiyo's, noting the different sounds their weapons made, but he never slowed down. He reached a stream, crossed over, and rode about twenty yards until he suddenly found himself in a mud bog. The ground around the area did not drain well and remained covered in water. In the harsh winters, the below zero temperatures often froze the ground deeper than in most areas. The mountains on either side kept the bog in the shadows year around. It had thawed slightly and refroze for centuries, breaking down the rocks and dirt until they were mixed like cake batter.

His horse struggled through the thick layers of wet, oozing peat moss with some slow progress. Spotted Owl urged his horse forward, but the animal ignored him and picked his own way. From time to time, Spotted Owl thought he heard something to his rear and jerked his head around expecting the riders.

For ten long minutes, the horse slipped numerous times as it struggled through the bog. Its belly was now covered in black mud, but finally it reached solid ground, and just as he made it up the bank, the horse flinched

216

at the sudden sound.

Boom!

Windtalker missed Spotted Owl, who had fallen forward as the horse made his way up the bank, but the shot caught the animal in the neck. The big exhausted horse abruptly fell forward to his knees, flinging Spotted Owl forward and head over heels into the brush.

Though it knocked the breath from him, somehow Spotted Owl managed to hang on to his spear. He scrambled to his feet and made his way deeper into the brush.

Boom!

Windtalker tried a second shot, hitting a limb just beside Spotted Owl's head. The limb shattered, sending sharp pieces of wood into Spotted Owl's face. He flinched at the pain, but made himself move deeper into the trees and out of sight.

Kiyo arrived and they both studied the bog. "Did you wound him?"

"No, but I shot his horse. He didn't have a bow."

Kiyo laughed. "The horse was trying to kill us? Don't you think it would have been better to shoot the man?"

Windtalker grinned. "I was aiming at the man. He moved just as I pulled the trigger and the horse suddenly lunged."

"Did he have an axe?"

"No, I think he has a spear."

Windtalker pondered the situation. "I'll cross the mud pits and continue tracking. Why don't you go upstream and look for dry land? Maybe you can get ahead of him. He's on foot, but be careful."

Windtalker urged his horse forward. Kiyo whistled for Emita to follow him to keep the dog out of the mud. Windtalker doubted the man would take a chance by flinging his spear at him, because if he missed, he had nothing left but a knife. If he succeeded, he would still be pretty much weaponless with Kiyo and Emita searching for him.

Spotted Owl wiped the blood from the numerous tiny wounds on his face. He removed several splinters. His ear hurt as a result of Windtalker's amazing shot from the fort. His forehead hurt from the cannon shrapnel. He cursed and quickly made his way back to the trail where he began jogging in an attempt to flee. He knew the trail would go upwards towards a ridge covered with giant boulders, but on the other side, he would soon reach one of the scouts protecting the village.

THIRTY-SEVEN

Kiyo made quick time along the stream before crossing about three hundred yards ahead of Spotted Owl. He searched the ground for tracks and found none, though tracking an Indian wearing moccasins on a hard trail would be difficult. He didn't see any blood drops. The trees remained scattered amongst the boulders. He pulled his horse behind a cluster of several big boulders and tied him off. Together, Kiyo and Emita made their way through the rocks until he found one that he wanted to scale so he could see. He laughed at how hard he struggled to climb, while Emita just scrambled up the loose rocks on four paws with ease. Emita was sitting and resting at the top by the time Kiyo arrived. Kiyo smiled and rubbed his ears.

Windtalker finally made it across the difficult mud bog. The black fertile stuff clung to the belly of his horse, as well as Windtalker's boots. They walked on solid ground to the area where he accidentally shot Spotted Owl's horse. To his amazement, the horse remained alive, but critically wounded. It made him feel sad, but he knew it was best to put the animal out of its misery. He drew his pistol and shot the horse in the head to relieve it from its agony. The horse died instantly. He began following the trail, but carefully searched left and right for the man with the spear. He lifted his nose into the air, hoping to pick up his scent. Without Emita, he would have to keep a sharp eye and keen ears. He knew that if he made one mistake, Spotted Owl would kill him.

Spotted Owl saw the mountain pass up ahead. He sighed with great relief that he was almost free. Thinking ahead, he left the trail, and worked his way to the right to come in and around the boulders while avoiding the chance of leaving tracks on the path. He knew he would have to ambush and kill one man at a time to survive. He could not outrun them on foot, but perhaps if he killed one, he might be able to take his horse and flee.

A sudden movement to his far right startled him. He didn't think they were that close to him. He had expected the mud bog to slow them down for a while. Unsure of what to expect, he instinctively brought up his spear and ducked into a crouch position while anticipating a shot from an arrow or gun. Hearing none, he peered carefully around a rock while taking small, quiet steps. Twenty yards above the rocks, his heart sank when he spotted a large mountain lion.

Spotted Owl sighed heavily at his misfortune. He had two armed, experienced hunters tracking him, no horse, no bow, and now he had discovered a male lion. He couldn't turn back, and it wasn't wise to try to hide near a lion that could easily sniff and pick up his scent. As silently as possible, he slowly moved around the next rock and hoped the lion would not consider him prey.

As he reached the third rock, the lion suddenly snarled and began descending with skillful grace, making no sounds, and stopping just ten yards above Spotted Owl's head. The lion suddenly roared loudly, as if trying to scare the warrior away.

Kiyo heard the lion just as he reached the ledge at the top of the rock. Quickly, he grabbed Emita; quite fearful the dog would run towards the lion. He brought his rifle up, and ratcheted a shell into the chamber while cocking the gun. "Stay," he whispered to Emita as his eyes searched the terrain, both for the lion and the warrior.

Windtalker also heard the lion, saw the big boulders up ahead, and spotted Kiyo on a rock. Kiyo saw him as well, and pointed below. Windtalker slid off his horse, retrieved his rifle, and made sure there was a shell in the chamber. He also checked his pistol, replaced a spent shell, and put his pistol back in his holster without the riding strap, fearing he might need the gun in a hurry. Out of habit, he almost tied off the horse, but with a mountain lion about, he knew the horse might need to protect itself.

He turned, cocked the Sharps rifle, and began making his way up the trail, but found no sign of the man. He assumed he had left the trail. He studied the terrain and felt the man would go right, so he left the trail in the same direction to make sure he didn't double back on him. Twenty steps later, he saw a fresh, partial mud print on the edge of a puddle of rainwater. It was the same black mud that he carried on his boots from the bog. Carefully, he continued moving forward.

As he came around a big rock, he saw the mountain lion about the same time the lion saw him. The animal growled fiercely, but stood its ground. Windtalker's heart pounded in his chest.

Kiyo saw Spotted Owl as he slowly made his way around a rock and moved towards the pass. He took aim, but the chief wisely darted from rock to rock.

Windtalker spotted the man, too. Spotted Owl quickly crouched behind a rock just fifteen feet in front of him. The man moved to the next position and so did Windtalker as silently as possible.

Boom!

Kiyo took a shot that grazed Spotted Owl's left forearm. Though painful and bleeding, it did little to slow him down. Bravely, he ran forward before Kiyo could load a shell and take another shot.

As he did so, Windtalker took quick aim, but failing to get a good line of sight, he waited, and continued following the man, until finally, he knew his chance had come. His finger twitched.

Suddenly, he heard the sound of a loose rock, followed by the sharp crack of a stick, and the unmistakable sound of the lion's roar. He turned quickly from his target and saw the lion in the air leaping towards him. The claws were extended in his massive front paws, and his large mouth revealed a mammoth and monstrous set of gnashing teeth.

Windtalker pulled the trigger, but the big cat's surprise leap left him little time to get the rifle fully around. The lion continued sailing through the air. Windtalker defended himself with his rifle, deflecting the lion to the ground. The lion got a swipe at him with his left paw before rolling into a bush, scrambling to his feet, turning around in a flash, and preparing to lunge once more.

Hearing the shot and the growl, the frightened warrior made a dart through the pass. Kiyo stood up slightly to see if Windtalker killed the lion, but hearing the growl, he feared not. He got a quick glimpse of Spotted Owl, but fired too late.

Windtalker knew he had no time to load another shell in his rifle. He kept the rifle in his left hand hoping to discourage the mountain lion, but drew his pistol as the animal charged him.

Boom! Boom!

He fired twice and landed both shots, but the lion kept coming.

Boom! Boom!

The mountain lion hit him in the chest, flinging him backwards and landing on top of him while knocking the rifle and pistol from his hands. Windtalker struggled to pull his hunting knife while anticipating a big bite from the lion, but the two hundred and forty pound lion's body suddenly went limp, pinning the young man beneath him. Windtalker cautiously grabbed a paw and rolled the mortally wounded animal off him. Getting to his feet, he knew the animal would die soon, though most likely in pain. He picked up his pistol and shot him in the head.

Boom!

Windtalker sighed heavily. He had bleeding scrapes on his chest that ripped right through his shirt. Though they hurt a bit, he would live. He reloaded the pistol, and then put a new shell in his rifle. He looked at the monstrous mountain lion once more and sighed with relief. He gave the sound of the hawk and began tracking Spotted Owl once more.

Kiyo heard Windtalker's call that made him sigh with relief and smile. He and Emita reached the trail and began running after Spotted Owl. Windtalker saw him and caught up. Silently, Kiyo pointed ahead where they both saw Spotted Owl's head bounce up and down as he ran through the rocks.

After they gained on him, Kiyo went off the trail to the right while Windtalker kept coming forward. Emita stayed with Windtalker.

The terrain became a bed of nothing but boulders and ancient, decaying, giant fallen trees. Windtalker saw a cave about forty yards above his head. He assumed the cave would be a good home for a mountain lion, panther, or maybe a black bear. It was too small for a grizzly, he hoped.

Spotted Owl panted from his constant run and numerous close brushes with death. He knew the hunters were behind him, but he had no chance of outrunning them. Their horses walked freely behind the scouts and this gave him an idea. If he could make it to a horse, fling himself on it, and grab the reins of the other horse, he could soon gallop back to the north leaving them on foot.

Abruptly, he crouched down and made his way to the left side of the trail. For the first time, he saw Windtalker coming up the trail, and Spotted Owl's face became a sea of puzzlement. It wasn't a white man trailing him, but rather an Indian. The realization that one of his own had turned against him infuriated the chief. He wanted to kill him even more, but to stay alive, he had to make an escape and do it soon.

Kiyo found a partial print and began making his way towards the trail. Convinced the man would be trapped between the rock walls that went high above on both sides, and Windtalker coming up the trail, he felt sure they would get the leader between them. The big Indian probably assumed they were both together, and this would allow him to capitalize on surprise.

Spotted Owl went around a very large boulder followed by more granite giants that appeared to have dropped from the skies like marbles. Suddenly, he spotted the paw print of a big grizzly, as well as a fresh pile of scat. His shoulders sagged. As a boy, he had encountered a grizzly that terrified him, and this fresh track made his body literally shake with fear. With no options left, he cautiously followed the trail around the next rock.

Kiyo got a glimpse of him, but he didn't have a shot as Spotted Owl moved quickly across the trail. He spotted Windtalker, pointed in the direction of Spotted Owl, and then put his finger to his lips to remind him to stay quiet. Suddenly, they heard a stick pop loudly, followed by yet another large growl, but this time the pitch of the growl was much lower. Emita suddenly gave his body a big shake as the hair once again stood up on his neck. Quickly, the trembling dog moved around behind Windtalker.

Spotted Owl turned to his right as his eyes moved upward, and just twenty feet away stood a twelve-foot tall, giant grizzly bear. The big animal swung his giant claws in the air and growled repeatedly. Terrified, Spotted Owl forgot about the hunters and began running back to the trail. He ran directly towards Windtalker, hoping to steal his rifle and kill the bear.

Tracking the warrior's movements at just fifteen feet away from Spotted Owl, Kiyo also saw the bear. He had no shot at the Indian, but he wasted no time firing his Winchester at the bear. The bear dropped to all fours as the first shot hit him. Filled with anger and rage, the beast began charging. Kiyo ran up a boulder and fired again, hitting the animal in the back while hoping for a shot to his heart.

Windtalker could not see the bear, but in a flash he saw Spotted Owl rushing towards him. Before he could bring his rifle up, the Indian leaped on him. Emita began yapping at the warrior's feet as they struggled for the gun. Spotted Owl kneed Windtalker, but the scout didn't let go of the rifle. Spotted Owl kicked and cursed at him, calling him a traitor, while Windtalker fought back with a vengeance.

They managed to get to their feet with the rifle parallel to the ground as they both gripped it tightly. Behind them they could hear the grunts and growls from the bear. Kiyo shot the bear again, but it did little to stop him. The bear ran to the boulder, but wounded, he decided not to climb it to go after Kiyo. The animal heard the struggle between Windtalker and Spotted Owl down the trail and suddenly, he picked up the scent of Emita.

He lunged off the rock and disappeared around a big rock before Kiyo could shoot him again. Kiyo thought it best to stay on the rock, at least until he knew where the bear had gone. He began reloading his rifle.

Windtalker and Spotted Owl kept kicking and struggling over the gun, spinning around and around as Emita continued taking bites at Spotted Owl's legs, causing them to bleed.

Suddenly, the bear came around the rock behind Windtalker. Spotted Owl saw him, his eyes widened, and he shook with fear. Windtalker struggled to see the bear, but as he did, the grizzly stood up while swinging his paws, growling, snarling, and then suddenly, he dropped down and charged at full speed like a buffalo.

Emita high tailed it into the woods. The horses turned and galloped back down the trail.

Windtalker suddenly yanked the terrified Spotted Owl from his feet, and instantly spun him around on the trail. The bear hit the back of the warrior with the full force of a huge swipe of his right paw that sliced through the man's flesh as if made of paper. He took another swipe with his left paw. Blood spurted and sprayed everywhere. The blow sent both Windtalker and Spotted Owl flying backwards, as the rifle fell harmlessly to the ground.

Before they could get up, the bear pounced onto the back of Spotted Owl's legs, breaking them like dry twigs. The warrior screamed at the excruciating pain. Windtalker scrambled as he tried to back away. The bear then chomped down on Spotted Owl's buttocks with his big jaws, taking huge chunks of meat into his teeth. He then shook the warrior's body like a rag doll, lifting Spotted Owl off the ground, and thrashing him left and right as the flesh tore away. He dropped him, grabbed another bite and thrashed the man again.

Windtalker quickly crab walked backwards into the brush, got to his feet, and searched for his rifle. He eyed it on the ground not far from the bloody mess of Spotted Owl. He drew his pistol and began firing at the bear.

Kiyo ran across the trail and began emptying his rifle into the bear. At first, nothing stopped the grizzly as it bent down and took all of Spotted Owl's head in his mouth and clamped down, shattering bone and brains. The ooze squirted out between his teeth and lips as it sprayed the dirt.

His rifle now empty, Kiyo then picked up his pistol and fired all six shots as well. Slowly, the bear began to bleed out as the brutal force of powerful body failed him. He kept swinging his paws, with each swipe getting slower and slower, when abruptly, he fell with a big thud right on the broken bloody remains of Spotted Owl.

Windtalker quickly darted to fetch his Sharps, but the bear never moved again.

Kiyo asked, "Are you all right? Did he get you? You're bleeding."

Windtalker looked at his chest. "This is from the mountain lion. I'm fine. Let's go home."

Emita came running to them as they walked down the trail in search of their horses. "Good boy," teased Windtalker. "You really scared that big old bear with your tail between your legs. He was terrified of you." Kiyo began laughing.

The dog didn't know the words, but he wagged his tail rapidly as the Indians gave him a good rub. "Find the horses Emita. Find them." The dog took off running down the trail to the south.

After they walked a while, they stopped and embraced with great relief that the battle was finally over, and hopefully the end of the battles between the Indians and the settlers, though they doubted that to be true. They soon kissed before descending to the grass to hold each other and rest for a while. Kiyo ripped his shirt to prepare a bandage for Windtalker's chest.

Ten minutes later, they broke their deep kissing at the sudden bark from Emita. They opened their eyes and saw the dog about ten yards away with the reins for both horses in his teeth and trailing behind him.

They laughed as they got up. "Good boy," pronounced Windtalker as he gave the dog another good rub and his horse as well.

Kiyo spoke to their dog. "Very good boy, but you mustn't interrupt long overdue love making." Emita barked as he let go the reins.

Windtalker laughed. "Was that a yes bark or a no bark?" Emita barked again.

Kiyo slung himself up on his horse. "I don't know, but I'm starving, let's get back to the fort."

Windtalker replied, "Wait. Perhaps there's another mountain lion or bear we could chase down. Don't you want to go hunting?"

Kiyo laughed at him, spun his horse around, and squeezed his legs to encourage the horse to trot out of there. Windtalker swung up on his horse and began following.

Emita barked while running past Kiyo's horse and took the lead. It would be dark before long, but they didn't care as long as they were finally going home.

TJ Johnson
January 10, 2010

Author TJ Johnson

TJ began writing his stories in the eighties, mostly for fun and for friends. He was still working full-time for someone else and the career took up more time than he wished. In 2005, he began working for himself with hopes of spending more time on his writing. On the computer were several novels not yet produced, so while writing new material, he began searching for outlets for the books he'd completed. His favorite part of writing is the crafting of the rough draft, a period in the process when the words fly from the storage center deep in his brain like a movie stuck on fast-forward. The agonizing part begins with the painstaking restructuring as the editing begins, but it is a joy when the tale is finally finished. TJ often works on three stories at once, each in different stages of production. He does this to keep his creative skills at peak performance, and because he believes fiction is just too much fun!

His most recent releases: **Gay Grifters** about a gang of thieves robbing rich gay men. The **Raceboys** about a national champion forced to come out as a gay driver, and **A Writer's Fantasy** about his favorite college basketball team and their handsome star player. Also available is **The Will** and **Stranded.**

Currently, TJ is editing **Crosshairs,** a continuing story with the cast of Gay Grifters – an Eric and Tyler Story.

Fans of the War Series (**The War Apart - Part 1**, **The War Ahead - Part 2 Revised 2010**) will be pleased to know that the research is finished, and the editing has begun on **The War Beyond - Part 3**.

Requests for additional information and Inquiries can be obtained from **Hard Title Publishing,** at **Info@ItsFiction.com**

You may also signup for free publication notices, read a chapter from other books, and check out TJ's blog at:

WWW.ItsFiction.Com

Acknowledgements

This story is the result of a wonderful collaboration between the writer and my editor on this project, Bruce Foulkes. He is absolutely tenacious in finding the right solution, phrase or word, and his patience and humor have made the work not only insightful for the author, but lots of fun as well. His comments back to me about my word choices just make me laugh. I wish to thank him for all his indulgence and hard work, and look forward to taking on another project in the future.

Contact TJ Johnson at:

Info@ItsFiction.com

1. I try to answer all my email myself; however please read "Bio & Info" at www.ItsFiction.com before writing as your question – saving time for all! Many readers ask the same questions repeatedly.

2. Please do not add my email address to any group for jokes, thoughts, prayers, or riddles, etc. I always delete these without reading.

3. I do not open any emails with attachments as these may contain viruses or other nonsense!

4. Please do NOT write suggesting plot lines as I delete these quickly, too. I like to write my own stories. If your plot is good, write it yourself! Do not send your manuscript to me – I am a writer, not a publisher, and I do not have the time.

5. All characters and names are part of my imagination and indicate no one particular. If I like a person's name, I may use the first or the last name but never both at the same time. It is true some of the events in my books are historical in nature but many are not. Choosing which to believe is your job, but this is why fiction is fun.

6. If you do not receive a reply, perhaps "Bio & Info" contains the answer already, or your email address is not functioning correctly.

7. If you have read all the above, I cannot wait to hear from you!

8. If you think a sequel should be added to your favorite story, please send an email to the above address!

www.ingramcontent.com/pod-product-compliance
Lightning Source LLC
Chambersburg PA
CBHW070103260626
47160CB00004B/1302